JOHN SANDFORD
BURIED PREY

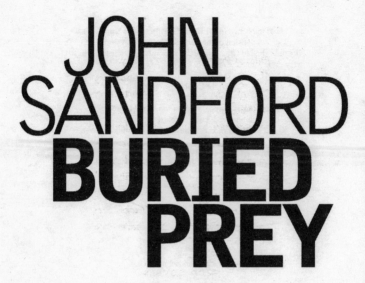

**SIMON &
SCHUSTER**

London · New York · Sydney · Toronto · New Delhi

A CBS COMPANY

First published in the US by G. P. Putnam's Sons, 2011
A division of the Penguin Group (USA) Inc.
First published in Great Britain by Simon & Schuster UK Ltd, 2011
A CBS COMPANY

1 3 5 7 9 10 8 6 4 2

Simon & Schuster UK Ltd
1st Floor
222 Gray's Inn Road
London WC1X 8HB

www.simonandschuster.co.uk

Simon & Schuster Australia, Sydney
Simon & Schuster India, New Delhi

A CIP catalogue record for this book is available from the British Library

Trade Paperback ISBN 978-1-47111-092-4

Book design by Nicole Laroche

Printed and bound by CPI Group (UK) Ltd, Croydon, CR0 4YY

For Michele

BURIED
PREY

ALSO BY JOHN SANDFORD

Rules of Prey	Easy Prey
Shadow Prey	Chosen Prey
Eyes of Prey	Mortal Prey
Silent Prey	Naked Prey
Winter Prey	Hidden Prey
Night Prey	Broken Prey
Mind Prey	Dead Watch
Sudden Prey	Invisible Prey
The Night Crew	Phantom Prey
Secret Prey	Wicked Prey
Certain Prey	Storm Prey

KIDD NOVELS

The Fool's Run

The Empress File

The Devil's Code

The Hanged Man's Song

VIRGIL FLOWERS NOVELS

Dark of the Moon

Heat Lightning

Rough Country

Bad Blood

1

THE FIRST MACHINES on the site were the wreckers, like steel dinosaurs, plucking and pulling at the houses with jaws that ripped off chimneys, shingles, dormers, and eaves, clapboard and brick and stone and masonry, beams and stairs and balconies and joists, headers and doorjambs. Old dreams, dead ambitions, and lost lives, remembrance roses and spring lilacs, went in the dump trucks all together.

When the wrecking was done, the diggers came in, cutting a gash in the black-and-tan soil that stretched down a city block. A dozen pieces of heavy equipment crawled down its length, Bobcats and Caterpillar D6s and Mack trucks, and one orange Kubota, grunting and struggling through the raw earth.

Now gone silent as death.

The equipment operators gathered in twos and threes, yellow helmets and deerskin work gloves, jeans and rough shirts, to talk about the situation. Slabs of concrete lay around the trench, pieces of what once had been basement floors and walls. Electric wire was gathered in hoops, pushed into a corner of the hole, to await removal; survey stakes marked the lines where new concrete would go in.

None of it happening today.

At one end of the gash, twelve men and four women gathered around a bundle of plastic sheeting, once clear, now a pinkish-yellow with age. It was still set down in the earth, but the dirt on top of it had been swept away by hand. A few of the people were construction supervisors, marked by yellow, white, and orange hard hats. The rest were cops. One of the cops, whose name was Hote, and who was Minneapolis's sole cold-case investigator, was kneeling at the end of the bundle with her face four inches from the plastic.

Two dead girls grinned back at her, through the plastic, their desiccated skin pulled tight over their cheek and jaw bones, their foreheads;

their eyes were black pits, their lips were flattened scars, but their teeth were as white and shiny as the day they were murdered.

Hote looked up and said, "It's them. I'm pretty sure. Sealed in there."

THE DAY WAS HOT, hardly a cloud in the sky, the July sun burning down; but the soil was cool and damp, and smelled of rotted roots and a bit of sewage, from the torn-up sewer lines leading out of the hole. Another woman, who'd walked into the pit in low heels and two-hundred-dollar black wool slacks that were now flecked with the tan earth, asked, "Can you tell what happened? Were they dead when they were sealed in?"

Hote stood up and brushed the dirt from her jeans and said, "I think so. It looks to me like they were hanged."

"Strangled?"

"Hanged," Hote repeated. "There appears to be some upward displacement of the cervical spine in both girls—but that's looking through a lot of plastic. Their arms go behind them, instead of lying by their sides, so I think they'll be tied or cuffed. Anyway—let's get them over to the ME."

"What else?"

"Marcy . . ." Hote was always reluctant to commit herself without all the facts; a personal characteristic. Most cops were willing to bullshit endlessly about possibilities, including alien abduction and satanic cults.

"Anything?"

"There's a lot of tissue left," Hote said. "They're mummified—it's almost like they were freeze-dried inside the plastic."

"Will there be anything organic left by the killer?" The woman meant semen, but didn't use the word. If they could recover semen, they could get DNA.

"If there was anything to begin with, it's possible there are still traces," Hote said. "Since hardly anybody had heard of DNA back then, we might find the killer's hair on them. . . . But, I'm no scientist. So who knows? Let's get them to the ME."

One of the cops in the back said, "Marcy? Davenport's coming down."

Marcy Sherrill, head of Minneapolis Homicide, turned and looked over her shoulder. Lucas Davenport, a dark-haired, broad-shouldered man in black slacks, French-blue shirt, his suit jacket hung by a finger over his shoulder, was trudging down the earthen ramp toward the group around the plastic sepulchre. He looked as though he'd just stepped out of a Salvatore Ferragamo advertisement, his eyes, shirt, and tie all entangled in a fashionable blue vibration.

She said, "Okay. This makes my day."

An older man said, "He worked on it. This." He gestured at the plastic.

"I don't think so," Sherrill said. "He'd have been too young."

"I remember," the old man said. "He was all over it. I think it was his first case in plainclothes."

SHERRILL WAS THE SENIOR active Minneapolis cop on the scene, a solid, raven-haired woman in her late thirties, with a great slashing white smile and what an older generation of cops called a "good figure." She'd had a reputation as a cop not afraid of a fistfight, and still carried a lead-weighted sap on a key ring. Sherrill had come on the police force at a time when women were still suspect when it came to doing street work. She'd erased that attitude quickly enough, and now was accepted as a cop-cop, rather than as a woman cop, or, as they were still occasionally called, a Dickless Tracy. She'd hardly mellowed as she moved up through the ranks and would someday, most people thought, either be the Minneapolis chief or go into politics.

There were five retired cops in the group around her, men who'd worked on the original investigation. As soon as the bodies had been discovered, the police had been called, and word of the find had begun leaking out. All over the metro area, aging cops and ex-cops got in their cars and headed downtown, to look for themselves, to see the girls, and to talk about those days: the hot summers, the cold winters, all the time on the sidewalks before high-tech came in, computers and cell phones and DNA.

DAVENPORT CAME UP, and the gray-hairs nodded at him—they all knew him, from his time in Minneapolis—and he shook hands with a

3

couple of them, and a couple who didn't like him edged away, and Sherrill asked, "How'd you hear?"

"It's gone viral, at least in the cop shops," he said, peering at the plastic sheeting. He worked for the Minnesota Bureau of Criminal Apprehension, and, with his close relationship with the governor, was probably the most influential cop in the state. Minneapolis was technically within his jurisdiction, but he was polite. He flipped a thumb at the sheeting and asked, "Do you mind if I look?"

"Go ahead," Sherrill said.

Hote pointed and said, "They're faceup, heads at that end."

Lucas squatted in Hote's knee prints at the end of the plastic, looked down at the withered faces for a full thirty seconds, then, paying no attention to the neat crease on his wool-blend slacks, got on his knees and crawled slowly down the length of the bundle, his face an inch from the plastic. After a moment, he grunted, stood up, brushed his knees, then said, "That's Nancy on the left, Mary on the right."

"Hard to know for sure," Hote said. "It likely is them—the size is right, the hair coloring . . ."

Lucas said, "It's them. Nancy was the taller one. Nancy was wearing a blouse with little red hearts on it, that she got from her father on Valentine's Day. It was the last gift he gave her. It's wadded up between her thighs. I can see the hearts."

Sherrill looked up at the sides of the trench and said, "I wonder what the address was here? We need to pull some aerials and figure out which one was which. I thought the guy who did it . . ."

"Terry Scrape," Lucas said. "He didn't do it."

She stared at him: "I thought that was settled. That he was killed . . ."

Lucas shook his head. "He was. I was there. I thought, back then, that there was a chance he was involved. But with this . . . I don't think so. There was somebody else. Somebody with a lot more energy than Scrape ever had. Somebody pretty smart. I could feel him, but I could never find him. Anyway, he hung it on Scrape like a hat on a witch, and we had us a witch hunt."

"I gotta look at the file," Sherrill said.

"Scrape lived way over by Uptown," Lucas said, remembering.

"There's no way he killed these kids and buried them in the basement of a private house, under the concrete floor. He was only here for a few weeks, homeless most of the time. He lived in a hole under a tree, for part of the time, for Christ's sakes. He didn't even have a car."

"Gotta get the addresses, see who was living here," Sherrill said again.

Lucas looked up out of the hole at the surrounding neighborhood, as Sherrill had, and said, "I knocked on two hundred doors. Me and Sloan. We never got within two miles of this place. Never crossed the river."

"Mark Towne owned a bunch of these houses down here," said one of the older cops. "The Towne Houses. I don't know if these were his."

Lucas said, "That seems right to me. Before the kids came in, it was mostly elderly. Retired railroad workers, lots of them. Towne was buying them up for a few thousand bucks apiece."

Sherrill said, "We'll check."

"Towne got killed in a car crash, maybe ten, fifteen years ago," somebody offered.

Lucas nodded at the bodies: "How'd they come out clean like this? So flat?"

A guy in a yellow helmet said, "I was pulling up the pieces of the basement slab, to load 'em up." He gestured at his Cat. "I got hold of that one block and tipped it up, and there they were."

"You could see them?" Lucas wasn't disbelieving, just curious.

"I could see the plastic and something in the plastic. I had to check in case . . ." He stopped and looked around the hole, searching for a place that didn't look back at him with bony eye sockets. "You know what? I got the creeps looking at it. I had a feeling it was something bad, before I ever got down to look."

Lucas nodded at him, said, "Bad day," and then turned back to Sherrill. "I'd keep the slabs around. He must've poured the concrete right over the top of them. You might find fingerprints, some kind of impressions. Something."

She nodded. "We'll do that."

"And you gotta find the Joneses, the parents, and let them know, right away. Before the news gets out. If you want, I've got a researcher who can find them, and I can have her call you with the phone numbers.

I heard they got divorced a couple years after the kids were killed . . . but I don't know that for sure."

"If you've got somebody who could do that . . . but have him call me."

"Her," Lucas said. And, "I will."

SHERRILL AND DAVENPORT drifted away from the group, and Sherrill asked, "Haven't seen you for a while. How've you been?"

"Busy, but nothing crazy," Lucas said. He touched her on the shoulder, and added, "This Jones thing. It was amazing, if you worked it. Big news—cute little blond girls, vanishing like that. The way things are now, I doubt anybody will care. It was too long ago. But the guy who did it is still around. We can't let it slide."

"We won't let it slide," she said.

"But you've got other things to do, just like I do. And the girls are dead."

"You sound like you've got a special interest," Sherrill said.

Lucas looked over to the plastic-wrapped bodies: "You know, all those years ago . . . I kinda messed up. I've always thought that, and now . . . here it is, back in my face."

A Channel Three TV truck slowed on the open street at the far end of the gash. One of the older cops called, "We got media."

Lucas said to Sherrill, as they stepped back to the group around the grave, "You got my number if you need anything. I'll get you that information on the Joneses."

She said, "I'm still a little pissed about the last time."

The winter before, Lucas had trampled all over a Minneapolis investigation of a series of murders that started in a Minneapolis hospital. It had all ended with a shoot-out in a snowstorm, to which Sherrill felt she had not been properly invited. Grenades had been involved.

Lucas grinned and said, "Yeah, well, tough shit, sweetheart. Listen, I remember a lot about this thing. If you need me, call. Really."

She softened, but just half an inch—she and Lucas had once spent a month or so in bed, and that month had been as contentious as their hands-off relationship since then. "I will." And, "How's Weather feeling?"

"Getting better; she was pretty cranky last month."

"Say hello for me."

Lucas said he would, looked a last time at the hole with the plastic-wrapped bodies: "Man, it seems like it was a month ago. That was the year of Madonna. Everybody listening to Madonna. And Prince was huge. Soul Asylum was coming up. I used to go to the Soul Asylum concerts every time they played Seventh Street Entry. And we'd ride around at night, look at the crack whores, listen to 'Like a Virgin' and 'Crazy for You' and 'Little Red Corvette.' Hot that summer. And I mean, Madonna was young, way back then."

"So were we," said one of the old cops. "I used to dance."

Another asked, "What're you gonna do about this?"

"We've got one more guy to catch," Lucas said. "I hate to think what this cocksucker's done between now and then. Excuse the French."

LUCAS WENT BACK to his office, in the BCA building on the north side of St. Paul. It was a solid, modern building, which felt more like a suburban office complex than a police headquarters. He climbed the stairs to his second-floor office, with a quick flash of a hand at a friend down a hallway. His secretary said, "Hi, I need to—" and he said, "Later," and went into his office and closed the door.

The image of the dead girls hung in his eyes, the stony smiles asking, "What'll you do about this?"

Lucas pulled a wastebasket over beside his desk and propped his feet on it, tilted his chair back and closed his eyes, and let himself slip back to the first days of the Jones case. He took the investigation a day at a time, as best as he could remember it, and there wasn't much that he'd forgotten.

And when he got to the end of the review, he decided that right at the beginning, he'd done something worse than anything else he'd done in his entire career since then—even though some of the things he'd done since then were technically criminal. Criminal, but not immoral. What he'd done back then was immoral: he'd caved.

He'd been a still-impressionable kid eager to get into plainclothes, and a path had been laid out for him. That path meant putting the early days of his career in the hands of Quentin Daniel, a very smart and occasionally quite a bad man. Daniel wanted to be chief of police, and maybe mayor.

The Jones case was an ugly one, with all kinds of frightening undertones, and as the head of violent crimes—Homicide—Daniel was on the hot seat. He'd pushed a strong and legitimate investigation, but when a suspect popped up, somebody who was essentially unable to defend himself, and against whom there was substantial evidence, Daniel had grabbed him and held on tight.

Then the suspect got himself killed, and once you kill a guy, you own him, for good or evil. If he's innocent, and you kill him, your career may be over; if he's guilty, well, then, no harm done.

Scrape, Lucas thought, had seemed to him innocent even at the time; and now, almost certainly so. He could have pushed harder, he could have slipped more information to the *Star Tribune,* he could have publicly challenged the verdict on Scrape . . . but he hadn't.

He'd done some poking around, but then, as the youngest member of Daniel's team, he hadn't rocked the boat. Daniel hadn't been dumb enough to forbid him from continuing an investigation, but had simply joked about his efforts—and kept him on the hop with daily investigative chores in the middle of the crack explosion—and Lucas had eventually let the Jones case go.

Had caved, had given up. Had put the Jones girls in his personal out-basket.

God only knew what the killer had done after that. In the best of all worlds, he might have frightened himself so badly that he never again committed a crime. But in the real world, Lucas feared, his own . . . negligence . . . had allowed the killer to continue to kidnap and murder kids. That's what these guys usually did, after they started.

A thin cold blanket of depression fell over Lucas's thoughts. He ran his hand through his hair, once, twice, again and again, trying to make the train of thought go elsewhere.

The Jones girls, back for their summer reunion tour.

2

THERE WAS AN INSTANT, just before the fight, when Lucas Davenport's overweight partner said, "Watch it, he's coming," and he pulled his nightstick and Lucas had time to set his feet. Then Carlos O'Hearn came steaming down the bar, through the stink of spilled beer and hot dogs with relish and boiled eggs in oversized jars, came knocking over bar stools like tenpins, a beer bottle in his right hand, while the bartender leaned away and said, "Noooo . . ."

Ten feet out, O'Hearn pitched the bottle at Lucas's head. Lucas tipped his head to the right and the bottle went by and bounced down the bar, taking out glasses and ashtrays and silverware as it went, so it sounded like somebody had dropped a kitchen tray. A woman made a scream-like sound, but not quite a scream, because it seemed more *interested* than terrorized. Lucas didn't register much of that, because he was focused on O'Hearn, who'd spent some time as a Golden Gloves fighter, in what must have been the germ-weight class.

O'Hearn was one of three siblings known as the asshole brothers to cops working the south side. They also had an asshole mother, but nobody knew for sure about the father. Fleeing Mother O'Hearn may have been simple self-preservation by whoever had made the mistake of impregnating her three times, because she was as violent and crooked and generally rotten and no-good as her sons.

The O'Hearns usually did minor strong-arm robbery, but they'd gotten ambitious and had gone into the back of a True Value hardware store, from which they'd stolen a pile of power tools. Everybody knew exactly *what* they'd taken because of the video cameras that the asshole brothers hadn't noticed, up on the ceiling behind silvered domes. The cameras had taken photos that would have made Ansel Adams proud, if Ansel Adams had ever taken pictures of assholes.

Enzo and Javier were already in the Hennepin County jail, and the bar owner had called 911 to report that Carlos had come in, and was in a bad mood, which usually led to a fight and broken crockery.

So Lucas and his partner rolled, and here they were, O'Hearn coming down the bar with a Golden Gloves punch. Lucas set his feet, dodged the bottle, and, with a reach about nine inches longer than the Golden Glover's, and with an extra eighty pounds or so, and with a fist loaded with a roll of nickels, tagged O'Hearn in the forehead.

The punch had been aimed at his nose, but O'Hearn, too, could dodge, and though the punch crossed his eyes, his momentum kept him coming and they collided and O'Hearn got in two good licks to Lucas's ribs as they went to the floor, where Lucas pinned his arms and his partner started playing the Minnesota Fight Song on O'Hearn's back and right leg with his nightstick.

O'Hearn took about six shots before he whimpered the first time, then Lucas got back just enough to pop him in the nose with the weighted fist, and blood exploded across the bar floor and O'Hearn went flat.

After that, it was routine.

ALL OF WHICH EXPLAINED WHY, when Lucas rolled out of bed and stretched, a lightning stroke of pain shot through his left side, from the cracked ribs he'd taken from those two quick Golden Gloves punches. He stretched again, more carefully, then looked down at the soft round ass of a blond-haired woman and said, "DeeDee. Rise and shine."

"What?" She sounded drugged. She wasn't getting much sleep, she said, between her law practice and keeping two guys happy.

Lucas said, "Get up. You got a bitter woman to talk to."

DeeDee McAllister groaned and said, "Go away."

He smacked her on the bottom and said, "C'mon. You told me not to let you sleep. Let's go. You got a client. You got a three o'clock."

She pushed up and looked at the clock on the bedstand: two o'clock. Dropped back and said, "Ten minutes."

"Ten minutes," Lucas agreed.

They'd rendezvoused in his first-floor apartment in an old brick house in Minneapolis's Uptown. He had two rooms, and a three-quarters bath, with a compact kitchen at one end of his living room, and an oversized leather chair that faced an undersized television.

He headed for the bathroom—a shower, no tub—scrubbed his face, brushed his teeth, hopped in the shower, sudsed up, rinsed, and was out in five minutes.

He stopped to look at himself in a full-length mirror on the back of the bedroom door: he was tall, dark-haired, broad-shouldered, heavily muscled from twenty years of hockey, the last few as a first-line defenseman for the Minnesota Golden Gophers.

He'd lost some muscle since graduation, but that was okay. He'd stopped the obsessive muscle-building workouts, at the advice of the team trainers, and started spending more time on endurance workouts, with lighter weights and more reps. And he was running more.

"You think my dick is bigger than average?" he asked, looking at himself.

McAllister pushed herself up, saw him posing in the mirror, said, "Oh, for Christ's sakes," and fell flat again.

"Well, what do you think?"

"You've seen about a million times more penises than I have, since you spent your entire friggin' life in locker rooms," she said. "I've seen about four."

"Four?" He sounded doubtful.

"Okay, six. Or eight. No more than eight. You've seen a million."

"Yeah, but they weren't, you know, erect," Lucas said. He looked in the mirror again. "I think I'm fairly big."

"I'd say you're on the big side of average," she said. "Now let me get my last minute."

"You think I'm big," he said.

"Big side of average. Maybe. Now gimme my goddamn one minute."

He stood sideways: Big.

HE STEPPED AROUND a pile of hockey gear next to the bed, got out a fresh pair of shorts and a T-shirt. As he was pulling on a T-shirt, McAllister sat up and said, "One thing is, your body gets me hot."

"Gets me hot, too," Lucas said. He rubbed his nipples with the palms of his hands.

"Ah, Jesus." She rubbed her face. "He plays with his own tits." She watched him dress, and smacked her lips and scratched her ass.

11

"C'mon," he said. The apartment bedroom had a tiny closet, too small for his growing collection of clothes, so he'd bought an old oak clothing rack from a used furniture store. From it, he selected a clean pair of uniform pants and a shirt. DeeDee got out of bed and went into the bathroom, stared at her face in the mirror above the sink, and said, finally, "I almost look happy."

"That's good."

"I wish Mark could see me this way," she said.

"Would I have to be standing here?" Lucas asked. Mark was her husband; McAllister was a divorce attorney. She sometimes talked about Mark's gun collection.

"I'd have to think about that," she said. She stepped back into the bedroom and picked up her underpants. "He has a nasty temper and you could protect me. Make me kinda hot seeing two guys fighting over me. Like a princess."

"Everything gets you hot. A domestic protection order gets you hot," Lucas said. They both knew he was telling the truth.

"On the other hand," she continued, "it's considered somewhat déclassé for a prestigious divorce attorney like myself to be caught screwing a humble cop. Even one with an average dick."

"Large." Lucas checked himself in the mirror: Hair still damp, uniform shirt tight across the shoulders and loose around the waist, tightly pressed slacks. Chicks liked pressed slacks, even the hippies; or at least, he suspected they did. His study of women continued. "So you'd have to decide whether you'd rather get beaten up, or be considered déclassé."

"Yeah. I hate to think which way I'd go," she said. "Getting beat up only hurts for a while." He turned and watched her get dressed: she'd draped her clothes neatly on wooden clothes hangers, and hung them on a curtain rod: a woman's business suit, navy blue jacket and skirt over a white blouse, big pads in the jacket shoulders, a narrow red ribbon tie. She had fairly wide, feminine hips, and the combination of shoulder pads and hips made her look, from the back, like a duck.

Lucas didn't say so. His study of women had gotten *that* far. Quack.

Instead, he picked up his duty belt and strapped it around his waist, pulled the Glock from its holster, did an automatic check. He didn't much like the weapon—too white-bread, in his opinion—but that was what he'd been issued and was required to carry. When he made detective, he'd change to something classier. European or something.

McAllister was back in the bathroom, checked herself in the mirror, and came out, smiled, not shyly, but said, "Don't kiss me, you'll mess up my lipstick."

"I'd like to throw you back on the bed and do you one more time," Lucas lied. She was attractive, all right, and she wasn't short on enthusiasm, but he was itching to get out in the car. He liked working nights, and this night was going to be interesting. Early August, people all over the street, and the heat had been building for a week. Rock-out. "Or maybe twice."

"Save it," she said. "I gotta go talk to the bitter woman."

Lucas stuck a finger through the Venetian blind and peeked out: the sky was clear and blue and shimmering with humidity. No sign of her husband.

Party time.

LUCAS HAD BEEN A COP for three years. He'd graduated from the University of Minnesota after five years of study, and four years of hockey—he'd been a rare redshirt the first year, to pick up weight and muscle—with a major in American studies, which, he quickly discovered, qualified him to go back to school. He considered law, but after talking to a few law students, decided that life might be too short.

One of his AmStud professors suggested that he look at law enforcement. "My old man's a cop," the professor said. "You've got the attitude. I think you'd like it. Do it for a few years, *then* look at law school."

His mother was against it: "You'll get shot. Then there'll be nobody left."

She meant, nobody left in the family. His father had died of congenital heart disease when Lucas was in fifth grade. His mother had now been diagnosed with breast cancer, and had convinced herself that she wasn't going to make it.

Lucas had looked into it, sitting up in the university's medical library, and thought she was probably right. He tried not to dwell on that conclusion, because there didn't seem to be anything he could do about it.

Stopping cancer, he thought, was like throwing your body in a river to stop the water. You could weep, scream, demand, research, and pray, and nothing seemed to help. The only help he'd found was in denial: he didn't think about it, particularly when she seemed to be in remission.

He also didn't worry about his own heart—his father's mother had German measles during the pregnancy, he'd been told, and that accounted for the defect that eventually killed him. No genetics involved.

LUCAS WENT OFF to the police academy, scored at the top of his class—would have been at the top in any class anyone could remember—spent a few weeks on patrol, spent six months working dope, then went back on patrol.

Dope was interesting, but he didn't get to do much investigation. He mostly hung out, a white guy in a letter jacket who always knew the spread on college sports, and tried to buy dope in commercial quantities by making friends with the dealers he met. The dealers were everywhere—meeting them wasn't a problem. The problem was, some of them didn't seem like bad guys. They were more like guys his age who couldn't get real jobs. So they'd come up with a kilo, or a pound, and then the real narcs would move in, and bust the dealer. . . .

The whole thing smacked too much of betrayal. You made friends, you bought dope from them, you busted them. The accumulating bad taste moved him back to patrol, which was fun for an ex-jock, a hockey defenseman. There was some excitement, new sights—new insights—and the sense that he was doing something worthwhile.

But after three years, he'd decided he wouldn't do it for too much longer. They'd make him a detective, and pretty quickly, or he'd find something else to do.

What, he didn't know.

Law school. Something. The military? There were no decent wars in sight. . . .

LUCAS WAS OUT sitting on the hood of his assigned squad when Fred Carter, his partner, finally showed up. Carter had missed the second-shift briefing, said he'd been caught in traffic, but he smelled of an Italian meatball sandwich.

"What're we doing?"

"Usual," Lucas said. "Homer's pissed at you."

"I'll talk to him. It was unavoidable," Carter said.

Lucas said, "You got some tomato sauce under your lip. I'd wipe it off before you talk to him."

Carter was a fleshy, bull-necked man who looked like a cabdriver, with blunt features and fingers, and a growing gut. He wasn't stupid, but he was going nowhere in the police department. He knew it, and didn't care. He was in for twenty, and then out. He'd gotten fourteen, and now his main concern was to avoid injury, and to plot out his move to state government, for a second dip in the pension stream.

That attitude was the main bone of contention between them: Lucas enjoyed the occasional fight and didn't mind chasing a man through dark backyards. Carter said, "I don't care if you get your ass kicked, but the problem is, you pull *me* into it. Stop doing that."

"We're cops," Lucas said.

"We're peace officers," Carter snapped back. "Try to keep a little fuckin' peace, okay?"

Yeah, keep a little peace. But what did it mean if a guy went through life thinking about nothing but football—Carter was a big Vikes fan—and a pension? What kind of life was that?

ON THIS AFTERNOON and evening, they checked out their squad and started rolling around in south Minneapolis, taking in the sights; it was one of those late afternoons in the city when everything smelled like melting Juicy Fruit, spilled Orange Crush, and hot tar. Then a drunk Ojibwa, down from Red Lake, climbed up on a fire hydrant, for reasons unknown, gave a speech, fell off, and gashed his head on the top nut. They thought for a moment that he'd been shot, until a witness explained. They called an ambulance and had him transported to Hennepin General, and rolled again.

Carter was short of his quota on traffic tickets that month, so they hid at the bottom of a hill and knocked off three speeders in forty-five minutes, which put him back square. It wasn't a quota, it was a performance metric. The chief said so, with a straight face.

They hit a convenience store on Lyndale, scowled at the dope dealers, who moseyed off, and Carter got a fried cherry pie and a Pepsi. They rolled away, and the dope dealers moseyed back. A half-hour later, they checked out a report of a fight in the parking lot of a bar. There'd been one, all right, but everybody ran when the car pulled up, and there were no bodies and no blood, and nobody knew who was involved.

They got a couple more soft drinks, Diet Coke for Lucas, another Pepsi for Carter, and moved along, arguing Coke versus Pepsi, took a call about another fight, this one at an antique store.

When they got there, two women, one heavy and one thin, both with fashionable blond haircuts, were squared off on the sidewalk, the dealer between them, a clerk peering out from the gold-leafed doorway. The fight hadn't actually taken place yet, and Lucas and Carter separated the two women, one of whom told the other, "You're lucky the cops got here, or I would have stuffed that chiffonier right up your fat butt."

"Oh, yeah, bitch-face, let me tell you . . ." What she told her couldn't be reported in any of the better home furnishings magazines, Lucas thought, as it included four of the seven words George Carlin said you couldn't use on television. The fat one was definitely ready to go, until Carter said, "If we have to take you in, they *will* discover any chiffoniers you got up there. It's called a body-cavity search, and you won't like it."

That cooled them off, and they left in their respective Mercedeses.

"It's the heat that does it," Carter observed to the antique dealer.

"Maybe not," the dealer said. "It's a gorgeous chiffonier."

"WHAT THE FUCK is a chiffonier?" Lucas asked, as they rolled away.

"One of those coffee-serving things," Carter said. "You know, that go around in circles."

Lucas studied him for a moment, then said, "You got no idea what a chiffonier is."

"That's true."

"But I liked the way you handled it. That strip-search line," Lucas said. "Took it right out of them."

"Like I said: keep the peace," Carter said.

"Really. You shoulda been a cop or something."

AT FIVE O'CLOCK, Lucas spotted a man named Justice Johnson, who'd beaten up his old lady once too often; a warrant had been issued. They corralled him in the recessed entry of a locksmith's shop. He'd been eating a raw onion, as though it were an apple, and it bounced away into the gutter as they cuffed him. He didn't bother to fight, and bitched and moaned about his woman, who, he said, did nothing but pick at him.

"Bitch said I'm a dumbass," Johnson said from the backseat of the squad. He was breathing out onion fumes, which were not diminished in any way by his overindulgence in Drakkar Noir.

"You *are* a dumbass, Justice," Carter said.

"Hey, she ain't supposed to say it," Johnson said. "She's supposed to take my side, but she never does. All she does is bitch, you ain't done this, you ain't done that. . . ."

"So you beat her up," Lucas said.

"I slapped her."

"Broke her nose," said Carter.

"Didn't mean to do that."

"Shut up, dumbass," Lucas said. "And quit breathing on me."

He didn't. He sat looking out the window for a minute, then said, "I think I'm peeing my pants."

"Ah, Jesus, don't do that," Lucas said.

"Gotcha, cop," Johnson said. He laughed for a minute, going huh-huh-huh, then said, "And my name ain't Jesus. You think I look like a fuckin' Puerto Rican?"

"You shoulda made the cuffs tighter," Carter said.

"I shoulda put them around his fuckin' windpipe," Lucas said.

They booked him into the Hennepin County jail.

AT TWENTY MINUTES after six o'clock, they took a call on two missing girls. It was still full daylight, and the dispatchers sent them down to the Mississippi, below the I-94 bridge. The two girls had been known to play along the river, although they'd been warned against it by their parents.

In the three years Lucas had been a cop, he'd seen most of what he'd ever see from a patrol car: murders, actual and attempted, the aftermath of robberies and burglaries, and even a couple of those in progress, as well as suicides, fights, mini-riots, car and foot chases, even an emergency pregnancy run, the woman screaming for help from the backseat. The baby arrived one minute after Lucas put the car at the emergency room door, delivered by a doc and a couple of nurses right on the gurney. The baby, rumor had it, had been named Otto, after the car ride.

Carter said, "That's always the rumor. That they called him Otto."

"It's a pretty good rumor," Lucas said. "I've been telling it to everybody."

There'd been a couple of lost kids over the years, but they'd been quickly found. These two had vanished between four and five o'clock, when kids were walking home for dinner, not heading down to the river.

They parked the car and headed over to the slope down to the Mississippi. The river at that point was a few hundred yards across, a sullen dark green, with streaks of foam from the falls just up the river. The bank down to the water was steep and overgrown with brush, cut by slippery dirt paths down the slope worn by walkers, marked with thrown-away food wrappers, and here and there, a wad of toilet paper back in the bushes.

A concrete walk ran along the river's edge, leading both north and south, with an informal beach area where Lucas and Carter came down to the river. A fat woman in shorts was wading in the water up to her knees, and a kid in cutoff jeans was farther out, with a spin-fishing rod, casting out into deeper water. A few more people were scattered along the edge of the water, sitting, wading, or swimming.

None of them had seen the girls.

They'd finished talking with people at the beach when they were joined by cops from another squad, and the four of them split up, two north and two south, up and down the Mississippi, from the access path that the girls would have taken to the water. Three hundred yards downstream Lucas and Carter came upon a group of gays, at the gay beach. One of the men said that they hadn't seen the girls, either on the bank or in the water, and they'd been there all afternoon.

Lucas and Carter walked back upstream, Carter fulminating about the gays: "Fuckin' queer motherfuckers, buncha goddamn fudge-punchers walking around in jockstraps in the middle of the day. Did you see that guy? He didn't give a shit. . . ."

"You sound kind of excited about it, Fred," Lucas observed. "Kind of aroused."

"Screw you, skate boy," Carter said. "Where in the hell are the sex guys, is what I want to know."

"They didn't see the kids," Lucas said. "If the kids'd gone in the water, you'd think they would have seen them. They say the kids could swim."

"Yeah." Carter hooked his thumbs over his belt and looked out at the water, which was low and flat and smelled of carp. "Not very deep here, either. I got a bad feeling about this, Lucas. I don't think they're in the river."

"No?"

"I think somebody took them," Carter said. "I think they're getting raped, right now, while we're standing here with our thumbs up our asses."

"Gut feeling?"

"Yep."

Carter wasn't much of a cop, but his gut had a record of good calls. Fourteen years rolling around on the street seemed to have given him—or his gut, anyway—a sense of the rightness of particular behavior. If his gut said that he and Lucas were doing the wrong thing, they probably were, and Lucas had come to recognize that fact. "What do you think we oughta be doing?"

"Looking up there," Carter said, pointing at the top of the bank, but meaning the south side in general. "The kids were walking past a lot of houses with a lot of weirdos in them. We oughta be shaking them out."

"Somebody's doing it," Lucas said.

"*Everybody* ought to be doing it," Carter said.

The other two cops, who'd walked upstream, came back with nothing to report. "You get down to the fruit market?" one of them asked Carter.

"Yeah, they saw nothin'," Carter said. "Bunch of bare-assed perverts . . ."

THEY WERE TALKING to a bum who'd appeared from under the I-94 bridge when a thin, freckled, red-haired man came jogging down the bank and called, "You find them? Anybody see them?"

Lucas asked, "Who are you?"

"George Jones. I'm their father, I'm their dad. Did anybody see them?" He was in his middle to late thirties, panting, and his sweatshirt, sleeves ripped off at the shoulder, was soaked in sweat, which they could smell coming off him, in waves. He was wearing a green army baseball cap with a combat infantryman's badge on it, and was breathing hard. One of the other cops stepped up and said, "You gotta take it easy—we'll find them."

"They've never done this," Jones said, his eyes and voice pleading with them for help. "Never. They're always on time. They're three hours late, nobody's seen them . . ."

Carter said, "I don't believe they're down here, Mr. Jones. We've talked to people all along here; they didn't see them. Quite a few people down here on a hot Saturday, they would have been seen."

Jones said, "All right. All right, thanks. They're probably . . . god-damnit, I'm going to beat their butts when they get back; they're prob-ably at a friend's house." Still talking to himself, he jogged back up the bank and they heard him shout to someone out of sight, "They're not down there . . . nobody's seen them."

One of the other cops said, looking out at the dark, drifting river, "Coulda stepped in a hole and got sucked under . . ."

Carter shook his head. "They ain't down here," he said. "We're wasting our time."

GEORGE JONES, the girls' father, belonged to a lefty ex-military organiza-tion, and he'd put out a call for help. Members of the Vietnam Veterans Against the War began showing up at seven o'clock, still not dark: a mis-cellaneous collection of haunted-looking men wearing pieces of military uniform, mixed with anti-war buttons and patches. A few dozen strong, they began working their way through alleys and backyards, within a half-mile of Jones's house, staying in touch by calling back and forth.

Just before it got seriously dark, Lucas and Carter were flagged by a vet off Thirty-fourth Street. When they stopped, the vet leaned into the car window and said, "We got a girl's blouse. Nobody touched it, but somebody needs to take a look."

They parked and called in, and Lucas walked down to an alley to where a bunch of vets had gathered around what looked like a rag, lying beside a hedge, as though somebody had thrown it out a car window. Lucas squatted next to it, and shined his flashlight on it. A girl's blouse, all right, blue with little white speckles. He called in again, on his shoulder set. Then he stood up and said, "We got some detectives coming. I don't know if it's anything, but good work, guys."

Carter said, "Good eyes."

"I hope it's not hers, I hope it's not," said a thin, crazy-looking man with a six-day beard. He was wearing an army OD uniform shirt with the sleeves cut off just below a buck sergeant's black-on-green stripes. "I got girls of my own, I mean . . ."

A car turned in at the mouth of the alley, and a man got out: Harrison Sloan, a youngish detective not long off patrol. He ambled down the alley, and Lucas pointed. Sloan squatted, as Lucas had, and Lucas put his flashlight on the blouse. Sloan looked at it for a minute, then said, "Goddamnit."

"Is it one of theirs?" asked one of the vets.

Sloan said, "Could be." He stood and looked around, and then asked, "Who found it? Who exactly?"

One of the vets raised his hand.

Sloan worked the group, taking notes, and a couple more plainclothes guys showed up, then Quentin Daniel, the Homicide lieutenant, and Carter muttered to Lucas, "It's her shirt. They know it. They're gone."

Daniel took his own long look at the shirt, shook his head, said a few words to the three detectives now talking to the vets, then turned and walked back to Lucas and Carter. "We need to go over this whole block, foot by foot. Carter, I already talked to Phil"—Phil Blessing was the head of the uniform section—"and he's rounding up twenty guys to get down here and walk it off. You think you can organize that?"

"Sure, I guess," Carter said.

Daniel turned to Lucas. "This is gonna be a mess. I'm borrowing you. Go home and put on a shirt and tie. You got a shirt and tie?"

"Sure."

"All right. I'm hooking you up with Sloan. I want you guys door-to-door. We're gonna interview every swinging dick for a half-mile around. Take the squad: I want you back here in twenty minutes."

"You got it, Chief," Lucas said.

Daniel had been his boss when he was working dope, just out of the academy. Daniel had taken an interest, enough that Lucas wondered briefly if he was queer. But he realized after a while that Daniel was interested in the way other people saw the world; other people including new cops. He also learned that Daniel expected to be chief, one day, and didn't mind being called that.

And Lucas knew that he wasn't being promoted. He was being used to pump up the apparent number of detectives working the case. There'd be four or five more patrolmen walking around in shirts and ties before the night was done.

He could think about that later. He climbed in the squad, drove it to the end of the block before he hit the lights and sirens, and took off, the traffic clearing out in front of him, pedestrians stopping with their toes on the curb, watching him go by. Wondering, maybe, about the smile on his face.

HE WAS BACK at his apartment in six minutes, and took another thoughtful six minutes to get into a pair of light khaki slacks, a short-sleeve white shirt, and a navy blue linen sport coat with a wine-colored tie. He hesitated over the short-sleeve shirt, because *Esquire* magazine despised them; but then, *Esquire* editors probably didn't have to walk through slum neighborhoods in ninety-degree heat.

He accessorized with black loafers, over-the-calf navy socks, and, from behind his chest of drawers, a Smith & Wesson Model 40 revolver with a belt-clip holster. He checked himself in the mirror again.

Lucas liked clothes—always had. They were, he thought, the chosen symbols of a person's individuality, or lack of it; not a trivial matter. They were also uniforms, and it paid a cop to understand the uniform of the person with whom he was dealing, to distinguish between, say, dope dealer, hippie, gangbanger, biker, skater, artist, and bum.

In addition to his intellectual interest, he liked to look good.

He did, he thought, and was out the door.

Still a little worried about the short sleeves.

3

LUCAS WORKED WITH Sloan late into the night, slogging up and down the dark, declining residential streets, pounding on doors. Ordinarily, there might have been enough bad people around—crack cocaine had arrived that spring, and was spiraling out of control—to inject some extra stress into the work. On this night, there were so many cops on the street that the bad people moved over.

"Weird thing happened with crack," Sloan observed, as they tramped between houses, and the dark shadows between streetlights and elm trees. "The pimps got fired. We used to think that the hookers were slaves. Turns out it was more complicated than that."

"I gotta say, I haven't seen some of the boys around," Lucas said.

"They're gone. They've been laid off. Had to sell their hats," Sloan said.

Lucas said, "When I was working dope, nobody even heard of crack. You had a few guys freebasing, but other than that, it was right up the nose."

"Chemical genius out there somewhere," Sloan said.

"Sales genius," Lucas said. "Toot for the common people."

Sloan was a few years older than Lucas, a narrow-slatted man who dressed in earth colors from JCPenney. When he wore something flashy, it was usually a necktie, probably chosen by his wife; and it was usually a glittery, gecko green. He'd been developing a reputation as an interrogator, because of a peculiar, caring, soft-talking approach he took to suspects. He was as conservative in lifestyle as in dress, having gotten married at eighteen to his high-school sweetheart. He had two daughters before he was twenty-one, and worried about insurance. As different as they were, Lucas liked him.

Sloan had a sense of humor, and a good idea of who he was. He was quiet and cool and smart.

"The word is, you're moving to plainclothes right away," Sloan said, as they moved across the dark end of a block, ready to start on another circle of houses. "Compared to patrol, it's a different world. Patrol is like football; plainclothes is like chess."

"Or like hockey," Lucas said.

Sloan looked at him suspiciously. "I'll have to assume that's your sense of humor talking," he said.

"Why's that?" Lucas asked.

"It's well known that hockey guys are almost as dumb as baseball players."

"I didn't know that," Lucas said.

"It's true," Sloan said. "In the major college sports, football's at the top of the intelligence ratings, then wrestling, then basketball, then golf, swimming, hockey, baseball, and tennis, in that order."

"Tennis is at the bottom?"

"Yup. Not only that, the further west you go, the dumber the athletes get," Sloan said. "By the time you get to the Midwest, tennis players are dumber'n a box of rocks. Across the Rockies? Don't even ask. The tennis players out there are not so much human, as dirt."

"Dirt?"

"Dirt."

"Something else I didn't know," Lucas said.

"Well, you *were* a hockey player."

THEY PUSHED THROUGH the gate on a chain-link fence, toward a clapboard house with a narrow front porch with a broken-down couch sitting on it, and a light in one window. Sloan pointed his flashlight into the side yard, at a circle of dirt around an iron stake, and said, "Bad dog."

"Could be a horseshoes pit," Lucas said.

Sloan laughed. "So you go first."

Lucas moved up to the door and knocked, and a dog went crazy behind the door.

"Bad dog," Sloan said behind him. "Sounds like one of those bull terriers."

Nobody answered for a minute, then two. Lucas pounded again, and a light came on at the back of the house. Another minute, and a man appeared, opening the door just an inch, looked at them over a heavy chain lock. "Who're you?"

Sloan explained, and the man started shaking his head halfway through the explanation. "I didn't see no white girls doin' nothin'," he said. The dog was snuffling at the man's pant leg, its toenails scratching anxiously on the linoleum. "I gotta go to bed. I gotta get up at five o'clock."

Walking back down the sidewalk, Sloan asked, "You hear what happened to Park Brubaker?" Brubaker was a Korean-American detective, now suspended and looking at time on federal drug charges.

"Yeah. Dumb shit."

"He had problems," Sloan said.

"I got problems," Lucas said. "I don't go robbing people for their Apple Jacks."

They came to a door on Thirty-fifth Avenue, answered by a heavyset white man with a Hemingway beard and a sweaty forehead and an oversized nose. A fat nose. He said, "We didn't see nothin' at all. Except what was on TV." A woman standing behind him said, "Tell them about John."

"Who's John?" Lucas asked.

"Dude down at Kenny's," the man said, with reluctance. "Don't know his last name."

"He's got a suspect," the woman said.

The man scowled at her, and Lucas pressed: "So what about John?"

"Dude said that there was a crazy guy probably did it," the man said. "Crazy guy's been running around the neighborhood."

"You know the crazy guy?" Sloan asked.

"No. We heard John talking about him."

"We've seen him, walking around, though. The crazy guy," the woman said.

"Did John say why he thought the crazy guy did it?" Lucas asked.

"He said the guy was always lookin', and never gettin' any. Said the guy had a record, you know, for sex stuff."

25

"He call the cops?" Sloan asked.

"I dunno. I don't know the guy. I don't know the crazy guy, either, except that I see him on the street sometimes."

"Gotta call it in," Sloan said.

He had a handset with him, and walked back down the sidewalk while Lucas talked to the man, and especially past him, to the woman. He asked, "What do you know about John? We *really* need to find him. If he knows anything . . . I mean, these two girls might not have much time. . . ."

He got a description—John was an overweight man of average height, with an olive complexion and dark hair that curled over his forehead. "Italian-looking," the woman said.

Lucas said, "You mean good-looking?"

"No. He's too fat. But he's dark, and he wears those skimpy T-shirts—the kind Italians wear, with the straps over the shoulders?—under regular shirts that he wears open. He's got this gold chain."

The last time they'd seen him, he was wearing jeans and a blue long-sleeved shirt, open over the wife-beater. She added that he liked some of the *girls* who came in, and she put a little spin on the word "girls."

"You mean, working girls," Lucas said. "I didn't know they hung at Kenny's."

"They don't, but there's that massage place across the street," she said. "They come over, sometimes, when they don't have clients. I don't like to see them in there, myself. I mean, what if somebody thought *I* was one of them."

The guy said, "I wouldn't mind a massage," and the woman punched him on the arm, and he said, "Ouch."

THEY DIDN'T HAVE much else. A moment later, Sloan came back up the walk. "Cherry and McGuire are coming over," he said.

"What for? We got what there is," Lucas said.

"Because they don't think we got what there is," Sloan said. "We're supposed to wait until they get here, then knock on some more doors."

"Fuck that," Lucas said. "We need to get over to Kenny's."

"Closed two hours ago," the man said.

"Might still be somebody there," Lucas said.

Everybody shrugged, and Sloan said, "They want us to finish knockin' on the doors."

CHERRY AND MCGUIRE showed up, two fortyish veterans, and took over. Lucas and Sloan moved on down the block, and got nowhere, Lucas fuming about being knocked off the only positive hint they'd gotten.

"We did the work, man, they oughta let us take it."

"Get used to it," Sloan said. "Takes about four years before you're a pro. That's what they're telling me. I got three to go."

"Fuck a bunch of four years," Lucas said. He hadn't told the older detectives about the massage parlor girls who might know John. Let them find it out themselves.

They worked for two more hours, and Sloan finally quit at the end of his shift and went home to his wife. "I don't even know what we're doing," he said. "We think the kidnapper'll come to the door and confess?"

"Somebody must have seen something," Lucas said. "Seen the kids getting in a car. Seen them going through a door. They can't just go away."

"Somebody would have called, if they were gonna talk," Sloan said. "When we found that blouse . . . we should have looked around at the baddest guy on the block, and squeezed his pimple head until he coughed them up."

Lucas shook his head. "That blouse wasn't right."

"What?"

"Wasn't right. Why in the hell would you throw a blouse out a car window? I can see throwing the girl out, if nobody was looking. But why would you throw a blouse out? Tell me one reason."

Sloan thought for a moment and said, "The guy killed her, took her blouse as a trophy. The bodies are already in a dumpster somewhere, and he was driving around with the blouse over his face, smelling the chick, getting off on it. At some point, he gets tired of it, or can't smell her anymore, so he throws it out the window."

Lucas grinned at him and said, "That's perverted. I kinda like it."

★

THE NIGHT WAS still warm, for August, with a hint of rain in the still air. They drove back to Lucas's place in Sloan's Dodge, arms out the side windows, Lucas thinking how quiet the city was, and for all they knew, somewhere in its quiet heart, two little girls were being tortured by a monster.

Sloan dropped him, and went on his way. Lucas went inside, got a beer, sat at the kitchen table and looked at a blue three-ring binder stuffed with paper. In school, he'd lived in an apartment inhabited mostly by nerds from the computer center. Despite his jock status, he had been pulled into some of their role-playing games. Then he wrote a module, which had impressed the nerds, who said it was as good as the commercial modules.

Talking around with the computer guys, he developed an idea for a football-based strategy game, similar to the war games popular in the seventies, but that would be played on a computer. A computer guy promised to program it, if Lucas could write the scenarios. The work had been harder than he'd expected, and had been delayed when he'd had to take a course in statistics: he wanted the game to be *real*.

He sat and looked at paper, which, after the day hunting for the girls, looked like *silly paper*. Games. Something awful was happening outside, and he was sitting at the kitchen table looking at *silly paper*.

He fooled with the coaching modules for a while, then gave up and got a second beer, glanced at the clock. Two o'clock in the morning. He wondered if Cherry and McGuire had gone down to Kenny's, and what they'd found.

Restless, he picked up his sport coat, climbed in his Jeep, and headed downtown, left the car at the curb, and walked into City Hall. The place was dark but busy, with cops all over the hallways. Lucas stopped a uniformed guy named Morgan and asked what had happened. "Nothing," Morgan said. "No sign of them. People are talking about the river again."

"I don't think they're in there," Lucas said. "How many guys are working it?"

"Right now? A half-dozen. Daniel's still here, but people are starting to freak—the TV people are driving around in their truck. It's turning into a circus."

"You seen Cherry or McGuire?" Lucas asked.

"Not for a while."

Lucas went down to Homicide, stuck his head in the office, spotted Daniel with his feet up on a desk, talking to a couple of detectives. Lucas went in, idled off to the side for a minute, until Daniel said, "Davenport. What's happening?"

"I wondered if Cherry and McGuire got anything at Kenny's?"

Daniel shook his head and said, "Not much more than you got." He looked at a piece of paper on his desk. "The place was closed, but they talked to the manager. He says it's a guy named John. Nobody knows where he lives, or how to get in touch. Just a guy."

"So they struck out," Lucas said.

"Well, it's something," Daniel said.

"Right," said one of the detectives. "We've got a suspect named 'John.' That narrows it down."

Daniel ignored him: "How come you're still running around?" he asked Lucas.

"Couldn't sleep," Lucas said. "I was thinking, you know, if it's all right with you . . . I might go down and hit that massage place across from Kenny's. Unless Cherry and McGuire already did."

"No, they didn't," Daniel said. "Why would they?"

"Didn't they get that? That John knows some of those chicks? Maybe that's why they call him John. Maybe he is one," Lucas said.

An annoyed look crept across Daniel's face. "I guess they didn't get that. You didn't mention it?"

"They told us to take a hike," Lucas said. "So . . . I'm not doing much."

"Step outside with me," Daniel said, standing up.

In the hall, he said, quietly, but showing some teeth, "You're not fuckin' with us, are you? Withholding information so you can get a shot at it? With these two girls, this wouldn't be the time to make points."

"Hell no," Lucas lied. "I wouldn't do that."

"You should have told Cherry and McGuire what the woman said."

"They didn't want to hear it," Lucas said. "They were like, 'Uh-huh, go knock on doors, rook.'"

Daniel looked at him for a minute, then said, "I can't pay you overtime. But if you go down there, I'll back you up if anything comes out of it."

Lucas nodded. "Okay. How long you gonna be here?"

"Not much longer. Don't call me unless you get something serious—but call me if you do." He gave Lucas his office and home phone numbers.

"Did we get anything tonight? Anything?"

Daniel shook his head. "We got that blouse, and it was Mary's. Nobody knows how it got there. We think the kids might have walked past Andy's Cleaners. One of the desk girls says she saw them. That's only about a block from their house, so maybe she did. It was early, before they were missing."

"But they were together?" ·

"That's what the girl says," Daniel said.

"Were they walking toward their house, or away?"

"Away."

"Any blood on the blouse?" Lucas asked.

"Not sure. There's a small discoloration, could be blood that some-body tried to wash out. We'll know tomorrow morning."

"You think they're dead?" Lucas asked.

"Probably not yet. But they will be, soon."

PAUL'S THERAPEUTIC MASSAGE occupied the end store in a five-busi-ness strip that included a movie rental place, a coin laundry, a dog groomer, and a medical-oxygen service. Lucas parked in front of the massage parlor. A light shone from one window, but a red neon "Open" sign had been turned off.

When Lucas climbed out of the Jeep and slammed the door, a curtain moved in the window, and he caught the pale flash of a wom-an's face. He walked up to the entrance, tried the handle: the heavy steel-cored door was locked. He pounded on it, got no answer. He pounded louder, still got no answer, so he kicked it a few times, shak-ing the door in its frame, and heard a woman shout, "We're closed. Go away."

Lucas pounded again and shouted, "Police. Open up."

He waited for a minute, then kicked the door a few more times—carefully, with the heel, since he was still wearing the loafers—stopped when he heard a bolt rattling on the other side of the lock. The door opened a couple of inches, a chain across the gap, and a narrow blond woman asked, "Cop?"

Lucas held up his badge: "We're looking for two missing girls. I need information about a guy you know."

"What guy?"

"His name is John. You guys hang out with him sometimes at Kenny's. That's all I know," Lucas said.

The door opened another couple of inches. "Did he do it?"

"He was telling people that he knows who did," Lucas said. He pushed the door with his fingertips, and she let it swing open a bit more. "So who is he?"

She looked back over her shoulder and shouted, "Sally."

Lucas pushed on the door again, and she let it open. He took that as an invitation, and stepped into a ten-foot-long room with a Formica counter and yellowing white-plaster walls, like in a dry-cleaning shop. A couple of chairs sat against the window wall, with a low wooden table between them, holding an ashtray and a table lamp with a shade that had a burned spot on one side. A gumball machine sat in a corner, half empty, or half full, depending. Not a place that people would linger for long, Lucas thought.

A short dark-haired woman came out of the back, behind the counter, looked at Lucas and said, "I'm all done."

"He's a cop," the blonde said. "He's looking for this guy John . . . you know, *John*, the joker."

Sally shook her head: "Why would I know where he is?"

The blonde said, "You'd know better than me. They're looking for him about those two girls."

Sally's right hand went to her throat: "*He* took them?"

"He's been talking about who might have," Lucas said. "We need to talk to him."

"I really don't know him," Sally said. "He's come in a few times, I got him, you know, gave him a massage. He's kinda funny, tells jokes and shit."

"He ever say where he lives? Ask you to come over? Give you any hint . . . ?"

She shook her head: "No, but I'll tell you what. He charged the massage last time. I bet we got the slip."

Lucas ticked a finger at her: "*Thank you*. Who do I see about the slip?"

"Me," the blonde said. "But since we don't know his last name, I don't know how we figure out . . ."

Sally pressed her palms to her eyes and said, "Let me think," and a minute later said, "Fourth of July. He was joking about fireworks, you know, when . . . never mind. Anyway, the night of the fourth. Don had a baseball game on the radio, so it couldn't have been too late."

The blonde went around the counter, took out a metal box, and began running through charge slips. Lucas said to Sally, "You said he's okay. That means, what? He didn't want anything peculiar?"

"Hey, it was a therapeutic massage."

"I'm sure it was," Lucas said. "Look, I don't care what he wants, or what you do. I'm trying to figure out these girls and whether he might be weird. Can you tell me that? Is he weird?"

Sally shrugged: "He wants the Three—start with a hand job, end with a blow job. Is that weird? I dunno. A hundred and twenty bucks, plus tip. I don't remember the tip, but it wasn't . . ." She dug for a word, and came up with one: "Memorable."

"So he's got some money."

"He's got *some*, anyway," the woman said. "But I ain't going to Vegas on a tip I can't remember."

The blonde said, "I got a one-forty at eight forty-five Friday . . . that's it, probably. Says his name is John . . ."

"That's gotta be him," Sally said.

Lucas took the slip and walked it to the table lamp. The ink imprint was shaky—the name was John Fell, Lucas thought, but the number was clear. Lucas took down the information, then asked, "You got a Xerox machine?"

"No . . ."

"I'm gonna take this," he said, waggling the paper slip. "You need the information to make the charge?"

"We already made it," the blonde said. "We send it in while you're still in the room."

"Okay." Lucas flipped a page in his notebook: "I need both your names. I want to see driver's licenses. I need to know how often he comes in."

The blonde began, "You said . . ."

Lucas shook his head: "I'm not arresting anybody. If he turns out to be somebody, I need to know who I talked to."

The blonde's name was Lucy Landry, and Sally's name was Dorcas Ryan. John Fell had come in at least once in the past ten days, had been cheerful, funny, even, had been satisfied with the service and paid cash. Ryan had seen him at Kenny's afterward, and he'd bought her a drink.

"He bought you a drink, but he didn't chat? Didn't tell you about himself?"

Ryan frowned: "You know what? Almost all he does is tell jokes. Like, 'You heard the one about the priest who caught the sonofabitch?' That's what he does. He's got a million of them."

Lucas used their telephone to call Daniel at home, who answered and, when Lucas identified himself, said, "This better be good."

"The guy's name is John Fell and I've got a credit card slip on him. How do I get an address off the credit card?"

There was a moment of silence, then Daniel said, "What I usually do is call Harmon Anderson, and he does something on the computer."

"So we gotta wait until he comes in?"

"No, no, I'll bust him out of bed," Daniel said. "Where're you?"

"Down at the massage place," Lucas said.

"Go on downtown. I'll have Anderson meet you there."

He hung up, and Ryan was telling Landry, ". . . so the Pope takes off his hat, puts his feet up on the table, and says, 'You know what? You fuckers are all right.'"

Landry only half smiled: "It's not that funny."

"I didn't say it was great," Ryan said. She looked at Lucas. "I told her John's *sonofabitch* joke."

Lucas shrugged: "I missed it. Can you break a dollar? I need a gumball."

BOTTOM LINE, Lucas thought, on his way downtown: he didn't know how to get an address for a credit card. He needed to fix that. He

33

chewed through the gumball in two minutes, threw the wad of gum out the window and drove faster.

He got there before Anderson, and had to wait. Anderson showed up twenty-five minutes later, sleepy and annoyed, sat down at his desk and turned on his computer. Lucas was looking over his shoulder and asked, "What're you doing here?"

"A credit check," Anderson said. "All the credit information is in computers. I can get in and look at some of the information for credit card holders. Including addresses and so on."

"Neat," Lucas said. "I'm thinking of getting a Macintosh."

"Wait awhile—there're rumors that they're going to 512K this fall. The 128K just isn't enough."

"Can't afford it for a while, anyway," Lucas said.

"You patrol guys know all the crack freaks," Anderson said. "You oughta be able to get one wholesale."

"Pretty fuckin' funny," Lucas said.

"No offense," Anderson said.

He sounded insincere, Lucas thought. He shut up and watched Anderson work. Five minutes after he started, Anderson had a name and address: "It's a post office box."

"That's not good." He wasn't a detective yet, but he knew that much.

"The post office will have a name and address for the renter," Anderson said. "But the thing is, credit card companies don't usually take post office boxes. Did the hookers get paid?"

"They said so," Lucas said.

"Huh. Well, something's not right."

THE POST OFFICE worked twenty-four hours a day, seven days a week. The front end was closed, but Lucas found his way in through the loading dock in the back and showed his ID to a couple of guys throwing canvas mail bags off a truck. One of them went inside and came back with a bureaucrat.

"I can't tell you that," he said. He was a fat little man, fish-pale with what must have been a permanent night shift. "It's privileged information."

"We got two girls missing—"

34

"I'm sorry, but it's against the law for me to give you that information," the bureaucrat said. "Come back with a search warrant and give it to the postmaster."

"This guy could be killing them," Lucas said.

"The law says—"

"Then give me the number for the postmaster," Lucas said.

"I can't do that. It's the middle of the night."

At some level, Lucas realized, the man was enjoying himself, sticking it to the cops. It was possible and even likely that there was a law or regulation about releasing the names of post office box renters; but, he thought, there sure as hell wasn't a law about calling up the postmaster, even in the middle of the night.

Lucas got his face close to the bureaucrat's. "I'll tell you what. One way or another, I'm gonna get the name off the box. And if these girls are killed, I'm gonna take this conversation to the newspapers and I'm gonna hang it around your neck like a dead skunk. When they find these girls' bodies, you'll have reporters standing in your front yard yelling at you."

The man flushed: "You can't threaten me. The law—"

Lucas crowded closer: "The law doesn't say you can't wake up the postmaster. Does it? Does the law say that?"

The man was furious, and said, "On your head."

"On yours," Lucas said. "You're now gonna come out looking like an asshole no matter what you do."

The bureaucrat said, "Wait here," and disappeared into the post office.

One of the truck loaders said, "He *is* an asshole. That's his job."

"Yeah, well, I got no time for it," Lucas said.

THE BUREAUCRAT CAME BACK a minute later, and said, "I got the superintendent of mails on the phone."

Lucas talked to the superintendent of mails, who said, "I'm waiving the confidentiality reg in this case because of the emergency, but I'm going to need a letter from your chief outlining the problem. I need to file it."

"You'll get it," Lucas said.

"Put Gene back on the line."

Lucas left the post office ten minutes later with the paper in his hand: John Fell at an address on Sixth Street SE, Minneapolis. Five minutes away, the sun coming up over St. Paul.

In his first year as a cop, working patrol and then, briefly, as a dope guy, he'd felt that he was learning things at a ferocious rate: about the street, life, death, sex, love, hate, fear, stupidity, jealousy, and accident, and all the other things that brought citizens in contact with the cops.

Then the learning rate tailed off. He'd continued to accumulate detail, to see faces, to interpret moves, but at nothing like the rate of his first ten or twelve months.

Now, investigating, the feeling was back: getting credit card numbers off computers—cool. Manipulating hookers. Threatening bureaucrats. He was crude, and he knew it, but it was interesting and he'd get better at it.

HE'D LEARN ABOUT DISAPPOINTMENT, too, he found out a few minutes later.

The address on Sixth Street was a shabby old three-story Victorian house that smelled of rot and microwave food, with six mailboxes nailed to the gray clapboard on the porch. All but one of the mailboxes had names, none of which was Fell. None of them had a John or a J.

The one unlabeled mailbox was for Apartment Five. He curled up a long zigzag stairway, half blocked at one landing by a bicycle chained to the banister, and pounded on the door to Apartment Five until a woman shouted from Six, "Nobody lives there. Go away."

He stepped across the hall and rapped on her door: "Police. Could you open the door, please?"

"No. I'm not crazy," the woman shouted back. "What do you want?"

"I'm looking for a John Fell," Lucas said.

"There's nobody here named John Fell. Or anything Fell," she shouted.

"You mean, in your apartment, or in the house?"

"In the house. There's nobody named John Fell. Go away or I'll call nine-one-one."

"Call nine-one-one. Tell them there's a cop at your door named Lucas Davenport. I'll call them on my handset. . . ."

She did that, and opened the door three minutes later, a woman in her early twenties with bad sleep hair. "It *is* you. You played hockey with a friend of mine. Jared Michael? I'd see you on the ice."

"Oh, hell, yes," Lucas said. "I haven't seen him lately, maybe a couple years . . ."

"He's in marketing at General Mills," she said. "He works twenty-two hours a day. You're looking for those girls? I didn't even know you were a cop now."

"Yeah, I am, and we're looking for a guy named John Fell," Lucas said. He described Fell, and she was shaking her head.

"Everybody in this house is a student. Three apartments are Asians, I'm by myself, Five is empty and has been empty all year—it's got a bad smell they can't get out. The previous tenants put rat poison inside their walls because they could hear rats running, and I guess all the rats died and now they're in the walls rotting and there's no way to get them out."

"Nice story," Lucas said.

"Yeah, well." She took a moment to sweep her hair back from her face. "The last apartment, One, is Bobby and Vicki Arens, and Bobby's got red hair and he's about six-six."

"Who's been here the longest?"

"Well, me . . . and the Lees, in Four. We both got here two years ago. The Lees, you know, are Chinese, they're studying medicine. They're really nice."

"Okay. Shoot. I'm sorry I woke you up," Lucas said.

"Listen, come on in for some Rice Krispies," she said. "We can think about it. I won't be able to get back to sleep anyway."

"Huh," he said. He looked at his watch. A little after five-thirty, and he could use a bite, and she was a pretty woman. "All right."

IN ADDITION TO a bowl of Rice Krispies, he advanced another inch in his education. The woman's name was Katie Darin, and she suggested that a student house would be the perfect place to set up a fake credit card, or a mail drop.

"Nobody knows who's coming and going—people move in and out all the time," she said. "The post office still delivers mail to my box for people who haven't lived here for years. So, you know, you want a fake ID, you have it delivered here. The post office doesn't know. Everybody's in class when the mailman comes. He comes at ten o'clock, and this place is empty."

"The guy I'm looking for set up his Visa account two years ago," Lucas said.

"When did he set up the post office box?" she asked.

"Six months ago."

"So he was picking up his mail here, for a year and a half?"

"I guess," Lucas said. "He didn't charge much, but he did from time to time."

"So the mail gets sent to Apartment Five, or wherever, and the mailman doesn't care, he just sticks it in the Apartment Five box," Darin said. "There's probably mail in it right now. This guy probably knows what day his Visa bill would get here, and he'd just come by and pick it up. No problem."

"The question is, why would he set up a fake ID?" Lucas asked.

"Because he's a criminal of some kind," she answered. "Or maybe, political."

"Political?"

"Yeah, you know, somebody who's underground," she said. "Somebody left over from the seventies."

Lucas scratched his nose: "I gotta think about it."

"How long have you been a detective?" she asked.

Lucas looked at his watch: "About eight hours."

She smiled and said, "So you got thrown in the deep end."

"I'll figure it out," he said. "You don't remember anybody like Fell? Do you think the Lees might? They overlapped by a year and a half."

"We could ask them." She looked at the stove clock. Six o'clock. "They'll be up."

THE LEES LOOKED like twins, same height, same haircuts, same dress; except that one of them had breasts. The one with breasts remembered Fell. "He was not supposed to take mail. He didn't live here. I ask him once, why do you take mail? He say, the post office still brings it by mistake. But after I ask him, I don't see him again."

That was, she guessed, about six months earlier. She added two details:

—Fell was missing the little finger on his left hand. "I see it when he opened the mailbox."

—He drove a black panel van.

Lucas took a few minutes to establish that the van wasn't a minivan, but Mrs. Lee was clear. He drove a panel van, with no windows in the sides. Lucas didn't say so, but it occurred to him that whoever took the girls must have had a vehicle, and a panel van would be perfect. More than perfect—almost necessary. It'd be tough to kidnap a couple of kids with a convertible.

When they left, Darin suggested that if Lucas became obsessed with finding Fell, he'd taken his eye off the ball. "You're looking for him because he said something about a crazy guy, and other people know the crazy guy. Maybe the other people would be easier to find."

"Good thought," Lucas said. She was not only pretty, she was smart. He looked at his watch again. Ten after six. He was due back in uniform in eight hours. "I gotta roll. Thanks for everything . . . maybe you oughta give me your phone number, in case I need more advice."

She smiled, then said, "All right."

HE WENT BACK to City Hall, to the licensing department, prepared to wait until somebody showed up. But when he got there and looked through the glass panel on the door, he saw a light coming out of an office. He banged on the door for a moment, until a man in a flannel shirt came out of the office and shook his head and waved him off. Lucas held up his badge, and the guy came over. Through the glass, he asked, "What?"

"I need a name."

The guy wasn't the right guy, but he knew how to work the computer, and he pulled up the owners of Kenny's, the bar where Fell had been hanging out, as a Steve and Margery Gardner from Eagan. A half-hour later, Lucas pulled into their driveway and pounded on the door until an irritated Steve Gardner came out from the back of the house in a bathrobe.

"What the hell?" he asked.

Lucas held up his badge: "We're looking for the two lost girls. You've got a customer named Fell, who was talking about a crazy guy. . . ."

They talked in the house's entry, and Margery came out after a minute. Neither one had any idea who Fell was. "You gotta talk to the manager, Kenny Katz," Steve Gardner said. "We own six bars, we're in Kenny's about three times a week for an hour a time. Talk to Kenny."

They had seen the crazy man. "He's been around all summer. He's tall, thin, he's been dribbling a basketball around. I've seen him down by the river a couple times, and he used to stand by the ramp onto I-94 with a sign asking for money. Said he was a homeless vet, but he doesn't look like a vet. I don't know how you'd find him—just drive around, I guess."

Lucas went back to his Jeep. *Just drive around, I guess.* Patrol cops—guys like him—could do that, of course, and probably *would* be doing that, if he couldn't come up with anything better.

He looked back at the Gardner house and filed away another fact: just because you figured out a possible source of information, and then figured out how to find them, and then rousted them out of bed . . . didn't mean they'd know a single fuckin' thing. He'd used up an hour learning that.

A thought popped in: the post office. There's probably a guy who systematically walks around the neighborhood every day. . . .

He headed back downtown, around to the back of the post office again. The old bureaucrat had gone at seven o'clock. The new bureaucrat decided that he wouldn't be breaking any regulation by letting Lucas talk to the mail carriers, who were sorting mail into the address racks. The new bureaucrat took him down to one wing of the post office and introduced him to four mail carriers who carried the near south side.

Two of them had seen the crazy man.

One of them knew where he lived.

4

A DILEMMA: LUCAS could call the information to the overnight guy in Homicide, or continue to push it on his own. If he'd already been a detective, he would have called it in, and gotten some help.

As a patrolman, temporarily in plainclothes—not even temporarily, as much as momentarily—he'd probably have the whole thing taken away from him, and given to people with more experience in investigation.

That had already happened once, and he didn't want it to happen again. He mulled it over only as long as it took him to get back to his Jeep. There was no way that Daniel would be back in his office yet, and since Daniel was his sole contact on the case, Lucas felt justified in running along on his own, until Daniel pulled him off.

Or until he turned back into a pumpkin, at three o'clock, and had to put his uniform back on.

HE'D BEEN UP for twenty hours, but still felt fairly clean. He climbed in the Jeep and headed over to the Mississippi, well downstream from the spot where, the day before, he'd been sent to look for the kids.

The crazy guy with the basketball, the mailman said, lived in a couple of plastic-covered Amana refrigerator boxes that he'd jammed in a washed-out space under an oak tree. The thick gnarled tree roots held, covered, and concealed the boxes, and the plastic sheets kept the water off when it rained.

The site should be easy enough to find, the carrier said, because it was right across a chain-link fence a few hundred yards north of Lake Street. "There's a big yellow house, the only one up there, and there's a hole under the fence about forty or fifty yards south of it, where you can scrape under. He's the only guy I've seen down there. The only bum."

The sun was getting hot, promising another warm day. Lucas drove down West River Parkway, into a neighborhood of older, affluent homes, carefully kept, spotted with flower gardens and tall overhanging trees. He parked his Jeep in a no-parking zone just south of the yellow house, put a cop card on the dashboard. When he got out, a man on the sidewalk, who was retrieving a *Star Tribune*, called, "You can't park there."

"I'm a cop," Lucas said, walking down toward him. He nodded toward the bluff. "There used to be a homeless man, living under a tree around here. The other side of the fence."

"He's gone," the man said. "We had the park cops out here, and they ran him off. Three or four weeks ago."

Damn it. "Where was he?" Lucas asked. "I need to take a look."

"You can take a look, but he's gone," the man said. He was a little too heavy, with a successful lawyer's carefully tanned face. He came down the sidewalk, his sandals flapping on the concrete; he was wearing a T-shirt and gym shorts, his black hair slicked back. He reminded Lucas a little of Jack Nicholson. "This way."

Lucas followed him up the street, and the man asked, "What's this all about?"

"We want to talk to him about some missing kids," Lucas said.

"The girls? He's the one?"

"Don't know that," Lucas said. "You ever see the guy around any kids?"

"No, I never did. But I never saw him much," the man said. "I'm usually outa here by eight o'clock or so, and I don't get home until six. My wife says he'd come out in the middle of the morning, go under the fence, but we never saw him come back. We figured he came back after dark."

The man pointed across the street to an aged, heavily branched oak: "He lived under that tree. There's a place just down the road where you can slide under the fence. Might tear your clothes up."

Lucas wrote the man's name and his phone number in his notebook: Art Prose. "I'd need to talk to your wife—I need to get a good description of the guy," Lucas said. "Will she be around?"

"Oh, sure. I'll tell her you're coming. Name's Alice. And I'll be here for another half-hour or so."

LUCAS WALKED DOWN the street to the tree. Looking through the chain-link fence, he could see what looked like toilet paper down the slope behind it, and plastic wrappers from food cartons, and a white plastic fork. He could see corners of the cardboard boxes, but not much.

A little farther down, he found the slide-under place, where water coming off the sidewalk had been flowing over the bluff toward the river. He'd get dirty going under, he thought, but what the hell. He took off his jacket, hung it on a tree branch that poked through the fence, and slid as carefully as he could under the wire.

A narrow dirt trail, no more than a foot wide, led from the slide-under place to the tree. The bluff going down to the river was steep, and he had to hang on to the brush to keep his balance.

The tree was huge, and canted slightly toward the river; the river-side roots were out in the air, and two empty boxes were wedged beneath them to make a cardboard cave. They were covered by a sheet of translucent plastic, like the kind painters used, but heavier. One edge of the plastic had been curled into a pipe that would collect water from the top of the boxes and empty a bit down the slope.

One of the boxes was pushed in horizontally, and was long enough to sleep in. The other was shorter, and upright, but high enough to sit in. The area around the boxes was littered with plastic and paper trash, the remains of magazines and newspapers. A green plastic Bic lighter was tangled in a bush down the slope, apparently discarded. Near the bottom of the slope, he could see tufts of rotting toilet paper around a clump of brush that was probably the man's toilet.

The water washing under the tree would collect in a shallow gully, and clean up the toilet from time to time, Lucas thought.

So: the boxes.

Not much to see, but he'd have to call it in—maybe there'd be fingerprints or something. He got down on his knees for a better look into the boxes, and noticed a slit in the back of the bed box, and a fold. Like a cupboard, he thought. He wondered briefly if he might get some disease by crawling into the box, then got down, and crawled in.

He could smell the man, even after a month. He tried breathing through his mouth, but it didn't help much. Well into the box, on his hands and knees, he reached back and pulled open the flap. It had been a cupboard, or something, he thought, a hole carved into the dirt, but it was empty now.

He crawled a bit deeper in and yanked the cardboard flap farther open . . . and saw the edge of several sheets of paper that had slipped down between the box and the dirt wall behind it. He pulled one of the sheets out, and for a moment, with the sheet upside down, didn't quite understand what he'd found.

He turned it around and said, "Jesus Christ."

He was holding a pornographic photograph, torn from a badly printed magazine. The woman—girl—in the photo was either very young, or looked very young. She was sitting astride a man, her head thrown back, the man's penis visibly penetrating her.

Lucas put the paper on the floor of the box and carefully backed out.

He dusted off his hands, noticed that they were shaking a little: adrenaline.

"Jesus Christ," he said again. And: he'd found something. He'd investigated, and he'd come up with something important, on his own. The rush was like kicking Wisconsin in hockey.

He hurried back to the hole in the fence, slipped under, got his jacket off the bush, and half ran back to the Proses' house. He knocked and Prose came to the door, now wearing a bathrobe, and Lucas said, "I need to use your phone. And talk to your wife. Like right now."

HE CALLED DANIEL at home. Daniel came up and said, "Davenport? It can't wait for breakfast?"

"I don't think so," Lucas said. "I found where that street guy was staying. He had a stash of porn, with some really young women in it. Like, girls. Young girls."

"Where are you?" Daniel asked.

Lucas gave him the address, and Daniel said, "I'll be there in fifteen minutes. You sit on that site, don't let anybody get close to it. You got that? You sit on it."

"I'll sit on it," Lucas said.

He actually sat on the Proses' front porch, talking to Alice Prose, a tall sandy-haired woman who looked like she should have been an English school mistress, and he drank a glass of the Proses' orange juice. Alice gave him a thorough description of the street guy: tall, not old but with a burned, weather-wrinkled face, brown and gray hair down to the back of his neck, a full beard. He wore a baseball hat, with a logo above the bill, but she'd never been close enough to see what the logo was. He carried a nylon backpack, stuffed with clothes or bedding. There was the occasional odor of cooking food around the tree, and sometimes a fecal odor, "which is one reason that people thought it was best if he'd find someplace else to stay. Someplace with a bathroom," she said.

She'd never seen him with anybody else, male or female. "He was always bouncing a basketball, but he didn't seem especially good at it. He was always losing it, and chasing it around."

"He's not just a bum, though," Lucas said. "People say he's crazy."

"Schizophrenic, I think," Alice said. "You could hear him yelling some nights. It sounded like an argument, like a violent argument, but he was all by himself, yelling and jumping up and down, like he was fighting somebody. Like fighting an invisible man. If you just heard it, and didn't see it . . . it was pretty convincing. It sounded like a fight. He'd be cursing and screaming. . . ."

"You never saw him with any girls, or women?"

"I never saw him with anybody. Ever."

"Did he ever show up in a car? Or a truck?"

"Never. Not that I saw."

LUCAS WROTE IT all down in his notebook, and fifteen minutes after he'd spoken to Daniel, walked down to wait in the street.

Daniel took nearly a half-hour to arrive; before he got there, an unmarked car pulled up, and a couple of homicide detectives got out, John Malone and Frank Lester. Lester asked, "Where's this stuff?"

Lucas pointed through the fence at the tree. "Right there. Under the washed-out roots."

Malone said to Lester, "We're gonna need better access," and to Lucas, "You get your prints all over everything?"

"On some of it," Lucas admitted. "The boxes were mostly empty, just a bunch of crap lying around. He hasn't been here for a couple of weeks, according to the neighbors. They had the park cops run him off.

There's like a . . . cupboard . . . thing cut into the back. I needed to go inside and see if there was anything in it."

"Hope you didn't fuck up a crime scene," Malone said.

"Get off his back," Lester snapped at Malone. "You would have done the same goddamn thing." To Lucas: "You did good, rook."

"I hope," Lucas said.

"Still need access," Malone said, tacitly conceding the point. "I'm gonna get some snappers."

He made a call from his car, and a squad showed up five minutes later. A uniformed cop named Willis climbed out, said, "Hey," to Lucas, and got a commercial bolt-cutter from the trunk. The cutter had steel handles almost as long as a baseball bat, and was mostly used for cutting the shackles off padlocks. Willis started cutting a man-shaped hole in the fence, and was finishing the job when Daniel arrived, driving a yellow, ten-year-old Corvette. Daniel nodded at Lucas and asked Lester, "Whaddya got, Frank?"

"Haven't been down yet," he said. "We're just going now."

Willis dragged the arc of cut wire out of the hole, and Lucas led the way down the slope to the base of the oak tree. "Smells like shit," Malone said.

"It *is* shit," Lucas said. "His toilet's right down the slope."

When they got to the mouth of the two boxes, they all squatted and Lucas pointed toward the niche in the back. "It's like a little cupboard cut into the dirt. That's where the paper is—I only pulled one out. That's it right there."

Daniel got down on his knees, crawled a couple feet into the sleeping box, picked up the paper, and backed out. They all looked at it, and Lester said, "That's not *Playboy* or *Penthouse*. That's really rough. That's a kid."

"No tits," Malone said. "But she could be older than she looks."

Daniel said, "That doesn't make any difference. The point is, she looks like a kid, and she's aimed at people who want to fuck kids."

They all looked at it for a few more seconds, then Daniel asked Lester, "You got some gloves?"

"Yeah." He took a pair of white latex gloves from his pocket, the kind surgeons used.

"Give them to Davenport," Daniel said. And to Lucas: "Crawl back in there and get the rest of the paper."

Lucas took the gloves, pulled them on, crawled to the back of the box, pulled the flap down, and retrieved the sheaf of paper. As he was backing out of the box, Daniel asked, "We got your prints, right?"

"Yeah," Lucas said.

"We'll need them to separate them from the prints this asshole left here. Let me see that stuff."

The porn was more of the same: young-looking girls having sex with older men.

Daniel said to Lucas, "He's our guy. We need to get all over this. I want you to find him."

"I go on at three o'clock. . . ."

"I fixed that. You're working for me for a while," Daniel said. "I want you to find this guy."

Lucas nodded, but said, "You know, I don't, uh . . ."

"I want you to *think* about it," Daniel said. "*Think about it.* And maybe go talk to the welfare guys or whatever. We need a description, we need everything you got. . . ."

"I got a description, but the main thing is, he's a street guy. He goes around dribbling a basketball," Lucas said. "The neighbor said that every time they saw him, he had the ball. That's the only street guy I ever heard of doing that. If you get the patrol guys looking for him, that'd be our best chance."

Daniel said, "We'll do that." To Lester, "We need to get some guys down here; we need to walk up and down this riverbank. If he killed them, he could have left them around here. He knows the area, he might have felt safe here. We need to look in the boxes and see if there's blood. We need to check old culverts down by the water, look for caves, holes . . . we need the whole riverbank swept."

"What about the kids' father?" Lucas asked. "Just out of curiosity."

"What about him?" Daniel asked.

"Is somebody taking a close look at him?"

"Yeah. Somebody is," Daniel said. "Don't worry your pretty little head about it. Get downtown, find somebody who knows this guy, and where he is. We want him."

"The girls are gone," Lester said.

"Maybe not," Daniel said. "There was that guy who kept the girl chained to the toilet. He didn't kill her for a week."

"One guy," Malone said. Then he said to Lucas, "You better hurry and find him."

Pressure. Lester grinned at him: "Life ain't fair, is it?"

BY THE TIME he left the scene, Lucas was feeling a little tattered. His clothes felt dirty, and he needed some sleep—he'd started twenty-two hours earlier with some vigorous sex, followed by an evening on patrol, then an overnight banging on doors, and then into the new day . . . and now he had the feeling that he was being judged by Daniel.

But he liked it: liked the pressure.

He *didn't* like the feeling of being slowed down. He'd spent most of his life playing hockey at a high level, and had grown to know the feeling of being not-quite-sharp. When you felt like that—not much off, but with a slightly blurred edge—you were looking at a bad game.

There were ways to take care of that. Instead of heading straight downtown, he detoured home, took a fast shower and washed his hair. As his hair dried, he went into the apartment's compact kitchen, dug a flat-bladed screwdriver out of a drawer, went to the entryway, and carefully popped off a baseboard. From behind the board, he removed an amber prescription-pill bottle he'd picked up on the street, shook out two Dexedrine tabs, tossed one to the back of his throat and swallowed.

He put the baseboard back in place and took the other pill back to his bedroom, where he dressed in a blue oxford-cloth shirt, chinos, and blue blazer. He dropped the second pill into a shirt pocket: he disliked taking three, because they pushed him out too far. But one or two were fine: by the time he got back to the Jeep, he was already building a new edge.

WHICH WAS WASTED over the next couple of hours: he worked through four separate welfare-related agencies, and found no one that knew, or had seen, a street guy with a basketball. He got the impression that most of their work was done in the offices, and that the people he spoke to had little regular contact with the street.

Later, he went down to the 911 center and started calling patrol cars. They'd all been put on the alert, to look for the guy, and he found two patrolmen who remembered seeing him at one time or another.

They agreed that he was usually in the neighborhoods adjacent to the river, between the I-94 bridge and the Marshall Lake bridge to the south. "I think he might have been camping out along the railroad tracks behind Brackett Park, but we went down there, and there's no sign of a camp. Maybe he split," one of the cops said.

AT NOON, he walked over to Hennepin Avenue to get a sandwich, but mostly to get away from the bureaucrats in City Hall, and to think. That's what Daniel had told him to do, and he hadn't been doing enough of it.

He took with him a file of arrest reports involving street people: the guy was so completely gone that it occurred to Lucas that he might be in jail. If he were, and that was discovered at some later date, they would all be embarrassed. He needed to check that. . . .

He was sitting in Henry's, a shabby bar-restaurant with a decent cheeseburger, flipping through the paper, finding nothing, when somebody said, "Jesus, they're letting the cops in here."

A thin man with wild blond hair and skinny paper-thin jeans stood in the dim light coming through the front door, fingertips in his jeans pockets, grinning down at him.

Lucas half stood and they slapped hands, and he said, "I caught you at Seventh Street. You guys are out of control."

"I saw you in the crowd. . . ." The man laughed, and said, "I love watching you dance. It's like watchin' a bear gettin' electrocuted."

"Hey . . . I'm physically talented."

Dave Pirner was the lead singer in the band Soul Asylum. He was a couple years younger than Lucas. They'd met in the rock clubs along Minneapolis's Hennepin Avenue when Lucas was at the university. Pirner slid into the booth: "So what're you up to?"

"I'm working on that thing with the missing girls," Lucas said. "Plainclothes, for a while, anyway."

"Read about the kids," Pirner said. He waved at a waitress. "They just take off? Or they get kidnapped?"

"Kidnapped, I think," Lucas said. "Some people say they fell in the river." Pirner made a rude noise, and Lucas nodded: "That's what I think."

The waitress came over and said to Pirner, "I love your hair," and Lucas leaned into the conversation, said, "Thanks, I cut it myself," and she rolled her eyes, and Pirner grinned at her and said, "Gimme a Grain Belt. He's paying for it."

"I'm not paying for a Grain Belt," Lucas said. "Give him a Leinie's."

They sat and drank beer, talked about Prince and *Purple Rain,* and Morris Day's feud with Prince, and about Madonna getting hot.

Pirner said Prince had come into Seventh Street with his entourage, and, "There was a bodyguard about the size of a mountain; he went through the crowd like a ship going through the ocean"; and he said Prince was interesting but "it's not really our kind of music, you know?" He said he was working on a rerelease of the first Soul Asylum album.

Lucas told him about the investigation of the missing girls.

"No suspects?"

"I'm trying to find a guy," Lucas said. He told him about the schizophrenic with the basketball.

Pirner leaned across the table and pointed the end of his Leinie's bottle at Lucas. "There's this chick . . . what's her name? She's kind of a groupie."

"Groupie for who?"

"For us, wickdick."

"Now I know you're lying. . . ."

"Karen . . . Blue hair. I'll think of it. She's a social worker for somebody. Some foundation or something. She knows every goddamn street guy in Minneapolis. She practically lives with them. There's a guy, she . . ." He straightened and snapped his fingers. "Karen, uh, *Foster.* Or *Frazier.* Something like that. Frazier, I'm pretty sure. Works for some foundation, but she went to the U for a long time. Like, years. Blue hair. She's at every show."

Lucas scrawled the name on a piece of paper. "I'll talk to her. We got nothin' else."

"She'll know the guy," Pirner said. "I swear to Jesus."

They finished a second beer, Pirner said they had another gig coming up, and Lucas said he'd be there. Pirner was meeting a couple of friends at Rifle Sport to do some shooting and invited Lucas to come along.

"I can't, man, I got this thing going, I can't stop," Lucas said, standing up.

He dropped some money on the table and Pirner headed out. Lucas went to the back of the bar to find a phone. He checked through a couple of supervisors in the welfare department and found a guy who told him that Karen Frazier worked for Lutheran Social Services.

Lucas got an address and headed that way.

A WOMAN at Lutheran Social Services told him that Karen Frazier was on the street somewhere, and when Lucas became persistent, went through the offices until she found somebody who said that Frazier planned to talk to a group of Hmong women about cultural violence, at an Asian grocery store in St. Paul.

Xiong's was on University Avenue, a near-slum of aging stores and small mechanical shops, now in the process of becoming a Hmong shopping district. Xiong's had once been a drugstore, then a secondhand shop, then abandoned, and now was back as a supermarket that smelled funny to Lucas's Western nose; an earth smell, like unfamiliar root vegetables. He found Frazier, with her blue hair, at the center of a group of Hmong women.

Lucas was a foot taller than any of them, and attracted some attention as he worked through the store: he waggled his fingers at Frazier, who frowned and asked, "Me?"

"I'm a police officer. I gotta talk to you right now—it's urgent," he told her.

"Me? About what?"

"About a transient over in Minneapolis. I was told you could help me," Lucas said.

"By who?"

"Dave Pirner. He's a friend of mine."

"Dave's a friend?" Now she was interested. She excused herself from the Hmong ladies, and they moved into an aisle of canned goods.

"I'm looking for a street guy who goes around bouncing a basket-ball," Lucas said. "We think he might know something about the two girls who disappeared last night. We really need to talk to him."

"You think he took them?"

"We heard some things in that direction," Lucas said. "And we found an old camp of his, under a tree . . ."

". . . off West Mississippi. I've been there," she said.

"So you know him?"

"Yeah, but why do you think he's involved?" she asked.

"Something a guy said, a guy we think knows him. Then, we were digging around under that tree, and we found a bunch of porn, with really young girls."

"Ah, boy," she said. She turned away from him and scratched her nose, working through the equities, decided, and said, "Okay . . . okay. His name's Terry Scrape. S-c-r-a-p-e. He was born around here, and he comes back in the summer. Most of the year he's out in California. Los Angeles. He's schizophrenic, he thinks he's in the movie business, he thinks he's an actor, he sees movie stars everywhere. The last time I saw him, he was into Harrison Ford and Michael J. Fox."

Lucas was making notes: "Any history of violence?"

"Not as far as I know—but you guys have busted him a bunch of times on marijuana charges," Frazier said. "Using, not dealing. Self-medicating. He does carry a knife, but most of them do, somewhere."

"He never threatened you, or anything?"

She shook her head: "No. He'll freak out sometimes. It's like . . . he has nightmares when he's awake. He might hurt somebody inadver-tently, but he's not a bad guy. He's suspicious, he's paranoid at times. He won't take his meds, they mess him up too bad."

"Where is he now?" Lucas asked.

"He's got a room. He had a room—I haven't seen him for a few weeks, so he's probably still there, or he's gone back to LA. Anyway, the big corporations—Target, Norwest—got their employees to kick in money to house the homeless, and he got one of the spaces. A Tar-get employee handles the money and finds the rooms."

She fumbled in her purse, took out a worn black address book, paged through it and said, "The Target guy's name is Mark Chakkour. . . ." She spelled the name and gave Lucas a phone number.

She had a few more details, and Lucas thanked her, got a phone number, used the phone in the back of the store to call Chakkour. He caught him on his way to a late lunch: "Yeah, we've got a Terry Scrape. What'd he do?"

"We don't know if he did anything, but we need to locate him," Lucas said. After a little more evasion, he got an address, and headed that way, and thought about his next step.

He was tempted to go in himself, just as he had been in the morning; no guts, no glory. On the other hand, Daniel already suspected that Lucas had held back information so he could work it himself. Maybe it was time to show some team spirit.

SCRAPE'S APARTMENT WAS in south Minneapolis, a mile west of the river, not far from Lucas's apartment in Uptown—a neighborhood mostly inhabited by people recently out of school, and working downtown. Lucas spotted the house, counted the mailboxes on the front porch, then went out to a shopping center and got on the phone to Daniel.

Another cop picked up, and yelled at Daniel that Lucas was on the line: "You find him yet?" Daniel asked without preamble, when he picked up.

"His name's Terry Scrape," Lucas said, straining to keep his voice nonchalant. "He's got a charity place in Uptown, one of those old houses converted to apartments. I'm standing outside. I haven't gone in yet."

"Don't go in. We'll be there. You say Terry Scrape?"

"Yeah. S-c-r-a-p-e. We should have a sheet on him. My source says he's been picked up a bunch of times. Possession of marijuana . . . carries a knife. Paranoid, schizophrenic, has waking nightmares. Not on his meds."

Daniel took down the address and said, "Fifteen minutes."

THIS TIME he *was* fifteen minutes. He and two other detectives came in two unmarked cars, Daniel alone, the second car driven by Sloan, the detective Lucas had worked with the night before. The third guy was a long-timer named Hanson, who wore a gray felt hat like men wore before John Kennedy changed the fashion; a hat with a brim.

Sloan asked Lucas, "You chicken out of going in by yourself?"

Lucas said, "I wanted to share the glory with you guys."

"Smart move," Daniel said.

They were parked a block from the apartment house, standing between the nose of Sloan's car and the trunk of Daniel's. "You seen anything moving over there?" Hanson asked.

"Nope. Not a single person, coming or going, since I got here. He's in Apartment F. The guy who got it for him says he thinks it's on the first floor, at the back."

"Where'd you get the information?" Daniel asked.

"I got it all written down," Lucas said. "I'll give you a list when we get back. Social worker, was the main one."

"There was a rumor that you were fucking a librarian at the *Star Tribune*," Hanson said.

Lucas shook his head. "Jeez, I hate that word."

"Then you're in the wrong fucking job, fuckhead," Sloan said.

"I meant 'librarian,'" Lucas said.

They all laughed, a little nervously, getting cranked for an entry, maybe even finding the Jones girls, dead or alive. They looked down the street some more, until Daniel said, "Well, hell." He looked at Lucas. "You wearin' your steel toes?"

"No. Why?"

"Might want you to kick the door, and I've got plantar fasciitis. Let's go on down there."

THEY WALKED DOWN the street two-by-two, looking enough like cops that a passing bicyclist checked them over, the way people check cops. They stayed on the opposite side of the street until they were directly across from the house's front door, then crossed and climbed the stairs to the porch. Lucas looked at the mailbox marked F, but there was no name on it. He opened it: no mail.

Daniel led the way inside, where they found a small foyer, with a stair going up, and a hall going back; smelling of boiled cabbage, or maybe broccoli. There were doors on either side of them, to front apartments, one marked A, the other B. Lucas held up a finger to the others, stopping them, and moved carefully down the hall, the wooden floor creaking underfoot. He found C and D opposite each other, halfway down the hall, and then saw E and F at the end.

He tiptoed back and said, "End of the hall, on the right."

They tiptoed back down the hall, the floor creaking, until they were opposite F, and Lucas breathed, "Knock, or kick?"

"You think you could get it with one shot?"

Lucas looked at the door. Some doors could be opened with a cough, but others resisted even sledgehammers. This house was a rehab, and the door looked like it might be trouble, at least for a kick: the lock was modern. He shook his head and muttered, "I don't know."

Sloan moved up and said, "I'll knock."

Lucas noticed that he had a gun in his hand, as did Hanson. He'd forgotten about his gun, put his hand back on it, then left it. Two guns were enough. Sloan looked at the three of them, then knocked and called, "Mr. Scrape? You've got a package. Mr. Scrape?"

They heard nothing for a moment, then the sound of heels, somebody either barefoot, or in stocking feet, coming to the door. Lucas said, "Stand back."

The others got behind him, and when Scrape opened the door—it was Scrape, the picture of the man described to him by Alice Prose—Lucas kicked it as hard as he could. The door smashed open, hitting Scrape in the face, and the man went down, screaming with pain, fear, and confusion, and Lucas and Hanson were on top of him. Hanson's hat popped off and rolled in a half-circle across the bare floor.

Scrape was an average-sized man, maybe an inch under six feet, with a long prematurely gray beard and pale blue eyes; he was extremely thin, and as he struggled with the cops, the ligaments stood out in his arms. He was screaming and thrashing and Lucas pulled his cuffs, and they rolled him, ignoring his thrashing, and bent his arms and Lucas got the cuffs on; and thought that Scrape smelled like some weird combination of smoke, rancid butter, and dirt.

Lucas patted him down, found an empty plastic baggie that might once have held some grass. Hanson spotted a butcher knife in a leather sheath on a rickety table next to the bed. He said, "Knife, over there."

They were all breathing hard, Scrape facedown on the floor, squealing now, and Daniel did a quick circuit of the spare room, looking for anything connected to the girls. Nothing. Daniel shook his head and said, "Let's get him downtown."

Sloan and Hanson helped Scrape get up, and Sloan brushed off his shirt and said in a soft voice, "If you've still got them, you could give them up. It'd be a big help to everyone."

Scrape asked, "Who? Who?"

Lucas would remember the tone of his voice: the utter confusion in it.

SLOAN KEPT TALKING to Scrape like a man talking to a nervous horse, and he and Hanson took him out the door. Daniel's eyes cut to Lucas and he said, "We had no time for a search warrant, I figured we were sort of in hot pursuit. We've got to have a warrant before we tear the place up."

Lucas thought that sounded a little shaky, but took a look around: one room, with a bed, a chest of drawers, a nightstand, and a wooden table and chair that might have been rescued from Goodwill. A key ring, with a bunch of keys, sat on the nightstand. A backpack, open at the top, and stuffed full of clothes, lay in the middle of the floor, with a basketball. There were two doors other than the one that went into the hallway: one stood half open, to reveal an empty closet. The other led to a compact three-quarters bath.

He asked Daniel, "Think it'd be okay if I took a leak?"

"If you don't see any blood, and if you really have to go . . ."

Lucas went in the bathroom, closed the door, checked the medicine cabinet—it was empty—and the shower booth, which showed only a sliver of soap, a miniature bar like those from hotels. No shaving cream or even toothpaste. There was a roll of unwaxed floss on the ledge behind the sink.

He flushed the toilet and stepped back out. Daniel, with no witness, had had time to check the closet, under the bed, the chest of drawers, and the nightstand. The clothes in the pack had been pulled out and stuffed back in. Daniel said, "Get the knife and let's go. We'll get some guys back to check his pack."

So he'd found nothing.

Lucas nodded. He picked up the knife, and the keys from the bed-stand. They went out, and Lucas selected the newest-looking key, found that it worked, and locked the door behind them.

Daniel said, "Be nice to know what those other keys do."

Lucas jangled them—a lot of them were old-fashioned skeleton keys, but some were modern. "We gotta ask him. And not nice."

5

THEY TOOK CRAPE, frightened, panicked, back to police headquar-ters, took his picture, printed him, tagged his knife, sat him at Sloan's desk, and Sloan went to work on him, with Hanson crowding in at Scrape's side, the bad guy. Lucas, Daniel, and a couple of other cops sat back and watched.

Scrape started out scared, but when Sloan asked him about the girls, he said he didn't know what they were talking about: and his confusion seemed real. He didn't read newspapers, watch television, or listen to radio. When Sloan gave him the news about the girls, he got angry, twisting in his chair to look each of them in the face, one after another, as if searching for an ally—or simply for understanding.

"I never would touch no girls like that," he said. "I never touch no good girls. You can ask anybody."

"You do like girls, though, right? You're not queer," Sloan said, lean-ing toward him.

"Heck no, I'm not queer. I got problems." He made a circling motion with his index finger, by his temple. "My meds don't help. But I'm not queer. I just . . . don't do much of that."

"Much of what?"

"You know. Girls," Scrape said.

"When was the last time you did?"

Scrape eased down in his chair, his eyes scanning the cops, calculating an answer. Finally, he said, "There was this woman down in the river . . ."

He stopped, and Sloan asked, quietly, "Where on the river? Down by your tree place?"

Scrape was puzzled again for a second, then snorted, as if at a joke, and he said, "Not this river. The LA river. I got run out of there by TVR, but that was the river."

"What's TVR?" Hanson asked. "That some kind of TV station?"

Scrape cocked his head. "What TV station?"

Hanson said, "You said, 'I got run off by TVR.' What's TVR?"

"Everybody knows that," Scrape said, taking on a slightly superior aspect. "The Toonerville Rifa. Bad dudes, man. I got the heck out of there."

They figured out that he was talking about a street gang in Los Angeles, and that he had never been around a woman on the Mississippi.

"So you backed down on a gang guy," Hanson sneered. "You yellow? You a chickenshit?"

"I'm just not a big-boned man," Scrape pleaded. "He was a big-boned guy. The only reason I'd ever back down, is if they're bigger-boned than me, then I disengage."

"They used to hear you yelling and screaming down there, by that box you had," Hanson said. "Were you yelling at the girls? Is that where you had them?"

"I never had any girls; I never did. When I'm having a bad day, I might do some yelling. They come crowding in on me, and I try to keep it to myself, but sometimes I can't. I have to yell it somewhere—"

"When who crowds in?" Hanson asked. "When the girls crowd in?"

"I don't know any girls," Scrape said, a miserable, yellow-toothed grimace pulling on his face.

THE QUESTIONING WAS MADE more difficult by Scrape's illness: he spoke his thoughts—"These cops are gonna kill me"—as a kind of oral parenthesis in the middle of answering a question. He claimed to have been in places where he couldn't have been—Los Angeles, that morning—and to have spoken to people that he hadn't spoken to—Michael

J. Fox and Harrison Ford. When Sloan made the point that the conversations were fantasies, Scrape became further confused.

"But I just talked to Harrison this morning. Or maybe . . . maybe yesterday. He was going to . . ." He paused, then said, "He was coming over with some friends. He was going to bring beer."

"Harrison Ford, the movie star," Sloan said.

"Yeah, he's a good friend. He loans me money sometimes."

He became confused by logical inconsistencies in what he was saying; became confused by the fact that he was in Minneapolis, and not Los Angeles, though at other times he knew for sure that he was in Minneapolis.

They brought out the porn they'd taken from his boxes above the river. He could barely look at them. "Not mine. Not mine. Somebody else's," he said, turning his eyes away, in what seemed like embarrassment.

"We found them in your place," Sloan said. "Your boxes, down by the river."

"You did not," Scrape said.

"We did," Sloan insisted.

"Where am I gonna get that?" he asked. "I'm gonna mail away for it, so they could bring it to my mailbox? I'm gonna spend good money on it when I got no food? Where am I gonna get that shit?"

Then he said something that did make sense: "Hey, if I had those in my box, wouldn't my fingerprints be on them?"

"Maybe," Sloan said.

"Sure they would," Scrape said. "I ain't got no gloves. You look at them pictures, they won't have no prints on them. Not my prints. You look."

"We will," Sloan said. "We'll look."

"That's the proof, right there," Scrape said. "No prints."

SLOAN WAS THOUGHTFUL and forgiving and mild-mannered, offered cigarettes and Cokes and coffee. Hanson was rude and demanding and skeptical. Between them, they tore everything Scrape said to shreds, except for three things: he'd never seen the porn, he'd never seen the girls, and he was a friend of Harrison Ford's.

He didn't know the girls, had never seen them, had never touched them.

So angry that he was shaking, his face red as a bullfighter's cape, he kept his hands down and his story straight: "NO: I NEVER SEEN THEM."

The ring of keys, he said, he collected: "I find keys, I put them on the ring. I like to listen to them at night. They're like bells. And who knows when I might need one? Maybe I could sell one, or something."

They gave it two hours, more or less, then Daniel brought in another cop to sit with Scrape, and he, Sloan, Hanson, and Lucas went into Daniel's office and shut the door.

"I don't think he did it," Sloan said. "But I'd be more sure if he wasn't nuts. Do you think it's possible that he could have done it, and then forgot he did it?"

"Doesn't seem like it," Hanson said. "He gets stuff confused, but he remembers it all."

Daniel looked at Lucas, who shrugged. "He looked like he was really confused when Sloan first asked him about them—it looked to me like he had no idea who we were talking about. I don't think he's smart enough to fake it. Or sane enough. Then, I've got to wonder about the prints on the porn. Are we looking at that?"

"We will," Daniel said. "So, we got a problem. I mean, we got nothing. We picked him up on a rumor started by a guy we can't find, and Davenport, here, thinks that guy's a crook of some kind, with fake addresses and phony credit cards. We can't even arrest Scrape on the knife, since he was in his own room, and he never had a chance to threaten anyone."

"They find anything else out at his camp?" Lucas asked.

Daniel shook his head: "I talked to Lester twenty minutes ago. They combed the riverbank for a half-mile, both directions, and didn't find anything. Not a thing."

"We gonna cut him loose?"

Daniel said, "If Sloan doesn't squeeze anything out of him." He looked at Sloan and said, "I want you to keep him going for another hour. Run through it, all over again, and if nothing comes up, cut him loose. I'm going to get a couple guys to track him. If he took the kids, he'll fuck up, and pretty quick."

"What if he just runs?" Hanson asked.

"We don't let him. He tries to get on a bus or hitch a ride out of town, we bust him again," Daniel said. "We don't let him get anywhere."

"If he gets to LA, he's pretty much gone," Sloan said.

Hanson picked up Daniel's phone and punched in a couple of numbers, listened, identified himself, then asked, "You got any inquiries about busts in the missing girls thing? Uh-huh. No, there's nothing here. Keep me up, though."

He hung up and said, "The papers don't know we picked him up. Not yet, anyway."

"So we cut him loose, in an hour or so, and tag him," Daniel said. "Put somebody on the house, front and back. We wanna be inside his sweatshirt."

Lucas asked, "What about me? You want me to follow him?"

Daniel said, "Nah. Go on home, get some sleep. We're done. I expect we'll be seeing you around."

LUCAS, DISMISSED, left Daniel's office a little down. He thought he'd done something with Scrape, and instead, they had, as Daniel said, "nothing." He went out to the Jeep, sat for a moment, thinking about the guy who started the rumor about Scrape. He'd like to find Fell, just to see if he could. To see what was going on there.

The Dexedrine was beginning to fade, but Lucas was still too jacked to sleep. Instead of going home, he drove down to Kenny's bar and introduced himself to the manager, Kenny Katz, who was sitting in a back office working over an old-fashioned mechanical adding machine. He looked at Lucas's badge and pointed him at a chair, and Lucas told him the story about John Fell and the panhandler named Scrape.

"John usually comes in about six or seven, stays for an hour or so," Katz said. "He showed up here three weeks or a month ago, and maybe every other night since. Usually around six or seven. He's not exactly what I'd call a regular, though . . . he doesn't exactly fit in."

"Why not?"

Katz hesitated, then said, "I don't know. There's something off-center about him. He comes in, has a couple of drinks, talks with people. But it's like it's not natural to him. The bullshit. It's like he went to a class. He tells a lot of jokes, and it's like he's got a joke book that he reads. It's not like he's got pals who tell him the jokes."

"Huh." They sat looking at each other for a moment, then Lucas asked, "You ever see this bum around? The guy with the basketball?"

"Oh, sure. He used to come in every once in a while, and ask to use the bathroom. I didn't encourage him, but if it's early in the day, and there aren't many customers around . . . You know, what are you gonna say?"

"Haven't seen him lately?"

"He stopped by maybe two weeks ago, said he got a room some-where, wouldn't need our bathroom anymore," Katz said. "He said thanks. Kind of surprised me. I said, 'You're welcome,' and that seemed to make him happy."

"You think he took those girls?"

Katz said, "Hell, I don't know. I mean, I just don't know."

"John Fell sort of put us on his trail."

Katz shook his head, his jowls waggling: "That's something else I don't know about. Why he'd think that? He doesn't seem like a guy who'd talk to bums."

"Fell used to go to the massage place across the street . . . and the girls sometimes come in here . . ."

"They do *not* solicit in here," Katz said. "This is a neighborhood place. They know better."

"But they come in," Lucas said. "Do they hang with Fell? Do they come in for him?"

"Not especially. But I'll tell you what, a guy that goes to a hooker, on a regular basis, isn't quite right," Katz said. "You know what I mean?"

Lucas nodded. "I think so."

"I mean, if you're really ugly, or you're handicapped, and can't get a regular woman, then, maybe. You gotta let off steam," Katz said. "But John, there's nothing physically wrong with him, not that you can see, anyway. Okay, he's a little fat, but a lot of guys are fat now. But if there's something wrong with him, it's up here." Katz tapped his temple.

"You say he's in around six or seven?"

"Most days," Katz said. "You plan to come back?"

"I'd like to talk to him," Lucas said. "We're pushing every button we got, and he's one of them."

"You think you'll get those kids back?" Katz asked.

Lucas said, "Most of the experienced guys don't think so. I'm too new and dumb to give up."

LUCAS WENT BACK out to the street and sat in his Jeep. The sun was still high, and it was hot, and he couldn't think of what to do. He finally headed home, cranked up the air conditioner, and fell on his bed, certain that he wouldn't be able to sleep.

He didn't for half an hour: his mind kept moving, looking for any crack that he could get ahold of, anything he could do. There wasn't much: as long as he was pulling on the Scrape thread, he had a line to work along. But that thread ran out, and he was dead-ended on Fell. There had to be some other way to get at Fell, but he could feel his own ignorance there. He knew that if he'd only been working longer, he would have thought of something.

Instead, he felt marinated in ignorance.

THE PHONE SURPRISED HIM: caught him asleep, and for quite a while, he thought. He popped up on his hands, in a half-push-up, disoriented, in the dark, his shirt twisted around his neck.

He found the phone, and Sloan was on the other end of the line: "Thought you might be interested. Nine-one-one got a tip that says ol' Scrape was seen throwing a box of stuff in a dumpster behind Tom's Pizza on Lyndale, yesterday about dark. You want to do some diving?"

"Aw, man, no," Lucas said. He'd gone dumpster-diving a few times on patrol. "I mean, I'd like to be there. . . ."

"Daniel's looking for one of us to go in," Sloan said. "You know, one of his guys. Junior guy usually does it."

"Who's junior if I don't do it?" Lucas asked.

"That'd be me," Sloan said.

Lucas smiled into the phone. "What's it worth to you?"

"C'mon, man. I'm in good clothes, I don't have time to change," Sloan said. "You're at home, you could just throw on some old shit."

"All right, all right," Lucas said. "I hope it's not for nothing."

"Bring a flashlight," Sloan said. "Listen, weren't you there last night when that soldier guy found the blouse?"

"Yeah, that was us."

"Well, Tom's is about two blocks up that alley. I think this could be something."

"Twenty minutes," Lucas said. "I gotta stop at Walgreens and get some Vicks."

He changed into an old pair of jeans and high-topped hiking boots, a T-shirt with terminally stained underarms, and a year-old canvas fishing shirt, still new enough to be stiff.

His biggest fear wasn't the filth of a dumpster; it was AIDS. The disease was exploding in the Cities, and the papers said that a major component in its spread, besides gay sex, was blood-to-blood contact with needles used by junkies.

And needles wound up in dumpsters.

Five minutes after Sloan's call, he was back in his Jeep. He made a quick stop at a Walgreens, picked up the thickest pair of yellow-plastic kitchen gloves they had, and a jar of Vicks VapoRub.

TOM'S PIZZA WAS a failing storefront pizza joint distinguished by its low prices and juicy bluebottle flies. The flies looked a little too much like Tom's pizza ingredients for the high-priced trade, though some argued that they added a certain *je ne sais quoi* to the cheese-and-mushroom special.

Lucas parked on the street at the side of the building and walked around back, carrying the bag with the gloves and the Vicks, and the heavy shirt, and found Sloan, Hanson, Lester, and Jack Lacey, the owner of Tom's, standing in the alley looking up at the dumpster. The bright motion-sensor light shone down from the roof, onto the space around the store's back entrance, half illuminating the dumpster. A stepladder stood next to it.

Lucas said, "Hey," as he walked up, and Sloan said, "I owe you," and Lucas said, "You really do." Lucas made the mistake of sniffing at the dumpster and gagged and turned away: "Holy shit; when was this thing dumped?"

"They get it once a week," Lacey said. "It goes out tomorrow. It's been hot."

"Maybe they ought to get it twice a week," Lucas said. "This is disgusting."

"Only in the summer . . ."

"Listen, it's been nice chatting," Lester said. "So, let's get your ass in there."

Lucas looked at the dumpster, sighed, pulled on the heavy canvas shirt, unscrewed the jar of Vicks, put a daub in each nostril.

"He's a goddamned pro," Sloan said, with false heartiness.

"Gonna ruin everything I'm wearing," Lucas said.

Lester said, "Put in for it. I'll approve it."

"Yeah, yeah."

Lucas climbed the ladder and looked into the dumpster—and looking was almost as bad as smelling. The basic component of the mess inside was rotten cheese, along with rotten meat, rotten crusts, rotten grease, rotten greasy cardboard, and flies. He'd always wondered where flies went at night, and now he knew. He could see a couple of cylindrical cartons that once contained tomato sauce; and a rat, with tiny black ball-bearing eyes, each with a highlight from the overhead alley spot.

The rat saw him coming and ran up the far corner and over the side. Lester cried, "Man, look at the size of that sonofabitch," and Hanson said, "Don't get bit. It might have rabies."

Hanson had his pistol out, tracking the rat. Sloan shouted, "Don't shoot it, don't shoot it, the ricochet . . ."

Lester said, "Remind me to bring my old lady here for dinner."

Lacey: "Hey. There aren't any rats *inside*. . . ."

When the excitement died, and Hanson put his gun away, Lucas said, "Ah Jesus," put his hips on the edge of the dumpster, swiveled, and let himself drop inside. The mass of cardboard—it was mostly cardboard—was saturated with various fluids, and was soft and slippery underfoot, almost like walking on moss.

He was breathing through his mouth, but with a nose full of Vicks, couldn't smell much of the crap anyway. He said, "Get out of the way," and bent and started throwing cardboard over the side, watching carefully where he put his fingers, looking for needles. In two minutes, his gloves and lower legs were covered with rotting cheese and tomato sauce, and another rat made a break for it, running up the corner, and again the guys outside yelled at it, and Lucas threw more crap over the side.

He'd been digging for five or six minutes when a patrol car turned into the alley and the light bar flared, and Lester walked around and yelled, "Turn the goddamn light off," and the light died. A patrol cop shouted back, "We got a call on you guys. . . . What's going on?"

"Had to check the dumpster," Lester said.

Lucas peered over the edge of the dumpster at the car, and one of the cops inside said, "Hey, it's Davenport."

The other guy started laughing, and then called, "Hey, plainclothes."

"Fuck you," Lucas shouted back, and started throwing more crap out.

The car left, and Sloan asked, "How's it going?"

"Fuck you."

They all laughed.

HALFWAY DOWN, Lucas found the box.

It was sitting flat on its bottom, as though it had been carefully placed inside the dumpster, a box that you might use to move books, its top flaps carefully interleaved. "Got something," he reported.

"Get it out," Lester said.

"Sort of stuck in here . . ." He threw more crap over the side, excavating around it. The box had been soaked in sludge on one side—mostly grease, with a little tomato sauce—and had weakened. He cleared a space all the way around it, then slipped a hand beneath it, and lifted it out.

He put the box on the top of the stepladder, boosted himself onto the edge of the dumpster, swung his legs over, and carried the box down. He put it on the ground under the door light, moth shadows flicking crazily across it, and as the other four crowded around, pulled the flaps apart.

Inside were two small pairs of jeans, carefully folded, a small brassiere, and a white blouse.

"Motherfucker," Lester said.

"They're dead. I told you they were dead," Hanson said.

Sloan's hands were in his hair, holding on, as though he couldn't stand his thoughts. Lacey had been smoking a cigarette, and turned away, dropped it in the alley and stomped it out, as though he were angry at the butt.

Lucas carried the soggy box around to Hanson's car and put it in the trunk, and asked, "When are you gonna get Mr. Jones down there?"

"I'll call him from the office after I talk to Daniel," Lester said.

"I want to be there," Lucas said. "But I gotta get cleaned up. Wait for me."

"You're not important enough to wait for," Hanson said. "So you better hurry."

Lucas headed for his Jeep, and Lacey called after him, "Who's going to throw this shit back in the dumpster?"

"I investigate, I don't clean up," Lucas yelled back, and then he was in his Jeep and rolling.

AT HIS APARTMENT, he stripped naked, put all the clothes except his boots and the newer canvas shirt in a garbage bag and threw it at the door. He put the shirt in another garbage bag, and left it on the kitchen table; he'd take it to a laundromat and wash it for an hour or so. The boots he carried back to the shower, and washed them with soap and hot water, until they looked clean, then left them on the floor to dry out. He scrubbed himself down, washed his hair, dried, dressed, picked up the garbage bag by the door, threw it in the trash on the way out, and headed downtown.

The box was on Daniel's desk, sitting on top of a pile of newspaper. Daniel was sitting behind his desk, while Sloan and Lester took the two guest chairs. Hanson wasn't around. An amused look flitted across Daniel's face when Lucas walked in, and he said, "They tell me you smelled worse than the box."

"They were right," Lucas said. "I ruined about fifty bucks' worth of clothes, if I manage to save the boots. You'll be getting the bill."

"Go ahead and put in for the boots," Daniel said. "A little bonus."

"Is Jones on the way?" Lucas asked.

"Talked to him five minutes ago," Sloan said. "He's coming."

"But it's theirs," Daniel said. "The girls'." There was no doubt in his voice.

They all sat there, for a moment, in silence, and then Lucas said, "I'd like to know a little more about that nine-one-one tip."

The tip, Daniel said, had come from somebody who identified himself as a neighbor who didn't want to get involved. He said he'd gone into the alley to move his car, and saw the guy with a basketball and a box, and saw him stop and loft the box into the dumpster, and then walk around the corner at Tom's. He said he knew about the basketball from neighborhood rumor—that the cops were looking for the guy with the basketball.

"So everybody in the world knows Scrape," Lucas said.

"Not the whole world," Sloan said. "But the neighborhood around Matthews Park is pretty contained—and when you're talking about a pedophile, the word gets around fast."

Lester: "The thing about Scrape is, all he does is walk. He walks up and down every street down there, every day. They all know who he is."

"I still don't like it," Lucas said. "We get an anonymous tip that Scrape threw the clothes in the dumpster, and we're only chasing him in the first place because of a tip from a guy we can't find, who might be some kind of an asshole operating under a phony name." He remembered, then, and looked at his watch: eight o'clock. "Shit."

"What?"

"I had an appointment at seven tonight. Gotta make a call."

"What you're gonna find as you get into investigations," Lester said, "is that all kinds of weird shit happens."

"I already learned that," Lucas said. "Weird shit happens on the street, too—but there's weird shit and then there's *weird shit*. When it's too weird, you gotta think about it some more. I need a phone."

He went into the outer office, to an empty desk, got Kenny's number from the operator, and called. He asked for Katz, got him, identified himself. "Has John Fell been in? John Fell?"

"Not tonight. Not so far."

HE'D JUST HUNG UP when George Jones, followed by a frightened-looking woman who Lucas recognized from the papers as his wife,

Gloria, stepped into the office, trailed by Hanson, who'd apparently gone to meet them at the door. Hanson said, "This is Detective Davenport, who recovered the box for us."

The two nodded vaguely at Lucas, and they all went into Daniel's office. Daniel, Lester, and Sloan were all on their feet, and Daniel said a few words about how hard it all was, and then opened the top of the box.

Gloria Jones, a slightly too-heavy woman with red-tinted hair, began to tremble and her husband took her arm. Together, they peered into the box, and then Gloria reached into it and picked up the brassiere and said, "The kitty bra," and fainted.

She would have fallen if Lucas hadn't caught her, under the arms, and he eased her into a chair, but she was unconscious, and Daniel was shouting about an ambulance, and everybody but Lucas and George Jones went running.

Daniel was back in a few seconds and said, "We've got an ambulance on the way; it'll be here in a minute."

"I think she fainted," Lucas said. "She's coming back."

"Can't take a chance," Daniel snapped. "It could be her heart."

She came back, but then the medics were there to take care of her, and the cops all moved to the outer office. George Jones said, "The kitty bra—it was Nancy's first bra. It has a kitty face in the front."

And it did.

GLORIA JONES WAS WHEELED to the ambulance for the one-minute ride to the emergency room, and George went with her. The cops gathered back in Daniel's office, and Daniel said, "We're looking at a double murder, now. Anybody doubt that?"

They all shook their heads.

"There's gonna be tremendous heat," Daniel said. "We've gotta get Scrape back, right now. We need to know who called nine-one-one, even if we have to tear the neighborhood apart. I don't give a shit if the guy doesn't want to get involved, we find him."

Hanson: "Best to do it right now, everybody home from work but still awake . . ."

Sloan: "Oughta get an entry team this time, gettin' Scrape."

Daniel began issuing orders, and the detectives started moving, and Hanson turned back to Daniel's desk and looked into the box, and Lucas, who hadn't been told anything, asked, "What am I doing?"

Daniel looked up at him and said, "Uhhh . . . Lucas, man, you did really good. And I'm keeping you around for a few more days. But we've got something else for you."

Lucas didn't understand. "Something else? What the hell? I'm all over this one," he said.

"But this one, we're just chasing the guy down. We . . . don't need you to do that. So now, you're gonna get all over the other one," Daniel said. "And it's important. The Smith murder. Capslock caught it this morning, but Sandola is on vacation, and we don't want Capslock wandering around by himself interviewing gangbangers."

"Smith murder? What's the Smith murder? What're you talking about?" Lucas was tired, and now was a little pissed.

Daniel spread his hands, as if explaining the real world to a moron: "Life goes on, even when kids get kidnapped. Billy Smith, a little dipshit gangbanger and crack salesman, got his ass stabbed to death. We found him this morning. He's over at the ME's office right now. We need to get a clean white face on it, and you're the guy."

"A clean white face?"

Hanson stepped in: "See, Billy had him some friends in the community, and if we don't step up and take it seriously, they'll call the mayor and their councilman, and they'll call the chief, and the chief will call QD here . . ."

"And I hate that," Daniel said. "I hate to get called. So even though we know we won't catch the killer unless somebody calls us, we gotta look like we're serious about it. That means sending white guys in good clothes down there, to talk to folks, and take notes on what they say. Capslock caught it, and he needs a partner."

"Fuck me," Lucas said, his hands on his hips.

"Yesterday, you were walking around with a flashlight picking up drunks. Today you're investigating a murder. Just take it," Daniel said. And: "Capslock's getting dinner at the XTC. You need to get over there and introduce yourself."

"Goddamnit," Lucas said.

Daniel: "You taking it?"

Lucas ran his hands through his hair, walked a tight circle around the office, then said, "Yeah, I'll take it—I'm taking it. Right in the ass. I oughta be on the girls, because I'm all over that. But I'll take it."

Sloan came back: "We're pulling the team together. They're coming in. Dick and Tim are down on his door, so there'll be eight or ten of us; should be enough for one guy."

"Let me just come for the entry," Lucas said to Daniel.

Daniel said, "Lucas, just . . . help me out here. Get on over to XTC. There's not a damn thing you could do when we pick him up. You'd just be another guy standing there with his thumb up his ass. Go see Del."

HE DID, STILL PISSED.

The XTC was a gentleman's club that used to be a strip joint on a side street where Minneapolis turned into St. Paul. During the day, it looked like a piece of shit, a purple-painted concrete-block single-story building with a cracked-blacktop parking lot that usually had a couple of used rubbers cooking on the tarmac. At night, it looked only slightly better. Lucas had been there a few times, called by the bouncer when a gentleman got too rowdy or was suspected of carrying a gun, or objected too strenuously to the champagne bill.

He'd never been there in civilian clothes, and felt a little sleazy as he went slinking down the street toward the entrance, hoping that no past, present, or future women friends saw him going in.

When the strip joint became a gentleman's club, the owner took down the NUDE-NUDE-NUDE red-blinking neons and put up a green one that said, "Gentlemen." Other than that, not much had changed; the first bar stool by the door still had a strip of duct tape covering a slash in the vinyl cover, and it still smelled of cheap disinfectant, layered over by even cheaper lilac perfume.

Del was in the back, playing shuffleboard bowling with a tall, heavy-set man with a drunk-red face under a white Sparkle Drywall hat with the bill turned up. A dozen empty Bud bottles were sitting on a table behind them. Lucas marched past the three main poles, two with active

71

dancers, one down to her G-string. The other peeled a pastie as Lucas went by, then cupped her breasts and pointed them at him.

"Stick 'em up," she said.

He kept going, not amused.

Del was looking at a six-seven split on the shuffleboard machine, and Lucas came up, crossed his arms, and stared at the back of his head. He'd worked with Capslock a couple of times as a drug decoy, and he'd seemed a little out there.

After a couple of practice strokes, Del let the puck slide, took out the six and cleanly missed the seven, said, "Rat poop," and without turning around, reached for his beer.

The drywall guy, peering through small drunk eyes at Lucas, asked, "What're you looking at, college boy?"

Lucas, still pissed at being pulled off the Jones kidnapping case, snapped, "Not you, fat man. I got better taste."

The drywall guy put down his beer and started around Del, as Del straightened, saw Lucas, put his arm across the other man's chest, and said, "Whoa. Slow down, Earl. He's a cop, he was third team all-Big Ten in hockey, he can press three twenty-five and he likes to fight."

"And if you keep coming, I'll beat your ass into one big bruise and then put it in jail," Lucas said. "I am *not* in a good mood right now."

Earl saw it in Lucas's eyes, and slowed down. "I'd kick your ass if I wasn't so drunk," he said.

"Go away," Lucas said. "I got business with this clown."

Earl picked up his beer and went to stare at a pole dancer. Del said, "Clown?"

"Third team?"

Del smiled, his teeth still yellow in the subdued light: "So we're even."

"I didn't know if the fat guy knew you were a cop," Lucas said. "Or I woulda called you Ossifer Capslock."

"Well, thank you."

DEL WAS A THIN, middle-height man with salt-and-pepper hair that seemed premature, and a short, neatly trimmed beard. His face was weathered, and his arms were dark with the sun. He was dressed in jeans and an antique Bob Dylan T-shirt ripped at the neckline, with a silver Rolex on one wrist. He led the way out of the bar to his vehicle, a '77 Scout pickup convertible that somebody had painted white with a brush. He settled in his seat and said, "We've got four interviews—friends and relatives."

"Why in the middle of the night?"

"Because that's when they're home and we can find them," he said, as he put the truck in gear. "They don't have straight jobs."

They found friends and relatives, but nobody knew anything about the killing, and Lucas tended to believe them. Smith, they said, was out doing his thing, which mostly involved wandering around, talking to his homeys. Everybody knew he'd been pounding the crack, and sometimes sold it, and was often holding. So the belief was, somebody needed some crack and they took it.

One guy angrily told them that "That shit is everywhere and it's fuckin' up everybody and you ain't doing a damn thing about it. Not a damn thing."

Del told him, "I don't know what to do. You tell me what to do."

"Do something," the guy said. "Anything. Arrest them. Put them in jail. They're a buncha animals, they're fuckin' up the whole neighborhood. If we were white, you'd be all over it."

His wife was standing behind him, arms crossed, nodding.

MOVING AROUND with Del felt weird.

As a uniformed cop, Lucas generally assumed that the people with whom he came in contact were the enemy, until proven different. In the course of covering traffic accidents or making traffic stops, breaking up fights, chasing down robbers or burglars, calling ambulances, talking to victims, uniforms really didn't need to project much empathy. They were like the army: not there to make friends. And sometimes, rolling through the dark across hostile neighborhoods, inside a car filled with weapons, radios, and lights, he *felt* like he was in an army, and in hostile territory.

Del, on the other hand, solicited help, listened carefully, displayed great patience, and when the guy went off about crack, he was nodding in agreement, and when the guy finished, he said, "Don't tell the boss I said this, but I agree with you."

And he got some cooperation, but no real information, probably, Lucas thought, because nobody had any.

AT TEN O´CLOCK, Del had gotten involved in a convoluted discussion with a minister who'd once run a church that Smith and his mother had gone to. Lucas had drifted off down the street, toward the corner where they'd parked, when he saw a thin young white man walking toward the same corner, from the right-angle street. The man was wearing what cops had called a pimp hat, a wide-brimmed fuzzy thing that had gone out of fashion sometime in the seventies, when disco died. Long knotted Rasta braids flowed out from under the hat, and Lucas said, aloud, "Randy."

The man stopped, saw Lucas, did a double take, turned, and started running. Lucas went after him, fifty yards behind.

The thing was, Randy Whitcomb could hoof it, like skinny people often can. He wasn't in the same class athletically as Lucas, but he wasn't carrying the weight, either. Lucas heard Del shout, "Hey! Hey!" as he went around the corner, and then the race was on. Lucas could close by ten yards or so every short block, but there was traffic. Sometimes he caught it wrong, going across the street, and Randy stretched his lead, and sometimes Randy caught it wrong, and lost ground. Five blocks and Lucas was getting close, fifteen yards back, and Randy swerved into an alley and as he turned, Lucas caught a flash of plastic going over a hedge; so Randy had off-loaded his crack, coke, or grass, hoping that Lucas hadn't seen it.

Toward the end of the block, Lucas was four feet behind him, then two feet: Randy glanced back in desperation, hearing the footsteps, and lost another foot in looking, and Lucas hit him between the shoulder blades. Randy went down on his face and Lucas was on top of him, one hand on Randy's neck, his weight on Randy's upper back.

"You little cocksucker, I told you to get out of my part of town," Lucas said. He banged Randy's face on the alley's concrete one time, then maneuvered to put the cuffs on. "What'd you throw in that bag, Randy? Yeah, I saw it. You got a little crack in there? You got five years in there?"

"I'm gonna kill you, you motherfucker," Randy said. "I'm gonna cut your fuckin' nuts off."

Randy Whitcomb was a twenty-year-old refugee from suburban St. Paul. He gave every sign of believing that he was a black pimp, though he was so pale that he almost glowed in the darkness of the alley. Not only did he believe that he was black, but a stereotypical TV gangster black, with the fuzzy hat, the cocaine fingernails, the braids, and even a ghetto accent, picked up from MTV. It might have been laughable, if he hadn't been such an evil little fuck, attempting to recruit runaway girls to hustle for him, beating them blue when they failed or didn't work hard enough or held out on him.

Lucas got the cuffs on and jerked Randy to his feet, and started marching him back down the alley to the hedge where he'd thrown the bag. "You know what's in the bag, dickhead? There's one-half ounce of weed, which will get me about, uh, an hour in jail, you piece of shit," Randy said. "Good going, Davenport, you're a real fuckin' . . . you know . . . that guy with the hat."

"What?"

"The fuckin' cop with the fuckin' backwards hat."

"Fuck you, Randy," Lucas said, with no idea of what Randy was talking about. But if he was telling the truth, the weed hadn't been worth the chase.

Then Lucas said, "You can take that weed and stick it up your ass, as far as I'm concerned. You're going down for the Billy Smith murder, you little shit."

"What? What the fuck?"

"We just got fuckin' tired of you," Lucas said. "We got the knife he was stabbed with, and guess whose fingerprints are gonna be on it? Man, I been waiting three years for this day. . . ."

"You wouldn't do that," Randy said, trying to twist around to see Lucas's face.

"Bullshit, I wouldn't," Lucas said. "So would every other cop on the south side. We solve a murder, we put you away for eighteen fuckin' years, get you outa our hair."

"But I didn't do it," Randy said. "I didn't do it."

"But you've done all kinds of other shit. We'll just call it even," Lucas said. "You get away with that, we frame you for this. Everybody's happy. Especially those three-hundred-pound weight-lifting homos out at Stillwater. They're gonna love your little red ass."

They came to the point in the hedge where Randy had tossed the bag, and Lucas steered him through a hurricane fence gate, and found the bag sitting on the back lawn of a darkened house. Lucas picked it up between two fingers, not getting prints on it: weed, all right, and probably not much more than a half-ounce. He stuck it in Randy's back pocket. "Oh, look—he's still got the weed."

"You fuck."

"And you murdered that poor Billy Smith boy."

Then Randy said, "Davenport, listen, goddamnit. I got something for you. You know when Rice got stabbed the other week? I know who done that."

"Rice?" Lucas knew about a guy named Ronald Rice getting stabbed on the north side, out of his territory, but hadn't heard much more about it.

"Yeah. I know who done that, and I know who'll tell you about it. You let me go . . . you got nothing here with this little bit of weed . . . you let me go, I'll give you the name. Just you and me."

"Randy, you're going to prison. Right now. You're off—"

Randy smelled the interest. "No, no, no, man, I got these names. They're good names, honest to God. I just don't want to go to jail tonight, and I don't like this asshole anyway, he gives me a lot of shit, so I'll give the name to you. And the name of the chick who can back it up."

Lucas thought about it, standing in the alley. Then he said, "If there's one thing I hate more than you, it'd be you punkin' me," Lucas said. "You punkin' me, Randy? If you are, I swear to God, I'll find you and I'll choke you to death and I'll throw your body in the fuckin' Mississippi River."

Randy felt the deal coming: "Okay. Okay. Here's the name: Delia White. She lives on the corner of Cornwall and Eighteenth, in a big red house. You know that big red house?"

Lucas did. "Delia White."

"That's right. The guy who stabbed Rice is her brother-in-law, which name is El-Ron Parker. And she'll talk, because she thinks El-Ron killed her sister two years ago."

"Did he?"

"How in the fuck would I know? And who cares?"

Lucas looked at Randy for a minute, then said, "How do you know this?"

"Because I sell a little medicine to Delia and her friends."

"Crack?" Lucas asked. A crackhead wouldn't be the best witness.

"Not crack, just a little weed."

"If you're punkin' me . . ."

"I'm not, I swear to God."

Lucas looked at him another moment, then said, "You get off the south side. I don't care where you go. You go up north, you go over to St. Paul. I don't want to see you on my turf."

"I'm outa here," Randy said. He held his cuffed hands out to the side. Lucas looked at him for another long moment, moved him over into the light from a streetlight, and popped the cuffs. Randy rubbed his wrists, moving away, then turned and ran. Lucas moved more under the light, wrote "Delia White" and "L. Ron Parker" in his notebook, circled them, and drew a line to "Ronald Rice."

A block down the street, Randy turned again and began screaming: *"You cocksucker . . . you cocksucker . . ."*

Lucas saw Del's truck coming down the street, and stepped out and flagged it down. When he looked back after Randy, Randy was gone.

Lucas got in the truck and Del asked, "What the hell was that all about?"

"Little asshole I've been trying to get rid of," Lucas said.

"You get rid of him?"

"Probably not," Lucas said. "You get anything?"

"I got a rash. I think my underwear's too tight."

AT ELEVEN O´CLOCK, they were ready to quit, and headed back toward the river to drop Lucas; they were talking about cars.

Del confessed that his heart beat a little harder every time he saw a Camaro IROC-Z. "Zero to sixty in seven seconds, thirteen grand to put it in my driveway."

"We called them dork-mobiles, over at the U," Lucas said.

"What?"

"Yeah. Dork-mobiles. You get one, you'd have to grow a mullet."

"Now you ruined it for me," Del said.

"I'm thinking Porsche," Lucas said. "They'd, like, *eat* a fuckin' IROC-Z."

"Along with your paycheck for the next ten years," Del said. He pointed off to his right and said, "Smith was killed about three blocks over there."

Lucas frowned. "Over there?"

"Yeah, right over there."

"Let's go see it," Lucas said.

"It's dark, man," Del said. "There's nothing to see. There wasn't much to see in the first place."

"I wanna see it," Lucas said. "It'll take you what, two minutes?"

Del shrugged and took the next right, and they went back around the block, took a left, went four more blocks down and took another right, and another right into a narrow alley, and rolled a few car lengths into it. Del did a little jog so his headlights played across the side of a garage and an adjoining hedge. "That's it. He was stabbed right by the garage door, we think, and thrown into the hedge beside the garage."

"And the garbage guys found him at six this morning, and the ME said he'd been dead for quite a while, but they weren't sure how long because it was so hot."

"Yeah."

"And he was stabbed by a long knife with a heavy blade," Lucas said.

"Where're we going with this?"

"We're about a five-minute walk from the Jones girls' house. We got a tip that the killer was this guy—"

"The bum with the basketball. Crank, or whatever his name is."

"Scrape. We took a long knife off him. Butcher knife."

Del looked at him in the thin ambient light and said, "Ah . . . fuck me."

They considered that statement for a while, then Del added, "This asshole, Smith, was killed by some other asshole for six dollars' worth of crack cocaine."

Lucas said, "Probably. But, you gotta consider the possibilities. A guy gets stabbed with a long butcher knife, and a crazy dude, who is a suspect in a kidnapping-murder in the same place at *exactly* the same time, is picked up with a long butcher knife. Probably a coincidence, but you gotta look at it. Am I right?"

Del said, "You're gonna cause a lot of trouble in this goddamn department. We gotta talk to somebody."

Lucas took out his notebook. "I got Daniel's home phone number. If we can find a phone, I'll give him a ring."

"You're a braver man than I am," Del said. "But if you'll talk to him, I know the location of every single fuckin' pay phone in Minneapolis, and there's one on the back wall of the Ugly Stick. We can be there in two minutes."

"Got a quarter?" Lucas asked.

DANIEL TOOK THE PHONE from his wife and said, "Davenport . . . goddamnit. It's almost midnight. Why'd I give you this number? I really need the sleep."

Lucas and Del were in the back room of the Ugly Stick, a pool parlor on Lake Street, thick with smoke and wiseasses. Del leaned against the wall and dug around his teeth with a toothpick, and listened as Lucas made the call. Lucas asked, "What'd we do with that knife we took off Scrape?"

"It's in an evidence locker. Did you hook up with Del or what?"

"Del's right here—he's the one who insisted we call," Lucas said. Behind him, Del clapped a hand to his forehead. "Listen: Scrape's in jail, right?"

There was a moment of dead silence, then Daniel said, "No. He took off. Snuck out. We don't know how—probably out a side window—but we can't put our hands on him. We checked his cave, he's not there. We're looking for him . . . but I don't want to talk about this in the middle of the night. What the hell are you doing?"

Lucas was dumbfounded. "He got away? Weren't we watching him? What was that thing about being inside his sweatshirt?"

"Davenport . . ."

"Smith got killed at the same time the girls disappeared, and he was stabbed to death with a butcher knife with a long heavy blade," Lucas said. "That was four blocks from the Jones house. You can't see it unless you're down here, how close they are. The girls could have been walking out to the stores on Lake, there's all kinds of stuff down there that kids might go for. And they would have gone right by this alley. Or through it. We need to look for Smith's blood on the knife."

Daniel said, "Aw, for Christ's sakes . . . Del's there? Let me talk to Del."

Lucas pushed the phone at Del: "He wants to talk to you."

Del took the phone and listened for a minute, then said. "Right. Talk to you tomorrow." He hung up and said to Lucas, "Thanks a lot for that 'Del insisted' bullshit."

"No problem," Lucas said. "What'd he say?"

"He said to go back and knock on every single door where the house shows lights," Del said.

"All right," Lucas said. "Now we're cooking with gas."

"I was cooking before," Del said. "Now, we're gonna be out here until two in the morning."

"I say we knock on every door, lights or not," Lucas said.

"Anybody ever tell you to go fuck yourself?"

"All the time," Lucas said. "Just about every fuckin' day."

6

THEY STARTED WITH the house closest to the murder site, Lucas always in front, looking more like a detective than Del, Del sidling around the edges with follow-up questions.

At the second house, they woke up a couple who, after listening to Lucas's explanation, told them two things: they knew the two girls by sight, they believed. "If it was the same two girls, we were talking about it at the dinner table," the wife said. But they hadn't seen them for several days. The girls sometimes walked past the house, and, the husband said, he thought he'd seen them cutting through the alley.

"You think that black guy getting killed had something to do with the girls?" the wife asked. She no longer looked sleepy, but she looked scared. "We've got girls."

"We don't know, but there have been some indications that we can't talk about," Del said. "You should keep those girls tight."

Lucas took down their names and the details of the conversation in his notebook, and asked who had the sharpest eyes for the street. They were passed along to another couple, who they shook out of bed for another sleepy interrogation. Those two had also seen the girls, but not in the last few days. And they had definitely seen them in the alley.

"I think they were back there pretty often, walking through," the wife said. "I've seen them more than once, and I don't go out there that much."

Lucas took down their details, and when they were back outside, said to Del, "Man, we're onto something here."

Del said, "Don't get excited. We got nothing yet. Nobody saw them the afternoon they disappeared."

"You think we got something or not?"

"Maybe we got something," Del conceded. "I'm glad I insisted on calling Daniel. At least I'll get the credit."

Lucas said, "You can have it. Who's next? Maybe we ought to do all the lights, then go back after the darks."

SO THEY WORKED their way around the block, and found an elderly single woman who'd also seen the girls. As they were leaving, she said, "You know, I was driving down to park in my garage and I slowed down to look at the place where that colored boy was killed. I think it was there . . . I think I saw a little zori in the street, like somebody had thrown it away. Like a girl's zori."

"A what?" Del asked.

"A zori. A flip-flop. Like plastic shower shoes. It looked like it had been run over a bunch of times, so I thought maybe it fell out of a garbage can. But kids wear them."

Del looked at Lucas and asked, "Were the kids wearing flip-flops?"

"I don't know. I haven't heard anybody talking about flip-flops," Lucas said. "Did you guys pick anything up when you were doing the crime scene?"

"No flip-flops . . ."

Lucas said to the woman, "Thank you, ma'am." And when they got out in the street, to Del, "We need our flashlights."

They spent fifteen minutes working through the alley, until a man shouted out of the back of a house, opposite the house where they'd started, "Get out of there. We called the cops."

Lucas yelled, "We *are* the cops. We need to talk to you."

Lights came on in the house next door, and Del pointed at the house and said, "I'll go talk to these guys."

The shouting man's name was Mayer, and he and his roommate agreed that they'd seen the girls walking by the house, but knew nothing about a flip-flop. They had been in Eau Claire the day of the murder and the girls' disappearance, they said, in answer to Lucas's question, and hadn't gotten back until that morning.

"Not to put too fine a point on it, we're not really interested in girls," Mayer said.

Del came pounding up the front steps and across the porch, and then he knocked and stuck his head through the door and said to Lucas, "C'mon. The guys next door said they got a flip-flop."

Lucas thanked Mayer and followed Del out the door, where an older man was waiting with a flashlight. They followed him down the side of his house and through a gate into the backyard, into his garage, and looked in his trash can. Inside was a single, badly beaten-up flip-flop.

"Well, shit," Del said.

"But this is good," Lucas said. "Maybe."

"This means we gotta call Daniel again."

"Okay, that's not good." But then Lucas laughed and slapped Del on the shoulder. "I'm so hot," he said. "I'm *so* hot."

The old man said, "I don't think you should be laughing about this. Those little girls, that boy being dead and all."

DANIEL SAID, "Okay, Davenport, listen carefully. You listening?"

"Yeah."

"Call a patrol car, get some crime-scene tape, and tape it to that garage. Leave the flip-flop in the garbage can, seal the garage, and go home. Okay? Go get some sleep. I will see you at that garage at nine o'clock tomorrow morning. You think you got that? Or do you want me to repeat it?"

"I got it, Chief," Lucas said.

"Davenport, I'm not the chief."

"You will be," Lucas said.

"Okay. And I actually like the ass-kissing, so I won't order you to stop," Daniel said. "But you: go home."

ON THE WAY BACK to Lucas's car, Del said, "I had a thought."

"Is it complicated?" Lucas asked. "You want to stop driving while you tell me?"

"Stop wiseassing me for a minute," Del said. "If the kids were really taken in that alley . . ."

"Then the kidnapper had to have a car or a truck of some kind, and Scrape the ragman doesn't, and probably doesn't even know how to drive. I thought of that."

They drove for another block, then Del asked, "What else did you think of?"

"That we've been running on clues given to us by people we don't know and can't find. Everyone else we've talked to is happy to chip in whatever thoughts they have—not a single person has been unwilling to help. Even the hookers were out front about what they knew. But everything good that we've gotten, it's all been anonymous, and perfectly timed, and it all points us at Scrape."

"Does seem too easy," Del said.

"And I've thought of the fact that Smith was killed by somebody who overpowered a muscular, violent young gang member without leaving a trace. Scrape has trouble dribbling a basketball."

"What does that mean?"

"Probably that Smith was killed by some other violent young gang member who he thought was a friend, and it has nothing to do with the girls," Lucas said.

"What else?"

"That it would be a big fuckin' coincidence, a HUGE fuckin'

83

coincidence that Smith got killed at the same time the girls were being kidnapped, in an alley that the girls used, without the two things being connected. You know what I mean?"

"What else?"

"That the first thing we should do tomorrow is find out if the flip-flop belonged to one of the girls, and where the girls would go down that alley. They had to be going somewhere, maybe out to Lake Street to buy shit. Popsicles, or something. Ding Dongs."

"Ho Hos."

"Sno Balls."

"Moon pies."

"Eight balls?"

"Not eight balls," Del said. Eight balls were one-eighth-ounce Saran-Wrapped cocaine favors.

After another moment, Del said, "Half of what you think is internally contradictory."

"Does that bother you?" Lucas asked.

"No, but it does highlight the fact that half of what you think is, *ipso facto*, bullshit."

"*Quid pro quo.*"

"*Nolo contendere.*"

"*Post hoc ergo propter hoc.*"

"Bullshit," Del said. "There's no such thing as that."

"Sure there is. Logic one-oh-one. *After this therefore because of this.* Look it up," Lucas said.

"Fuck that. I'd rather get my balls busted than waste time looking it up."

DEL LEFT LUCAS on the street looking at his watch. One-thirty in the morning. He should be ready for bed, but the afternoon nap, and his normal night-shift life, had him awake. He could hit a couple clubs, or find a party at the university; on the other hand . . .

He went back to the XTC, found the phone, and dialed a number from memory. Catherine Brown answered: "Library."

He asked, "So you clipping the papers?"

"That's what I'm doing. And it's very cold and lonely up here."

"Bet it's boring, too," he said.

"But they depend on me," she said. "What would happen if the reporters actually had to file their own stories, instead of having me clip them for them?"

"I can't begin to contemplate the awfulness of it," Lucas said. "You like mushrooms?"

"Love mushrooms—and pepperoni. I'm starving. But I don't get off for another hour and a half."

"I can get four slices and be there in an hour," Lucas said.

"I'll be down by the door at exactly three o'clock."

He had an hour to kill, not much to do: he could pick up the pizza anytime, at Red's, an all-night pizza place on Hennepin Avenue. He looked at his watch, then pulled the notebook from his pocket. Red house, corner of Cornwall and Eighteenth. He headed back across town, farther south and a bit west of where he and Del had been working. Traffic was light, and he was cruising Cornwall in fifteen minutes: the big red house showed a light. Just one, but that, he thought, was enough for a knock on the door.

He parked at the curb in front of the house, looked up and down the street, then crossed the lawn, climbed the porch steps and knocked on the door; he could hear a radio or a stereo playing inside, and then he heard somebody say something, and he knocked again, louder.

A pretty woman came to the door, pulled back the curtain that covered the glass inserts, looked at him, turned on the yellow bug light, looked at him again, obviously puzzled that a guy who looked like Lucas would be knocking on her door at two in the morning, and she asked, through the glass, "What?"

Lucas held up his badge and said, "I need to talk to Delia White. That you?"

"What do you want to talk to Delia for?"

"She might be able to help me with an investigation," Lucas said.

"It's two o'clock in the morning."

Lucas looked at his watch, frowned, and said, "Jeez, I must have lost track of time."

A smile flicked across her face and she turned and called back into the house, "Mom!"

Another woman came out, the first one turned away and met her a few steps from the door. Lucas couldn't see them anymore because of the curtain, but he could hear them talking, and then the second woman pulled the curtain back, looked at him, and snapped, "What do you want?"

"I'm a police officer. I need to talk to Delia."

"About what?"

Lucas wanted to get inside, but didn't really know how, so he just said it: "I understand Delia saw L. Ron Parker stab Ronald Rice. I need to talk to her about it."

The curtain slid back across the glass, and he could hear the women talking, but couldn't make out the words. Then the curtain slid back again, and the older woman, Mom, gave him a long look, then unlatched the door.

Once inside, sitting on the front room couch, Lucas re-apologized for running so late, but told them about the Jones investigation, and said, "So I was talking to a guy and he said that Miz White might be able to help me with this L. Ron Parker thing."

"If El-Ron thought I was talking to the police, he'd stick me," the pretty woman said, and Lucas understood that she was Delia.

"That doesn't happen much," Lucas assured her. "You gotta make up your own mind—I won't say it never happens—but we can usually take the guy off in the corner, and whisper into his ear, and he'll leave you alone. Unless he's nuts."

"El-Ron *is* nuts," the older woman said. She looked at her daughter. "But I don't know if he's crazy enough to go after you."

"Especially after what he did to your sister," Lucas offered.

The two women turned back to him, faces gone hard, and Mom asked, "What'd you know about that?"

"I heard about it," Lucas said. Nobody said anything for a long time, and Lucas took out his notebook and said, "So . . . to start, what does the L. stand for?"

"What L?" Delia White asked.

"In L. Ron Parker?"

"It's not L, like the letter," Delia said. "It's El. E-L. His name is El-Ron Parker. E-L-dash-R-O-N. That's his name."

"Did he kill your sister?" he asked Delia.

She said, "Can't prove it, but he did it."

"What was her name?"

"CeeCee."

"Did he stab Mr. Rice?" Lucas asked.

The story came out slowly. Delia and a man named George Danner had gone out to get some tacos and were eating in a parking lot by the Taco Bell when El-Ron Parker went by in a hurry, and they could tell he was looking for trouble, right there. They stepped around the Taco Bell, and they saw Parker approach Rice between two cars. They started arguing even before they got close, and then Parker went after the other man. They thought he was hitting him, but when Parker came running out from between the cars, they saw the knife in his hand.

"Does he know you saw him?"

"He does. He came over the next day and tried to make friends with me again."

"What about your friend, this Danner guy?" Lucas asked. "Wouldn't he testify against him?"

"George went back to St. Paul, and I haven't seen him since. He's a pretty peaceful man."

"But he knows El-Ron."

"Yeah, he does."

Lucas said, "Huh. What about Mr. Rice? Has he identified Parker as the one who stabbed him?"

"Stop calling him mister," the older woman said. "Ronald Rice is just another fool. But, he ain't woke up yet. He might not wake up, is what the newspaper says."

Lucas looked at his watch: time to go get pizza. He said, "This whole deal wasn't my reason for being here. But I'm gonna look into it. We'll protect you. He probably won't even remember you by the time he gets out of prison. Has El-Ron got any prior arrests?"

"About a hundred," said the older woman.

"There you go. He'll be going on vacation for a long time, if you're willing to testify," Lucas said. "Think about your sister . . . and I'll come back and talk to you some more. Think about CeeCee."

HE WAS TEN MINUTES late to the *Star Tribune*'s loading dock. Brown said, "I thought you'd forgotten. I was about to go back upstairs," and they climbed the back stairs with the pizza box. She was a moderately overweight blonde wearing a thin blue cotton-paisley dress, almost but not quite a hippie dress, which let the roundness of her figure shine through. He watched her hips as they went up the stairs and began breathing a little harder than the climb warranted.

There was hardly anyone in the building, and they walked down a couple of dark hallways toward the light coming out of a single office; Lucas could hear the police radios as they came up.

The radios were in a small room down the hall, and the blind man who monitored them said, as they went by, "Hello again, Catherine," and she said, "Yup, it's me," and they went on into the library. She closed and locked the door behind her, though if there were any reporters left in the building, the guy in the monitoring room could buzz them through.

They got the pizza inside and they messed around for a couple minutes, squeezing and petting, then she buttoned her bra and they settled behind the counter to eat the pizza. Catherine asked, "What have you been up to?"

"This has gotta come from an anonymous source," Lucas said, around a pepperoni and mushroom.

"I've already gotten you in the paper about six times. . . ."

"No, no. This time, I don't want to be in the paper," Lucas said. "In fact, you can't mention my name. Maybe you could feed it through the radio guy?"

"What is it?"

He told her how he'd been put in plainclothes to look for the girls, how he'd been switched to the Smith investigation, and how the two investigations might become one—how there was at least a possibility that Smith had been killed by the same person who took the girls.

"*You* figured this out? Wow," she said. Her eyes were large. "Wait a minute, I just clipped the story. . . ."

She went through a file of stories clipped from the next day's paper, and said, "Here . . ." She scanned it, and then looked up: "There's not a single word about a suspect. About this street guy."

"We've been holding it tight. But here's the thing: instead of giving it all to the reporter, have them ask the question: Did you arrest a bum, a transient, and then let him go? Are you looking for him? Do you have a photo? And ask if the Smith murder was involved."

"What do you get out of this?"

Lucas grinned at her: "Friendship?"

She blushed and said, "I could use a little friendship. But I've got to finish clipping."

LUCAS WATCHED her clip the rest of the papers, stuffing the day's stories in little green envelopes, and thought about the stuff he'd given her, and smiled to himself. A few questions about Scrape would crank up the pressure, might bring in some tips about where he was and how he got loose after his arrest, and keep Lucas on the job.

He really didn't want to go back to the patrol car. Not after the taste he'd had; and he wanted to stay in front of Daniel as long as he could.

As Catherine finished the clipping, Lucas went into the vault, an inner room of the newspaper library, and pulled a tied bundle of papers off a shelf. Some historic issue about Hubert Humphrey, judging from the headlines. Well, fuck a bunch of Hubert Humphrey. He spread the papers out on the floor, an inch or so thick.

When he came back out, she said, "What were you doing?"

"Hubert Humphrey's suffered a tragedy," he said. "Only a trained librarian could put it right."

She came to look in the vault, turned to him and said, "This is a disgrace."

AN HOUR LATER, on their way out of the building, Catherine leaned in the door of the radio room and said, "Roy . . . listen, I was talking to a guy—"

"The guy with you?"

"No, no. This is just a friend," she said.

89

The radio guy said, "Hi, friend."

Lucas: "Hi."

Catherine said, "Anyway, this guy says there was a ruckus down in his neighborhood tonight, right around midnight. There were some cops there—"

"Got that. The fight down at the Mill?"

"No. Listen, here's the thing. My guy says somebody should ask the cops if it's true that they arrested a transient in the case of the Jones girls, and then let him go, and now are trying to get him back. And they should ask if it's true that the killing of the black kid the other day, Bobby's story, if that guy was killed by the same transient who took the girls, at the same time."

"The cops think a transient killed Smith, and kidnapped the girls?" The blind guy was skeptical.

"That's what my guy heard. They were searching that alley where Smith got killed, at midnight, and they weren't looking for evidence about Smith—they were looking for evidence about the girls. And he says they found some. They say Smith might have tried to interfere in the kidnapping. He might be a hero, not some dead dope dealer."

"Pretty heavy-duty if it's true," the blind guy said.

"Thought you might get some cred if you pass it along," Catherine said.

"I'll do that. Thanks, Kate."

They went down the back stairs, and Lucas walked her to her car in the parking lot across from the front of the building. She said, "You never come to my place. I think you're afraid it might turn into a relationship."

"That's completely wrong," he said. "With my hours . . ."

"You're not going anywhere now," she said. "So follow me."

"Kate . . ."

But she was already rolling.

THE THING ABOUT BIG GIRLS, Lucas thought, the next morning, as he parked his Jeep outside the entrance to the alley, is that sometimes they can take more punishment than you're prepared to hand out. He half limped around the corner and found Daniel, Sloan, Hanson, and Del staring through the open garage door at the trash can.

"Jesus, what happened to you?" Del asked. "You look like you fell out a window."

Lucas shook his head: "Just tired. Been working too hard." He looked into the garage, where a guy had pulled the flip-flop out of the trash can and set it on a plastic bag, and now was probing deeper into the trash. "Is that . . . have you talked to the Joneses? Were they wearing flip-flops?"

"Mary was," Daniel said. "They were red and white, like this one, Miz Jones thinks. They got them at a Kmart, and we'll be checking for size and brand and style."

"Well, hell, it's her flip-flop," Lucas said. "What are the chances?"

"There's always a chance it isn't," Hanson said. "The problem is, we got that box."

"And?"

"We got some prints on it. They look like Scrape's."

Daniel said that they'd gotten a dozen partials off the box, none good—but when compared to the prints they'd taken from Scrape the day before, there seemed to be a few apparent matches.

Lucas scratched his ear and said, "Huh."

Daniel said to Lucas, "We're gonna take this flip-flop around to Miz Jones and have her look at it, and Sloan will check the Kmart connection. For you—that chick who knew where Scrape lived. I want you to find her again, and tour her around to all the places that he might have gone."

"He could be halfway to California," Hanson said.

Daniel: "He could be, but I doubt it. He had four dollars when we picked him up and he skipped at night. I think he's hiding. We've got the highway patrol and every cop in Minnesota looking at hitchhikers."

"Look at the trains," Lucas said.

"What?"

"Have somebody check the train yards over by the university," Lucas said. "Bums still ride trains—I was talking to a railroad security guy last year, after that guy got his legs chopped off. He said they still got all kinds of bums riding the boxcars. Especially out to the West Coast."

Daniel said to Hanson: "Check that. Like right now. Get onto railroad security."

Lucas said, "I've got a phone number in my notebook."

Daniel said to Del, "I want you down at the place where he was living. Knock on all the doors, talk to the residents. Anything they know . . ." Del nodded, and Daniel said, "So let's go. Go, everybody. Go away."

AFTER A COUPLE of phone calls, Lucas found the blue-haired Karen Frazier standing at a bus stop just down the street from her office. He pulled up, leaned across, and popped the door and said, "I'll give you a ride."

"What do you want?" she asked, not getting in.

"More help," he said. "Come on, get in. I'm not gonna bite."

She got in and pulled the door shut: "So?"

"So where're you going?"

"Back home. I live in Uptown."

"So do I," Lucas said. "But listen—this is confidential. We found a box last night with some of the girls' clothes in it. Their mom fainted when she saw it."

"Oh, no." Her hands went to her face. "It was theirs? For sure?"

"For sure. One of them was wearing a bra with a kitty face on it."

"Ah, God. I don't want to hear that," Frazier said.

"What I need is, a tour of the places where you think Scrape might go to hide. He took off in the night, after we let him go. He had no money, we're checking hitchhikers and the freight trains, but we think he's probably hiding out somewhere. Somewhere he could get in the dark."

She thought for a minute, then said, "Scrape's pretty good at hiding. He doesn't go where the other transients go. Doesn't hang out with them, doesn't use the Mission. He's not stupid, either—he's just really schizophrenic, which can make him look stupid, but he's not. If he wants to hide . . ."

She thought for another minute, then said, "The idea of the trains . . . I don't think he rides trains. I've never heard him say that. I think he hustles around for bus money. . . . But there're abandoned sheds and buildings all over that area, north of University Avenue, and some of them are built up on stilts and you can get under them. And there are old shipping containers all over the place, that you can get into, and old truck trailers at some of the trucking companies . . . Guys who ride the trains use them to hide—the train cops know most of them, but that would be one place. He could walk there from his room in a couple of hours."

"Where else?"

"Well, he was living under that tree. He likes it outdoors, and there are all kinds of little caves and nooks and holes where he could be, along the river. There are some sewer tunnels you can get into, and they cross through old caves and things. Some of the guys know those places; Scrape does. But most of them smell pretty bad, from sewage and gas, so they stay out. If he's hiding in there, it'd be hell to get him out. I went down in one once, and you could walk right past him, and never know he's there."

"Where else?"

"Well, the other places—you'd never find him unless people see him coming or going. They go under houses, in old garages, anyplace that has a roof and they can't be seen. Apartment neighborhoods, with old houses, like over by the university. You find gangs of guys under the main highway bridges; they'll be camping out, hanging out together."

"Where would you go, if you were Scrape and you thought the cops were after you?"

"Honestly, there's no way to tell, exactly," she said. "He could go to any of those places."

"C'mon."

She sighed. "I'd go with the river. That's where he always lives, except when he can get a gig like this apartment. If you get set up in a cave, especially one with water, you can be safe, dry, hidden, and you can even keep yourself clean. Scrape likes to stay clean, when he can."

Lucas said, "Huh. Where are these caves and sewer things?"

"All along the riverbank. Best thing to do is, find people who are living there now," she said. "Ask them. They'll know."

"And if they don't want to talk to me?"

She looked out the side window and said, "I hate telling you this stuff."

"Why? The girls . . ."

"I feel terrible about the girls, which is why I'm talking to you at all. But talking to cops, if any of the guys see me, and figure I'm a snitch . . . it doesn't help my work, and might even cause me trouble. Most of them are harmless, but *some* of them are crazy. *Very* crazy. If they thought I was working with the cops, I don't know what they'd do."

"Okay. I see that," Lucas said. He waited a beat, and then said, "You were going to tell me something, that you didn't want to."

She turned back to him. "They hate going to jail. They don't do well there, not well at all, because of their handicaps. If I were desperate to find somebody, and wanted to get information from these guys, I'd threaten them. You know—'How'd you like to spend a couple weeks in jail?' That kind of thing."

"Good," Lucas said. "Specifically, the riverbank . . ."

"I'd start at Hennepin Avenue, and work south. Like I said, he's not stupid: I don't think he'd go back to the part of the riverbank where he was before."

"Thank you," he said. "Where can I drop you?"

She popped the door. "Thanks anyway, I'll just take the bus."

TEN MINUTES LATER, Lucas stood on the edge of the Mississippi River, looking up and down the bluffs, and realized that the idea that he might search it himself was ridiculous. He also realized that if he were running from the cops, and needed to hide out for a couple of days, he'd head for the river.

And that's what he told Daniel, at police headquarters.

"There are all those bridges, there's two spans to each one of them, I could see at least one catwalk under a bridge, which means people could be living up there, right under the road deck. If we're gonna do a search, we're gonna need twenty guys, and it's gonna take a couple of days, at least. We'll probably need people from St. Paul—"

"I'll have to talk to the chief," Daniel said. "The problem is, the *Strib* is all over us. They know something happened. They know we picked somebody up and turned him loose again. I think the Joneses might be talking to them . . . so the shit's about to hit the fan."

"I could go back out alone . . ." Lucas yawned.

"No, no, I hear what you're saying about the river," Daniel said. "We got railroad security checking the rail yard, but the riverbank is just too big."

"Maybe you ought to talk to the paper, call a press conference," Lucas suggested. "Get yourself some airtime. We got a good mug of Scrape, put it out there. The more eyes the better."

Daniel thought about it, then said, "That's an idea. I'll talk to the chief. You, go home. Get some sleep. You been up for two days."

"I can handle it for a while."

"Ah, you did pretty good. We'll take it from here."

Lucas saw himself back in uniform, searching the riverbank in a line of cops: "Wait a minute. I don't want to quit this. We got this other possibility to think about, that Scrape didn't do it. That the kids were picked up in a vehicle. I've got this guy I'm looking for. I got this feeling . . ."

Daniel was shaking his head. "We can cover that. This is turning into a snake hunt. When we find Scrape—"

Lucas leaned forward: "Listen, Chief, I'll take vacation days. I'll work free. Just back me up for a shot at this other guy."

Daniel pursed his lips, eyebrows up, then he said, "All right. Don't take vacation, though. I'll keep you on for three days. I got Del still working on Smith; get with him, talk this thing over, and between the two of you, figure out Smith and figure out this missing guy you got. I'd like to know who he is, myself—and what the hell is he doing?"

"I'm outa here," Lucas said.

"Hey, hold on," Daniel called after him. "Del works late. Get some sleep. You really do look like shit."

LUCAS CALLED DEL, who answered on the eighth or ninth ring. "What?"

"This is Davenport. You up?"

"Jesus, it's not even noon yet," Del said. "What do you want?"

"We're hooking up, looking for Mysterio," Lucas said. "What time do we meet?"

"Ah . . . six o'clock. Meet me at six. No, wait: seven. Downtown. Don't call back."

7

FIVE HOURS OF sleep wasn't enough—he would have killed for seven—but the alarm blew him out of bed at five-thirty. Lucas cleaned up, put on khaki slacks, a black golf shirt and a sport coat, regulation black steel-toed uniform shoes, with the Model 40 in a shoulder rig.

When he got downtown, he found Daniel in his office, cleaning off his desk, ready to go home. "What happened?" Lucas asked.

"The chief had his press conference, we're still looking for Scrape," Daniel said. "We got fifteen guys on the street, and we're getting jack shit. Don't know where he could've gone. His face is all over the TV."

"We get a hard time about turning him loose?" Lucas asked.

"Not yet, but we will, sooner or later," Daniel said. He kicked back in his chair, put his feet on his desk. "But the chief can tap-dance. He made it sound like brilliant police work, picking him up the first time. Then, we're civil liberties heroes, letting him go. Now we're all working together, the people and the police, hand in hand, getting him back."

"Wish I'd seen it," Lucas said.

"Taught me one thing: I gotta learn how to tap-dance," Daniel said. "What're you doing here?"

"Waiting for Del. We're going out on the Smith thing again. Different angle this time. Was Smith a hero? Maybe loosen some people up. And we're gonna see what we can find out about Fell."

"Good luck. I don't think there's anything there, but—good luck."

DEL SHOWED UP at six-thirty, yawning, rubbing his unshaved face with the back of his hand. "You look like a cocker spaniel, your tongue is hangin' out," he said to Lucas. "Let's get some coffee, somewhere. Something to eat. Fries. Figure out what we're doing. Maybe you could do some push-ups, or something."

"I could attract some women for us," Lucas offered. "Just as a personal favor to you."

"Coffee. Fries. You can fantasize on your own time."

"Jealousy is hard to live with," Lucas said. "But there are government programs for the handicapped. Maybe I could find one for you. . . ."

They walked over to the Little Wagon, ordered coffee, two twenty-one shrimp baskets with fries, and Lucas sat for a few minutes beside a uniformed cop named Sally, working through her latest romantic trauma, before moving back to Del when the food arrived.

"You *are* a goddamned hound," Del said.

"Just trying to help her out," Lucas said. "Her boyfriend smokes a little dope, but now she thinks he might be moving into retail. She's wondering if she should bust him, and if she does, if that would adversely affect their relationship."

"I'd get one last terrific piece of ass before I did it," Del said, pouring a quarter bottle of ketchup on a mound of fries. "Of course, that's the male viewpoint. And that assumes that the guy's terrific in bed. 'Course, most dope dealers are. That's what I hear."

"And that's why you don't get laid. You see everything from the male point of view," Lucas said, around a mouthful of shrimp breading, and not much shrimp. "I try to see these things from the woman's point of view. That's why I got women crawling all over me. That and my good looks and charisma."

"One: I get laid all the time, and, two, that sounds pretty fuckin' cynical for a fifteen-year-old, or however old you are."

"Not cynical. I'm sincere," Lucas said. "I really do try to see it from their point of view."

Del looked skeptical.

"Really," Lucas said. "I'm serious. I try."

THEY SAT AND TALKED, getting acquainted. Del had been on the force for nine years, after two years of college, and had worked patrol for only six months.

"I went on in October, got off in April. Coldest winter in twenty years," he said. "Honest to God, there were nights so cold that the car wouldn't heat up. I'd walk down the street, and my nuts would be banging together like ball bearings. I was directing traffic around a big fire downtown one night, it was nineteen below zero with a thirty-mile-an-hour wind. The fire guys were spraying the building, and we had *icicles* blowing back on us."

Like Lucas, he'd done drug decoy work out of the academy, but unlike Lucas, he'd liked it, and stayed on, started working with intelligence and the sex unit, off and on, before his short stint on patrol. "They had a nasty long-term intelligence thing come up. I took it, and the payoff was, I got to stay on with Intel," he said.

Lucas told him about his time on patrol, and how he'd like to get off, the sooner the better: "If I'm not off in the next couple of months, I'm gonna apply for law school for next year. I already took the LSATs and I did good."

"You really want to be a fuckin' lawyer?" Del asked. "Look in the yellow pages. There are thousands of them. They're like rats."

"Yeah, I know. I don't know what to do. I used to think I could be a defense lawyer, but now, you know, after looking at four years of dirtbags, maybe not," Lucas said. "So then I'm thinking about being a prosecutor, but then I see the prosecutors we work with, and the political bullshit they put up with, and I'm thinking . . ."

"Maybe not," Del finished.

"But there's gotta be something in there," Lucas said. "Maybe get a law degree, I could go to the FBI."

"Ah, you don't want the FBI. Maybe ATF or the DEA, and you don't need a law degree for that," Del said. "The FBI . . . there's not much there. They mostly call each other up on the telephone. If you want to hunt, you need to be a big-city cop."

"I wrote a role-playing game when I was in college," Lucas said. "I was in this nerd class, introduction to computer science, and these guys were playing Dungeons and Dragons. I got interested and wrote a module for them, and they played it, and they liked it. There's some money in that. . . . I'm writing another one, on football. I don't know. There's a lot of stuff out there that I could do. I think I could be an investigator, but if I've got to spend much more time on patrol, I'm not gonna do it."

"Daniel likes you and he's got clout," Del said. "Have a serious talk with him. Something'll get done."

SALLY, THE UNIFORMED COP, stopped on her way out, patted Lucas on the shoulder and said, "Thanks for all that. I gotta think. Maybe we could get a cup of coffee."

"Anytime," Lucas said. "But hey: stay loose. And if you need help, call."

She patted his shoulder again and when she left, Del said, "I can barely stand it."

Lucas grinned and said, "Sincerity. That's all it is. So—let me tell you about John Fell, and you can tell me how to find him."

When Lucas finished explaining his ideas about Fell, Del said: "Interesting. So we've got a bunch of people who know him, who've seen him. Let's go talk to them."

"I talked to them—"

"But from what you tell me, you haven't *conversed* with them," Del said. "You interviewed them, you got a bunch of facts. What we want is all the ratshit they've seen and know about. Have they seen him in the neighborhood? What kind of a car does he drive? Does he smoke dope? Snort cocaine? If he does, I might get something on him, with my people out on the town. Oh—and we get Anderson in again, and instead of a credit check, we get his Visa bills. We want to know where he spends his money."

Lucas said, "That's good."

Del said, "No, it's not—it's just a bunch of words. We're just sitting here bullshitting."

They called Anderson, the computer guy, and asked him to try to get Fell's Visa bills. Anderson said he'd go back to the office and see what he could do, and leave the results on his desk, in a file marked for Del.

Then they headed over to Kenny's, and found Katz, the manager: "Haven't seen him—it's been a while now."

"Since the night the kids were kidnapped," Lucas said.

"That's right," Katz agreed.

Lucas said to Del, "See. That's part of the pattern. We can't find the tipsters. Or tipster—maybe there's only one."

"Who else ever met him?" Del asked Katz. "Any other people here?"

Fifteen or twenty people were sitting around the bar: Katz checked the faces, then said, "Yeah, there are a few people here who knew him. I'd rather not point them out, you know . . ."

"Be all right if I made an announcement?" Del asked.

Katz shrugged. "Be my guest."

Del dragged a chair from a side table into the middle of the bar and stood on it: conversation stopped, and he looked around and said, "I'm a Minneapolis police detective, my name's Capslock, and my partner and I are looking into the disappearance of the two Jones sisters. We need to get in touch with John Fell, who has been a semi-regular here. He provided some very useful information about the key suspect, but now we can't find Mr. Fell. We're asking that anybody who knew him, come chat with me and Detective Davenport, in the back booth. No big deal, just a chat. We pretty desperately need the help. . . . If you've been watching TV, you know what I'm talking about. Anyway—in the back."

He hopped down off the chair and walked with Lucas to the back of the bar. In a minute, four people had pulled up next to their booth, and a fifth had moved down to the end of the bar, from where he could watch and listen.

"Anything will help: nothing's too small," Del repeated.

Two of the people said they'd seen Fell getting into a black commercial van; one thought it was a Chevy, with cargo doors. One of those two said he thought Fell worked in electronics, that he'd said something about that. But a third, a woman, said she thought he might have been a teacher—now an ex-teacher.

"He said something about having tried teaching when he got out of school, but found out he couldn't stand high school kids. He said they never thought about anything but themselves, that they were a bunch of little assholes, and that teaching them was impossible."

"So he's a college grad," Lucas suggested.

"I think so."

"You know where he taught?" Lucas asked.

"No, I don't," she said. "He never said much about it."

"He's got a Minnesota accent," said one of the men. "He says 'a-boat,' like a Canadian."

"But you don't think he's a Canadian?" Lucas asked.

"No, I got the same feeling that Linda did—that he's from here."

"He didn't really talk about himself that much. He mostly told jokes," the fourth man said.

The fifth man slid down from the bar stool and came over with a beer in his hand. "I think he might've got fired from the school."

"Why's that?" Lucas asked.

"One time he went on a rant about school administrators. It sounded like stuff you say when you get fired. You know, they didn't know what they were doing, they were incompetent, they were jealous, all of that. Like when you get fired."

Del bobbed his head: "Okay. That's good. Anybody ever see him on the street? Outside the bar?"

"I might've," the woman said. "I think I saw him down by the university, walking down the street."

"Just walking?" Lucas asked.

"Yes, like he was going to lunch or coming back from lunch. Didn't have anything in his hands, he was just walking along. But—I'm not completely sure it was him. It just seemed to me that it was. I didn't think about it."

"Has he been in with women?"

"Girls from across the street," one of the men said. "The hookers."

"They hang out here?"

"They'll come in for a drink. You know. Kenny doesn't allow any hustling, or anything. But, they knew him," the man said.

"I get the feeling that he's from right around here," Lucas said. "Sees the girls across the street, hangs out here."

"Doesn't hang here much," a man said. "He only came in, the first time, maybe a month ago." The others nodded in agreement. "Then he was here pretty often. I haven't seen him for a few days, though."

"He was talking about seeing this transient—" Lucas began.

"The Scrape guy," the woman said.

"Yeah. What'd he say about Scrape? Any of you guys hear about that?"

"He said Scrape had some sort of sex record," one of the men said. "Is that true? You guys oughta know. . . ."

"He's been arrested about a hundred times, but we haven't found anything about sex so far," Lucas said. "It's mostly just, you know, loitering, or sleeping outside, pot, that sort of thing."

"He's one weird-lookin' dude," one of the men said. "And weird-actin'."

"So's John Fell," the woman said.

Del pounced on it: "Why?" he asked her. "Why do you say that?"

"He just makes me . . . nervous," she said. "I don't like to sit around with him. You have the feeling he's always sneaking looks at you. And then, he goes across the street. And that, you know . . . that's kinda freaky."

THERE WAS a little more, but nothing that would nail Fell down. Del said to Lucas, "So let's go talk to the girls again."

On the way out the door, a guy with a waxed mustache and muttonchops held up a finger and said, "Hey, you know about Dr. Fell?"

Del: "What?"

The guy said, "It's a nursery rhyme: 'I do not like thee, Dr. Fell / The reason why I cannot tell / but this I know, and know full well / I do not like thee, Dr. Fell.'"

Lucas said, "Uh, thanks."

The guy shrugged. "I thought you should know about it. It was written about a guy named John Fell."

Dell frowned. "But it was like a . . . nursery rhyme?"

"Yeah. About a professor. Way back, hundreds of years ago. In England. Dr. Fell."

Lucas said, "Huh," and, "How'd you know about it?"

"I'm an English teacher."

"Okay. You ever talk to John Fell? This John Fell?"

The teacher shook his head. "No, I never did."

"All right." He nodded at the guy, and they went out. He asked Del, "What do you think?"

"You say there is no John Fell—that it's a phony name. A guy who sets up a phony name is a criminal. So he picked a name for himself . . . and who'd know about a Dr. Fell?"

"Maybe he likes nursery rhymes . . . or maybe he was a teacher."

"That's what I'm thinking," Del said. They jaywalked across the street to the massage parlor, and he added, "Maybe . . . I don't know. There wasn't much in that nursery rhyme, the way the guy said it. So maybe it's a coincidence."

"Hate coincidences," Lucas said.

"So do I. One interesting thing: that chick who didn't like to sit next to Fell. Women have a feel for freaks. Makes him more interesting."

On the way across the street, Del burped, said, "Excuse me."

"What do you expect? You ate about fifteen of my twenty-one shrimp, and all of yours, and most of two orders of fries."

"I'm still growing," he said.

Lucas said, "I don't want to sound like an asshole, but you know what fries are? They're a stick of starch, which is basically sugar, designed to get grease to your mouth. Those shrimp are mostly breading, which is starch, also designed to get grease to your mouth. And, of course, shrimp are an excellent source of cholesterol."

"You sound like an asshole," Del said.

"Ask me about cigarettes sometime," Lucas said.

"Mmm, Marlboros," Del said.

THERE WERE FOUR WOMEN working at the massage parlor: three waiting for customers, one with a customer. Lucas went back and knocked on the door where the fourth woman was with the customer, and called, "Police—we need to talk. No big hurry, though. Take your time."

Back in the front room, Del said, "Very funny," in a grumpy voice, but then he started a low rolling laugh, almost like a cough, and the three women giggled along with him. One of the women was Dorcas Ryan, whom Lucas had already interviewed; the other one, Lucy Landry, was off.

Ryan said, "I've been thinking about him, ever since we talked to you. I can tell you, I think he works with his hands, because they're rough, and his fingernails need cleaning. Not like he doesn't clean them, but like, they get dirty again every day."

"Never said what he does, though."

"Not that I remember," Ryan said.

"Does he spook you guys?" Del asked. "If you were here alone, and he showed up, would you let him in?"

Ryan said, "Not me." Another one of the girls said, "I've only seen him a couple of times, but he has . . . a cruel lip. You know, his top lip: it's really tight and cruel-looking. I wouldn't let him in."

"But he's never done anything? Anything rough?" Lucas asked.

Ryan shook her head: "He gets his rub and goes on his way."

The fourth woman came out of the back and said, "Okay, that was mean. You scared the poor guy half to death."

"He's gone?" Ryan asked.

"Yeah, I let him out the back." She was a thin woman, with an over-tanned face already going to wrinkles, though she couldn't have been more than twenty-five, and an out-of-style Farrah Fawcett hairdo. She looked at Lucas, then at Del: "So what's up with the cops? You need a little shine?"

"We're looking for John Fell," Lucas said.

"I heard that," she said. "I think he works at Letter Man."

"What's Letterman?" Del asked.

"A silkscreen place, up off I-35 by Stacy. I used to go by there, on my way to school. He came in wearing a Letter Man shirt, and I mentioned I used to live up there, and I like the shirt, and he said he could get as many as I wanted. He never did get me any, though."

"When was this?" Lucas asked.

"A month ago, maybe . . . No wait, longer than that. Maybe . . . May. I remember thinking it was still a little cool for T-shirts. But he's one of those stout guys, who doesn't feel the cold."

"Letterman is one word? Or two words?" Del asked.

"Two," the woman said. "Letter Man. Like a man who has letters. You know, they do advertising T-shirts and hats and shit."

"He ever get rough with you?" Lucas asked.

"No, but I wouldn't have been surprised if he did," she said. "He seemed like he might . . . like to, but was holding back. I think he could be a mean bastard."

THEY USED THE PHONE in the massage parlor to call Letter Man, but it was apparently closed for the evening, and the woman who knew about the place didn't know who ran it.

When the conversation ran down, Del looked at Lucas and said, "So let's go see if Anderson got anything." He gave the women his business card: "Don't mess with this guy. If he comes in, call me. I won't give you away, I'll catch him later, on the street. But call. We're thinking, he could be dangerous."

Outside, Lucas said, "Dangerous," and, "I gotta get some business cards."

"I am getting a bad vibe from the guy," Del said. "I'd just like to see him. Have a few words. I think you might be on to something."

"We ought to go up to Stacy right now," Lucas said. "We could be there in a half-hour, forty minutes. If we knock on enough doors, we'll find the guy who runs the Letter Man place. We'll be talking to him in an hour."

"Anderson—"

"Anderson's stuff will be there when we get back," Lucas said. "Let's go."

"Checking Anderson will take five minutes, and we can have the comm center run down the Stacy cops for us—find out who we can talk to."

"You think they got cops?"

"That's why you check before you go," Del said.

ANDERSON'S FILE SHOWED seventy-two charges to the Visa account over its lifetime, the last a month before, at the massage parlor. They scanned down the list of charges; a dozen or so were local, at what Del said were three different massage parlors. The others were apparently mail-order places scattered around the country.

"A bunch of them in Van Nuys, California, different places . . . you know what? I bet it's pornography," Del said. "I bet he's using the card for sex stuff that he doesn't want attached to his name."

"Because why? He drives around in a van, he's not some big shot," Lucas said.

"I don't know why, maybe he's just embarrassed," Del said. "But if it is porn, it's another thing to throw in the pot. Porn addiction, goes to hookers . . . and you said Scrape denied that the porn you found was his."

Lucas nodded. "Fell doesn't know we're checking on him," Lucas said. "We talk to the post office guys, watch the box when he picks up the next bill."

"Two weeks away," Del said.

"But we know he's up to something crooked."

"Not good enough. I know two hundred people who are up to something crooked, but I can't prove it," Del said.

"All right. But if we know who he is, then we got something to work with," Lucas said.

"Good point. You always want to know the players. Even if you can't prove anything against them." Del looked at his watch. "Let's talk to the commo guys. Get up to Stacy."

STACY DIDN'T HAVE COPS: the city was patrolled by the Chicago County sheriff's office. The comm center got in touch with the night duty officer at the sheriff's department, and between them they arranged to have a patrol officer meet Del and Lucas at County Highway 19, just off the I-35 exit.

They took a city car, and left Del's truck parked: the tranny needed work, he said, and he didn't trust it for the ninety-mile round-trip. The drive north took forty-five minutes, and just before they got there, the comm center radioed to say that the cop they were supposed to meet had to take a call, and he'd be a few minutes late. They turned off the highway and drove around town, looking for the Letter Man office; Stacy was a small place, a few blocks of houses this way and that, mostly new, ten or fifteen years old.

"People getting out of the Cities," Del said.

"Long commute."

"But pretty fast . . ."

They saw a guy walking a dog, stopped, and he told them that the

106

Letter Man was a small storefront back on County 19. They drove back, found it. Dark, nobody around.

"This isn't that much like the movies," Lucas said, as they leaned back against the trunk of the car. "I'm thinking, 'law school.'"

"Man . . ."

The sheriff's deputy showed up five minutes later, introduced himself as Ron Howard, said he had no idea of who ran Letter Man, but knew who would: a local city councilman who knew everybody. They followed him to an older house, with a porch light on, where he knocked; a gray-haired man came to the door, saw Howard, smiled, and said, "Hey, Ron, what's up?"

"Dave . . . these guys are with the Minneapolis PD. They need to talk to whoever runs Letter Man."

"Rob Packard . . . what'd he do?" Small moths were batting around the porch light, and the older man moved his hand inside the door and turned the light off.

Del said, "Nothing, as far as we know. We're looking for somebody who he might know, either as a customer or an employee."

"He's only got three or four employees, far as I know," the man said. "His wife and daughter and a couple of girls."

"Does Packard live around here?"

"Yeah, he lives up north of here. Let me get the phone book."

They got an address and the deputy led the way north, eight blocks, into a circle of the newer, suburban, ranch-style homes. There were lights in the window, and they got out and knocked on the door.

Rob Packard wasn't John Fell: Packard was a short, thin man, maybe fifty, wearing jeans and a University of Minnesota sweatshirt with cut-off sleeves, and he didn't know a John Fell. Neither did his wife, but his daughter, whose name was Kate, said that judging from Fell's description, she might.

"There was a guy who came around three or four times. He bought some shirts, asked me about getting some made," she said.

Her father said, "Katie runs the front counter and does the design."

Kate said, "I think he works around here. He sort of hit on me, but you know—I wasn't interested."

"Why not?" Lucas asked. He was checking her as she spoke: in her mid-twenties, he thought, but slender, and white-blond with small breasts: and he thought of the young Jones girls.

"He just was . . . I don't know. Not my style," she said.

"Creep you out?" Del asked.

"Oh, he never did anything. But, yeah, you know . . ."

Lucas: "Did he tell you jokes?"

"Every time," she said. "Really stupid ones."

Lucas said to Del, "That's him." And to Katie: "A fat man?"

"Yeah, that too . . . sort of like a young Alfred Hitchcock."

Del asked, "Do you have any idea where he works?"

"No, really, I don't. I can tell you that he drives a black van, like a plumber or a contractor . . . but I don't think he's a plumber. Or a contractor. He sorta doesn't talk like one."

"How about a teacher?" Lucas asked.

She thought for a moment, then said, "Maybe. Yeah, maybe."

"What kind of shirts did he want?"

"The first time, he said he was checking prices for a rock band, some stupid name, I forget." She paused, her eyes floating up, then dropping back to Lucas: "No, wait: it was 'Baby Blue.' Or 'Baby Blues.'"

"Never heard of them," Lucas said.

"Neither have I, and I still haven't," she said. "He came in again, about that, about the band, then the next time he came in, he was asking about buying seconds. We've always got some seconds, that we sell cheap. The last time, I don't know. I think he was just looking me over. He took some seconds. They were for Wyman Archery. Says 'Wyman Archery' in a target, with a hunting arrow under the words."

"He's an archer? A bow hunter?"

She shook her head, "No, it was kind of a wicked-looking shirt. He just pulled them out of the seconds basket."

Lucas asked her about the Letter Man shirt he'd been wearing. "We have samples, we sell them at cost—four dollars. I don't remember selling him one, but maybe I did. He did buy some shirts."

She hadn't seen him around town, didn't know whether he was

going east or west when he arrived. "What time did he come in?" Lucas asked. "Same time?"

"Middle of the afternoon," she said. "Yeah. Every time, around two or three. Between two and three. It's our slowest time of day."

Lucas said to Del, "He might be doing factory work, going in to the second shift."

Del asked Kate, "You get any feeling that he was watching you? You know . . ."

She was shaking her head: "I never saw him outside the store. He'd come in, he'd go away. I thought he was interested in talking to me, you know, but . . . he got the idea."

"You never saw a black van around when you were out walking?"

"Now you're scaring me," her father said.

"I don't remember any, especially, but . . . there are vans all over the place. I guess you see them all the time. You don't even look at them."

THERE WASN'T ANYTHING MORE—a bit of a description, but nothing significant. The Packards knew of three or four assembly plants in the area, mostly smaller places putting together electronics, the kinds of places that came and went every few months. And she hadn't seen Fell for at least four or five months, Kate said.

On the way back to the Cities, Lucas said, "I'm coming back up here tomorrow. I'm going to hit every one of those factories. If we get a time card, there'll be eight ways to track him, even if he's not working there anymore."

BUT HE DIDN'T DO THAT.

8

THEY SPENT THE drive back to the Twin Cities speculating about John Fell. Lucas said, "He's at least as good a suspect as Scrape. Look, think

109

about this: Somebody needs a fall guy. Who's better than a guy like Scrape, who can't even defend himself, because he's crazy? And he looks crazier'n hell, who'd believe him? So this guy tracks both Scrape and the girls, steals stuff that Scrape has used, like that box in the pizza dumpster, and then he calls nine-one-one to feed us the clues."

"Sounds too much like a movie," Del said.

"It does," Lucas admitted.

"I've never known one of those movie plots to work out," Del said.

Lucas looked out the window at the rural darkness, just a scattering of lights off to the west. "Neither have I."

DEL HAD A LIST of eight more people he wanted to interview about Smith, with addresses. Though it was late, they found four of them with the lights on, but got no help. After the last one, Lucas followed Del back down the street to the car, and Del asked, "You know what the perfect crime is?"

"You're gonna tell me, right?"

"It's when you walk up to a guy you don't know that well, because you want the crack in his pocket. You look around, there's nobody watching. You pull your gun and *Bam!*, you kill him. You take the crack and you walk away," Del said. "Nobody gives two shits about a crack dealer, so there's not gonna be a big deal investigation. There're gonna be two guys walking around with notebooks, for maybe a week. There's a million potential suspects, and no real connection between the killer and the killee, and an hour after the killing, the evidence has already gone up somebody's pipe."

"But somebody *could* see you—"

"Eh—no. Or they turn away. Smith wouldn't be standing out in the middle of the street, handing it off. That's why dope dealers get killed. Get killed all the time. Because they're vulnerable and they're worth killing. The guys doing it are desperate for a hit, they don't have a hell of a lot to lose, and they don't have two brain cells to rub together. So, they don't worry about it, they don't talk about it, they don't plan it. It's just walk up, look around, pull out the piece, pop him, and go."

"All right—but when was the last time you picked up a dead black crack dealer in the alley behind a bunch of houses where all the people are white?" Lucas asked.

Del held up an index finger. "That's another reason I like your whole spontaneous, semi-accidental murder theory. It's possible that our crack-freak killer doesn't exist. At least, not this one. So we're looking for the wrong dude. He doesn't exist. Maybe your dude does."

"My dude exists—he snatched the girls," Lucas said.

"Unless Scratch did it," Del said.

"Scrape."

"Yeah, Scrape. The point remains: we are wasting our time, right now," Del said. "We aren't gonna hang the Smith murder on a neighborhood guy unless an eyewitness turns up, and even then, we'd probably need to kick a confession out of the guy. Because (a) there's no link to follow, and (b) nobody gives a shit. There's no logic to a crack killing. No puzzle you can figure out. Only hunger."

"You got me convinced," Lucas said. "But you gotta keep your eye on the other ball, too."

"What ball?"

"The political ball," Lucas said. "The ball that requires two white guys to be out roaming around the black community so it looks like somebody cares, when nobody does."

"I don't like that ball," Del said.

AFTER A WHILE, when the lights started going out around the neighborhood, they went home. Lucas thought about the case while waiting for sleep to catch up with him. It was confusing, but in a pleasant way: it was intricate, like a puzzle, like a really magnificent game. You could make a million moves, and prove yourself a complete fool.

He was still sleeping soundly at eight o'clock the next morning when his phone rang. The comm center was calling to say that some woman was trying to get in touch, and she'd said it might be an emergency. Lucas dialed the number she left, not recognizing it, and the blue-haired Karen Frazier picked up.

"All right, Scrape's name is all over the place and the whole street is all freaked out, and I was talking to a guy named Millard and he told

111

me that he saw Scrape last night sneaking along the riverbank across from the falls. On the east side."

"Where are you?" Lucas asked.

"Right there, on Main. I was looking around for him."

"For Christ sakes, don't do that," Lucas said. "Even if he didn't do it, he's still nuts and we took a great big long knife off him. He's probably got another one by now."

"I thought of that. That's why I'm calling you," Frazier said. "You think he did it?"

"I don't know—there's some other stuff going on, but there's some evidence, too. Against him, I mean. So you sit tight: I'm coming over. Give me twenty minutes. I'll meet you at the end of the bridge there."

He'd planned to go back to Stacy, to look for Fell. Instead, he rolled out, brushed his teeth, skipped the shave, was in and out of the shower in one minute, and in two more, was dressed. He thought about calling in, as long as the phone was right there. On the other hand, if he picked up Scrape on his own . . .

He gave the phone a last look, and with only the slightest of misgivings, was on his way.

FRAZIER WAS SITTING on a bench south of the Central Avenue bridge. Lucas pulled in, flipped his "Police" card onto the dash, locked the door, and walked over. She saw him coming and stood up.

"Everybody's scared," she said. "The newspaper had this huge story about letting him go, and how maybe he stabbed some black man. And you guys are hassling everybody. People are running out of town—"

"We're still thinking about the girls," Lucas said. "There's not much chance anymore, but we gotta try."

She looked doubtful: "It seems more like you're doing it for television, than really looking."

"We're really looking," Lucas said. "And I haven't rousted anyone. I've been working the Smith killing."

She turned away and looked off down the river.

"Anyway," Lucas said. "There's a guy named Millard, right? Where is he?"

112

"I don't want you to talk to Millard, because he'll put two and two together, and figure out where you got his name."

Lucas shook his head: "I gotta know. I'll cover you. But I gotta talk to him."

"I can tell you what he said. He said, Scrape was right under the bridge when he saw him, but then he started walking down the bank. Millard said there are a bunch of old cave openings and drains down there, that go up under the bank. He thinks Scrape is in there."

"I need to talk to Millard," Lucas insisted. "I need to bring him down here."

They argued for a minute, but Lucas knew her soft spot—the chance the girls were still alive somewhere—and she finally agreed to ride around with him, looking for Millard, and said she'd point him out.

"I feel like a Judas," she said, as they walked back to the car.

"Yeah, I know," Lucas said. He told her about working undercover on drugs, and the bad feeling he'd gotten from it. "Drugs kill people. Getting the dealers off the street is important. But I didn't want to do it."

And a few minutes later, "Is Millard his first name, or last name?"

"Don't know," she said. "He's just Millard."

"Like Madonna."

She didn't smile.

THEY FOUND MILLARD at a free store a half-mile off the river, a place run by a bunch of old hippies who'd drifted into charitable work. Millard was sitting on a stoop at one end of the store, next to a table full of used shoes. He had a stack of shoes on the steps next to him, and he was trying them on, one pair at a time. A battered backpack sat on the sidewalk next to him.

Lucas dropped Frazier a block away, out of sight, then went around the block, pulled up across the street from the store, hopped out of the car, and walked across the street.

"Hey, Millard," he said.

Millard looked up, and then sideways, as if trying to figure out a place to run. Lucas said, "Don't run. I'd catch you in thirty feet and then I'd have to take you downtown."

"Cop," Millard said. He was a tall man, emaciated, windburned, with a long gray beard, and pale blue eyes under white eyebrows. He wore a thirties-style gray felt fedora, crushed on his skull like an accordion bellows, and a gray cotton shirt under an ancient navy blue wool suit.

Lucas said, "Yeah," and then, "Donny White saw you with Scrape this morning, over by the Hennepin Bridge," he said.

Millard was confused. "I never . . . Who? White?"

"The newspaper guy," Lucas said, inventing as he went along. "Said he saw you with Scrape. The fact is, my man, you're going off to prison, if that's true."

"I didn't . . . I wasn't with Scrape," Millard said.

"You were seen," Lucas said.

"I wasn't with him," Millard said, his voice rising toward a shout. "I wasn't . . ."

One of the old hippies came out of the store, a short, square man with a red beard, and he asked, "Is there a problem?"

"Minneapolis police," Lucas said. "I'm talking to Millard, here. You can go on back inside."

"Could I see some ID?"

"Sure." Lucas pulled his ID, hung it in front of the hippie for a moment, then slipped it back in his pocket.

"Maybe I should call a lawyer."

Lucas shrugged. "Do what you want; but right now, go away. This is an official investigation."

The hippie said, "I'll be back."

Lucas turned back to Millard. "So, I'm probably gonna have to arrest you. At least you'll get three squares a day."

"Look . . . look . . . I might have seen him, but I wasn't with him," Millard said. "I might have seen him down the river from the bridge."

"Where'd he go? If you can show me, I'll cut you loose."

Millard shuffled around in a half-circle, thinking about it, eyes averted, and then said, "I can show you. But no jail."

"Put on your shoes," Lucas said.

★

LUCAS WALKED HIM across the street, put him in the Jeep, threw his pack on the backseat. Millard hadn't washed for a while, and Lucas dropped the windows. "How long you known Scrape?"

"I don't know him," Millard said. "I just know who he is."

"You ever see him with a basketball?"

"Uh-huh. He's had a basketball all year," Millard said. "I don't know where he got it. Pretty good ball, though."

He took Lucas to the riverbank, and then south a couple hundred yards, farther than Lucas expected. "Right down there," Millard said, pointing over the embankment. "There's a cement thing that sticks out of the hill. That's where I seen him."

"I want you to sit right here, on the Jeep," Lucas said. "If you run, I'll catch you, and then you will go to jail. We ain't fooling around here, Millard. You help me out, you'll be okay. You fuck with me, you're going to jail. Okay?"

"Yeah, yeah."

"You sure you got it?"

"Yeah, I'll sit here on the Jeep."

Lucas skidded down the embankment, through brush and broken glass, holding on to weeds to keep his balance. Two-thirds of the way down, he found what looked like the end of an old concrete storm sewer set into the riverbank. A barrier made of steel bars had been bolted to the concrete, but had rusted over the years, and one side of it had been broken free. The drain was dark, but Lucas could see trash from food wrappings inside the mouth of it, as well as the remains of campfires. If it no longer functioned as a drain, it'd be dry and safe, or at least easily defensible, with the iron bars over the entrance.

The floor was covered with a layer of sand, and what appeared to be new footprints were going in and out. He called, "Scrape? Scrape? Come out of there."

He saw nothing in the dark, but a minute after he called, he heard a scuttling sound. Somebody was headed farther back into the tunnel.

"Scrape? I can hear you. Don't make me come get you."

Nothing but dark.

Lucas climbed back to the top of the riverbank, half expecting

Millard to be gone; but he was still sitting on the Jeep, looking worried. Lucas asked, "Where are you staying? And don't lie."

"Mission," he said.

"All right. You hang out here, in case I need to talk to you again. I don't want to have to come find you, okay? If I have to come find you, I'll pick you up and put you in jail, so I can find you when I need you. Okay? You hide or run, you go to jail. You understand?"

"Yeah . . . Was he in there?"

"Somebody is," Lucas said.

"It's him. He goes all over in there."

"How deep is it?"

"Oh, it's way deep," Millard said. "You can go all over the place, in there. It's like a big cave. There's like water in there; you don't want to be in the deep part when it's raining—it fills up."

"All right. You sit tight."

"You got a couple bucks for a coffee?" Millard asked. "I'll just go to the Lunch Box."

Lucas considered cuffing him to the bumper of the Jeep, but the guy might freak and scratch up the truck. So he fished in his pocket, came up with a ten and a twenty, looked at them for a moment, then gave the ten to Millard and put the twenty back in his pocket. "You hang at the Lunch Box. If I need you, you better be there."

LUCAS WALKED BACK down the riverbank, looked in the entrance to the drain, shouted, "Scrape? Don't make me come in there. . . ."

He was trying to push Scrape back into the drain, to let him know that there was still somebody waiting, while he found a phone. That done, he climbed back up the riverbank, saw Millard a block away, headed toward the Lunch Box. He jogged across the street to Jay's Electronic Salvage. A half-dozen people were browsing through racks of electronic circuitry. Lucas went to the back, showed his ID to a clerk, and got the phone.

Daniel was at his desk. Lucas said, "I got a line on that Scrape guy. He's in a sewer."

After a moment of silence, Daniel said, "Sewer?"

"Yeah, he's hiding in a big sewer pipe south of the Central Avenue

Bridge, by that power thing. I guess it goes back into some kind of cave. We're gonna need some lights. A lot of lights."

"A cave? Is it too much fuckin' trouble to find him in a supermarket or something? What's this cave shit?" But Daniel sounded happy.

"I guess there's some water in there, too," Lucas said. "Probably gonna need some boots. And some sewer guys. Guys with sewer maps. You know. That kinda stuff."

He gave Daniel the details, and in the next hour, got six cops and four sewer guys, in boots ranging from green-rubber Wellingtons to buckle-front galoshes. Daniel was there, in a suit, and had no interest in going into the cave. Instead, he went down and looked at the entrance. "I'm more of an administrator," he told Lucas. "You're more of a guy who totes the barge. And goes into dumpsters and sewers and so on."

One of the sewer guys had an extra pair of Wellingtons that were too large for Lucas, but better than nothing. Sloan showed up with a pair of galoshes; the sewer guys had work lights, instruments for detecting lethal gas, and maps.

One of them, named Chip, laid the maps out on the hood of Lucas's Jeep. "This isn't actually a sewer. It used to be part of a drainage system for the old power plant. It's been closed up for years."

"If it's not a sewer, how do you know about it?" somebody asked.

Chip said, "There are some connections between the storm sewers and the tunnels, caused by erosion. We're planning to go in there, when we can get the money, and block everything up. We've had bums work their way a half-mile from the river, and come popping up through a manhole in the middle of a street."

He began tracing the sewer routes out of the city down to the river, with the cops looking over his shoulder. "The power plant part is pretty much in this area," he said, tapping the map with an index finger. "And there are a couple of different levels and some old abandoned machinery. Your guy could be hiding in there—we've found campfires and litter and stuff in there. But there's also a broken-down abutment and a crack in the rock that breaks into the sewer system . . . here." He pressed a thumbnail into the map. "If he's gone through the crack into the sewer system, then he could get quite a way back, and maybe up through a loose manhole somewhere."

"What's the floor of the sewers like?" Lucas asked. "Is there sand, or water, or what?"

"Some water, and there's always some sand. . . . It hasn't been raining, so there'll be quite a bit of sand, a thin layer on the bottom."

"So we'll be able to track him," Sloan said.

"If he's in the sewer, you can do that. He's really got no way out and no way to cover his tracks. Though, in some of the older sewers, there are also erosional features . . . holes and gaps and little caves . . . where he could hide. But there'll be tracks leading up to them."

"What about the smell? Are we gonna be wading in shit?"

"Nah, not so much," Chip said. "The first part is the power plant, and that's just damp. The sewer part is storm sewers, not sanitary sewers, and they're not so bad right now."

They looked at the maps for another couple of minutes, then Daniel said, "Let's get the show on the road. And, the most important thing, nobody gets hurt. Okay? Watch for this guy, we know he carries a knife. Take him down easy, don't get yourself hurt."

Everybody nodded, and Chip said, "Check your lights," and they all checked their lights, and then Daniel said, "Altogether now, what'd I say was the most important thing?"

Somebody said, "Don't get hurt."

9

CHIP LED THE WAY down the bank to the entrance. There were nine of them, sliding down the dirt track, seven cops including Lucas and Sloan, plus Chip and one more sewer guy, everybody with flashlights, Chip and the other sewer guy carrying heavy battery-powered work lights. They spent a moment pulling back the metal grate, then squeezed through the enlarged opening.

Lucas was the third man through, into the dark, damp air, smelling of wet sand, dead fish, old concrete, and an undertone of sewage.

"Been somebody here," one of the leading cops said, shining his light toward the ceiling. There were bench-like shelves at the top of the concrete walls on either side of the entrance. A plastic garbage bag, fat with weight—clothing, apparently—sat on each of the walls. The floor was littered with paper, some old, some new: wrappers from packages of cookies, crackers, candy bars, along with plastic wrappers for fast-food meat, wieners, sausages, adding their own rank, rotten-grease odor to the underground mélange. A few steps inside, the concrete ended, and the walls became cave-like, cut through natural rock.

They edged inside, slowly, climbed a cave-in, found themselves in a wider section with a rusted metal superstructure overhead, its use obscured by the rust and damage. They played their lights over it, and something flapped past them, and they all ducked, and the second sewer guy, whose name was Russ, said, "We got bats."

"Scared the shit out of me," one of the cops said.

Somebody else said, "You fire a gun in here, it's gonna ricochet all over the place."

"So don't be shootin' any guns," somebody else said.

"We oughta be armed with tennis rackets," said a fourth voice.

Chip said, "Bats can have rabies—let them go, don't mess with them."

Sloan, who was a step behind Lucas, said, "This is a good afternoon. I'm chasing a bum through a sewer filled with rabid bats. I can't wait to tell my wife."

"See, this isn't a sewer—" Russ began.

Sloan said, "It was a figure of speech. Let's keep going, or get out of here."

Up ahead, a dark hole.

They left two cops to guard the exit, while the rest moved on until Chip said, "Look."

Lucas looked where he was shining his light. A thin stream of water cut across the floor, coming from who-knows-where, bordered on both sides by a half-inch of fine sand. A single set of tracks were pressed into the damp sand, heading deeper into the dark.

They went past a short shaft going straight up, like an upside-down well. An intersecting shaft went off to the right, perhaps fifteen feet up. "If he had a rope, he could get up there and nobody could get at him," somebody said.

But Chip said, "Yeah, but . . . see?" He pointed to a partial track in the sand, six feet past the intersection, going deeper into the tunnel. "And I've never seen a rope or anything going up there."

They moved on, then somebody spotted a hole in a wall to the left. Lucas climbed a short slope to the hole, pushed his light in: there was a low-ceiling space, a kind of pot full of water. He could hear more running water, but couldn't see anything inside the room except a pile of metal trash and some rotting wooden beams.

He hopped down and said, "Nothing."

They found another hole, and this one carried a human stench. Sloan looked and he said, "Somebody's using it as a can. Hang their ass off the wall, and let go."

"More tracks," somebody called, from up ahead.

SCRAPE WAS FAR AHEAD of them, carrying a cheap aluminum flashlight with a weak bulb: but he knew where he was going. He got in the main room, under the power plant, tiptoed across the wet concrete, careful not to leave footprints, boosted himself up on a damp concrete revetment, then onto a rusting steel beam that sat on top of it. Once on top, he slid down into a narrow space on the other side, and lay on top of the concrete revetment. He barely had room to move his shoulders and hips, but he was practically invisible. They wouldn't find him unless they climbed a ladder that led up toward the power plant, and then shined a light down. . . .

If they did that, he was cooked.

As he lay there, in the dark, listening to the cops coming down the tunnel, he began to feel his muscles clenching up and down his body, in fear and anger. If they caught him, they'd put him in a hospital, and the hospital people would do experiments on him, as they had in the past. Experiments . . .

He'd known when the cops released him that they'd be back. Scrape was crazy—and knew it, and regretted it, and suffered for it, nothing to be done about it—but not stupid. Once they had a taste of him, he believed, they'd be back if they didn't find the little girls with somebody else. He was just too good a target, and in his experience, if cops couldn't solve a bad crime, they began to look for somebody they could hang it on.

An old story on the street. Some people said it was bullshit; others swore it was true, said it had happened to them. Scrape believed it to be true. He'd been arrested too many times for nothing, for simply being there, crazy, on the sidewalk, to have any faith in the honesty or efficiency of cops.

What good did it do to take him down to court? He didn't have any money, putting him in jail didn't cure anything, so why did they do it?

Because, he thought, that's what cops did. They got grades on a paper, somewhere, on how many arrests they got. He was an easy one.

The night before, he'd tricked them, sliding out a side window after dark, creeping like a shadow down the hedge and across the yard, staying in backyards for half a mile, before breaking to the river. He'd thought he'd be safe, for a while, in his tunnels, but somebody had talked. . . .

Now they were coming for him again, and they'd put him in a hospital and they'd strap him to a bed, and they'd do more experiments; he lay behind his beam and closed his eyes and tried to pretend that they weren't there.

That the nightmares weren't there: but this time, they were.

WHILE SCRAPE SETTLED into his hiding place, the cops pushed on, like a National Geographic caving expedition made up of stupid people, splashing through pools of water, stumbling over debris and rotting lumber, swearing, shining their lights around. They turned a couple of corners, explored shafts going left and right. One of them showed what appeared to be an attractive, golden-brown wall. Then the wall twitched, and a cop, looking closer, suddenly back-pedaled and said, "Jesus, those are cockroaches. Millions of them."

"Don't mess with them, don't mess with them . . ." The wall shimmered and they all backed up.

Moving ahead, they found more footprints, which Lucas now

recognized from a series of round treads on the bottom—running shoes—and followed them.

Chip took them down a branch and over a wall, then through a narrow natural crack half filled with dirt. They were squat-walking now, under a four-foot ceiling, which led to a hole in the top of a dry storm sewer. They shined their lights down the hole and found another thin stream of water, and more sand, with no sign of footprints.

"He could have gotten down there, but I can't believe he'd have landed in the water and never made a print," Chip said.

Lucas said, "If he did, he could have gotten out, right?"

"Yeah, he could've walked back into town, got out at a drain, if he could find a loose one. There probably are a couple. Or, he could follow it out to the river, but the exit is barred."

Lucas looked both ways and said, "He can't dribble a basketball. He didn't jump down there and not make tracks. Let's back out."

THEY BACKED OUT of the crack and found that the other cops had pushed on, down a ledge and into a cavernous room that might have been a dungeon in a post-industrial vampire's castle. The ceiling was invisible in the murk, and the place was full of huge rusty pipes, more unidentifiable superstructure, and a couple of shafts, with steel ladders and wrist-thick ropes that disappeared into the gloom. "They go up to the power plant," Chip said. "You can get up there, but the entrance at the top is always blocked off. Didn't used to be, but they had some bums set up housekeeping a few years back."

Somebody called in the dark, "I got some tracks."

They went over and looked, and found the prints they'd been following in. They went even farther back into the room.

Sloan asked Chip, "Is there any way out of here?"

"There are some tunnels, but they're all dead ends, and not far now. There's a pretty good storage cave over there to the left. That's probably where he's hiding. Little nooks and crannies back in there."

Sloan said, "All right, everybody, we think he's still in front of us. Take it slow, keep your lights way out in front of you. No hurry—we take it slow."

They spread out and checked the rest of the big room, eventually moving to a cluster in the back, around a seven-foot-high tunnel, maybe twenty feet long, that showed a black patch to the left, down at the end—a big dark space. Lucas and Sloan led the way in, and as they came up to the cave, found another smaller branch going off to the right. A uniform cop crawled down it, came back a few seconds later: "Nothing. Dead end."

Lucas and Sloan shined their lights into the cave. As Chip said, it was deep, and fairly wide. Squared off, it had been carved into the sandstone by humans, rather than by water. They couldn't see quite to the end of it.

"It smells awful," a cop said.

"Like something's been dead for a while," Lucas said.

"Bat shit," Chip called, from the end of the line. "Lots of bat shit. Guano."

"If he's in there, and he's got a gun, we're done," one of the cops said.

"I don't think he's ever had a gun," Lucas said. He turned: "Hey, Chip, Russ? Could we get those lanterns up here?"

The two sewer guys came up, and the extra light was enough to show them the end of the cave. There was no sign of Scrape, not even footprints. Lucas pointed at a band of sand ten feet in: "He either flew over that, or he's behind us."

Russ the sewer guy said, "There's a small side room down to the left. He could be in there—it's about the only place left."

Lucas nodded, moved ahead with the light. Another cop pulled his gun and said, "If he comes after you with something, just get flat and out of the way."

Lucas went in, saw the side hole, again as a patch of black. He edged up to it: "Scrape? Hey, Scrape? We don't want to hurt you, man. Come out of there. . . ."

Not a sound. He stuck his head around the edge of the hole, shined the light in. Empty. There seemed to be a cavity in the roof. He got on his knees, crawled inside, and shined the light up the hole: just enough space to stand up in, and it was empty, and smelled of water and something else, like clothes left too long in a washer. And the wall moved, and he realized his face was inches from another school of cockroaches, or whatever they were. He quailed, and knelt, and got out.

He said to Sloan: "He's behind us."

At that moment, a cop called, "Hey, Jesus, Jesus," and a swarm of bats flew through them, spiraling out of the cave and into the large outer room. Lucas froze, creeped out, and when they were gone, moved back to the tunnel. They'd left two cops in the outer room, and the two of them shouted warnings at each other as the bats came through.

IN THE MAIN ROOM, Scrape remained hidden until he heard what he'd feared: one of the cops said, "I think I'll climb up there and look around. Maybe he's in one of those crannies behind those pipes."

Another voice: "You'll fall on your ass."

"Shoot, I use to climb up on top of water towers just to look around."

"If you're gonna do it, take the big flash."

"Let me see . . . ladder feels fine."

"Careful, there . . ."

A cop was climbing, and in two minutes, he'd put a light on Scrape. He was behind them, his only chance was to drop down and run for it. Maybe more guys outside, but he'd have to take the chance, Scrape thought. He shivered with fear: have to take the chance. If he just lay there, they'd get him and put him in the hospital and they'd tie him down and do their experiments. . . .

He could hear the cop climbing up the ladder, one step at a time, the other cop shining a light up on the higher rungs. Then he could see the cop, still climbing. When he turned, with the flashlight, Scrape would be right there.

Scrape pushed himself up on his elbows, cocked his knees. When the cop seemed to have turned his head away, he pushed himself to his feet and looked down at the other cops. He was in luck: the other cop had his back to him.

He hooked a hand around a piece of rebar to brace himself, felt the rebar move; and he jumped, holding on to the rebar to keep himself upright, and hit with a thud. He saw the cop turn, and Scrape took off, the rebar still in his hand. He'd pulled it out, he realized, maybe he'd have a use for it, maybe God put it there.

He had a good lead going into the tunnel, and he knew where he was going. . . .

LUCAS WAS THIRD in line again, heading back out. He said to Sloan, "Another ten million cockroaches . . ." Then there was a clatter, metal on metal, and one of the cops in the big room shouted, "Hey, stop, stop," and a second later, "There he is . . . there he is . . . he's coming out, he's coming out. He's coming out. . . ."

Lucas and Sloan ran back to the big room, too late to see what had happened, but saw the two cops they'd left behind, running toward the exit, their guns drawn. They shouted again, "Watch out, he's coming."

Sloan said, "Oh, shit."

And three seconds later, a single shot: *BAM*. The noise was muffled by the branching of the caves, but there was no question of what it was, and the cops all headed toward the exit tunnel, trailed by the sewer guys. They could hear more shouting, and two or three minutes later, back at the exit, they found four cops crouched over a body.

Lucas came up and looked down: Scrape, lying faceup, looking not so much tired, as resigned. His eyes were moving, but glazed, and his heels scraped at the sand, as though trying to push himself out into the light. He had a hand-sized patch of blood on his chest.

"Get a goddamn ambulance," Lucas said. Lucas headed for the entrance, but another cop was there, shouting, "What? What?" and had a gun out.

"He's dead," said a crouching cop, from behind him. Lucas turned, took a step back, and looked again. Scrape was gone, his eyes still open, but deathly still.

Another one, the shooter, said, "Jeez, I never even aimed. He had that iron thing—"

"It's not you, man, you did the right thing," a third cop said. "He was coming right for you."

A two-foot-long piece of rusted rebar lay just down the tunnel from Scrape's body.

Sloan said, "Jesus. Okay. Freeze everything. You guys back off. We need an ambulance down here."

"He's dead, Sloan," one of the cops said.

"I'd rather have a doctor tell me that," Sloan said. "'Cause if he blows

125

a bubble five minutes from now, and the papers ask us why we didn't get a doc on him, I don't want to say because Larry Plant told me so."

Lucas pushed through, squeezed past the bars, saw Daniel at the top of the bank, and shouted, "We need an ambulance. Right now."

Daniel shouted back, "Who's hurt?"

"Scrape. He came out with an iron bar in his hands. He's dead, but Sloan is asking for a doc."

Daniel nodded and hurried off, and Lucas went back into the cave.

A cop was saying, "The only bad thing about it is, we can't ask him where he stashed the girls."

Somebody said in a hushed voice, "Christ, remember that thing down in Florida where that girl was buried alive?"

They all thought about that and looked at the body, and then the cop who did the shooting said, "I saw him coming with the bar and I didn't know if it was a rifle or something and he lifted it up . . ."

"Like a baseball bat," said another cop. "If he'd hit you with that, that'd be you laying there. . . ."

DANIEL CAME DOWN and moved them all out of the cave, except for one guy to keep an eye on the body, although there would be nobody to interfere with it, except the bats. A few minutes later, an ambulance arrived. Two medics were taken down the riverbank, and a minute later were back: Scrape was dead.

The crime-scene specialists showed up next, went down to the cave. Daniel, who'd been talking to the shooter, took Lucas aside. "How'd you find him?"

Lucas told the story about Karen Frazier calling him at home, about his interview with Millard, about hearing somebody moving in the entrance.

"You think this Millard guy is still down at the Lunch Box?"

"Yeah. I had him pretty scared," Lucas said. "If he's not, he'll be easy enough to find. He's staying at the Mission."

Daniel slapped him on the back. "You did good on this, Lucas. I'm gonna talk to the chief. Del tells me you're pretty hot to get out of uniform."

"I am," Lucas said. "To tell you the truth, I'm not sure Scrape took the girls. There are too many questions."

"There are a few," Daniel said. "What I need for you to do is, I need you to give a complete statement, with everything you think. I got some of it from Del, and it worries me. Don't leave anything out."

"If we could just put hands on this Fell dude. That's all I want—just to talk to him."

"What I need to do is find those girls," Daniel said. "I'm not gonna rest right until we do it. We need to turn this cave inside out, we need to search every goddamn cave on these bluffs. . . ."

"He couldn't get them down here without a vehicle," Lucas said. "I keep stumbling over that. Where's his vehicle? He couldn't have just marched them down here."

Daniel said, "Yeah, yeah. I need to get you back to the office. God-damnit, too much to do. Tell you what: you go down and get this Willard guy. Is that right, Willard?"

"Millard," Lucas said.

"Get him, and bring him back here. We're gonna need to squeeze him. Ah, Christ, look at this . . ."

And here came the media: the Channel Three truck. They were quick and close, but the other stations would be right behind them.

Daniel took Lucas by the arm and steered him up the slope. "You get Millard, get him back to my office. Just sit him there. I'll be back as quick as I can. And we're gonna need statements. Lots of statements . . ."

LUCAS FOUND MILLARD sitting outside the Lunch Box. "They never let me sit inside, even when I got money."

"I gotta take you downtown to make a statement," Lucas said. "Let's go."

"You're not gonna put me in jail?"

"No, no—just need a statement. No jail, as long as you keep your shit together."

"What happened to Scrape?" he asked, as Lucas pushed him toward the Jeep. There were eight or ten squad cars around the shooting scene, two TV trucks, thirty or forty spectators.

"Got himself shot," Lucas said. "Went after a cop with an iron bar."

"Don't sound like Scrape. He was afraid of everybody," Millard said.

"Well, that's what happened."

"How bad was he shot? Is he gonna be okay?"

"No, I don't think, uh . . . it's gonna work out that well."

A DOZEN COPS were standing around outside the Homicide office, not knowing what to do, now that a suspect was down. Lucas turned Millard over to another cop, got an empty desk and started typing up a statement. Daniel came back, and he and another cop talked to Millard for ten minutes, then sent him on his way. Lucas gave Daniel his statement, and Daniel read it, came back with a half-dozen questions, and told him to rewrite it.

Lucas was working on the rewrite when he heard one of the cops talking to Daniel about Ronald Rice. He turned and looked at them, and the other detective was flipping through a stack of paper, explaining something, and Lucas said, "Hey."

Daniel looked over and Lucas asked, "What about Ronald Rice?"

"He got stabbed," Daniel said, and he started to turn back to the other cop.

"I know that," Lucas said. "Did he wake up?"

Daniel: "No."

The other guy said, "He croaked."

Lucas: "He died?"

"Lucas, write the statement," Daniel said.

"But I got a guy who told me who stabbed Rice, and who the witnesses were, but I sorta let it go—he wasn't dead," Lucas said. He held his hands out in a "What the hell?" gesture: "I was gonna bring it up," he said.

The other cop said, "What?"

Lucas gave them a quick summary, and Daniel shook his head. "Okay. Give it all to Dick." He turned to the first cop. "Dick, you go talk to this Delia. I mean . . ." He turned back, and sputtered: "Jesus Christ, Davenport, you were gonna *bring it up*?"

BY THE TIME Lucas finished, Daniel had gone off to talk to the chief and the mayor.

Del came in. "I hear you bagged him," he said to Lucas.

"Not me. It was Ted Hughes," Lucas said. "I don't think he meant to, he sort of jerked off a shot."

"I meant, you were the guy who tracked him." Del sat down in a chair across from Lucas's desk.

Lucas said, "You know what? Daniel was telling me about the evidence they got—that box from the pizza place. I kinda don't believe it. I want to find this Fell guy."

"Maybe you can work it some other time," Del suggested.

"I was thinking, tonight . . ."

Del was shaking his head. "Look, Lucas . . . They've got a dead suspect, and they've got all kinds of evidence against him. If there was a little less evidence, or if he was a little less dead, then maybe they'd let you look for Fell. But now that Scrape is dead, they *need* him to be the bad guy."

"The girls—"

"The girls are gone," Del said. "Everybody knows it. That was blood on the blouse . . . man, they can't afford to have Scrape be innocent. That'd open a huge can of worms. They'd have shot an innocent guy, and screwed up the investigation. What I'm telling you is, I guess, it's done."

"Doesn't seem right," Lucas said.

"I'm just sayin'. Not sayin' it's right." Del shook his head. "It happens, and I can smell it coming."

"What do you *think*?" Lucas asked.

"I'd like to find Fell," Del said. "I'd really like to find him. But there's a lot of evidence against Scrape. So, I don't know. I just don't."

Lucas ran his hands through his hair. "I'll tell you what. I'm gonna find the guy. I don't give a shit what anybody says. I'm tracking his ass down."

Del shrugged. "Good. Nice to have a hobby. C'mon. Let's go get a Coke. You gotta tell me about this whole Ronald Rice thing. I just got the story from Roy Patterson. You were gonna bring it up?" Del started laughing. "You broke a murder case in your spare time, and you were *gonna bring it up?*"

Lucas got the feeling that he'd done something unusual.

★

129

THERE WAS a press conference later that day, Lucas standing in the back of the crowd, in which a mournful chief of police said, "We know we got the killer, and there's every sign that the little girls are gone. Have been killed. We haven't found them yet, and will press on with every available man. We *will* find them. . . ."

BUT THEY NEVER DID.

THAT NIGHT, Daniel took Lucas aside and said, "I talked to the chief. You'll be temporarily assigned to Intelligence, but you'll be working with me. Can't promote you yet, we don't have the slot, but you're the next guy up—you'll have it in six months, max, and you'll be working in plainclothes until then. You're gonna be a goddamned fantastic detective, Lucas. You broke this case, and you took the Rice case and stuffed it. Un-fuckin'-believable. I've never seen anybody do it better, and you're a rook."

"I never found my guy," Lucas said, with some bitterness riding on his voice. "I never found Fell."

"You need to evaluate," Daniel said. "Fell is a person of interest, all right? But we have that cardboard box with Scrape's fingerprints on it, and we're looking for the witness who saw Scrape throw the box in the dumpster. We're really looking."

"Yeah . . ."

"Listen: in every case you have, for the rest of your career, there'll be loose ends. Things you can't explain," Daniel said. "This isn't the kind of job where everything ties up in a knot. We're walking in a fog, man. Every once in a while, it clears up enough that you can see something, but then it comes right back down. You'll have to learn to live with that. But I'll tell you what, it's more interesting than any other job you could ever find. More complicated. Sherlock Holmes was a fuckin' piker compared to us, compared to what we do."

Sherlock Holmes, Lucas thought. He was the guy that Randy Whitcomb had been talking about. The cop with the backward hat.

LUCAS TOOK WHAT DANIEL told him, and moved into plainclothes the very next day. In his off-hours, for a while, he looked for Fell. With

Anderson working the computer, he found that Fell never again used the Visa card.

Nor did he go back to Kenny's, or the massage parlor. Lucas wondered, at the time, why he hadn't. Did he know that Lucas was checking for him? Had somebody tipped him?

Lucas kept checking for nearly a year, but he got hot as an investigator, buried in cases that piled up with the crack craze.

After a year, he let it go.

10

LUCAS SHOOK HIMSELF out of his Jones girl reverie—was that the right word?—and called his researcher, and told her to find the girls' parents. He gave her what he had about them, then spent ten minutes reviewing a series of proposed statements from the governor, concerning crime, and generally taking credit for its decline. He initialed them as he read, and dropped them with his secretary.

The researcher came back with names and addresses for the Jones girls' parents, whose names were George and Gloria—he'd forgotten them—and he called Marcy Sherrill at Minneapolis.

He gave her the names and asked, "Are you going to call them, or have somebody else do it?"

"I'll have a chaplain do it," she said. "John Kling. He's got a really nice manner and he was around back when the girls were killed. I already talked to him."

"It's gonna be on TV pretty quick," Lucas said.

"He's standing by—I'll have him call right now. You still pretty bummed?"

"Ah, you know. Another day in the life."

HE COULDN'T GET AWAY from the Jones girls all afternoon. He went to a long meeting, filled with lawyers, about the prospect of taking

DNA samples from every person arrested in Minnesota, for crimes other than routine traffic offenses. Civil libertarians argued that it was a further intrusion into the privacy of the citizenry; those in favor argued that it was no different from taking a mug shot and fingerprints, which were routinely done on arrest.

Lucas's position was supine: that is, whenever he heard people arguing about it, he wanted to lie down and take a nap.

Still mulling over the discovery of the bodies, he told the story during dinner, which started a long, tangled discussion of forensics. In the evening, a banker named Bone stopped over with his wife, and they ate cookies and talked about portfolios and the stock market, and about fishing.

Lucas's wife, Weather, a surgeon, was working the next morning, and went to bed shortly after the Bones left.

Lucas went for a walk around his neighborhood, chatted with a couple of dog walkers, spent some time at the computer when he got back, and finally went to bed and dreamed about the Jones girls.

Weather was sound asleep when he woke up at four o'clock, the dream popping like a bubble, gone forever. He tried to get it back for a moment, then gave up, opened his eyes, and rolled toward Weather. She'd thrown off the sheet and lay with her legs wrapped around a long, soft pillow, which propped up her distended abdomen. She was pregnant again, six months down the road, and the ultrasounds suggested they'd be getting a sister, rather than a brother, for their three-year-old Sam and fifteen-year-old Letty.

A Gabrielle rather than a Gabriel.

Lucas was as excited by the prospect as Weather: the idea of another daughter. Girls are always good. More girls are even better. Lucas already had one natural daughter, whom he saw only once or twice a month, for a few hours at a time, as she was settled in with her mother and a terrific second family; and he loved her to death.

And there was Letty, whom he and Weather had adopted. Letty was a handful, but Lucas loved her as much as he would any natural daughter; and was confident that she loved him back, despite her tendency to terrorize him.

Lucas turned toward Weather, watched her for a moment, her hip high on the pillow, her small body twisted toward the corner of the bed. She hadn't been sleeping well, but she'd had a similar sleepless stretch in her first pregnancy, from about five and a half months, to about seven. Stress, anxiety, whatever . . . he hadn't been able to help much, and he was pleased to see her sleeping so soundly this morning. He worried about her: neither one of them was a kid, with Weather edging into her forties, Lucas looking at fifty.

He closed his eyes, and dozed, and his dream seeped back: he was a young man again, driving around in a squad with Fred Carter. Carter's grumpy disposition, his tendency to avoid conflict . . .

Lucas had seen him a few months before, working as a security guard at the Capitol, no longer youngish, still carrying a gun on his hip. Carter was generally happy with the work, but straining toward retirement, now only a year or so away.

"The thing is," he'd told Lucas, "you can never tell where the terrorists will hit next. What if they decide on a big city, but one out of the limelight? One that no one expects?"

"Like Minneapolis or St. Paul," Lucas had suggested.

"Yeah. And what would they hit? The Capitol." Carter had looked up. "That big fuckin' dome. Man, I can see it: I'm two days from retirement and some fuckin' raghead with a dynamite belt drops the dome on my head."

"Well, at least your wife would collect your retirement," Lucas had said.

Carter waved his index finger like a windshield wiper: "Don't even joke about that, man. Don't even joke about it."

Carter's whole life had been pointed toward retirement; and he had such an enormous gut on him, Lucas thought it unlikely that he'd live for more than a few years into it.

The thought of Carter again brought up the faces of the dead Jones girls, grinning their bony smiles through the yellow plastic at the bottom of the condo excavation. The Jones girls . . .

JUST AFTER DAWN, Lucas rolled out of bed and padded down the hall in his boxer shorts and T-shirt, down the stairs to the front porch. He cracked the front door and peeked outside. There were three newspapers scattered down the walk, the *St. Paul Pioneer Press*, the *Star Tribune*, and the *New York Times*.

The *Times*, the one he didn't want at the moment, was closest; the *Pioneer Press* was six feet farther out, the *Star Tribune* five feet beyond that. He didn't want to go running out in his shorts if, say, a troop of Girl Scouts were passing by. No young girls were in sight, and he pushed the door open, trotted down the sidewalk to the *Star Tribune*, grabbed it, snatched the *Pioneer Press* on the way back, and got to the door two seconds before it closed and latched itself.

Someday, he thought, it'd snap shut with him outside. Probably in the winter. The obvious solution would be to unlock the door, but then he'd forget to lock it, as would everybody else, and the door would be open all the time.

Besides, he got a little thrill from beating the door in his underwear.

The *Star Tribune* had the Jones story on the front page, front and center. The *Pioneer Press* had it on an inside page. They'd missed the story, Lucas decided, probably saw it on the ten o'clock news, and then tried to recover. They hadn't, very well.

Lucas dropped the *Pioneer Press* on the floor by the door and carried the *Star Tribune* into the den, kicked back in his work chair, read through the story. The *Strib* had gotten to the Jones girls' parents—now divorced, the story said, both remarried, George Jones with more children, though his ex-wife was childless. A second tragic story there, Lucas thought, thinking of Weather, pregnant, up in the bed; of the children who would comfort him in his old age.

He finished the story, read through comments by the Minneapolis chief—they'd throw everything they had at the case. Right. Still sleepy, Lucas went back upstairs, and found Weather getting ready to go in to work.

"Where're you working this morning?"

She yawned: "Regions."

"Anything interesting?" he asked.

"It's all interesting . . . but no."

"I'm going back to bed," Lucas said.

*

HE FELL ASLEEP immediately, woke up three hours later, feeling sharp, picked up his cell phone from the bedstand, turned it on, and dialed.

Del came up, and Lucas asked, "You read the paper this morning?"

"Yeah. I was wondering if you'd call."

"I want to get in on this," Lucas said.

"I wouldn't mind, but the politics will be a little crude," Del said. "It's a Minneapolis case."

"They won't do it as well as you and I would," Lucas said.

"That's true," Del said.

"Besides, we wouldn't have to tell them . . . right away."

They thought about that for a minute. An unstated rivalry existed between the Bureau of Criminal Apprehension and the cops in Minneapolis and St. Paul. If you asked a Minneapolis lead-homicide detective, he would say something like, "A guy at the BCA probably handles twenty murders in his career. I see twenty in a year."

The BCA guy would say, "Yeah—gangbangers. You catch the guy sitting on a couch with a beer and a gun. When we go in, we go in late, and they're always the hard ones."

To which each side would say to the other, "Bullshit."

Lucas asked, "You remember John Fell?"

"I remember the name. That's the guy you were looking for," Del said.

"There's a good chance that he's the killer. Even at the time, I thought there was some chance, but now that Terry Scrape is pretty much ruled out, I think we need to find him," Lucas said.

"Long time ago," Del said.

"Yeah."

"We oughta get a cup of coffee, sit and think."

"Give me an hour—I'll see you down at the café."

"Bring your notebook," Del said. "We're gonna need a list."

SO THEY went down to the café on Snelling, sat in a booth with a coffee for Del and Diet Coke for Lucas, and Lucas opened a sketchbook that he used for planning, and they started making their list.

1. Fell was fairly young—in his twenties—in the mid-eighties. "That means he didn't quit with the two girls," Del said. "He might've quit by now—a lot of the psychos poop out in their forties. But he kept going for ten or fifteen years. We need to look at cold cases where young thin blondes vanished."

2. He could have been arrested for a sex crime at some point—most sex criminals were. Lucas couldn't remember everything about the description of the guy, but he was overweight, dark hair, told jokes instead of engaging in regular conversation. "I think he might be missing a finger," Lucas said. "I think I remember that." That combination might be enough to identify him either to investigators, or to serial offenders who had spent a lot of time in jail.

3. At the time the girls disappeared, he may have been fired as a high school teacher. "Since he wasn't very old, he must've been fired fairly recently when I was looking for him," Lucas said. "And if he was fired that quickly, I wouldn't be surprised if there was a sex thing involved . . . or suspected, anyway. So we're looking for a guy with a rap sheet involving sex, who was a local schoolteacher back in the early eighties."

4. Del said, "If we can find old checks that he wrote to cover the John Fell Visa account, we might pick up some DNA—and if he's in the sex database, we'd have him." Lucas shook his head: "I don't think they keep paper checks anymore. We can look."

5. "We gotta check every utility record we can find on that house," Lucas said. "His name should be somewhere." Del nodded, but said, "Minneapolis will be all over that angle." Lucas said, "Wonder if they'll check on next-door neighbors?" Del: "They will if they really pull out all the stops, like they say. But, we oughta check."

"Think Marcy will let us look at the Jones case file?" Del asked.

Lucas said, "I don't know how she could turn us down, if we asked, but she might get pissed."

Del suggested that they might find a pressure point, and Lucas asked, "How about this . . . you know James Hayworth at St. Paul?"

Del nodded.

Lucas said, "He just came back from Quantico. He's really big on the behavioral science stuff. He'll know that guys like Fell don't quit . . . so what if we feed him to the *Star Tribune*? He's all fired up right now, all that new information in his head, he'll tell them a story that'll scare the shit out of everybody."

Del half smiled and shrank back into the booth: "Man, if Marcy found out, she'd shoot you."

Lucas said, "Yeah, but if she doesn't, and we perform just the right amount of suck . . . I'll bet we get invited in. You know, to spread the blame."

"Where do we start?" Del asked.

"I can get Sandy to do the research on missing children," Lucas said. "She'd get it a lot faster than we would. We don't want to bump into any Minneapolis guys any sooner than necessary, so . . . I think maybe we start with the schools."

"When?"

"I'll get Rose Marie to yank you off the task force for a while, and we can start this afternoon. What I'm thinking is, it'll be an employment record, which the bureaucrats hold pretty close, so we might need a subpoena. Maybe we just get a subpoena that applies to all school board employment records in this area . . . we need to know how many school districts there are, and where they're at."

"You find that out, and get the paper," Del said. "I've got some task force stuff I have to clean up. I'll be ready to go tomorrow morning."

AT THE OFFICE, Lucas found Sandy, the researcher, told her his theories about Fell, about what may have been a fight in an alley between Fell and Smith, the crack dealer, and outlined what he needed to know about missing girls; she would start immediately.

Then Lucas started working the schools by telephone—and found there were more than fifty school districts in the metro area, and he'd have to go after them individually. He began with the larger, close-in districts, was told that he would need a subpoena to look at the employment records.

He asked the first record keeper, "Do I need a subpoena to find out if you fired anyone in that period of time? Or could you just tell me 'yes' or 'no'?"

"Sure, I could tell you that," he said. "Let me look at my records, and I'll get back in an hour or so."

So he sat for five hours, breaking for lunch, patiently dialing phone numbers, reciting the same set of facts to all the various record keepers, and by the end of it, he'd learned that twelve of fifty-five districts had fired male schoolteachers during the relevant period.

"I can't give you the name, but I can tell you that this guy's record suggests that there may have been a parental complaint without any follow-through . . . which could mean sex," one man said.

"Straight sex?"

"Uh, can't tell. Didn't occur to me that it might be otherwise, but I can't tell. The thing to do is, get your subpoena, and we'll dig everything out and you can take a look at what we've got."

"See you tomorrow," Lucas said.

Two more of the twelve districts also had fired or released male teachers under unclear circumstances, which the record keepers thought might suggest a sexual basis for the dismissals. "That stuff doesn't get talked about or written down, because there's the possibility of legal action."

The other nine were fired for a variety of behavior, most often drunkenness or drug charges, which were clearly not sexual.

AT THE END of the day, he called Marcy Sherrill at Minneapolis: "You get anything on the Jones girls?"

"We're working it—things are a little slow, so we had some folks we could throw at it," she said.

"Shit hit the fan with the media?"

"Maybe not as much as I expected," she said. "This whole thing happened before the Channel Three reporter was born, and anything that happened before she was born is obviously not important . . . so, yeah, people are calling up, but it's been reasonable."

Lucas said, "So you're saying you got the media under control, and you haven't got jack shit on the Jones case."

"I wouldn't say that. Not yet. The ME thinks there's a chance they might take some DNA off the girls."

"I wouldn't hold my breath," Lucas said.

"Well, if it's there, we could be all over this guy in a couple of days. I mean, any strange DNA that we find on them would almost have to belong to him. They were gone for two days, probably getting raped multiple times, so . . . there should be some DNA somewhere."

"Good luck. Did you get any names off the houses in the neighborhood?"

"A few. We're looking at utilities, of course, but they seem to have all been paid by Mark Towne, the Towne House guy. Apparently they were all rented with utilities paid . . . though not telephone. But, we've got no telephone for that address at that time. So, we're looking. Trying to find old neighbors and so on."

"All right. Well, keep me up on it."

"Don't bullshit me, Lucas," Sherrill said. "I know damn well you're looking at something over there. What is it?"

"Doing some research, is all. I've got a woman looking for other missing children of the same appearance from the same time. We're doing the metro area, then I'll have her do the state, then surrounding states. I don't know if it'll be of any use."

"That's fine," Marcy said. "That's the kind of support we appreciate. If she finds anybody, let me know."

"It's not a matter of finding anybody," Lucas said. "She's already got about twenty possibilities. Probably have fifty by the time she's done. The problem is, figuring out who ran away, who snuck off to the other parent, and who got murdered. It's pretty murky."

"Well, keep pluggin'," she said.

Lucas hung up a minute later and thought, *She's really gonna be pissed when she finds out.*

However dark the killer might have been, Lucas thought, the case lacked the urgency of a crime that happened yesterday: it was interesting in an archaeological way. Solving it would be a feather in Marcy's cap, but she didn't have the visceral drive she would if she'd been chasing a guy who was operating *right now*.

Lucas did—a little, anyway, because he'd been there when the mistake had been made. After talking to Marcy, he leaned back in his office chair and closed his eyes, trying to remember those far-off days. Where had the time gone? Parts of it seemed so close he should be able to go outside and see it; but, on the other hand, it simultaneously seemed like ancient history.

He remembered that during that summer, when the Jones girls disappeared, he'd had a brief and satisfactory relationship with a divorce attorney in her late thirties, and not long ago, he'd heard that she'd retired to Florida.

Retired . . .

SANDY POKED HER HEAD in the office: "Got a minute?"

"Sure." He pointed at his visitor's chair.

"Something interesting," she said. She had sandy hair that was neither really blond nor really brown; so she was well-named, Lucas thought. She was a self-described hippie, who showed up in shapeless, ankle-length paisley dresses and sandals, under which she had a figure that Lucas found interesting. She was pretty, in a bland way, with brown eyes that were touched with amber, behind old-fashioned round hippie glasses. Beneath it all was an intelligence like a cold, sharp knife.

Lucas's agent Virgil Flowers had once dallied with her, Lucas thought, and had gotten cut . . .

She fussed with a yellow legal pad, then said, "I've got one *very* interesting case, so interesting I pulled it out for a special look. A stranger molestation, or attempted kidnapping, 1991 in Anoka County. The girl's name was Kelly Bell, and from the photos we have, she looks like a sister to the Joneses. She was twelve, thin, blond, she got jumped while she was crossing a park on her way home from school. A man wielding a knife. Dark-haired, overweight. He tried to force her into a van, but she started screaming and fought back. He slashed her, cut her hands and forearms, but she ran away from him. She thinks the vehicle was a red cargo van, and you mentioned black cargo van when you briefed me. The colors are different, but if you're right about how the kidnapping happened, and the murder . . . technique's the same, and the description of the guy is perfect for this Fell person."

Lucas said. "They ever ID the guy?"

"No. Which I thought was another interesting aspect. It was like the Jones thing—where nobody saw anything. Same here. He picked out a place where he knew she'd be, and jumped her," Sandy said. "It was too well-planned to be a mistake. The sheriff's deputies got some tire tracks, which they identified as Firestones, replacement tires, and fairly worn. The van was old enough that it needed an alignment—there was some cupping on one of the tires."

"This woman's name was . . . ?"

"Kelly Bell."

"I need to know where Kelly Bell lives, and the cops who did the investigation. I take it we weren't involved?"

"No. Anoka PD," she said. "Vital records shows Kelly Bell got married in oh-five, changed her name to Barker. Husband's name is Todd Barker. They live down in Bloomington."

"You got the address?"

"Of course. And their phone number," Sandy said.

"You ever think about getting your ass certified, and becoming a cop?" Lucas asked. "You'd get paid more, and we'd find a place for you here."

She was shaking her head. "I'm going to law school. When I finish there, maybe the feds."

"Like Clarice Starling . . . *Silence of the Lambs.*"

"That's what I'm thinking," she said, with her shy, hippie smile.

BECAUSE IT WAS LATE in the day, and the pressure was not that intense, Lucas went home for dinner—his daughter Letty was experimenting with vegetarianism, so they ate wheat-based fake-chicken cutlets, which Lucas secretly thought weren't too bad—got the latest news on the pregnancy, and the gossip from the hospital, and then, when the housekeeper was hauling the dishes away to the dishwasher, he slipped into his den and called Kelly Barker.

She picked up on the third ring, and when he explained who he was, and that he'd like to talk to her about the attack in '91, she asked, "Does this have anything to do with those girls they dug up?"

"It might have," Lucas said. "The man I suspect of killing the Jones girls would have been fairly young at that time, and these kinds of predators don't usually give up when they're young. If they don't get caught, they keep doing it, and the attack on you is pretty similar to what I think might have happened to the Jones girls. And the guy sounds the same. We don't know who he is, but we may have a description. So if I could sit and talk for a bit . . ."

"Would we be talking to any TV stations?" Barker asked.

Lucas leaned back, surprised a bit. "Well, I wouldn't. That's not really part of an investigation track."

"I ask because I have an ongoing relationship with Channel Three. They did my biography after the stabbing, and I was on several times, few years ago, when Michael McCannlin got arrested for those child murders."

Lucas remembered McCannlin, who'd killed three children and wounded two adults in a shooting spree that involved property lines and a kids' soccer game.

"I don't . . ." Lucas began, then, "McCannlin didn't have anything to do with your case, did he?"

"No, it's just because of my attack, I've been asked to comment on other ones," she said.

"I'm not looking for television, although Jennifer Carey is an old friend, if you know her," Lucas said.

"Oh my God, I love her," Barker said. "So, sure—come on over. When do you want to do it?"

RIGHT NOW, he'd said. She lived about twenty minutes from Lucas's house in St. Paul, so he checked out with Weather, climbed into his Porsche 911, and headed across the Mississippi to Bloomington.

Another warm night, a night like those when the Jones girls were taken, stars drifting through a hazy ski, humidity so thick you could almost drink the air. Lucas flashed back to the night he'd gone dumpster diving, and had come up with the box of clothing that would kill Scrape; the same kind of night.

He took I-494 west past the airport and the Mall of America, through Bloomington, then south, and more west, into a neighborhood of sixties ranch-style houses, many of them still lived in by the original owners: not so many kids around, few bikes or trikes, a single Big Wheel over by a lamppost, looking discarded.

The Barkers lived in a gray-and-white rambler with a cracked driveway and a narrow two-car garage. A sidewalk curled from the driveway up to the front door.

Lucas got out, rang the bell, and Todd Barker opened the door. "Don't want to be impolite, but have you got some kind of ID?" he asked.

"Sure." Lucas fished out his ID and handed it over. Barker glanced at it, and said, "Okay. Come on in. . . . Uh, I have a pistol here that I'm going to put away. We didn't know for sure who you might be."

"Okay."

A woman was sitting on a couch facing a television, which had been muted. She said, "Todd was a little upset that you were coming over."

Todd said, "Not exactly upset . . ." He put a Smith & Wesson Airweight in a drawer that popped out of the side of a six-foot-tall grandfather clock, and pushed the door shut. "More like careful. We try to stay in Condition One at all times. Cocked and locked . . . Can I ask what you carry?"

"Uh, sure," Lucas said. He pulled back his jacket to show his pistol in its shoulder rig. "Colt Gold Cup."

"Terrific," Todd said, enthusiasm showing in his face. "Cocked and locked, or . . ."

"No, I don't keep a shell in the chamber; I keep the—"

"Israeli draw," he said. "Not quite as quick that way."

"I've never really needed a quick draw," Lucas said. "If I think something is coming, I take the gun out and jack a shell into the chamber."

"Yeah, yup, yup," Todd said. "I got a carry permit, myself, but my employer doesn't allow guns on the premises; a mistake I hope he never lives to regret."

BOTH THE BARKERS appeared to be in their early thirties. The house had a starter-home feel to it, with mass-market furniture and inexpensive carpeting, an unpainted-furniture-style hutch in one corner, full of old dishes. An antique buffet, carefully polished, had pride-of-place in the living room, under a wall-mounted flat-screen television.

Todd Barker dropped onto the couch beside his wife, and gestured at an easy chair for Lucas. Lucas took it, gave them a quick summary of the Jones case, including the recovery of the girls' bodies, and recited the details, as he remembered them, of the descriptions he'd accumulated on the man who'd called himself John Fell.

"Fairly big guy, but chunky to fat," Lucas said. "Dark hair, black or dark brown, and curly. Broad face. If he's the one who took the Joneses, he might also have killed a drug dealer who witnessed the kidnapping. The drug dealer was stabbed several times—many times—and that murder was never solved, either. But, if it's him, he used a knife."

"That sounds like him, and he used a knife on me, that's for sure," Kelly Barker said. She stretched her arms toward Lucas, and traced a finger down thin white scars on her forearms. "He really cut me up. He stuck my hand, too, right through my palm." She held up her left hand so Lucas could see a wedge-shape scar in the palm. "I kept screaming, and trying to run backwards, and he stumbled and that gave me room and I ran. He ran after me for a little way, but then, he was too fat, he couldn't catch me, and he ran back to his van. I ran out of the park and waved at people on the street and this man stopped and took me to the hospital."

"Weird that you got in a car with somebody after that," Todd said. "You know, a strange man."

"He was a really nice guy, actually. His name was Nathan Dunn, he was a salesman, an older guy," she said. "Anyway, he took me right to the hospital. I got blood all over his car. I was afraid I was going to bleed to death."

Hospital officials had called the Anoka police, and the cops had quickly started a search for a red van driven by a dark-haired fat man. "They never found him."

"Do you remember him well enough that if I put you with a police artist, you could put together a picture of him?"

"The Anoka police already did that," she said. "Way back when it happened. Wait just one minute . . ."

She hopped off the couch, went into a side room; Lucas heard a file drawer open, and a minute later she came back, digging through a manila folder. "Here."

She passed Lucas a sheet of paper, with a man's face done with an old-fashioned Identi-Kit. He took it in, blinked: the face fit the description of Fell, though the Identi-Kit made it thinner. That wasn't uncommon with eyewitness photo-sketches—police artists tended to go to averages, and if somebody was fat, they tended to lose weight in the sketches.

"We've got a little better computer tech now," Lucas said, passing the sketch back to her. "If you have any time at all to come up to St. Paul . . ."

She did, and she would.

He dug for more details, and she had a few. Her attacker had parked the van off the park road, backing it into the bushes so it was right up against the walking path. "I saw it really close—it looked like some kind of . . . prisoner thing. There was a screen behind the driver, so you couldn't get at him from the inside," Kelly said. "I remember the screen. And there was more screen on the back windows, hung off bars, so you couldn't break the glass. There were no side windows. That's what I remember . . . the inside of the van. It was like a prison van."

"What'd he say when he tried to grab you?" Lucas asked.

"I don't really remember that. Even right afterwards. I was walking down this sidewalk in the park, and there was this place where bushes closed in—lilacs, I think—and he came out of them and grabbed me and waved the knife at me, and I saw the van and he was pulling at me and I was fighting him, and I broke out of his hand, and started backing up and he was trying to talk to me but he was slashing, too, and then he tried to grab me again and I yanked away and I ran. . . . He came after me a little but I ran faster and faster, and I looked back and I saw him going into the bushes and then I heard the van, and I got off the sidewalk because I was afraid he'd chase me, and I could see the street up ahead and I ran as hard as I could . . . but he never came after me."

"But you were right there: face-to-face."

"Oh, yeah," she said. "He was talking and . . ." She put a hand to her face. ". . . spitting. He got some spit on me, he was so close."

"Do you remember what kind of knife?"

145

She shuddered: "Do I ever. It was this long curved meat knife, like you use for cutting roasts or something. Not like a big heavy butcher knife, but a long curved knife."

"A kitchen knife, not a hunting knife or a jackknife."

"Definitely a kitchen knife. Like one of those Chicago Cutlery things, with the wooden handle."

"Then you ran and the Dunn guy came along. Did he get a look at the attacker?"

"Oh, no—I had to run down this path, through the bushes. Mr. Dunn didn't even see me until the last minute. He almost ran over me. And I went to the hospital," Kelly said. "But I can tell you, when I was fighting the guy, I scratched him, and I had blood and skin under my fingernails, and the police took it away. And there was a hair—I remember the guy at the hospital took it out from under my fingernail and he said, 'Got a black hair.'"

"Ah—that could be important. Thank you," Lucas said.

"Can you still get, you know, DNA from stuff that old?" Todd asked.

"If they've still got it, we can," Lucas said. "The good thing is, people who do this kind of thing usually get caught, sooner or later, and we've got a DNA bank for criminals. So does the FBI. If he's been arrested and convicted, he could be in the bank."

"That is so exceptionally excellent," Kelly said.

They talked for a few more minutes, but she had nothing more that really contributed to the case. Didn't remember anything about a missing finger.

The DNA possibility was interesting. DNA had been used to clear quite a few men improperly convicted of rape or murder, but had been used to nail just as many who thought they'd gotten away with it, only to have a long-ago crime snatch them right off the street.

Barker also convinced Lucas that Fell, whatever his real name, was the killer, and that he'd continued operating after the Jones murders. If the Jones girls' kidnapping was his first killing—and it might or might not have been—and Barker was another attempt, there'd be more.

As he was leaving, Kelly Barker asked, "Listen, do you mind if my agent gets in touch with Channel Three, and they give you a call? I'm pretty sure they'd be interested." She said it earnestly, one showbiz personality to another.

"I can't talk to them on the record, at least at this point," Lucas said. "If you do talk to them, and they want to do some film, be sure you let me know. I mean, this guy might be watching. And there's a woman at the Minneapolis Police Department, Marcy Sherrill, the head of Homicide—you should call her. She might have some ideas for you. Remember—you might be the only living person who could identify him."

"I think we can take care of ourselves," Todd Barker said, with a square-chinned grin. "Look around—there are four guns in this room. I can get to one of them in two seconds, from the threat-alert to trigger."

Lucas nodded: "Hope you have the two seconds."

"Two seconds is nothing," Barker said.

"Average high school kid, on a track, can run a hundred yards in twelve seconds or so," Lucas said. "That's about fifty feet in two seconds . . . from your front door to your backyard."

"You think I should get a shotgun?" Barker asked.

"I think you should get good locks," Lucas said.

LUCAS WALKED BACK down the dark sidewalk to the Porsche, stood there for a minute, looking up at the sky, thinking. Gun nuts made him a little nervous. He always had the feeling that they were looking for something to shoot. They had a kind of tight-jawed routine—"Better to have a gun and not need it, than need one and not have it"—but behind that, he thought, was an urge.

And the idea that they could take care of themselves was an illusion: put an asshole behind a bush, in the night, with a shotgun, and you were gonna get shot.

Lucas had shot a number of people in his life, and found shootings always involved a bureaucratic nightmare and sometimes a few lawsuits; all in all, with a couple of exceptions, he'd prefer not to shoot. For Lucas, shooting wasn't important; what was important was the hunt.

Now he felt a quickening at the heart.

Because he'd gotten a sniff of the quarry, he thought. John Fell was eighty percent the man who'd attacked Barker. The hunt was under way.

11

DEL WAS PLAYING with a new camera when Lucas came in the next morning. "That fuckin' Flowers got me interested," Del said. "I'm taking a photography class at night."

"Weather gave me one," Lucas said. "Kinda interesting. Wish I had more time for it. . . . So did you get free?"

"I'm cool," Del said. "What'd you find out yesterday?"

Lucas told him about talking to Marcy Sherrill, about calling the schools, about Sandy finding Kelly Barker, and his conversation with Kelly and Todd Barker.

"I may be wrong, but I've got the feeling that if we go to a full-court press, we'll track him down pretty quickly," Lucas said. "I'm at least eighty percent that it's Fell who went after Barker, and ninety-five percent that Fell killed the Jones girls. If we get a name, all we need to do is get a DNA sample and run it against the Anoka sample."

"Won't necessarily get him for the Jones killings that way," Del said.

"You told me back the first time I met you, that knowing was pretty important. Once we know . . ."

"Sure—but it's a bigger deal with drug dealers and burglars and people like that," Del said. "People who are committing crimes five times a week. If you know, you'll get them, sooner or later. But if they're committing a crime once a year, and if they quit doing it ten years ago, that's a whole different problem."

"It is," Lucas agreed. "But not an insoluble one."

THEY SAT in Lucas's office for an hour, plotting and making phone calls. The first went out to Anoka County, where, after some runarounds, Lucas talked to a detective named Dave Carson. He gave Carson a quick explanation of the Jones case, and then got the bad news: "There was apparently some tissue collected at the time, but the DNA analysis got screwed up . . . by, uh, you guys," Carson said. "It was right after the lab opened, and there wasn't much tissue, and the test failed. I don't know why."

"Was any tissue saved?" Lucas asked.

"No. It's gone. We've been told since then that if we'd stored it for a few months, or a year or so, until techniques got better, we'd have been okay," Carson said. "As it is . . . we got nothing."

"Who knows about it?"

"Well, a couple of us guys here," Carson said. "And maybe a couple guys at the BCA, if they're still at the lab. I mean, it was twenty years ago, pretty near."

"Okay. Listen, if the question comes up, don't mention this," Lucas said. "We might want to put a little pressure on the suspect—let him think that we've got the DNA."

"Fine by us," Carson said.

"That didn't sound good," Del said, when Lucas got off the phone.

"It wasn't." He explained what Carson had told him. "Goddamnit, if we had the DNA, all we'd have to do is identify the guy, and we'd have him." He turned and looked out his window, where a police van was just pulling up to evidence intake.

Another nice day. Hot, but not too hot.

They sat and thought about it.

"Are you going to talk to Ruffe? See if you can light a fire under Minneapolis?" Del asked after a while. Ruffe Ignace was a moderately trustworthy reporter at the *Star Tribune*. Trustworthy because he had an acute sense of where, how, and by whom his bread got buttered; but only moderately trustworthy because he was intensely ambitious.

Lucas said, "Yeah. If we do it now . . ." He looked at the clock, found Ignace's number on his computer, picked up the phone, and punched in the number.

Ignace came up on his cell: "What?"

"This is Davenport, over at the BCA."

"Tall guy, dark hair, constantly relives his glory days as an amateur hockey player," Ignace said, "while overestimating his abilities on a basketball court."

149

"That's me," Lucas said. "I got something you may be interested in, or maybe not."

"I got nothing today—if you got a cat in a tree, I'm interested," Ignace said. "In fact, I'd encourage you to *put* a cat in a tree."

"What about the Jones case?"

"Day before yesterday's news. Nobody's got anything," Ignace said. "We got one guy, called up Scrape's relatives, and asked them if they were going to sue. They said no, they weren't the suin' kind. Our guy said they didn't remember him very well."

"Won't sue? My God, where do they live?"

"I don't know, but it must be someplace so primitive they haven't even developed trial lawyers."

"Pretty fuckin' primitive," Lucas said.

Ignace said, "Okay, I'm starting to yawn, here. Always happy to talk to a source, of course, but I gotta polish my shoes. . . ."

"This can't come from me," Lucas said. "There's a guy over at St. Paul who just got back from the FBI school at Quantico."

"James Hayworth. 'Call me James.' Yeah, but I'd cut my wrists before I wrote about some guy doing an FBI school," Ignace said.

"The thing is, he got really freaked out by the behavioral science thing. He now sees serial killers in his garbage can," Lucas said. "So: I think if you called him about the Jones case, he'd probably tell you that the killer didn't stop with the Jones girls. That he's probably been killing right along. That there are God-only-knows how many victims, buried in lonely old basements."

"Huh. But it's a Minneapolis case, and he's St. Paul," Ignace said, not uninterested. "You think he'd say something anyway?"

"He'd talk to Rudolph the Red-Nosed Reindeer if Rudolph asked him about sex killers," Lucas said. "I'm thinking you could talk to him, take what he has to say, and then blow it all out of proportion."

"That's true, and a worthy goal in itself," Ignace said. "But an equally interesting question is, what does Davenport get out of it?"

"Just trying to help out an old newspaper friend," Lucas said.

"You too often lie by reflex," Ignace said. "You should consider your lies more carefully."

"Well, hell, I'm dealing with the press," Lucas said. "So, what do you think?"

"If I go with this, will I wind up looking like a fool? Or will it turn out that he actually has killed more people?"

"Off the record?"

"For now," Ignace agreed.

"We think we have at least one more attack," Lucas said. "So we think he kept doing it. And you won't wind up looking like a fool anyway, because if it doesn't pan out, nobody'll remember it: just another piece of paper for the bottom of the birdcage."

"Yeah?"

"Yeah. So what do you think?"

"I think it'll be on the front page tomorrow," Ignace said.

"There you go," said Lucas.

DEL SAID, "If Marcy finds out . . ."

"Ah, Ruffe can keep his mouth shut," Lucas said. "But, I oughta call Marcy and tell her about Barker." He got back on the phone, was told that Marcy Sherrill was in a budget meeting. He left a call-back.

"Want to do schools?" he asked Del.

"No, but what else have we got?"

Armed with a batch of subpoenas set up by Sandy, the researcher, they started with the schools the farthest out, in south Washington County, then drove north to Mounds View schools, then over to Minneapolis.

The first firing, of a forty-four-year-old male teacher named Hosfedder, in south Washington County, was actually a double firing. Hosfedder and a female teacher named Dubois, who had also been fired, had been involved in an extramarital affair, according to an assistant superintendent. The affair had been consummated, at least once, on a table in the chemistry lab on a dim Saturday afternoon in the late fall. Unfortunately for them, the coupling had been witnessed by a group of students who'd been in the school for a music program, and who'd gone quietly down to the lab for reasons not disclosed and presumably not relevant.

"Probably to neck," Del suggested to the assistant superintendent.

"At least," the guy said.

"No kids involved, I mean, no kids approached by Hosfedder," Lucas said.

"Nothing recorded here," the assistant superintendent said, thumbing through the file.

The second case *had* involved teacher-student sexual contact, a teacher named Lewis and a seventeen-year-old girl named Pelletson, but Del said, "Uh, we've got a problem, Houston."

He tapped a line in the personnel file: Lewis was fifty-three at the time of the contact.

Lucas said, "Dirty old man," and, to the school principal, "Thank you for your cooperation."

MARCY CALLED as they were heading to Minneapolis. Lucas told her about Sandy finding the case involving Kelly Barker. "So I ran over there last night and talked to her, and I'll tell you what—I think she was attacked by the same guy."

"By the guy you say set up Scrape."

"That's right," Lucas said.

"Okay. Thanks for the call," Marcy said. "I'll have somebody run down and check." She sounded bored.

"Anything more on who lived in the house?"

"Not at the moment," she said. "We've got a name for somebody who lived next door, but we haven't gotten to her yet. She moved out to Fargo."

"Let me know," Lucas said.

"What's happening with them?" Del asked, when Lucas rang off.

"Ah, they're dead in the water," Lucas said. "Marcy's just not much interested yet."

"She's usually a go-getter."

"She's not a believer—doesn't believe this is going to turn into anything except another pain in the ass. What she really likes is a nice run-and-shoot murder where she can put on a vest and smoke somebody out of a basement."

After a minute, Del said, "Well, that *is* pretty fun."

"Well, yeah."

★

THE THIRD SCHOOL CASE, in Minneapolis, involved teacher-student, male-female contact again, but the teacher was black.

"That doesn't help," Lucas said.

They stopped at a McDonald's for a quick lunch, got back to the office in the middle of the afternoon, just as Todd and Kelly Barker walked out the front door. "You do the Identi-Kit?" Lucas asked.

"Just got done—it's a lot better than it used to be," she said. She handed Lucas a printout of the reconstruction. He looked at it, passed it to Del, and said, "We need to dig up the people who met Fell, way back when, and show them this—I hope somebody's still alive."

"Well, we are," Del said, handing the picture back to Kelly. "Must be some more. Maybe those hookers. They were pretty young. You still got their names?"

"Gotta be in my reports from back then," Lucas said.

"You comfortable asking Minneapolis for that?"

"Man's gotta do . . ." Lucas said. He turned back to the Barkers. "Whatever happened to the TV thing? You talk to your agent?"

"We're waiting to hear back," Kelly said. "I think it's gonna fly, especially with this." She flapped the computer likeness at them. "And especially now because of the Joneses."

"We're not sure of that connection yet," Lucas said.

"All possibilities should be examined," Kelly Barker said.

UP IN LUCAS'S OFFICE, Del asked, "What do you want me to do?"

"Check the Visa stuff under the John Fell name. We need to find out how he paid the account. If it's postal money orders, we're screwed, and I wouldn't be surprised if that's what it is. But if he had a checking account under the same name, then it gets more interesting. More complicated . . ."

"He'd have to have an ID for that," Del said. "Did anyone ever check to see if he went for a driver's license under that name?"

"Yeah, we checked at the time, but he didn't have one," Lucas said. "I suppose we could look again. But take a close look at how he paid those bills. If he had a checking account, we could probably find out quite a bit just by who he was paying."

"What are you going to do?"

"Maybe talk to Marcy again," Lucas said, "And then I'm going home for a nice vegetarian dinner with my wife and kids."

"Kill yourself now."

"No, no, it's fine, a nice tofu steak with quince sauce, maybe, some corn," Lucas said. "Organic applesauce for dessert."

"I'm having some pig," Del said. "I'll call you and tell you about it."

"God bless you," Lucas said, and Del left.

HAD TO DO SOMETHING. Right now.

On the phone to Marcy: "I'd like to come over and look at the file on the Joneses, if that's okay with you," Lucas said.

"What are you looking for?"

"My notes. I wrote a couple of reports; I want to see if I can get some names."

"You're really getting into this," she said.

"It's interesting," Lucas said. "I'm not working on anything hot right now, so I thought I'd hang around this for a while. If it doesn't bother you."

"No, not really. As long as you don't overreach, and keep us up to date. Come on over, the file's on Buster's desk."

Lucas made it over to Minneapolis in twenty minutes, and left his car in a police-only slot outside City Hall. He'd gone in and out of the Minneapolis City Hall probably ten thousand times during his career, and always marveled at how the original architects had managed to contrive a building that was at once ugly, inefficient, cold, sterile, charmless, and purple; and yet they had. Much of it was given over to the police department, and the long hallways of locked doors didn't make the place any more cheerful.

He walked back to Homicide through the empty corridors, peeked into Marcy's office. Nobody home. A lone Homicide guy was reading a *New York Times* at his desk, had looked up to grunt when Lucas came in, and said, "She's gone to talk budget," when Lucas looked into Marcy's office.

"Where's Buster's desk?" Lucas asked.

"The one with the big-ass files sitting on it," the guy said. His name was Roberts or Williams or Richards or Johns or something like that; Lucas knew him, but couldn't put his finger on the name. "Marcy said I should watch to make sure you didn't steal too much."

"Just a few names," Lucas said. A name popped into his head: Clark Richards. "How you been, Clark?"

"I been fine. You need help?"

Lucas looked at the five bankers' boxes sitting on Buster's desk: "If you got the time. I'm actually looking for my own written reports on the Jones kidnapping."

They started going through the boxes, which were pleasantly musty, and halfway through the first one, Lucas found two brown office-mail envelopes, fastened with strings, that said "911 Tapes" on them. He opened them and found two cassette tapes.

"You have a cassette player around?" he asked.

"Yeah. Rodriguez has one in his bottom drawer."

Lucas set the two tapes aside and continued looking. Richards found the reports in his second box, a big wad of cheap typing paper fastened with clasps. "Probably in here," he said, thumbing through it.

Lucas took the paper, sat down, began flipping, and found his own contributions two-thirds of the way to the end. The hookers' names, he found, were Lucy Landry, Dorcas Ryan, and Mary Ann Ang, and he'd taken down their driver's license numbers along with their names.

"Just a child, but I was already so good," he muttered, as he wrote them in a new notebook.

"Got what you needed?" Richards asked.

"Yes, I do," Lucas said. "I wonder if you could get on your computer and look up some names for me, from the DMV. I want to listen to the nine-one-one tapes. . . ."

HE SAT in Marcy's office with the tape recorder and a pair of earphones, made sure he was pushing the right buttons, and listened. Neither tape was longer than thirty seconds:

The first one:

"Nine-one-one. Is this an emergency?"

"Maybe. I think so. I heard about those two girls who are missing,

155

and I don't want to get involved, but there's a transient guy who walks around here dribbling a basketball, and the rumor is, he's got a record for sex crimes."

"Do you know his name?"

"No, I don't talk to him, I only see him. You guys need to pick him up."

"Do you know where he lives?"

"Not exactly. I know he used to live in some boxes down the river bluff off West River Road."

"What's your name, sir?"

"No, no, I don't want to get involved. Find the guy with the basketball."

At that point the conversation ended, and two seconds later a different voice from the first two gave a time and date for the call, and added that it came from a number traced to a phone booth on southeast Fourth Street on the east bank of the Mississippi, a half-mile or so from the place where the girls had been buried.

The second call:

"Nine-one-one. Is this an emergency?"

"Yes. I think so. You're looking for Terry Scrape, that transient who kidnapped the Jones girls. I know who he is, because he dribbles a basketball all the time, and I saw him walking down an alley behind Tom's Pizza last night, and he was carrying a box and he threw the box in a dumpster behind Tom's Pizza. I don't know if it's important, but I thought I should call."

"Thank you. If we could get your name—"

"I don't want to get involved. Okay? Check the box."

Two seconds later, a different voice gave a time and date for the call, and said that it had been traced to a phone booth near the University of Minnesota—not the same place as the first, but close: walking distance.

Lucas listened to the two calls, twice each, and made a few notes. He checked his notebooks, and found that the first call had come in about the time he and some other detectives—Sloan? Hanson or Malone? And Daniel?—had been looking across the street at Scrape's apartment. The 911 call had been irrelevant at that point, not that the caller would know it. The second call had come in that night, while Lucas had been asleep. Sloan had gotten him out of bed to do the dumpster-diving. . . .

RICHARDS CAME and leaned in the door frame as Lucas was taking off the headphones, and Lucas asked, "What'd you get?"

"They all still live here—around here. One's out in Stillwater," Richards said. "I took them right from the ID numbers you have, up to the present. Names, addresses, phone numbers."

"Terrific," Lucas said. "Now, I need something else. I need you to listen to these two tapes. Take you two minutes."

Richards sat down, put the headphones on, listened. When he was done, he frowned and asked, "A little strange—that was the same guy both times, right?"

"I was hoping you'd say that," Lucas said. He looked at his notes. "In both calls, the operator asks if the call is an emergency, and he says, 'Maybe' in the first one, and 'Yes,' in the second, but then, in both of them, he says exactly, 'I think so.' Then at the end of the tape, he refuses to give up his name, with almost the same words: 'I don't want to get involved.'"

Richards said, "I was listening more to his voice. He's got a kind of prissy way of talking, you know what I'm saying?"

"English teacher," Lucas said.

"Yeah, like that."

Lucas put the two tapes back in their envelopes, took out his cell phone, and called Marcy. She picked up and said, "I'm in a meeting."

"I know, but I needed to ask you something. If you don't mind, I'm going to take the two tapes of the nine-one-one calls and have a voice guy look at them," he said.

"Why?"

"Because I think the two tips came from the same guy, which, if you listened to what he's saying on the tapes, is unlikely, unless he's the killer. So, if it's okay with you . . . I'll leave a receipt with Clark."

"Why don't you just sit tight for five minutes?" She crunched on something, a carrot or a stalk of celery. "We're about done here, and I'll be back there."

157

"Really five minutes? Not twenty minutes?"

"Really five minutes."

SHE WAS BACK in ten minutes, crunching on carrot slices from a Ziploc bag. They went in her office, and she listened to the 911 recordings, and said, "Same guy. Okay, take them." She popped the second tape out of the recorder and pushed them across her desk.

"Thank you," Lucas said.

"You're really into this, huh?"

"Yeah. I wish you were, a little bit more."

"I'm interested. I've got Hote working on it full-time, and if we see anything at all, I can pull another guy," she said. "But I've got that Magnussen thing going, and we're tracking Jim Harrison . . . you know."

"So you're busy," Lucas said. "So don't give me any shit about looking at the Jones girls. I'll keep you up to date, and if I can, and if we identify someone, I'll get you there for the kill . . . if I can."

"Try hard," she said, a little skeptically.

He grinned and spread his arms and said, "I always do."

She laughed and asked about Weather, and about Letty, and the conversation rambled back to the good old days. They'd once gone off to the Minnesota countryside where Lucas had gotten in a fistfight with a local sheriff's deputy. "If I hadn't talked our way out of that, you'd probably still be on a road gang somewhere," Marcy said.

"*You* talked our way out of it? What are you talking about, I negotiated," Lucas said.

"Negotiated, my ass," Sherrill said.

"I did negotiate your ass, if I remember correctly," Lucas said. "I was so weak when I got back from that trip I could barely crawl. . . ."

And they were laughing again, talking about taking down the LaChaise gang, and Sherrill said, "It was all pretty good, wasn't it? I gotta tell you, by the way—just between you and me—the Democrats want me to run for the state senate. Rose Marie's old seat, it's coming up empty."

"You gonna do it?" Lucas asked.

"Thinking about it," she said. "I feel like where I am now—I mean,

I kicked this job's ass—I feel like I'm on a launchpad. I'm good on TV, I've got a rep. I could go someplace with politics."

"You'd have to hang around with politicians," Lucas pointed out.

"You say things like that, but you hang around with politicians yourself," Sherrill said.

"So go for it," Lucas said. "You want me to whisper in the governor's ear? He's always had an eye for hot-chick politicians."

"Well, if you find your mouth pressed to his ear, someday, instead of that other area, and can't think of what to say . . . you could mention my name."

Before he left, she patted the envelope with the tapes and asked how long it would take to confirm that the caller was the same man on both.

"Maybe tomorrow, or the day after," Lucas said.

"So call me tomorrow and tell me what you got," she said.

"Yes, dear," Lucas said.

ON THE WAY HOME, he thought, *Good old days*. Not always so good: Marcy had been shot twice over the years, both times seriously. She was lucky she was still alive . . . but so was Lucas, for that matter.

With that thought, he went home and had a vegetarian dinner and talked to his kids and spent some time in the bathroom with Sam, who was having a little trouble with toilet training—"He knows what to do, he's just being stubborn," Weather said. "He needs some encouragement from his father."

Then he sat alone in the den and thought more about the Jones case. They had a number of entries into the case, and any one of them might produce Fell. The most promising, he thought, was the probability that one of the massage-parlor women would identify Fell as Kelly Barker's attacker, through the Identi-Kit picture.

If that didn't work, he'd give the picture to the media; that might well produce an ID, especially if Fell had stayed in the area.

And, he thought, if Barker talked Channel Three into putting her in front of a camera, and if Fell saw it, and believed that she was the only witness against him, and if he were genuinely mad . . . might he not be tempted to get permanently rid of the only witness who could identify him?

Something more to think about.

A trap?

But probably not: too much like TV.

13

THE JONES GIRLS killer sat in his living room staring blankly at the TV, a rerun of a *Seinfeld* show, which he'd seen twenty times, the one about the Soup Nazi. He was dead tired, sat drinking a Budweiser, eating corn chips with cream cheese, trying to blink away the weariness as he waited for the old man to show up.

The killer was a large man, dressed in oversized jeans and a gray T-shirt; rolls of fat folded over his belt, and trembled like Jell-O down his triceps. He had thick black hair, heavy eyebrows, dark eyes, a small, angular nose, and a petulant, turned-down mouth. A mouth that said that nothing had worked for him: nothing. Ever.

His living room was small and cluttered. Off to one side, in a den not much larger than a closet, a half-dozen rack-mounted servers pushed the temperature in the room up into the eighties. He could take eighty-three or eighty-four, but any higher than that, he couldn't sleep. He was right at that level, he thought, and sure enough, the air conditioner kicked on.

And started eating his money.

NOT THAT he could sleep anyway.

He'd never slept more than five or six hours a night, except when he was popping Xanax, and that might get him seven hours for a week or so. He suspected he needed eight or nine hours, long term, to stay alive. He wasn't getting it. He'd get up tired, be tired all day, go to bed tired, and then lie there, staring at the dark.

He suffered from anxiety, and felt that he had a right to. He had high blood pressure, high cholesterol, was grossly overweight, and had a set of vicious, burning hemorrhoids that might someday put him on an operating table.

And now the Jones girls had come back to haunt him.

Then there was the old man.

THE KILLER, back in the day, had been an almost-college-graduate; and then, after college, he'd worked at a half-dozen jobs in electronics. Computers, everybody had said, were the machines of the future, and people with a computer education were assured of success.

The reality, the killer found out, was that a half-dozen courses in electronics would get you the same status and income as a TV repair-man—not even that, after people began to accept the idea that computers were disposable. Then, they simply threw them away, rather than fix them when they broke.

He trudged around the edge of the computer business for ten years, and finally, and almost inevitably, given his deepest interests, he wound up selling porn. He ran a half-dozen porn sites out of his den, collecting barely enough to pay for food, taxes, and the mortgage. Porn suppos-edly was a mainstay of the Internet, an easy way to get rich. Maybe it was, but if so, where was *his* money? Back at the beginning, when the Net was just starting up, he'd worked hard at it, gathering hundreds of thousands of porno shots from around the world, plus thousands of short videos.

Now, he let the servers do the work. He had a computer kid over at the U who kept the site going—turning over the daily offerings so they didn't recur too quickly, and stealing videos and photos from other sites when he could—in return for free access to the porn for himself and his friends, and a hundred dollars a week. The Jones killer did the books, processing the credit card numbers as they trickled in, a few every day, but, it seemed, fewer every day.

He had money worries.

The porn brought in two grand a month, after expenses. Nothing, really.

He made the rest of his money on eBay, reselling almost anything he could turn up that might be of value to somebody, somewhere.

Over the years, he'd developed an eye for money-makers collecting dust in the back of junk stores; knew the back rooms of every junk store between the Ozarks and the Canadian line, from the Mississippi to the Big Horns. His latest score had been a bunch of silk kimonos that turned up in a bundle of rags from Japan. He bought sixty of them for twelve dollars each, sold them for an average of fifty to a hundred, depending on color and condition.

Enough to keep going for another couple of months.

But he needed money for his travel, and he needed to travel. The need was growing. He really would like to go first class, because he'd become large enough that tourist class was starting to hurt, especially on the long flights.

THE KILLER WAS a borderline manic-depressive, currently sliding down the slope into depression. That hadn't been helped when the cops turned over the basement of his old house by the university, and found the bodies of the Jones girls.

He was mostly worried about the neighbors from back then. He'd never been a social butterfly, but still, some might remember him, if the cops could find them. He didn't worry too much about the landlord, who was dead, and had been for years; and he'd always paid the rent in cash, for a ten percent discount, which the landlord had recouped by not paying taxes on the cash.

In his manic phases, the killer had spent twenty years running his porn sites and collecting both junk for resale, and incautious young girls. He'd taken seven of them between the middle eighties and the middle nineties, and once kept one for almost a month before she died. Three, including the Jones girls, had come from Minnesota. The others had come from Iowa, Missouri, and Illinois. The Illinois girl had been an experiment, a bone-thin black girl from East St. Louis, taken to see if black girls were sexually different, like he'd heard. They weren't, and he decided he didn't like black. He cut her throat the same night he took her, and threw her body in a ditch off the Mississippi up in Granite City.

Then, in the middle nineties, he'd discovered the sex tours to Thailand.

You could get whatever you wanted in Thailand, if you had the right contacts. No fuss, no muss, no risk . . . and he liked the little yellow ones.

HEADACHE.

He stood up, went into the bathroom, pulled off six feet of toilet paper, folded it into a pad, and used it to pat sweat off his forehead and the top of his chest. The house smelled, he thought. Pizza and beer and black beans and beer-and-black-bean farts. He'd open the window, but it was just too damn hot.

He went into the second bedroom, where he kept the junk, and retrieved a pair of antique wooden Indian clubs. He'd had them up on eBay for $99, but hadn't gotten any bids; he'd wait for a week or two, and put them back up, under a different name, for $69 OBO.

The clubs, originally used in exercise routines imported from India to Europe, and then from Europe to the U.S. at the end of the nine-teenth century, were nineteen inches long and weighed almost exactly two pounds each—about the weight of a baseball bat, but less than two-thirds the length of a bat.

Shaped vaguely like bowling pins, they were made to swing, and to juggle, and to build flexibility and muscle.

He put them on the carpet under the couch table.

A LIGHT FLASHED across his window, and he went to the front window and peeked out between the drape and the wall. The old man was getting out of his Cadillac. The killer watched as he stood in the driveway for a minute, scratching his ass—the hemorrhoids were another genetic gift passed down through the family—and then plodded up toward the door.

Plodding, yet another gift. They all plodded.

The killer went to the door and pulled it open. The old man came in, sniffed, looked around, then looked at the killer and almost shook his head. "What you up to?" he asked.

"Nothing much," the killer said. "Sit down. You want a beer? I got Budweiser and Budweiser."

"Yeah, I'll take a Budweiser." The old man dropped on the couch, looked at the TV. "What's this shit?"

"Seinfeld," the killer said from the kitchen. He twisted the top off a Budweiser, brought it in, handed the bottle to the old man, who took a hit and said, "Hot outside."

"So what's up?" the killer asked. He sat on a beanbag chair opposite the couch. "You sounded a little cranked up on the phone."

"You remember way back, twenty, twenty-five years ago, there were these two girls kidnapped in Minneapolis? Disappeared? The Jones girls? A tramp got shot, a bum, a couple days later, found his fingerprints on a box full of the kids' clothes."

The killer shook his head. "I don't remember it."

"You oughta read the papers," the old man said. "You were pretty interested in it, at the time. We were talking about it every night."

"Okay, I'm thinking I remember that," the killer said. "The tramp was shot in a cave?"

The old man tipped a bottle toward him. "That's it. The thing is, they found the girls' bodies yesterday. They were putting some condos up, over off University, digging up some old houses, and they found them under the basement. Apparently, whoever did it buried them under the house, and poured concrete back on top of them."

Well, not exactly, but pretty close, the killer thought. "I don't know," he said. "I don't read the papers, much."

The old man looked at him, his eyes a watery, fading blue. "The thing is, the house is right near that place you used to live. I thought . . . you had that problem back when you were teaching school, you know, and if they start doing some research, there could be some questions coming at you."

"Well, Jesus, I didn't have anything to do with that," the killer said, letting the impatience ride up in his voice. "They had fingerprints on the bum, right? It's all settled."

"Not all settled," the old man said. "A couple of the old guys on the force say Marcy Sherrill, she runs Homicide . . . they're saying she doesn't think the bum could've done it. He didn't have a car, so the question is, how'd he get them all the way across town from wherever he picked them up? Anyway, there's a guy named Davenport, works with the BCA. He was on it back then, and I hear he's all over it again.

164

Between, they're gonna push it to the wall. They'll be talking to every swinging dick who lived within a mile of that house."

"Ah, man," the killer said. He stood up, brushed his hand through his long hair, said, "This is just what I needed." He wandered around behind the couch and picked up one of the Indian clubs.

The old man said, "I don't think you have—"

AND THE KILLER HIT him in the temple with the club, a long flat snapping swing that crushed the old man's skull and killed him before his body hit the floor.

The killer took another hit on the bottle of Budweiser, looked at the body folded on the floor. He'd never much liked the old man, not even as a kid. As to this discussion, he'd seen it coming; he'd heard it in the whining tone of the old man's voice, when he'd called earlier in the evening. And once the old man knew for sure, he'd be downtown talking to his pals on the force.

No way that could happen.

THE KILLER SIGHED, went over to the body, and dug the car keys out of the old man's pocket. Took his wallet, his change, grabbed the body by the shirt collar, and dragged it down the stairs. No blood to speak of. Have to find a permanent place to put him . . .

He felt not a single spark of regret. He'd noticed that when he killed the girls—he regretted not having the sex, of course, but the killing, that wasn't a problem. Once they were dead, he rarely thought of them again.

Now he hoisted the old man's body into the freezer, dropped him on top of a dwindling pile of white-wrapped deer burger, and packages of frozen corn. When the old man was inside, he reached beneath him and swept the food packages out from under, folding and refolding the limp body until he'd gotten it as compact as he could. That done, he pushed the packages of venison and corn over the body. Didn't really hide it, but maybe if somebody just glanced inside, they wouldn't see it. Maybe. Have to get rid of it, but no rush. If the cops showed up and looked in his freezer, he was already finished.

And as for the final disposal, he'd had some experience with that.

The killer was tired. Really tired. While he'd waited for the old man to show, he'd worked out his next steps, and those had made him even more tired. Nevertheless, they had to be taken.

He went back up the stairs, picked up the old man's hat, put it on his head, turned off his porch light, and when he was sure there was nobody out in the street, walked out to the Caddy, got inside, and backed it down the drive.

Really tired.

FOUR HOURS LATER, at ten minutes before one in the morning, with the lights of Tower, Minnesota, in the distance, he took a hard left out to Lake Vermilion. The old man had a cabin there, one of a line of small cabins on the south shore of a peninsula. He pulled up the drive next to the cabin, went inside, turned on a light, waited a bit, and turned it off. Realized he was about to fall asleep: set an alarm clock for three o'clock in the morning, and two hours later, was knocked out of a sound sleep.

Getting off the couch was painful, but he did it. Moving as quietly as he could in the dark, he went down to the dock, lifted the kayak that sat on the dock into the sixteen-foot Lund that was tied next to it, then untied the Lund and, using the kayak paddle, began to paddle out into the lake.

The night sky was clear, with twenty million stars twinkling down at him. The lake was flat, and quiet, other than the odd *plonks* and *plunks* you always heard around lakes. He saw one other boat, a long way north, running at some speed from left to right, and then out of sight. Vermilion was a big place, and it was easy to get lost. . . .

He paddled for ten minutes, a few hundred yards offshore, then fired up the four-stroke engine, which was relatively quiet, and motored another half-mile out. Somewhere out here was a reef, he thought, where the old man often went walleye fishing. Didn't matter too much . . .

Black as pitch; only a few lights on shore to guide him. He dropped the old man's hat in the boat, lifted the kayak over the side, and eased into it. When he was settled, he horsed the boat around until it pointed back out into the lake, pushed the tiller more or less to center, and shifted the engine back into forward. The boat puttered off. He watched it for a minute, then turned the kayak back to shore. A half-hour later, he lifted the kayak back onto the dock and walked in the dark back up to the cabin.

He'd been out an hour. Couldn't risk any more sleep. He locked the cabin, went to the garage, opened the side access door, and wheeled the dirt bike out onto the gravel. Closed the door, and started pushing the bike up the drive toward the road.

Heavier work than it looked, and he was sweating heavily by the time he got to the blacktop. Once there, he fired it up, and took off.

It'd be a long trip back to the Cities.

And he was so tired . . . so dead tired.

13

LUCAS GOT UP early the next morning, shaking out of bed as the Jones killer hit the northern suburbs on his bike; neither would ever know about that. But the killer was hurting. To ride a dirt bike from Vermilion to the Twin Cities was absurd, even for a regular rider. The killer wasn't a regular rider, and on top of that, he was fat. He felt at times like the bike's seat was about three feet up his butt.

When he finally got back to his house, he pushed the bike into the garage at the back and staggered inside, left his clothes in a heap and lurched into a shower. He had saddle sores, he thought; he couldn't see them, but he could feel them, flat burns on the inside of his legs. As to the hemorrhoids . . .

LUCAS, ON THE OTHER HAND, was completely comfortable, and perhaps even self-satisfied, especially after he went out to recover the *Star Tribune*. As Ignace had suggested, his story was on the front page: "Cop Says Jones Killer Probably Murdered More Girls." Excellent. Marcy would have a spontaneous hysterectomy when she read that, and the Minneapolis cops might actually start working the case.

He left the house an hour later with three names and addresses written in his notebook—the three former massage-parlor women, Lucy Landry, Dorcas Ryan, and Mary Ann Ang, whose last name was now Morgan. He'd interviewed the first two on his own, back in the eighties, and the third one with Del. He hadn't remembered any of their names or what they looked like, but recognized Dorcas Ryan when she opened the screen door of her St. Paul Park home and he introduced himself. She said, "Man, it's been a while."

"Yes, it has," Lucas said.

Ryan's house was a little run-down, and not the neatest of places, but no less tidy than his would have been if he'd been living alone, Lucas thought. Like most people, he carried certain models in his head for old acquaintances. He'd often seen hookers go from fresh-faced high school girls to broken-down, sorry-looking creatures of twenty-two or twenty-three, with coke or meth habits, who seemed destined to slide into a grave before they were thirty.

Ryan, on the other hand, looked pretty much like a schoolteacher or bookkeeper in her late forties or early fifties, one who took care of herself. She was dressed in jeans, a neat collar blouse, and loafers. She invited him inside, offered him a Coke. He declined, sat in her one easy chair while she took the couch.

"You remember why I came to talk to you back then?" he asked.

"Oh, yes. The Jones kids. I was amazed when they were dug up—I guess you were, too."

"I was," Lucas said. "You remember the guy I was looking for? John Fell."

"Sure. We were talking about him for weeks. He never came back."

Lucas took a bundle of papers out of the briefcase he'd brought with him, and handed them to her. "I want you to look at a bunch of faces, and see if Fell is one of them."

"All right . . . Huh. Not real photographs . . ." She began shuffling through the Identi-Kit pictures, taking them one at a time, slowly. "They're all pretty much alike . . ."

Lucas had chosen a dozen faces, all with dark hair and round, heavy faces. She went through them, pulled a couple, compared them, and handed one to Lucas. "There's something about this face. It's got something. I think it might be him."

She'd chosen the face that Barker had put together, and Lucas felt the hunter's pleasure uncoil in his stomach. Most cases had a moment or two when a fact or an idea snapped into focus, when you knew you'd just taken a large step, and this was one of those times.

He nodded at her: "Thank you," he said.

"Are you looking up the rest of the girls?"

"Lucy Landry and Mary Ann Ang," Lucas said. "Those were the ones I could find, along with you."

"Lucy's had a hard time," Ryan said. "First she got Jesus, probably fifteen years ago, and that didn't work out, so she tried Scientology, and that didn't help, but it cost a lot of money, so she tried Buddhism and yoga, and those didn't work, so she started drinking. I think that helped, because she's still drinking."

"Sorry to hear that," Lucas said. "What about Mary Ann Ang?"

She shook her head. "Haven't thought about her in years. I can barely remember her face. I do remember that she married a rich guy—like maybe a doctor. Had some kids. I'm not sure that anybody knows that she ever worked with us. She was only there a couple of months."

"Think it would mess her up if I interviewed her?"

Ryan tipped her head: "That was not a good time, back then, you know . . . for any of us. We're lucky we lived through it. If she's doing good, jeez, it'd be an awful shame to mess her up."

LUCY LANDRY LIVED in an apartment on the edge of St. Paul's Lowertown, one of those districts of old brick warehouses that the planners thought they could make artsy. He called her from the street, got lucky. She was home and buzzed him into the lobby. She was on the eighth floor, and he went up in an old freight elevator that groaned and stank of onions and took its own sweet time.

Landry came to the door in a dressing gown, looked at him through half-drunk morning eyes, and said, "Yep, it's you. You look tougher than you used to."

"You okay?" Lucas asked.

"Yeah, I'm fine," she said, pulling the gown tight around herself. "Come on in. I work late, I should be sleeping for another couple of hours."

She had one bedroom, a small living room with a kitchen to one side, a round wooden table to eat at, a corduroy-covered couch to sit on, and a TV peering across the couch. Lucas sat on one end of the couch and took out his pictures.

She went through them, pulled out the same picture that Ryan had. "That's the closest," she said.

"Just close, or do you think that's him?"

"If I were putting a face on him, with this computer or whatever it is, that's what I'd draw. There's something not quite right around the mouth, but it's pretty good." She stood up, absently scratched her crotch while looking around the living room, then tottered off to the kitchen area and came back with a pencil and a book. She put the paper on the book and then used the pencil to touch up the mouth. After one try and an erasure, she said, "There. That's better."

She handed it back to Lucas: she'd made only a small change, but one of significance—she'd changed the line of his lips, from squared-off, to a descending curve. She asked, "Do you think he killed the Jones girls?"

Lucas said, "I think maybe he did. I think this time I'm going to get a chance to ask him."

"I saw on a Channel Three promo that some woman was attacked by him and got away. She's on at noon."

Kelly Barker had gotten her wish, Lucas thought. "She's the one who gave us this picture," he said.

"So he was still trying to snatch girls like years later," Landry said. "You think he got some that nobody knows about?"

Lucas stood up, stuffed the pictures of Fell back in his briefcase. "I hate to think about that," he said.

He took the stairs down instead of the elevator and was slowed by two men, artists, he supposed, carrying a four-by-eight sheet of plywood down the stairs. When they turned it around the corner, he saw that it was painted with a picture of a dancing man, like Lucas had seen on tarot cards.

Back at his car, he decided not to go after Mary Ann Ang/Morgan.

He might have screwed up a few lives through simple inexperience, way back when, but he didn't need to screw up another, by showing up on her doorstep with questions about a massage parlor.

He would locate and identify Fell—he probably had enough now, he thought—and doubted that Ang/Morgan would be able to speed that up much. Now, it was all research.

WHILE LUCAS WAS TALKING to Landry, the killer was lying facedown on his couch. Just as he had gotten out of the shower, he'd suffered a series of muscle spasms in his back and legs, and he was afraid the ride might have done something to his spine. He found a bottle of oxycodone, left over from an oral surgery, popped three of them.

After an hour on the couch, he felt good enough to eat. He turned on the TV and headed into the kitchen. He was putting together three fried-egg-and-onion sandwiches on Wonder bread when he heard a promo for a woman who might be able to identify the killer of the Jones girls.

He went into the living room to watch, eating the sandwiches, swilling Diet Pepsi. He had to wait ten minutes, through the last part of a gardening show, before the noon news came up. Kelly Barker was the first story.

He remembered the bitch with perfect clarity. He'd cut her up, but she got away—one of only two women to get away from him. The other had been in Kansas, under similar circumstances. But he'd made his move too soon then, and never got close enough to touch.

With Barker, he'd gotten close enough, but she'd fought him and then she'd gotten a couple of steps on him, and she'd run like the wind. He'd made the executive decision to get the fuck out of there.

Now she was on TV—and she had a picture that looked something like him.

He unconsciously licked egg and grease off his fingers, shook his head, and when she'd finished, went off to lie down and think about it.

LUCAS GOT BACK to his office at five minutes to twelve. He turned on the TV, to Channel Three, for the *Midday Report*. Del wandered in as he was waiting for the show to come on: "I talked to a security guy at

Wells Fargo," he said. "They have a file of three cards they issued at different times, and they think they might all be linked to the same guy. John Fell was the first one. The others were a Ronald James Hubbard and a Tom Piper."

"Nursery rhyme names," Lucas said. "Mother Hubbard and Tom the piper's son."

"Yeah, the Wells Fargo guy picked that up, too. He wasn't working with them, then, Norwest Bank issued the cards before it took over Wells Fargo, but the old Norwest file had all three guys already pulled out. No idea who he was, but he did the same thing with all three of them: had an address to start it, had it linked to a checking account he'd opened a couple of years earlier, changed the address to a post office box, emptied out the account, and skipped on the last credit-card bill. The first two final bills were small change, but the last one, he skipped on four thousand dollars. He worked it as a con, that last time."

"Checks?" Lucas asked.

Del shook his head: "It's all electronic. We can get facsimiles, but not the originals. They've all been recycled."

"But we know what he was paying for . . ."

"Yeah, we got that. But it's all pretty obscure. Small amounts, scattered all over the place. Maybe porn, like we were thinking. Could be books or records. That kind of money. Except that last one, toward the end, he bought a lot of stereo and TV stuff—stuff he could sell, I think."

"But why would he hide books or money on a fake account?"

"That's why I'm thinking porn, or something like it. Sex toys or something. I can't find any of the account names at their address, so they were small-time, whatever they were. I'll keep looking."

The news came up on Channel Three, and Lucas used his remote to push the volume. After a story about a woman who cleaned out the accounts of a local charity to support her Vegas habit, Barker came up, sitting on a couch, talking to Jennifer Carey, the woman with whom Lucas shared a daughter.

"She's on some kind of anti-aging sauce," Del said. "She looks terrific."

"Got the cheekbones," Lucas agreed.

Barker said, ". . . came as a complete surprise. I agreed to cooperate, of course, so I went to the BCA office in St. Paul, and talked to an imaging expert named John Retrief, who helped me put together the image of the man who attacked me."

The image of Fell flashed up full-screen, stuck for a moment, then pulled back, and down, to reveal the two women again.

"And this man they're looking for, this John Fell—he matches that image?" Carey asked.

"He matches exactly, according to Agent Davenport," Barker said, with a solemn turn of her lips and eyes.

"Jesus, I didn't say that," Lucas said.

Del said, "You did now."

She continued, "And if you read the *Star Tribune* this morning, there's a story on the case, where a serial-murder expert says he almost certainly killed more girls." The camera shot changed to catch her square in the face: "I'm probably the only survivor. . . ." She began to shake, and tears appeared on her cheeks, and she said, "And I'm permanently scarred . . ." and held up her hands.

"She can do it," Del said. "She's only about an inch away from Oprah."

"She might get Oprah, if we find Fell and pin the Jones murders on him," Lucas said.

"Hope her alligator mouth don't get her hummingbird ass in trouble," Del said. "If Fell sees her . . ."

"I thought about that," Lucas said. "I didn't do anything about it."

Jennifer Carey said, "If any of our viewers have any idea who this John Fell might possibly be, his real name, or his current name, notify the Minneapolis Police Department or BCA agent Lucas Davenport immediately, at the numbers on your screen. Do not attempt to apprehend . . ."

After the Channel Three broadcast, the other four stations jumped on the Identi-Kit picture, and Barker did tape for both KSTP and KARE for the evening news, variations on Channel Three; KARE also ran tape of James Hayworth, the St. Paul cop interviewed by the *Star Tribune*. Hayworth repeated his contention that there were almost certainly more dead girls.

During the afternoon, Del found four successor companies to the ones who took charges from Fell. "We were right—they were porn and sex toys," he told Lucas. "None of them have records from back then. Just too long ago."

During the afternoon, too, seven calls came in for Lucas, based on the Channel Three broadcast, with tips on people who resembled John Fell. Minneapolis got twelve more.

Lucas worked biographies on all of them during the afternoon, pulling criminal records, driver's licenses, credit reports, personal histories. Four had minor criminal records, none for sex. Judging from driver's license photos and data, two of the seven didn't have dark hair, and four, including one of the brown-haired candidates, were too young. He was left with two possibilities, and he didn't have much faith in either.

He talked to Marcy Sherrill, who said of the twelve tips they got, three were still considered possibilities. "We'll have more calls coming in overnight," she said. "I figure the chances we'll get him are like four to one, against."

"That's about right," Lucas said. "But if he's still around, we're gonna scare the shit out of him. That might get us somewhere."

He took another tip, shifted up by the BCA operator. A man who said, "I don't want to say my name, but the guy you want is named Robert Sherman. He's a sex freak and he's the spitting image of the guy on TV, and he's the right age—early fifties."

Lucas checked the number: the guy was calling from a bar.

The guy said, "He lives on Iowa Avenue. In St. Paul."

And was gone.

Lucas looked at his watch: he could hit Iowa on the way home, check the guy out. Or maybe after dinner . . .

He did a quick dip into the driver's license records, decided the guy did look like Fell, but Fell with a mustache. He got an address and date of birth, went out to NCIC to check criminal records, found nothing.

No record, but he was a sex freak?

Called Del on his cell. "What're you doing?"

"I'm on my way home for dinner. What's up?"

"You got time after dinner to make a quick stop up in north St. Paul?"

"Sure, as long as I don't get shot. What're you doing?"

"Going home," Lucas said. "But I got a guy I want to look at. Pick you up at your place, at seven?"

"See you then."

HE WAS HOME by six; watched the KARE broadcast with Letty and Weather.

"All in all," Lucas told them, "a fairly satisfactory day. We've got the guy's nuts in a vise."

"Lucas, watch the language," Weather said.

The housekeeper stuck her head in from the kitchen: "Everybody come on. Food's getting cold."

"Okay, testicles," Lucas said, as they all headed for the dining room.

"What do you think about the whole concept of nuts-in-a-vise?" Letty asked.

"Letty . . ." Weather began.

Letty said to her mother, "Something I'm curious about. You see these movies where a guy gets racked in the nuts, and they fall down. But I once shot a guy and he didn't fall down. In fact, he walked away. So what I want to know is, is racking a guy in the nuts really that powerful? Or is that a myth? I mean, what if I'm attacked someday? Should I kick the guy in the nuts, or what?"

Weather said, "Speaking as a medical doctor . . ."

Lucas waved her down and focused on his daughter. "Here's the thing. If you give a guy a really good shot in the nuts—like, if he doesn't see you coming, and you kick him from behind, right in the crotch, you're gonna hurt him. He's gonna hurt bad.

"But—and this is what you need to know: First, guys whack themselves in the nuts every once in a while, by accident, from the time they're young. We develop really good reflexes for protecting ourselves. You try to kick a guy in the nuts from the front, all he has to do is flinch, and you wind up kicking him in the leg, instead. And, you piss him off.

"Second, when you hit a guy in the nuts, from the front, even if you give him a solid shot, it takes a couple of seconds for the full reaction. You don't drop him like a sack of . . . rocks. And what you've done, by kicking him, is you've gotten close enough that he can get his hands on you. And no matter how bad his nuts hurt, he can hang on to you. And he can kill you. With all the pain, he is seriously pissed, and he just might do that.

"Thing to remember: the average guy is a lot bigger and stronger than the average woman. Best way to protect yourself is to scream and run. If he gets you and pulls you in, go with it. Go in, and go for his nose—try to bite it. Hard—like you were trying to bite through an overdone steak. He'll let go of you, to try to push you off. When your hand comes free, go for his eyes with your nails. A kick in the nuts, it's too hard to score, and even if you do, there's a good chance he'll still take you down."

"What if you don't want to really hurt him, you just want him to quit what he's doing?" Letty asked.

"If a guy's a serious threat, you hurt him," Lucas said. "If he's not a serious threat—if he's just messing you around—don't hurt him. Don't rip his nose off or his eyes out, don't kick him in the nuts. But if he's serious, tough shit. Take him any way you can. Okay? Is that what you wanted to know?"

"That about covers it," Letty said.

"I hope the new one didn't hear that," Weather said, patting her baby bump.

WHILE LUCAS AND LETTY were reviewing testicular vulnerabilities, the killer was cruising Barker's home in Bloomington. He'd looked her up on Facebook, had taken her husband's name from that, and then looked them up in the phone book.

And there they were.

He had the old man's Glock with him. Didn't need to be a genius to use it. He'd fired it any number of times up at the cabin, back in the woods. Thirteen rounds. Enough to start a war.

Just point and shoot.

He was a little scared, but not too. Quiet neighborhood, close to a freeway where he could quickly get lost.

If he decided to do it.

14

LETTY WAS GOING to a snobby friend's pre-junior-year party. Letty wasn't a snob, but something about the whole insider-clique idea appealed to her sense of investigation. She'd dressed carefully, and carefully suggested that it might be good if she were to arrive at the party in a Porsche. With the top down.

Letty had Lucas whipped, so Weather took her in the Porsche, with the top down. And so Lucas was driving the Lexus SUV when he pulled over to pick up Del. Del was standing at the curb outside his house, talking to a guy in a St. Paul Saints hat who had a wiener dog on a leash. Del said goodbye to the guy, climbed in the car, and said, "Maybe I oughta get a wiener dog."

"You got a toddler, why would you need a dog?" Lucas asked. "Teach the kid to retrieve."

"Wiener dogs don't retrieve. They were bred to go down into badger dens and fight the badgers."

"Hey, that'd be right up your kid's alley, from what I've seen."

Del refused to rise to the bait: "No, really, I think a kid ought to grow up with a pet. It's another way to get socialized."

"When the hell did everybody start worrying about socialization?" Lucas asked. "Look at you. You're not socialized, and you've done okay. Well, I mean, you're not in jail, anyway."

"I'm trying to make a serious point," Del said.

So they talked about it on the way to Robert Sherman's house on Iowa Avenue. Lucas knew where he was going, he thought, and, despite St. Paul's insane method of assigning street addresses, didn't bother to punch the address into the truck's navigation system. When they ran out of street before they got to the number, they wound up driving around, running into more dead-end streets, muttering to each other, until finally Lucas pulled over and laboriously punched the address into the navigation system.

Iowa Avenue, it turned out, existed in several pieces. The piece that they'd been looking for was a nice-enough neighborhood of older clapboard houses, with a touch of brick here and there, garages added later, full-grown maple and ash trees along the streets, and mailboxes out at the curb.

Sherman's house sat ten feet or so above the street, with a newer concrete driveway leading to a four-car garage in what had once been the backyard. There were lights in the window. Lucas and Del got out of the car, and Del hitched up his pants, which gave him a chance to touch his pistol, making sure it was in exactly the right spot.

Lucas said, "Somebody's playing a piano," and they both turned and looked for the source. The sound was coming from a house across the street, Lucas decided, where somebody was playing a familiar tinkly movie theme that he couldn't quite name. Something old.

"And somebody's cooking pork chops," Del said.

Lucas said, "That's it—we're cooking out next weekend. Brats and sweet corn. If nobody wants to eat with me, I'll eat it all myself."

"Attaboy," Del said.

They went on up Sherman's driveway, the music notes falling about them like raindrops.

SHERMAN CAME to the screen door, a heavyset man wearing sweatpants and a St. Thomas T-shirt, and as soon as Lucas saw him coming, he thought, *Wrong guy*. He *looked* like the Identi-Kit picture of Fell, but he also had a cheerful, hang-out face, and that was not Lucas's idea of John Fell. He had a can of beer in one hand.

Sherman, behind the screen, said, "You don't look like Jehovah's Witnesses."

Del said, "No, we're with the state Bureau of Criminal Apprehension," and held out his ID. "We'd like to have a word with you, if we could."

Sherman peered at Del's ID, then opened the screen and stepped out on the porch. "What's up?"

"We got a call from a source who said you might be able to help us with our investigation of the murder of the two Jones girls—"

"Ah, man, you think I look like that guy, don't you?" Sherman said.

"My wife said that. She saw the picture on TV and said, 'You look like that guy.'"

He had a wife; Lucas didn't think John Fell would be married. "Our source said that you may have had some problems with sexual issues," Lucas said.

Sherman started getting hot: "Sexual issues? What does that mean? You mean, somebody said I was a pervert? Is that what?"

"Well, somebody suggested—" Lucas began.

Del said, "Take it easy—"

Sherman said, his voice rising, "That's bullshit. I never . . . I've never been arrested, I mean, I got some speeding tickets back a few years ago, but I never . . ." And then he swiveled his head to the left, looking over Del's head, and shouted, "You motherfucker."

Lucas looked that way and saw another man, looking out from the open door of his garage. On his face was an expression compounded of rage and glee, and he shouted back, "Now you're gonna get it, dick-head. Now you're gonna get it."

Del said, "Ah, man . . ."

Sherman took three quick running steps down the porch and Lucas tried to grab his arm, but Sherman was heavy and moving fast, and Lucas fumbled it, and Sherman was loose and heading across the lawn. The other man, who was much smaller but just as angry, came out to meet him, and when they were ten feet apart Sherman threw his beer can at the other man's head, and a half-second later they were wrapped up on the ground, ineffectively punching at each other, and tearing at each other's hair.

As Lucas and Del ran across the lawn to separate them, a woman came out behind them and shouted, "No, no, Bob, don't . . ."

And then a thin woman with fly-away hair popped out of the neighboring garage and shouted, "You shut up, you whore," and she started for the property line.

The neighbor was shorter and lighter than Sherman, so Lucas grabbed him by the collar and yanked him away from Sherman and threw him at Del, who grabbed one of the neighbor's flailing arms and levered him onto the grass, facedown, his arm locked straight up behind him.

Sherman was trying to get up, and Lucas shouted, "Stay down, stay down," and then the women started, circling each other like a couple of Mexican fighting cocks, yelling at each other. Lucas pushed Sherman down and got between the two women, who were getting the nails out. He shouted, "Everybody shut up, or you're all going to jail. Everybody shut up."

The neighbor, still pinned, was shouting, "You're killing me, you're killing me," and Sherman, now on his feet, wild-eyed, said to Lucas, "It's the fucking garage. It's the fucking garage."

Lucas had the two women separated, and he looked at Sherman and said, "You think you could hang on to your wife here?" Sherman hustled over and got his wife around the waist and walked her back to the porch, and then came back and shouted at the neighbor, still on the ground, "It's the fucking garage, isn't it? You called them because of the fuckin' garage."

They took five minutes to get the story. The two couples had never liked each other, and Sherman's kid had been a high school football star, and the neighbor's kid had been cut in tenth grade, and then Sherman built the Taj Ma-Garage in his backyard, looming over the neighbor's backyard, throwing half of it into shadow.

"Where'm I supposed to grow my tomatoes?" the neighbor bleated at Lucas. "You can't grow tomatoes in full shade. And he goes back there with that saw all the time and it used to be all peaceful back here and now he runs that saw at all times of day and night."

And, he thought, Sherman was a dead ringer for the guy who killed the Jones girls and attacked Barker.

When the neighbor had calmed down, Del had let him up, and the two men were shaking grass off their clothes. The two women were standing with arms crossed twenty feet away from the circle of men, on opposite sides, throwing in an occasional word of encouragement.

Lucas finally said, "Look—no harm done at this point. Okay? You want to sue each other, that's your problem. But I don't want to take you downtown, and you don't want to go. It's really unpleasant. Okay . . ."

And they were nodding and muttering around, and Lucas suggested that they shake hands. Sherman stepped forward, and so did the neighbor, and when Sherman stuck out a hand, the neighbor hit Sherman flat in the nose, and the big man staggered and one second later they were at it again and the women were screaming, and Lucas ripped the neighbor off Sherman and threw him at Del again and said, "Cuff him, he's under arrest."

Two more neighbors from down the street came running in, and Lucas held up his hands and said, "Police . . . we're police . . . stay off the lawn, stay off."

One of the new guys said, "This is about the garage, isn't it?"

Sherman was bleeding from his nose, but not too bad. He was trying to pinch it off, and Lucas said, "Go inside, lie down, put some ice on it. If it doesn't stop, get your wife to take you down to the emergency room, okay? Got that?"

Sherman said, "Ah, I'b hab a bloody nose before," and asked, "Wha' 'bout Berg?"

"He's going downtown," Lucas said.

THEY HAD THE NEIGHBOR, whose name was Eric Berg, in the back-seat of the Lexus when Lucas took a cell phone call from an agent named Jenkins, who shouted into his phone, over what sounded like a screaming car engine, "Where are you?"

"Up on Iowa Avenue, off Rice Street."

"We'll meet you at the corner of Rice and Maryland, in that tire company lot, lights and sirens, man. . . . Get down here."

"What's going on?"

"Just . . . just get your ass down here. We'll be there in two minutes. . . . Fuckin' get down here. Go."

15

MARCY SHERRILL MISSED Kelly Barker's performance on the noon news, but heard about it, and then caught her on KARE at six o'clock. She'd known the Jones case was going to be a headache, and the headache had only gotten worse with Davenport working it.

She appreciated the fact that he had a personal stake in the investigation, and when that happened, it was usually like Sherman's March on Atlanta: nothing stood in his way. Among other things, she believed, he was manipulating the media to put pressure on the Minneapolis PD to dig up every scrap of information they could find on the mystery man, John Fell.

Davenport really didn't care about their other problems—though, to be fair, their problems weren't all that bad. The murder rate was continuing to drop, rape and armed robbery were down, the gangs were continuing to fade. Part of that, she thought, was that coke and meth sales were down, while the quality of marijuana continued to increase.

In her humble opinion, a guy lying on his living room floor with a B.C. blunt, a bag of nachos, and *Wheel of Fortune* on the TV was less likely to do serious civic damage than some freaked-out tweaker looking for another hit.

And, to be doubly fair, Davenport had generally played the media as much when he was a Minneapolis cop, as when he'd left for the BCA. In fact, Marcy thought, she'd helped him do it often enough. . . .

But, annoying. The chief was going to call her up and ask, in his sideways, we're-all-pals voice, "Have you had a chance to talk to that Barker woman? I've seen her on all the channels."

The chief spent a lot of time watching all the channels.

SHE WAS SITTING in her office, feet up on her desk, looking at a small flat-panel TV when Barker came on. When Barker was done, she called out to Buster Hill, in the next room, "Hey, Buster. Get me an address and phone number for this Kelly Barker. She's someplace down in Bloomington."

Buster, a man who claimed to be an endomorph, rather than simply fat, came and leaned in her doorway and asked, "We gonna talk to her?"

"Got to," Marcy said. "She's been all over the TV, she's got that BCA face . . . we gotta talk to her."

"For real, or for PR?"

Marcy yawned. Her boyfriend was in Dallas, and she was restless and a little lonely: "PR, mostly . . . she's told that story so often I got it memorized."

"You want me to do it?"

"I want you to come along when I do it—follow me over there. I can go home from there. You can take notes. Somebody's got to take notes."

Buster got the address from the DMV, and a cell phone number from someplace else. Kelly Barker would be pleased to talk to Sherrill; she'd be at home all evening.

So Marcy and Buster headed out in two cars, down I-35W through south Minneapolis, past the airport and then west on I-494 and south again, a half-hour of easy driving, the sun slanting down toward the northwestern horizon.

Marcy thought about Davenport—he really was an arrogant bastard in a lot of ways, good-looking, rich, flaunting it with the car and the outrageously gorgeous Italian suits. But they'd once been involved in a case that led more or less directly to bed . . . forty days and forty nights, as Davenport referred to their affair. It had been short but sweet, and she still had a soft spot for him.

If he ever left Weather, would Marcy go back? Well, he was never going to leave Weather, for one thing. He was so loyal that once you were his friend, you stayed his friend, even if you didn't want to . . . and he was married to Weather and that would last right up to the grave, no doubt about it. But, speaking of the grave, if Weather got hit by a train, and Davenport, after a suitable interval, expressed a need for some female companionship . . .

Maybe. But what about Rick? Well, Rick was interesting, but he made his money by calling people up on the telephone, and talking to them about investments. He liked having a cop on his arm, and insisted that she carry a gun when they went out at night. She would have anyway; she'd always liked guns.

Still, she wasn't much interested in being somebody's trophy. She'd gone out with an artist for a while, a guy who reminded her of a crazier version of Davenport—in fact, he'd been a wrestler at the U at the same time Davenport had been playing hockey, and they knew each other, part of the band of jock-o brothers.

Huh. The artist had been . . . hot. Crazy, maybe, but hot. After they'd split up, he'd gone and married some chick he'd known forever, and Davenport had told her that he and the chick even went and had a kid.

Had a kid.

She'd like a kid . . . but, it'd have to be soon. Rick wasn't the best daddy material in the world. He had the attention span of a banana slug, and didn't seem like the kind who'd be interested in the poop-and-midnight-bottle routine.

There was another guy, too, an orthopedic surgeon who wore cowboy boots and rode cutting horses on the weekends, out of a ranch north of the Cities. He was divorced but getting ripe, looking at her, from time to time, and she felt a little buzz in his presence. And she liked horses.

Possibilities.

She smiled to herself and turned on the satellite radio. Lucinda Williams came up with "Joy," quite the apposite little tune, given her contemplation of the boys in her life. . . .

WHILE SHE WAS HEADING SOUTH, the killer was roaming around Bloomington, going back again and again to Kelly Barker's house, not knowing exactly what he planned to do; whatever it was, he had to wait until she got home, and she'd already kept him waiting so long that he felt the rage starting to burn under his belt buckle.

He was one morose and angry motherfucker, he admitted to himself, and things weren't getting any better. He had no life, had never had one. He had a crappy house, a crappy van, a crappy income, and no prospects. He collected and resold junk. He was a junk dealer. He had a bald spot at the top of his head, growing like a forest fire at Yellowstone. He was so overweight he could barely see his own dick. He had recurrent outbreaks of acne, despite his age, and the cardiologist said that if he didn't lose seventy-five pounds, he was going to die. And he had dandruff. Bad.

Dumb and doomed: even in Thailand, he could see the disregard, the contempt, in the eyes of the little girls he used. They weren't even frightened of him.

Might just want to stick a gun in his mouth . . . some other time.

Some other time, because right now he was in an ugly mood, and the mood was feeding on itself, and he had that gun, and he had the address of the only woman who could identify him for sure.

He went around the block and this time, there were lights on in the window, and he saw a shadow cross a drape. They were home.

All right, he thought; time for tactics.

He did a few more laps, took a long look at the neighbors. The Barkers' street was quiet enough, but there were lights in almost every house. On the street behind the Barkers', though, two dark houses sat side by side. If he parked on that street, he could cut between the two houses, walk down the side of the Barkers' place, and around to the front door.

Ring the bell, kill the bitch, and wheel. If her husband answered, knock him down with a couple of shots, go in after the woman, put her down, and go out the back.

He pulled into a parking lot and parked, getting his guts up; sat and thought and then reached out to the glove box, opened it, and lifted out the fake black beard. Wouldn't fool anyone from two feet, but it'd be good enough from eight or ten or fifty. It had little pull-off tabs that uncovered sticky tape. He pulled them off, threw them on the floor of the car, and stuck the beard on his face using the rearview mirror to get the position right. When he was satisfied, he pressed the tapes hard, ten seconds each, then smacked his lips to make sure it was on tight.

Ready to go.

Careful not to leave any DNA, not to touch anything. Let the bullets do the talking.

Speaking of which . . .

He checked around again to make sure he wasn't being observed, took the shells out of the pistol's magazine, and polished each one with a Kleenex, taking care not to touch them again as he pushed them back into the magazine, one by one.

Thirteen rounds.

Barker's unlucky number.

BUSTER HILL SAID, as they crossed the street, after parking, "When you see her on TV, you gotta think she's having a good time. I mean, she's been doing this for what, almost twenty years?"

"She likes it," Marcy agreed. "If you're a victim, at least you're something. You're not just another nonentity."

"Got some drama in your life," Hill said.

"Exactly," Marcy said. They got to the door and Marcy rang, and Kelly Barker answered, a puppy-like eagerness on her face.

"Officer Sherrill? Come on in—you have to excuse the house, we've been running around like mad dogs since this started."

Her husband was smiling in the background, as eager as his wife. Marcy could smell coffee and coffee cake, and smiled, and led Buster inside.

She could use some coffee cake.

THE KILLER COULDN'T BELIEVE that he was going to do it, but he was. He just . . . did it. He parked on the street behind the Barkers' house, got out, looked up and down the street—lots of lights, no people, all inside eating dinner, or watching TV, though it was a beautiful evening.

Started walking. When he got around the block, there was a new car parked on the street across from the Barkers' but nobody in sight. That was the last moment that he might have turned around.

Instead, he put his hand on the Glock, in his jacket pocket, made sure the safety was off, and walked quickly across the yard and down between the two dark houses, pushed through a sickly hedge, and continued through the Barkers' backyard, down the side of their house, and around to the front.

Looked up and down the street, saw nobody watching, rang the doorbell. Heard the faint cadences of people talking, and footfalls on the floor inside. The knob turned, and he was looking at a thirty-something guy, a guy with an eager white face over a JCPenney suit. . . .

The killer shot the guy three times, *bap-bap-bap*, and he went down, and the killer took a step forward, following the muzzle of his gun, saw three people frozen on the living room couch and then a dark-haired woman was moving and a big fat guy, and they seemed to have guns and the killer ripped out ten shots without stopping, just pointed the gun and let it rip, fast as he could move his finger, and saw people falling and then something tore at his side and he was running . . .

Didn't think, didn't hear, didn't do anything but run.

MARCY HAD A SWEET ROLL in one hand—tasted good, she hadn't had anything to eat since lunch—when the doorbell rang. Todd Barker got up and said, "I'll get it, it's probably Jim," and went to the door. Kelly Barker said, "Jim's from just down the street. He was going to record all the TV—"

And Todd Barker opened the door and there were three shots and he went down, and a black-bearded fat man was there with a gun and Marcy made a move for her pistol and could feel Buster making a move . . .

Then it all went away for Marcy Sherrill, as swiftly and surely as the light fleeing a shattered bulb; gone into darkness.

No more Davenport and his suits, no more Rick or the hot artist, no more lunches with pals at the police force, no more fistfights, no more surgeons on cutting horses, no more politics, no more anything.

The killer's fifth wild shot, sprayed across the room, caught Marcy Sherrill under the chin, blew through her throat and spinal cord, and she died without even knowing it, without being able to say goodbye or feel any regret, with the taste of a sweet roll on her tongue. . . .

Nothing, again, forever.

16

LUCAS DROPPED THE hammer on the Lexus, burning down Rice Street, blowing through a red light at Arlington, with barely a hesitation. Berg, cuffed in the backseat, called, "Whoa, whoa, whoa," and Del, holding on to an overhead hand grip, said, "I wonder what those crazy fucks have done this time?"

"I don't know. I don't know why they wouldn't tell me," Lucas said. "Why wouldn't they tell me?"

Maryland wasn't far. "Maryland? What's at Maryland?" Del asked. "Was there something going on there?"

"Not as far as I know," Lucas said. "They were working those home invasions down in South St. Paul. . . ."

Shrake and Jenkins had many sterling qualities, but discretion wasn't one of them: to hear them freaked and screaming for lights and sirens meant something bad was happening or about to happen. "Something bad, man, something really bad," Lucas said.

Del put his feet on the dash and dug his pistol out and checked it. From the back, Berg cried, "What's happening? What's happening?" and Del said, "Shut up, asshole."

Three blocks ahead, they saw Jenkins's personal Crown Vic slew across the intersection and then disappear into what must be the parking lot.

They were there in ten seconds, saw Jenkins and Shrake standing outside the Crown Vic looking up the street at them, and Del said, "They're just standing there," and he reholstered his pistol, and then Lucas put the truck into the parking lot, bouncing to a stop next to the two big agents.

He and Del were out, and Jenkins pointed at Berg through the back window of the Lexus and asked, "Who's he?"

Lucas asked, "Jesus, what's going on? What's going on?"

"Who's the guy?" Jenkins asked again.

His voice carried a peculiar intensity that made Lucas stop, and answer: "We're transporting him down to Ramsey on assault."

Jenkins said to Shrake, "Get him out of there," and to Lucas: "We'll take him."

Shrake went around and jerked open the back door. Lucas said, "Jenkins, goddamnit—"

"Marcy Sherrill's been shot," Jenkins said. "She was over at that Barker chick's house, and somebody came crashing in and shot the place up. Three people hit, the shooter's maybe hit, it's all confused, it's all fucked up."

Lucas grabbed Jenkins's arm: "How bad? Where're they taking her? Where're they taking her?"

Jenkins shook his head: "They're not transporting her."

Lucas's mind froze for a minute, then: "What?"

"They're not transporting, man." Jenkins moved up and threw an arm around Lucas's shoulder. "She's gone, man. That's what they're telling us."

LUCAS STARED AT HIM for a moment, and then Del said, his voice shaking, "We're going. Get that fucker out of there . . ." gesturing at Berg. Shrake yanked the thin man out of the back of the truck and slammed the door.

Del ran around to the driver's side, and Lucas said, "No, I got it," and Del said, "Bullshit, I'm driving. Get in. Get the fuck in the car."

Del drove fast, but not crazy, as Lucas would have, all the way across town, with Lucas yelling suggestions at him, onto I-94, off I-94 at Cretin Avenue, south down Cretin at sixty miles an hour, then across the bridge and past the airport and the Mall of America and down into Bloomington's suburban maze.

And all the way, with the sick feeling of doom in his gut, Lucas was yelling out reasons why it couldn't be right: one of the best hospitals in the metro area was five minutes from the Barkers' house; they would have transported her no matter what, there was a lot of confusion, that fuckin' Jenkins had it wrong.

Del just drove and once in a while, shook his head. Jenkins, he believed, wouldn't make that kind of mistake. He was a thug, but a smart one, and not insensitive. He didn't say it, kept his foot down and shook his head as Lucas shouted out possibilities.

THERE WERE BLOOMINGTON COPS all over the place, and the street down to Barker's house was blocked off. Del rolled the Lexus past the blocking black-and-white, hanging his BCA credentials out the window, and put the truck in a vacant spot a half-block from the Barker house.

They climbed down and jogged past a half-dozen uniformed Bloomington cops coming and going, cutting across a couple of yards, swerving around a loop of crime-scene tape to a detective standing out in the yard. He looked up as Lucas and Del came up and said, "I know you—"

"Davenport and Capslock, with the BCA," Lucas said. "We heard that Marcy Sherrill was down. Is she . . . ?"

The cop shook his head: "You were with Minneapolis, right?"

"Yeah, we both were. We're close friends of hers."

"I'm John Rimes, I'm running the scene right now. I'll let you go in," he said. "But you might not want to . . . have to go around to the side door."

"Man, she's . . ." Lucas held his hands out, palms up, pleading.

Rimes nodded. "She's gone. We got two more down, another cop named Buster Hill, and Todd Barker, the husband here—"

"Aw, man." Lucas stopped, put his hand to his forehead. Del put a hand on his shoulder. "Aw . . . can't be right."

"I'm sorry," Rimes said.

"I interviewed them a couple days ago; this is part of the Jones investigation," Lucas said, as they walked around to the side of the house. A kind of black dread was enveloping his brain. "I talked to Marcy a couple times today."

Del said, "Easy . . ."

Lucas shook him off. "I'm okay."

Rimes said, "Hill got off a couple of shots and it looks like he hit the guy—we've got a blood trail going around the side of the house over to the next street. Not much, but it's a trail."

Del asked, as they went through the side door, "Anybody get the tags?"

"No, but a guy down the street said it was a white cargo van. . . . Of course, there are only about thirty thousand of those."

Lucas said to Del, "It's him. It's the van. It's the guy."

Rimes asked, "Who?" but Lucas shook his head.

Then they were crossing a kitchen toward a crowd of people in the living room, and Rimes said, "Make a hole," and people stepped back and Lucas looked down and suddenly, shockingly, saw Marcy, eyes still open, faceup on the living room rug, only a small hole under her chin, but a big puddle of blood under her neck. She was wearing a white silky blouse with bloody handprints down the front, where somebody had tried to tend to her. Her eyes were blank as the sky.

"Aw, Christ," he said, and he began to shake.

Around her, the house was a shambles, overturned chairs and blood tracks on the carpet, telling the story.

"This Hill guy was hit in the leg. He started screaming for an ambulance, but she was gone," Rimes said. "He said he knew she was gone the minute he looked at the wound. Hill's gonna be okay, the husband's hurt bad, but he'll make it. He took two in the chest and one in the shoulder. . . . Sherrill was hit right under the chin."

"Took out her spinal cord," said a crime-scene guy. "Instantaneous. Like she was decapitated."

Rimes shook his head at the guy and said, "Thank you," and the guy looked at Lucas's face and went away.

Rimes said, "The woman, this Kelly Barker, she wasn't hurt. She said the shooter was a big fat guy with a black beard. We're gonna get DNA on him, so he's toast if we can put our hands on him."

Rimes's voice was quiet, but intense, a recitation of what he'd learned since he took over the scene. He asked Lucas, "You need to sit down?"

Lucas turned toward Del but he couldn't find his voice, couldn't even find any spit in his mouth, not enough moisture to force out a word, and he shook his head and went back through the kitchen and out to the backyard and sat down on the grass.

Del was on his cell phone when he came out a minute later. He clicked off, squatted next to Lucas, and said, "Come on, these guys are pros. They'll get it done. Let's get you home."

"Got to tell her folks," Lucas said, finding a few words. Tears started streaming down his face. "Somebody's—"

"Somebody does, but not you," Del said. "Come on. I'm taking you home."

LUCAS DIDN'T FIGHT HIM. He sat in the passenger seat, couldn't stop the tears. Del said, "This is the worst goddamn thing. It's the worst goddamn thing."

WEATHER CALLED on Lucas's cell and asked, "Where are you?"

"Coming home. I'll be there in ten minutes," he said.

"Are you driving?"

"No. Del is."

"Ten minutes," she said.

★

WEATHER AND LETTY were in the driveway when they got to Lucas's home. Del pulled in, and said, "I'll go downtown and take care of the paper on Berg—I wish we'd never talked to that fool."

Lucas nodded and climbed out of the truck, and Weather came and took him around the waist and said, "Shrake called, and Del. Lucas, I'm so sorry."

Lucas nodded and Letty asked, "What're you going to do?"

"I don't know. I've got to think about it. I'm so freaked out I can't think right now. This was like a freak shot, the guy was spraying the house. He shot the husband three times from four feet and didn't kill him, but he hits Marcy once from forty feet and she's gone. Ah, Jesus . . ."

Letty said, "You've got to find the guy who did it and take care of him. Personally."

Weather said, "Letty, let it go."

Letty said to Weather, "I'm not letting it go." And to Lucas: "If you don't settle this, get a hand in it, you're going to be screwed up for a long time. First the Jones girls and now Marcy. Dad—"

Weather said, "Letty, shut up. Look: just shut up for now. We can talk about it later. Lucas, let's go sit down."

"I need to talk to the guys at Minneapolis," Lucas said. "I need to talk to her partner, find out what happened. I've got enough to find this guy, and now we've got DNA on him."

"You're not going to do any of that tonight," Weather said. "Come on. I've got some hot dogs hidden away. We'll get something to eat . . . you need to think."

"All right," he said. "Gotta think." He put his arms around the shoulders of both women, and they walked into the house.

TIME PASSED; it always does, and the dead don't come back, and their death becomes more real.

Lucas sat in his darkened den while Letty and Weather bustled around the kitchen with the housekeeper. He could hear them banging around, like the distant sad/cheery sounds of Christmas to a bum on the street. And he could hear them snarling at each other from time to time.

Letty and Weather were close, but had radically different world-views. Weather, as a surgeon, was imbued with the medical profession's "care" mentality. Letty, their adopted daughter, had grown up in a harsh rural countryside without a father, and with a half-crazed, alcoholic mother: her attitude was, Hit first, and if necessary, hit again. If you made a mistake, you could apologize later. Her mentality was stark: take care of yourself, and your family and friends.

Weather would argue that the system would take care of Marcy's killer. That Lucas would only get in trouble if he made it personal. Letty's attitude was that Lucas would never sleep right if he didn't hunt the killer down, and finish him.

Lucas had never loved another woman as he loved Weather—but his attitude was closer to Letty's. He could feel the murder of Marcy Sherrill sitting like a cold chunk of iron in his heart and gut. It wouldn't go away; it'd only grow harder and colder.

The anguish and regret never faded, but the anger came on, and it grew.

Marcy had meant a lot to him: he'd known her from her first days on the police force, just out of the academy, a dewy young thing working as a decoy in both prostitution and drug investigations. She'd been hot: terrific in a short skirt and high heels, with a soft clinging blouse: Weather habitually referred to her as Titsy.

She and Lucas ran into each other when Marcy made detective. They hadn't worked out as sexual partners because, in some ways, they were simply too much alike: competitive, argumentative, manipulative, cynical. Both of them wanted to be on top; so they needed a little distance between them.

And while they were alike in their attitudes, they didn't always—or even often—see eye to eye on investigations. Marcy had always been a leader: on an important case, she would put together an investigative crew, as big as she could get, and methodically grind through it until the perpetrator was turned up. With Marcy, an investigation was almost a social event.

Lucas, on the other hand, was a poor leader. He simply wasn't interested in what he considered the time-wasting elements of operating in a bureaucracy. He was intuitive, harshly judgmental, and would occasionally wander into illegalities in the pursuit of what he saw as justice. In doing that, he preferred to work with one or two close friends who knew how to keep their mouths shut, didn't mind the occasional perjury in a good cause, and knew when to blow him off, if he got too manic and started shouting; and would shout back. Lucas's cops were outsiders, for the most part. The strange cops.

HE DIDN'T THINK about all that, sitting in the den: he mostly just saw Marcy's face on the floor in Bloomington, the postmortem lividity already showing as reddish streaks in her pale skin, and the eyes. He had to see that to know in his heart that she was dead, but now wished he hadn't.

WEATHER CAME IN, and they talked quietly, some about Marcy, and the times they'd been together; and about Letty at school and Sam at preschool. Then the housekeeper came and said Sam was ready for bed, and Weather went to put him down. Letty came in and pulled a chair around to face him.

"You're responsible for a lot of people," she said. "You gotta take care of this, but whatever you do, it can't be crazy. You've got to plan it out."

"I don't know if I'm going to do anything," Lucas said.

Letty said, "Please," like they do in New York, meaning, "Don't bullshit me," and then, "What I'm saying is, you can't go to jail and you can't lose your job. You've got to think. So think. Don't just start smashing people."

He showed a little smile: "Thanks for the advice. Maybe you should go do your homework."

"It's summer vacation," she said, and he said, "*Great Expectations*? All read?" and she said, "Fuck a bunch of homework. I'm serious here. I think you gotta do it, but you gotta think about it."

"I will," he promised.

"So where are you going to start?"

He closed his eyes and thought: "I've got to talk to Kelly Barker. Like right away. Tonight."

"What else?"

"We know the guy lives here. He's been here the whole time. He watches TV here. People know him, and we'll have processed the DNA in a couple of days. . . . All we have to do is identify him, and we've got him. The Bloomington cops have called all the ERs, so we'll know if any gunshot wounds come in. The guy's hurt . . . he's gotta make a move. It'll all be done pretty quick."

"Can you live with it if somebody else takes him down?"

Lucas thought for a few more seconds, then said, "Yes. I can. I'd rather do it myself, I'll kill him if I can, but if the Bloomington cops get him . . . I can live with it."

Letty leaned forward out of her chair and said, "Get with Del. If you wind up putting him down, Del's the guy you want with you."

Lucas nodded. "Of course." And, a few seconds later, "I don't think you need to review this conversation with your mom."

Letty said, "She's so smart—she knows what we're talking about. That's why she's upstairs with Sam, to get out of the way."

"Yeah, probably."

"So stop sitting there like a robot," Letty said. "Call people on the phone. Get Del over here. Get it going."

Lucas stared at her for a moment, unblinking; she didn't flinch. And he thought, *She's way too young to think like this.* But then, given her history, she really hadn't been young since she was nine; *that* had been the last year of her childhood.

17

DEL CALLED AHEAD, and showed up in the truck a little after ten o'clock. Lucas was waiting in the driveway and said, "Let's go over to Fairview. Kelly Barker's still over there."

"What's she got for us?"

"I want to see what she says. And I want to get her with Retrief, working up another head shot. Then we paper the TV stations with it overnight."

"Bloomington probably has that under way."

"I want to make sure—and I need to hear her talk. Want her to talk about John Fell."

"If it is John Fell—"

"It is. . . . You take care of Berg?"

"Yeah. He'll be out tonight. I don't want to fuck with it."

LUCAS TOOK THE WHEEL, and they headed across town to Fairview Southdale, a trauma center four or five miles north of the Barker house. They parked outside the emergency exit, threw the "Police" card on the dashboard, and went inside. Two Bloomington uniformed cops saw them coming and pushed off a counter they'd been leaning against. Lucas held up his ID and asked, "Is Kelly Barker still here?"

"Up in surgical waiting," one of them said, and pointed the way.

Barker, when they found her, was sitting upright in an overstuffed chair, but was sound asleep. A Minneapolis cop sat on the couch across from her, reading a copy of *Modern Hospital*. Lucas introduced himself and Del, and the cop said, "She's been trying to get some sleep."

Lucas said, "Kelly," and touched her shoulder, and she started, her eyes popping open. She looked at Lucas for a minute, as though she didn't recognize him, then shook her head and said, "Is he all right?"

"We just got here," Lucas said. "We don't know the status on anyone."

"That lady police officer died."

"Yeah . . ."

"She seemed nice. It's so awful," Barker said. "Everything was going so well this morning and afternoon, and then this man . . ."

It all came out in a gush; what they'd been talking about, the man at the door, the explosion of gunfire, the screaming of the wounded, the rush to the hospital.

"They say the man was shot, but I don't see how. The police officer, Buster, was upside down on the floor; he shot two times, I think, but they say he might have hit him."

"There was a blood trail," Lucas said. "It's the only good thing to come out of this whole disaster. All we have to do now is identify him: we've got all the proof we need, if we can just lay our hands on him."

"How are you going to do that?"

"I've got John Retrief headed this way with a laptop. Since you're waiting here on the operation, we were hoping you'd help revise the head shot."

"Sure. I'm lined up to go on WCCO and KSTP tomorrow. Channel Three wants me but I told them I couldn't do it until noon, and I told them all I needed like, heavy makeup, because I'm so distraught."

Lucas thought: she didn't look all that distraught, and he felt the anger burning away in his chest. He pushed it back and asked, "What about Todd? What've you heard?"

"Only that he's shot pretty bad, there're some holes in his lungs and they have to reconstruct his shoulder when he's recovered enough to do it," she said. "They brought Buster out a while ago; he's in recovery—or maybe he's out by now—there are some more police officers down there. If it wasn't for Buster shooting that nut, we'd all be dead now."

The shooter, she told him, had a heavy square-cut black beard like some Iranians she saw on television. "But it was him—it was my stalker, all right. I saw his eyes. I thought he was going to kill me."

They talked awhile longer, then Lucas called Retrief and was told that he'd just passed the airport and was probably fifteen minutes away. "As soon as you're done with Miz Barker, I want you to send copies to all the media outlets you've got," Lucas said. "Everyone in the state. And down to Des Moines, out to Fargo, over to Milwaukee, with a response back to us. Tag it with something about a Midwestern serial killer of young girls, so it attracts some attention outside the state. Localize it for them."

"I'll do it—too late for the regular news tonight, but they'll all have it at the crack of dawn tomorrow."

THEY LEFT BARKER on the couch, and stopped by the intensive care ward, where Buster Hill was sitting slightly upright. Two Minneapolis detectives were sitting with him, nodded when Lucas and Del stepped in.

"Thought you might come by," said the older of the two cops, a guy named Les MacBride. He turned to Hill: "Davenport and Capslock, BCA." The younger of the two detectives was named Clarence.

"Heard of you from Marcy," Hill said to Lucas and Del. "God, this is the most awful day of my life. She was such a great kid."

"How're you doing?" Lucas asked.

"Hurts," Hill said. "But . . . the thing about Marcy is what's got me really freaked out."

"Sounds like you did okay," Lucas said. "You tagged the guy."

"Shoulda killed the sonofabitch. Maybe I will yet," he said. "I will if I get the chance."

His story was only slightly different from Barker's, nothing more than a point-of-view variation. He hadn't seen Marcy get hit. As soon as the shooting started at the door, he said, he went for his gun, but Marcy's weapon was in her bag, and she went for the bag, but he didn't know whether she'd ever cleared the gun. He'd been hit right away and didn't see Marcy get hit—didn't realize she had been until the shooter disappeared, and he'd called out to her for help.

"Didn't come. I rolled over, and man, she was . . . gone."

The shooter, he said, emptied his Glock into the room and then turned to run, which is when Hill hit him, he thought. "I was on my back with my gun over my head, shooting upside down. Bad shot, off center, but he stepped into it. Looked to me—this was a pretty fast impression—that he got it above the elbow, left arm, entry wound in the back, going out the front. Maybe, maybe hit him in the side, not the arm. But right there. I had this image when I fired. Don't think it broke the bone, his arm didn't move much. I think it was all soft tissue."

MacBride said, "The blood trail was pretty thin. A splotch right at the beginning, but after that, it was mostly drips and drops."

"It's all good, they can get DNA out of nothing," Lucas said. To Hill: "You said, 'Glock.' You sure about that?"

"Yeah, I'm pretty sure. Had that matte-gray look, not like metal as much as plastic. That plasticky finish. I picked up on it all the way."

"Did he look like he knew what he was doing?"

Hill shook his head. "Naw. He was pumping with every shot. Squeezing as fast as he could, gun was jumping all over the place. I mean, he was trying to hit us, he just wasn't much of a shooter. Except for . . . you know."

They talked for a few more minutes, didn't get much more: from Hill's point of view, it'd been like getting hit by a car. He'd been chatting with Kelly Barker one second, and in the next second, he was upside down with a bullet wound.

"You did pretty goddamn good," Del said, and Lucas nodded: "That's right. We're proud of you, man."

Hill nodded. "Thanks . . . I only wish . . ."

IN THE CAR, driving back to St. Paul, Lucas said, "Fell is not much of a shooter. Except he was the only one who killed anyone."

After a moment of silence, Del asked, "What's next?"

"With Marcy, the Minneapolis cops will be working nothing but a million details. They'll knock down everything. I would like to get to the guy before they do," Lucas said.

"If you kill him, there'll be a humongous stink, sooner or later," Del said. "There are quite a few people around Minneapolis who don't completely appreciate your act. And they know that you and Marcy had that relationship."

"I'll think of something," Lucas said. "Forty days and forty nights, she used to say."

Del snorted. "It wasn't the most discreet romance. There was a rumor around that you nailed her on your desk downtown."

"Ridiculous," Lucas said.

"You're saying it's not true?"

"Of course it's not true." He looked out the window for a moment, then said, "We couldn't keep it on the desk. It was on the floor."

They both laughed, and then Del said, "Aw, Jesus. She did everything right. Ate right, exercised, never smoked, hardly drank . . . Why are we still here, and she's gone?"

★

WHEN LUCAS HAD BUILT his house, he'd designed a combination den and office where he could sit and think, when he needed to do that. It wasn't large, but it had a desk with a proper office chair, and two large leather chairs with tile-topped side tables. Everybody but Sam was still awake when they got back. Lucas got beers for himself and Del, and they went into the den and sat down, Lucas with his briefcase between his knees.

"Here's the thing," he said. He took out a sheaf of paper, his copies of his reports from the original investigation of the Jones girls' disappearance. "Ninety-nine percent of what's in the Minneapolis file is bullshit. That's because they were specifically going after Scrape, most of the time. I was the only guy looking at John Fell, so the only reports worth a fuckin' thing are mine, and I didn't know what I was doing."

"You did all right," Del said.

"Yeah, yeah . . . I fucked it up, is what I did. But, tonight, what I want to do is, I want you to look at the reports, read through them, then we talk about them. I don't think I'm missing anything, but you never know. . . ."

So Lucas sat and drank his beer, and Del drank his and read through the slender pile of paper. He said once, "You didn't type so bad."

"Yeah, I taught myself to touch type. Got a book."

"Huh . . . didn't know that."

Weather came to say that she was going to bed, and then Letty asked if there was anything she could do, and Lucas sent her off to bed, and finally Del looked up and said, "Nothing jumps out at me."

"Listen to the tapes," Lucas said. "These are copies of the nine-one-one calls."

Del listened to the tapes and said, "Boy—sounds like the same guy, doesn't it?"

"It's him. The calls came from two different pay phones, but in the same area, and not in Scrape's neighborhood."

They sat around and speculated some more, talked about the possibility that Fell had been a schoolteacher, and how he'd probably worked in some assembly plant up north, then Del sat up and snapped his fingers. "Hey, here's an idea. How old do you think he was?"

"Middle twenties, maybe a little older," Lucas said. "That's what people in the bar said."

"So—if most people go off to college when they're eighteen, and don't usually graduate in four years anymore . . . now it's more like five or six, must've been like that when you graduated."

"Yeah?"

"So what if he wasn't actually a teacher?" Del asked. "What if he was like a practice teacher or something? I bet the schools wouldn't even have a record of that. 'Cause they never would have actually fired him—he'd just be sent off. We'd have to go somewhere else to get his name. Like, you know, teachers' college or something."

Lucas wagged a finger at him: "That's decent. Not great, but it's decent. I'll get Sandy on that first thing in the morning."

AT ONE O'CLOCK, they hadn't thought of much else, and Del finally went home. "You gonna be okay?" he asked, in the doorway.

"Hell no," Lucas said. "I'm gonna be screwed up for a while."

"You got some people worried about you," Del said. "We don't want you doing anything goofy."

"Jeez, have a little faith," Lucas said. "I'm screwed up, but I'm not nuts."

WHEN DEL WAS GONE, Lucas went back to the den and gathered up all the papers, scanned them, sighed, and thought that the information was too thin. They had his voice . . . but it told them nothing, until they could find him. Once they had him, it might mean something.

Same thing with his face—maybe Barker could identify him, and Todd Barker had stood within inches of him, and might be able to identify him, but they had to find him first. And once they found him, the DNA from the blood was really all they'd need.

The problem was finding him.

Lucas was stuffing the two tapes back in his briefcase when a thought struck him. There was nothing in the voice, but what about the timing of the calls? He checked the times, then went back to his notes, and the summarized notes from other investigators. The summaries weren't enough to be sure, but the tips on Scrape and his whereabouts seemed to come precisely when the investigation was slowing because of a lack of information.

That is, when they were looking for Scrape, they got a tip on where he lived. It hadn't been used, because by the time they got it, Lucas had already located him.

But then Scrape was released, and they promptly got a tip on the box of clothing that had been thrown in the dumpster, and the tip had paid off with what looked like the definitive case against the street guy.

Both tips from the killer himself.

As though the killer himself had been inside the investigation.

LUCAS REACHED UP and turned off his over-the-shoulder reading lamp, and closed his eyes in the now darkened den.

Once, years before, he'd been a Minneapolis police lieutenant loosely assigned to special investigations and intelligence work. At the time, a serial killer simply known in the newspapers as the "Maddog" had been killing women around the Twin Cities, in particularly brutal ways. The case turned on a pistol that had been stolen from an evidence box in the police department—an evidence box to which Lucas had had access.

Early in the investigation, Lucas had been put under surveillance by Internal Affairs, with the thought that he might have been the killer. That had been quickly cleared up, when one of the murders took place while he was actively being watched.

But he'd been roundly pissed off, until the chief explained the circumstances—about the missing gun, about a profiler who said that the killer would be attractive to women, and charming, and probably a nice dresser, whose dress would bring women to trust him . . . a description that fit Lucas.

Could this killer be a cop? Buster Hill said that the shooter at the Barkers' house had been using a Glock, a fairly nondescript piece of weaponry that was also a common police sidearm in the Twin Cities area.

He'd known cops who were killers, but they were not common.

He hated to think that a Minneapolis cop might have been one.

Given the age of Fell, he'd almost have to be a patrolman, and Lucas knew all the young patrolmen at the time. He couldn't think of any who'd really fit both the personality and the appearance of Fell. . . .

Well: maybe one or two.

He'd think about it overnight.

Try to sleep on it.

TRY TO SLEEP ON IT—he hardly slept at all. Kept flashing back to Marcy. Weather always got up first, and did this morning. As soon as she got out of the bathroom, he rolled out of bed.

"Can't sleep?" she asked.

"Can't stop thinking about possibilities," he said. "I might as well get going. I want to check and make sure that poster got out to the TV stations. And I got a couple of things I want to look at over at Minneapolis."

"Good luck," she said. "Be careful."

18

WHEN THE KILLER had turned from the Barkers' doorway, he'd been confused by the crowd in the house, by the noise, and even by the gunfire itself, though he was doing the shooting, then by the sight of the cop coming out with the gun. Nothing rational was working through his brain: he was down on the lizard level, banging away as fast as he could, both scared and furious and righteous.

He saw one or two people going down and the muzzle flash from a pistol and then, as he turned, felt an impact under his armpit. He was confused about what it was, felt like somebody had hit him with a thrown rock, a sharp rock—and then he was around the house and running between houses, stuffing the pistol in his pants pocket, and across the neighbor's backyard, between more houses out to the street and into the van.

His heart pounding, he'd cleared the neighborhood in little more than a minute, turning corners, heading out to I-494. His arm didn't hurt that much, but when he scratched at it, his other hand came away covered with blood and he realized he'd been shot or had cut himself, or something.

He freaked. One thing he didn't like was the sight of his own blood. He was weaving around the highway, trying to see where it was coming from, then thought about the highway patrol—it'd be ridiculous, at this point, if he were pulled over by the highway patrol for drunk driving.

He swerved onto an exit, across the highway into a shopping center, parked in front of a Best Buy, and looked at his arm. Lots of blood. He probed at it, realized there was nothing there. He hadn't been hit in the arm at all, but in the side, near the pit of his arm.

He checked the parking lot, then carefully peeled up his shirt and found the wound. To his eye, it looked almost like a knife cut, straight, but deep and ragged. Not a hole, but a slice.

Not too bad, he thought; not too bad, but still bleeding.

He saw a newspaper stand outside a bagel place, dug some change out of his parking-meter stash, looked around again, hopped out of the van, walked over to the box, and bought a *Star Tribune*.

He'd once read that the inside pages of newspapers were fairly sterile. The pages were made with acidic wood pulp, with lots of heat in the process, and were untouched by human hands. He hoped it was true. He carried the paper back to the van, got inside, pulled out the sports pages, and used them to pad his armpit.

Needed to get home . . .

The beard was bothering him—and he wondered if the cops had put out a thing about a white van and a black beard. He pulled it off, the adhesive stretching the skin around his mouth and nose, pushed it down between the seats of the van. He looked in the mirror: still had adhesive on his face. He peeled it for a moment, then put the van in gear and headed out.

IF ONLY . . .

Most of his life seemed built on the phrase. If only . . .

If only the apartment building had been put somewhere else, if only the Jones girls hadn't been found. If only those things had happened, the old man would still be alive, and he'd still be peacefully pursuing his junk, building his stash for another trip to Thailand.

If only the Barker woman had been there alone, if only he hadn't been hit by the bullet. Who were those people, anyway? Must have been cops. Maybe bodyguards? Had it been a trap? He wondered if he'd hit them, thought he might have. He'd emptied the pistol at them. . . .

If they were cops, they'd never stop looking for him, especially if he'd hit one. He turned on the radio, looking for news, but none of the radio stations did news anymore. He turned it back off, tried to concentrate on his driving. His side hurt worse, the pain growing, and he started to sweat.

He could handle the pain, he thought. He could even handle the wound. He had that half-tube of oxycodone, left over from the root canal, along with some antiseptics of some kind.

But he needed to get home. Once he was home . . .

Sweat was running freely down his face by the time he turned into his driveway and pulled into the garage. He didn't know why he was sweating—he wasn't hurt that bad. There was some pain, but it was a dull ache, rather than agonizing.

He clambered out of the van and went inside, straight to the bathroom, pulled his shirt off, peeled the newspaper off his skin, and looked at the wound. Still bleeding, but not that much. All right. He dug through his medicine cabinet—got the tube of oxycodone, found another tube, from an ear infection, with some amoxicillin, two tabs. Not much else, besides some Band-Aids and a tube of Band-Aid antiseptic cream.

Then he remembered the first-aid kit that came with the van. He'd never bothered to open it, but wouldn't that have some gauze in it? He went back out to the garage, found the kit, found four gauze pads inside it, and a roll of medical tape. He carried it back to the bathroom, wiped some antiseptic cream over the wound, then covered the wound with the gauze pads. He tried the tape, and managed to stick the pads on, but they wouldn't hold, he thought. The tape was not long or strong enough, meant to go around fingers or toes. He got a bread bag, ripped off a piece of plastic large enough to cover the gauze pads, then taped it to his body with long strips of duct tape.

Not bad, he thought, looking in the mirror. He hurt, but he wasn't going to die, unless he got infected. He popped an oxycodone and one of the antibiotic pills, then, on reflection, popped another one of each.

Still hurt, but there was nothing more he could do about it. He went into his living room and lay down on the couch, moved around until he was as comfortable as he could get, and turned on the TV, flipped around the channels.

Nothing. The news wasn't up yet. Nobody was breaking in with a news flash—maybe nobody had been hit.

If he'd been really unlucky, somebody might have gotten his license tag numbers, but there was nothing he could do about that. And if they had, the cops would already be at his door . . . and they weren't.

With that thought, he dozed; tired from the action, knocked down by the dope.

WHEN HE WOKE, he was disoriented for a moment, looked at the time. After nine-thirty. The news would be coming up.

He was anxious, waiting for it. Anxious to see what he'd done, where the coverage was. Anxious to see how he'd been described. To see what they knew . . .

He went out to the kitchen, got three wieners out of the refrigerator, and a jar of sauerkraut; slathered the wieners in the sauerkraut, stuck them in the microwave, got out three hot dog buns, got a bottle of horseradish-mustard out of the refrigerator, squirted the buns full of the mustard.

The microwave beeped and the meal was ready: he sat on the couch watching the end of a complicated cop drama, and the news came on.

A woman standing outside the Barker house: "A bearded gunman who may be the killer of the two Jones sisters struck again this evening, murdering a Minneapolis police office, wounding another police officer, and also wounding Todd Barker, the wife of Kelly Barker, who is believed to have been attacked by the same gunman in 1991 in Anoka.

Officer Buster Hill is in guarded condition tonight, and Todd Barker is in critical condition at Fairview-Southdale Hospital in Edina. . . ."

The killer watched with dulled interest as the reporter recounted the shooting, and then interviewed a police spokesman, who said, "We believe Officer Hill wounded the gunman in the exchange of gunfire. We found traces of blood along what we presume to be the route the gunman took away from the house. The blood has been picked up by our crime-scene crews and will be taken to the BCA where we will . . ."

And then the police spokesman said the word that the killer hadn't thought about, but knew quite well. The thing that had, really, pushed him to Thailand.

The officer said, ". . . process it for DNA. When we find him, we'll then know that we have him for sure, and we think that finding him is now only a matter of time."

The killer knew all about DNA. DNA seemed like a cloud, something that contaminated everything you touched. He'd been afraid that if he simply continued taking girls, that someday he'd be tagged by DNA. Now he sat up, staring at the TV, felt like screaming at it. Felt like throwing one of the Indian clubs through it, to shatter the screen, but didn't.

Just stared, the chant going through his head: DNA, DNA, DNA . . .

Had to get out of here, he thought, looking around the house. Had to get away from the smell, the blinking lights on the porn servers, the junk that was scattered all over the place. Had to get away from this piece-of-shit life, had to find a den, had to get well. Had to heal.

Had to put a pillow over his head, shut out the world.

Hide.

19

MINNEAPOLIS POLICE headquarters was full of pissed-off people the next morning, buzzing like a nest of killer bees. Lucas slipped through the swarm around Homicide, found the room he was looking for, used for training—and on the walls, photos of every academy graduating class.

At the time of the Jones killings, everybody he'd interviewed about Fell agreed that he was in his mid to late twenties. If he were a young-looking thirty, just to pad the age range a bit, he could hardly have gotten out of the academy before the mid to late seventies—couldn't have been a cop for more than ten years, at the most.

Lucas went through ten years of classes, noting the names of the prospective cops who looked more or less like the Barkers' description. There weren't many. The killer was heavily built, almost square, she'd said. She emphasized the darkness of his hair, almost Mediterranean in tone, but said that his complexion was fair.

In ten years of photographs, there were nine possibilities. After noting down the names, he walked down to the office of Deputy Chief Marilyn Barin. Barin ran the Professional Standards Bureau, which included Internal Affairs. She was Lucas's age, but had come up through patrol. They'd been friendly enough over the years, but not good friends; she'd been a casual friend of Marcy's.

She looked up when Lucas knocked on her door frame. "Lucas. Thought you might come around today. This is brutal."

Lucas took a chair and said, "A long time ago, I worked the Jones girls' killing, and thought I had a lead on the killer. That was wiped out when we pinned it on a street guy. Turns out we were wrong about that—the guy who shot Marcy is the same guy who killed the Jones girls, and probably a few more over the years."

Barin nodded. "I heard a couple people talking about your theory . . . and you're a smart guy."

He said, "I *am* a smart guy, and it's way more than a theory, now. I wouldn't bullshit you on something like this. The thing is . . ."

He explained the sequence of the original investigation, and the 911 calls that had led them down the path to Scrape. "It looks like—this is a leap—like the shooter might have had a contact inside the department, or might even have been a cop. The shooter yesterday used a Glock, according to Buster Hill. Bottom line is, I have a list of names of cops and probably ex-cops or never-were cops, and I'd like somebody to pull some personnel folders and some IA files and tell me if I'm barking up the wrong tree. Or the right one."

Barin contemplated him for a moment, then swiveled in her chair and looked at a bulletin board above a bookcase, then swiveled back and said, "I gotta talk to the chief. I'll tell him that we've got to go with the request. But I've got to clear it with him."

"How long will that take?"

"Sit here," she said. She got up and left the office. Five minutes later she came back and said, "You're good to go. The chief called Cody Ryan down in IA. He's waiting for you."

"Thanks. I'll keep you guys up-to-date. It's sort of a reach. . . ."

"Do stay in touch," she said. "We're putting everything we've got on this thing. But if it should turn out to be a cop, or an ex-cop . . ." She rubbed her face. "Ah, God, I hate to think about that. I mean, at this point, I gotta tell you, I don't believe it'll be that way."

CODY RYAN WAS another cop who'd moved into his job after Lucas left the Minneapolis force; Lucas knew him not at all. Which was good, since Lucas had been pushed off the force by IA, after he'd finally beaten up Randy Whitcomb for church-keying the face of one of his street contacts.

Ryan was a bluff, square man with gold-wire-rimmed glasses and a red face, a white shirt, and a red tie and blue slacks. Lucas introduced himself and Ryan said, "I just looked up your file. You were a bad boy."

"I shouldn't have hit him the last thirty times," Lucas said. "The first thirty were pure self-defense."

Ryan gestured at a chair: "Yeah, well . . . saw the pictures of the chick who got church-keyed. That might tend to piss you off. So: who're we looking up?"

Lucas gave him the list of names, and Ryan started punching up computer files. He had records on six of the nine, nothing at all on the other three. "Makes me think they didn't work here," he said. "Might have gotten turned down for one reason or another. You'd have to go to the general personnel records for that. I don't know if they'd have them that far back."

"What do we have on the six?"

Ryan hit a *Print* button, and started passing the files over to Lucas. Four of the six were clean in IA's eyes—minor citizen complaints that didn't amount to much. Only one of the four was still on the force, a patrol sergeant working out of the second precinct. Lucas checked his dates: he'd come out of the last class that Lucas had looked at, which meant that he'd be close to the prime age for the killer. The file included an ID photograph; the guy wore glasses and really didn't look much like Barker's reconstruction. He was square, but not fat.

The other three had come out of earlier classes; two had quit the force relatively early on, one had retired. Nothing in the IA reports suggested that any of them had ever had problems with women.

Of the two with more serious IA reports, one was for excessive use of force on three separate occasions, but with nothing involving sex. The final one involved a complaint by a dancer that the officer, a Willard Packard, had pressured her for sex, suggesting that there might be some benefits in sleeping with a police officer.

Packard had replied that he suspected the woman of prostitution, and had moved her along when he found her loitering outside the club, talking with customers. He said she was clearly soliciting, and had filed the complaint as a way of getting back at him.

An IA investigator named John Seat had concluded that both might be telling the truth—that she had been soliciting, and that Packard might have pressured her for freebies. Seat had been unable to come up with any hard evidence, and when the complainant told IA that she was tired of the whole thing and wanted to drop the complaint, the investigation ended and Packard walked.

Packard continued with the force for another three years, then resigned, with a note that he'd gone to work with a suburban department east of St. Paul.

"Sounds to me like Seat was pretty sure he was pushing her, but what are you gonna do? It's all talk, no action, and no witnesses," Ryan said.

Lucas looked at a photograph: There was a resemblance to the Identi-Kit portrait, though Packard had a bulbous nose, and Barker had shown the killer's nose as harsh and angled. But eyewitnesses, like

Barker, were notoriously unreliable. That she could assemble a coherent image at all, that was picked out by other witnesses, was unusual. Getting a nose wrong—making it more "evil"—was a small enough thing. "Think I'll look him up," Lucas said. "Our guy used to go to a massage parlor. He liked his hookers."

"Long time ago, though," Ryan said. "He could be dead."

ON HIS WAY OUT, three different detectives hooked Lucas into quick conversations about Marcy Sherrill; by the time he went out the door, he was hurrying to get away from it. Twenty minutes later, he was back at the BCA headquarters in St. Paul. He called in Sandy, the researcher, and outlined Del's idea about possible practice teachers. Her eyes narrowed as he talked, and she said, "I'll try, but I'd be willing to bet that the schools don't track that stuff. I'd probably have to go out to the teachers' colleges, teacher-training courses. I don't know—"

"Give it a try," Lucas said.

When Sandy was gone, he looked up Willard Packard, and learned that he was still on the job. His driver's license ID showed a square-built balding man with dark hair and glasses—he had a corrective lens restriction on his license—weighing 230 pounds. He was clean-shaven.

DEL CALLED and asked what Lucas wanted to do: "I'm going out to Woodbury to talk to a cop. You could ride along."

"See you in ten minutes," Del said. "Want me to pick you up a Diet Coke?"

"Yeah, that'd be good."

Lucas needed to check off Packard, just to get the name out of his hair, but had lost faith in the prospect of Packard being the killer—too many things were a bit off. He didn't look quite right, and the man who shot Marcy, now that he thought about it, hadn't used the gun like a trained police officer. The *gun* itself might be a common police weapon, but the shooter apparently hadn't behaved like a cop.

Probably. But then you really couldn't tell how a cop would behave in a shooting situation, until you'd seen him in one. You hoped the training worked, but there was no guarantee.

He sat thinking about that for a moment, groped for something else, realized he was treading water. He picked up the phone and called Bob Hillestad, a friend in Minneapolis Homicide, on his cell phone. Hillestad said, without preamble, "It's a bitch, huh?"

"Yeah, it is," Lucas said. "Where're you hosers at? You got anything at all?"

"No. We got nothin'. Wait: we got that DNA, and we'll run it through the database. It's like everybody's got both hands wrapped around their dicks, saying, 'He'll be in the database.' Maybe he will be, but I don't believe it, yet."

"Heard anything from Bloomington?"

"A couple of people saw a white van leaving the neighborhood, pretty fast, at the right time. So Bloomington's getting a list of white van owners. You know how many that'll be? Someplace up in the five-digit area, is what they're telling me. They're saying it could go to six digits."

"Good luck on that," Lucas said.

"We're all scratching around like a bunch of hens," Hillestad said. "You guys got anything?"

"I decided to look at one guy based on nothing, and he's not gonna work out. You know who's getting that list for Bloomington?"

"No, but they're going through the DMV. You could check over there."

Lucas rang off, called the DMV, got routed around, and finally came up with a database guy who was doing the list for Bloomington. "I'm not a cop, but it's absurd. What're they going to do with it? On the other hand, it takes ten minutes and I don't have to print it out—I'm just sending an electronic file, so, no skin off my butt."

"Once you get the file, can you alphabetize it by the owners' names?" Lucas asked.

"Sure." There was a slurp at the other end; the guy had a cup of coffee. "You want me to shoot it to you?"

"Not yet—but put the list somewhere you can get at it. Hey, wait, could you do something to scan it, see if you've got a guy named Willard Packard on it?"

"Hang on. Give me a couple of minutes."

The guy went away, and Del came in and Lucas pointed him at a chair, covered the mouthpiece of the phone and said, "Just a minute. Talking to the DMV."

The DMV guy came back and said, "No Willard Packard on the white van list, but I looked up Willard Packard out in Woodbury, and he's got a champagne Toyota minivan and a blue Ford Explorer. Champagne, white, not that close, but they're both light."

"Thanks. Keep the list active," Lucas said. He hung up and said to Del, "Our guy owns a champagne minivan, but not a white one."

"Eyewitnesses suck," Del said. "Let's go jack him up."

THEY JACKED UP Packard about one-millionth of an inch, and then he unjacked himself. He lived in an apartment complex behind a shopping center, and came to the door in cargo shorts and a gray Army T-shirt with a sweat spot on the chest.

His hair, what was left of it, was cropped right down to the skin, giving him what looked like a cranial five-o'clock shadow. That didn't fit with what Barker had seen.

A golf bag was leaning against the wall of the entry, and over his shoulder, in the living room, Lucas could see six-foot-tall stereo speakers: the place reeked of a post-divorce crib. Lucas and Del, standing in the hall, told him why they were calling.

"Jesus—you guys are hassling me on something I was found innocent on, more'n twenty years ago? What's up with that?"

"We're running down everything," Lucas said. "Since Marcy Sherrill was killed—"

"All right. But man, you gotta get ahold of Dan Ball at Woodbury PD. You can get him through the station—he'll be in at three o'clock, or you can call him at home. Or call Bill Garvey, he was supervising yesterday: I was in a squad starting at three o'clock, until eleven. We were sitting outside Cub eating lunch when we heard on the radio about the shooting."

Lucas nodded. "So we're cool. If we come by and ask for a DNA sample, you wouldn't have a problem with it? Wouldn't need to mention it to anybody."

"I got no problem with that," Packard said. "So you got nothin'?"

213

"We got nothin'," Lucas said, turning away.

"I worked that Jones thing, in a squad," Packard said. "I kinda remember you. You were on patrol. You were a couple-three years younger than me, and I mostly worked west. Wasn't Brian Hanson big on that case?"

"Yeah. He was one of the lead guys," Lucas said.

"Reason I mention it, see, is he died a couple days ago. Kinda weird way," Packard said.

Lucas stopped. "Why weird?"

"Well, they know he's dead, but they can't find the body. They found his boat driving around in the middle of Lake Vermilion, up north, with his hat in it, but no sign of him. There's a thing in the *Star Tribune* this morning, inside. His daughter says he used to pee off the back of the boat; everybody tried to stop him doing it."

"Huh. Couple days ago?"

"Yeah. Same day the Jones girls were found. Or maybe the next day. Weird, huh?"

"Yeah, weird," Lucas said. "Huh."

OUT IN THE CAR, Lucas said, "You know, Hanson . . . Wouldn't have to be a cop—it could be a cop's friend, just asking about the case."

"I haven't had any breakfast," Del said. "Why don't we stop over at Cub and get something? And figure this out."

They sat in the parking lot eating deli sandwiches, and talked about Hanson, then started back to the BCA. They were a mile out when Shrake called on Lucas's cell: "Minneapolis SWAT's outside a place off Portland about Forty-second, not on Portland but over a block, it's like Fifth Avenue or something, no details but the word is, the guy inside is the one who shot Marcy."

"*What?*"

"That's what we're hearing, man," Shrake said. "Some biker guy. Supposedly some kind of grudge thing, Marcy had been bustin' his balls. Jenkins and I are on the way over. We'll keep you in touch—"

"That makes no goddamn sense," Lucas said. "That's crazy. This doesn't have anything to do with Marcy, it's Barker who's the one. That's who the shooter was after."

214

"I'm just telling you what I hear," Shrake said. "The guy's a doper."

"We're coming. We're on 494 coming up to 94; get us some better directions. I think we'll turn around and come up from the south."

"Might be quicker," Shrake said. "And you better hurry."

"I bet they got a nine-one-one tip on the guy," Lucas said.

"Why? We got DNA on the shooter; giving up the wrong guy won't help him."

Lucas said, "Yeah . . . maybe the guy doesn't know about DNA. Or maybe he's just fuckin' with us. Or maybe he's playing for time, maybe he's getting his shit together and trying to get out of town."

MINNEAPOLIS HAD BARRICADED a two-block radius from the target home on Fifth Avenue, an older white-stuccoed place on an embankment with a two-car detached garage in back. They parked outside the perimeter, walked past Jenkins's Crown Vic and through the perimeter, flashing their BCA identification at the uniformed cops barricading the streets.

They found Jenkins and Shrake loitering outside the SWAT team's command post. Lucas asked, "What's happening?"

"Still in there," Jenkins said. "They got a negotiator on the phone; he says the guy sounds pretty high."

"Probably flushing all their junk down the toilet, what they can't get up their noses," Del said. "How many are in there?"

"A guy named Donald Brett and his old lady, Roxanne. Maybe a kid. Probably a kid."

"I know that guy," Del said.

"Asshole?" Shrake asked.

"Oh yeah," Del said.

Lucas: "Crazy enough to kill a cop?"

"Probably," Del said. "He's your basic hometown psycho who's been self-medicating with crank and cocaine for years."

"Can't see anything from here," Lucas said, peering down the street at the target house.

"Couple guys went up and were getting ready to take the door down, a pit bull came around the house and started tearing up their ass, and they shot it. Dog's still there," Jenkins said. "When they went back to the door, Brett had pushed a table in the entryway. They can't get the door open now."

"That's a handy table," Del said.

"Probably done it before," Shrake said.

Lucas: "I'm gonna go find the guy in charge."

THEY FOUND the guy in charge, a Xavier Cruz, sitting on a tripod stool behind a SWAT van. Inside, another guy was sitting on the floor of the van, talking into a telephone, a finger in his off-ear: the negotiator. Cruz saw them coming and said, "Davenport. Del."

"How'd you figure the guy out?" Lucas asked.

"Got a nine-one-one tip," Cruz said. "Guy said he was bragging to friends over at the White Nights."

"You got the nine-one-one guy?"

"No, I don't think so."

"He said he didn't want to be involved," Lucas suggested.

"Something like that," Cruz said. "Why?"

Lucas said, "Because the guy on the phone was the killer. He did the same thing to us back on the Jones case. Did it twice; we still got the recordings."

Cruz said, "Huh," like, maybe yes, maybe no.

The negotiator was saying, "You gotta man up, Don. You gotta man up. You got responsibilities, you got a wife, you got kids. If you're not involved, it won't take long for us to figure it out."

Del said to Cruz, "If you put me on the phone, I can probably get him out of there in a couple of minutes."

Cruz studied him for a few seconds, then asked, "You pals?"

"Not exactly. But he knows me. I don't bullshit him."

Cruz shrugged: "Gotta ask the man," and flipped a thumb at the negotiator.

WHEN THE MAN TOOK a short break, they asked him, and he said, "I'm working him around. I don't need somebody setting me back."

"If you think I'll set you back, then let's not do it," Del said. "But I wouldn't. I think I could get him to come out."

216

The man looked at Cruz, who shrugged again and said, "Brett's got us by the nuts—we can't get in, we can't shoot in, we can't even gas in, without knowing who else is in there. We know there are at least two more. . . ."

They both looked at Del, and then the negotiator said, "I'll give you a couple minutes with him, if he comes back on the phone."

THEY GOT BRETT BACK on the line, and after a little back-and-forth, the negotiator gave the phone to Del.

Del said, "Hey, Don, this is Del. Yeah, it's Del. I saw you at Einstein's a couple weeks ago, you were getting a bag of bagels, and we bullshitted for a while. Yeah, the Jewish chick. Yeah, yeah." He listened for a minute, and then said, "Listen, Don, I *know* you didn't do it. I *know* you didn't. We're looking for a guy, and it ain't you. Not only are we looking for him, the guy was shot in the arm yesterday, and if you don't have a bullet hole in your arm, you're good. And we're getting DNA from the blood from his bullet wound, and if it ain't your DNA, then it wasn't you. Yeah, yeah, hey, it was on TV. You been watching TV, haven't you? Yeah, it's been on TV."

After a moment, Del took the phone away from his ear and said, "He's talking to his old lady. She was watching TV."

He listened on the phone for another minute, then said, "They're not gonna shoot you. If you want, I'll come up there, and you can come out behind me. We already told the SWAT boss that you didn't do it. Yeah, yeah. We told him. He's right here. Who's that crying?"

Another few seconds, then, "Of course she's scared. She's probably scared shitless. No point in staying in there, nobody here's going away. Yeah, they'll take you downtown, look for bullet holes, probably make you give them a DNA sample. . . . You just take a little swab and swab the inside of your cheek. The cheek in your mouth. Yeah . . . well, yeah, they're a little pissed about the dog, but you'd be a little pissed, too, if a goddamn pit bull was biting your ass. . . . Wasn't all that funny, from our point of view. Huh? Okay. Yeah, I'll do that. I'll come down and knock."

★

CRUZ ASKED, "You want a vest?"

"Yeah, might as well," Del said. "If he shoots me, I trust you to plug him."

"Think there's a chance of that?" Cruz asked. "If there is—"

"Nah, he's not gonna shoot me," Del said.

"But take the vest," Lucas said.

"You want to come with me?" Del asked Lucas.

"Fuck no," Lucas said. "He might shoot both of us."

"I was planning to stand behind you," Del said.

"You guys slay me," Cruz said, no sign of a smile. "A laugh a minute."

SO DEL WENT DOWN to the white house, walked up the bank to the front steps, and up the steps and peered in the window, then pulled open an outer screen door, and they saw him talking, and then talking some more, and then he opened the front door and they saw Brett in the doorway. He was a large man with a black beard.

"He looks right," Cruz said.

"Yeah, he does," Lucas admitted. "But it's not him."

"I think it might be," Cruz said.

"He wouldn't be coming out if he had a bullet hole," Lucas said.

"We'll see," Cruz said.

Brett stepped out on the porch, Del said something, and he put his hands on top of his head, POW style, and Del backed away and Brett followed him. A SWAT guy came off the corner of the house, then another one, and a minute later, Brett was sitting on the lawn, his hands cuffed, and SWAT was inside the house.

Lucas asked Cruz, as they walked toward the house, "Can I ask him one question?"

"Okay with me, if it's okay with him."

Del was standing over Brett, and Lucas came up and asked, "You give him his rights?" He could hear a girl child crying from up in the house.

"Yeah, the SWAT guy did."

Lucas squatted next to the doper: "I got one question for you, about who might've told the cops that you were the shooter. The guy who ratted you out. It's gotta be somebody about fifty years old. Fat. Black hair, big black beard. Know anybody like that?"

Brett shook his head in exasperation: "Man, I'm a biker. Everybody's heavy and fat and got a black beard."

Lucas stood up and shook his head at Del. "He's . . . ah, fuck it."

Del asked Brett, "You got any kind of bullet hole in you?"

"No, man, I never been shot."

"They're gonna look at you downtown."

"Man, I keep telling you, I haven't been shot," Brett said. "They can take all the DNA they want, I'll jack off in a bottle, whatever they need."

A SWAT guy came out carrying the girl. She was maybe five, and still crying, and her mother came out behind her, and she was crying.

Brett said to the SWAT guy, "Look what you did."

Lucas said to Del, "Come on, let's go. This is bullshit."

"It's not bullshit," Cruz said. "We had a credible tip."

"It's bullshit," Lucas said.

ON THE WAY BACK to the car, Del said, "Made more friends in the MPD."

"Fuck 'em," Lucas said. "We got led around by the nose when the Jones girls were killed, and they're being led around by the nose now."

"What if you're wrong?"

"I'm not wrong. I'm pissed, and frustrated."

They drove back to the BCA, mostly in silence, and finally Lucas said, "I'll call Cruz this afternoon, and kiss and make up."

And a few minutes later, he added, "Fell knows Brett. Somehow he knows him. Maybe if we talked to Brett a little more—"

"He isn't the brightest bulb on the pole lamp," Del said. "He started out stupid and then started sniffing glue, so I wouldn't expect too much."

BACK AT THE BCA, he walked down to the office where Sandy, the researcher, worked. She was poking at a computer, looked up when Lucas loomed, and said, "It's impossible. I can't even give you a probability, because too many records are gone, and too many people took teacher training."

"How many names you got?"

"I haven't counted them—must be a couple of hundred. But the problem is, this is all before everything got computerized. Personal computers were brand-new, and a lot of stuff was still kept on paper. I can keep trying—"

"Ah, give it up," Lucas said. He turned away, then turned back. "Hey, a guy from Minneapolis, a former cop named Brian Hanson, apparently fell out of his boat up on Vermilion. Could you see if there are any news feeds?"

"Sure." She rattled some keys, and a news story popped up. "TV station out of Duluth," she said.

Lucas read over her shoulder: neighbors heard him arrive, heard the boat go out, very early in the morning. The boat, a Lund, was found turning circles in the lake just after dawn, the motor running. Another fisherman had hopped into the boat, found Hanson's hat, fishing rod, and open tackle box. No body had been found yet.

"Not uncommon," Sandy said. "He was peeing over the side, like all men do, and he fell in, and the boat motored away. The water's cold enough all year round, he dies of hypothermia, and sinks. Happens all the time."

"Yeah, but . . . He worked on the Jones case, and died the day after they found the bodies. It worries me that they haven't found *his* body."

"You think he might have faked his own death?"

Lucas scratched his head: "*That* hadn't occurred to me."

BACK IN HIS OFFICE, working more from simple momentum than anything like intelligence, he called the St. Louis County Sheriff's Office, got hooked up with the deputy who'd covered the accident, and got the names of the two fishermen who'd chased down the empty boat. The cop said there was nothing especially suspicious in the disappearance: "It happens. And when it does, there's nothing really to work with. A guy falls over the side, the boat drifts away, he sinks, and that's it. No signs of violence, no disturbance . . . nothing. He's just gone—but he'll be back. Give him about ten days, he'll come bobbing up."

Lucas called around until he found one of the fishermen, an assistant manager at a Target store in Virginia. The boat, he said, "had been chugging right along."

"How fast?" Lucas asked. "I mean, fast as you could walk?"

"Fast as you could jog," the guy said.

"Big boat? Nineteen, twenty?"

"Uh-uh. Sixteen. The cops towed it back in, no problem."

"How big was the engine?" Lucas asked.

"A forty."

"Life jacket in the boat?"

"Can't really . . . you know, I don't think there was."

Lucas thanked him and hung up. Thought about it for a second, said, "Ah," to nobody, picked up the phone again, and called Virgil Flowers, a BCA agent who worked mostly outstate. "Where are you?" he asked, when Virgil came up.

"Sitting in the Pope County Courthouse. That Doug Spencer deposition."

"Got a question for you," Lucas said. "You used to have a little Lund, right?"

"Yeah. It's all I could afford on my inadequate salary."

"We got a guy who apparently fell overboard while he was fishing out of a sixteen-footer," Lucas said. "His hat was found in the boat, two fishing rods and tackle box, so he wasn't taking a fish off. The boat was found running, about as fast as you could jog. No body. So why did he fall overboard?"

After a moment of silence, Virgil said, "He was moving around, for some reason, stepped on something like a net handle or the rod handle, and he slipped and the gunwale caught him in the back of the legs, below the knees and he fell over backwards."

"There was a theory that he was peeing off the boat."

"Not that boat, not with the motor running like that," Virgil said. "You couldn't pee over the motor, so you'd have to stand off to one side, and with the motor running, and all that weight in the back corner, it'd start turning doughnuts. If he was peeing off the side, he'd have peed all over himself. You're gonna pee, you kill the motor."

"But still, you could think of a way that he'd fall over."

221

"Sure. Boat bouncing around in the waves, you lose your balance—"

"No wind, flat lake."

Another pause. "Step on a net handle."

"That's all you got?"

"It's not all that easy to fall out of a boat," Virgil said. "For one thing, in a boat that size, if you're alone, you don't really walk around. Not if the motor's running. What would you be doing? You sit. Walleye fisherman?"

"That's what I'm told."

"So, there's just not much reason to move around," Virgil said. "I don't know, Lucas. It's sure not impossible, but it's not too likely, either. On the other hand, he could have had *three* fishing rods, was playing a fish, reached too far over to lift it out of the water, had a spell of vertigo, and went in. It's not that easy to fall out of a boat, but people do, all the time. For no good reason. How old was he? Could he have had a heart attack?"

"Thank you. Are you pulling your boat today?"

"Of course not. I'm on government business," Virgil said.

LUCAS HUNG UP and thought about it—whatever anybody might say about it, it was a peculiar death, and it came at a peculiar time. He called Del and said, "I'm going up to look at Hanson's cabin. Talk to his neighbors and so on."

"Why?"

"Because it's what I got," Lucas said. "It's all I got. I'm scratching around."

"What do you want me to do?"

"Think about it," Lucas said. "What we need is ideas . . . maybe you could go back and talk to Don Brett again. Figure out how Fell knows him. If you could figure that out . . ."

"We'd have him."

"Yeah. Exactly." Lucas looked at his watch. "I'm gonna run home and get a bag, and take off. See you tomorrow."

20

LUCAS GOT DIRECTIONS to Hanson's cabin from a deputy sheriff, who told him that the cabin was temporarily sealed "until we figure out for sure what happened to him. If he doesn't show up in the next week or so, we'll let the relatives in."

"I need to get in," Lucas said. "Can you guys fix it?"

"When are you coming up?"

"I'm on my way," Lucas said into his cell phone. "I'm just clearing the Cities . . . so probably three and a half hours."

"More like four. How you coming? You been here before?"

"Yeah. I'll take 35 to 33 to 53 and then up 169 into Tower," Lucas said.

"You want to stop at Peyla, that's a crossroads just short of Tower, where 169 hits Highway 1 and County Road 77. You want to turn left on 77 . . ."

Hanson, the deputy said, lived on a peninsula that stuck out into Lake Vermilion fifteen or twenty road miles north of Tower. Lucas took down the directions and said, "See you in three hours and a bit."

"More like four," the deputy said.

MORE LIKE FOUR; Lucas went a little deeper into the Porsche.

Thought about Marcy all the way up: couldn't get her out of his head. He'd be driving along, looking at cars or the landscape, and he'd get a flash of Marcy, something they'd lived through. The flashes were as clear and present as if he were still living them. He said a short prayer that he didn't outlive Weather, or any of his children.

Like most smart people, Lucas was able to stand back from himself, at least at times, to examine thoughts, motives, feelings. He knew that he was running out of control. He felt pointed toward Fell's death, however that had to happen: he wasn't sure that he'd be able to perfectly control himself when he came into Fell's presence. When he imagined a confrontation with Fell, he could feel his blood pressure rising, could feel the adrenaline kicking into his bloodstream, could feel the anger surging up to his throat.

He realized he was having a hard time recognizing that Marcy was gone, and there wasn't a damn thing he could do about it, and that killing Fell would not answer the problem he was having with her death, would not bring her back, and could have devastating consequences for himself and his family.

The little man at the back of his mind could whisper all of that to him: and yet, that realization had little effect on the urge for revenge.

HIGHWAY 77 WAS a two-lane blacktop through scrubby tamaracks around the edge of Vermilion, one of the major lakes of northern Minnesota. He called the deputy, whose name was Clark Childress, when he was fifteen minutes south of the crossroads, and Childress said, "Jeez, you made good time, then. See you out there. . . . I'm in Tower, I'll leave right now."

Childress either stopped to do something, or was a slow driver, because Lucas caught him right at the crossroads, saw the patrol car make the turn, and fell in behind him. They took 77 through several twists and turns, then onto a narrower blacktopped road, and finally onto a lane barely wider than the patrol car. Childress pulled into a yard beside an older garage, with a green clapboard cabin closer to the lake. A floating dock stuck into the lake, and a kayak was overturned and tied on top of the dock.

Lucas got out of the car at the same time Childress did, and the deputy said, "I thought, God almighty, that can't be a cop driving a Porsche. That explains the fast trip." Childress checked out the car, then said, "You got lights."

"Don't use them much, but they've been handy a time or two," Lucas said. "Took a little heat from the highway patrol a couple of years ago."

"Yup, those guys are your eager beavers when it comes to spirited driving," Childress said. Then he laughed, a short little bark, and said, "I heard that 'spirited driving' thing on that British car show."

"No sign of Hanson's body?" Lucas asked.

"Not yet. His daughter is at a motel down in Tower. I told her you were stopping by; she's gonna come over, too. She's interested in why you're interested."

Lucas nodded. "Okay. The fact is, I'm running down a thin thread on the killing of an old friend of mine in Minneapolis, a detective named Marcy Sherrill."

"Read about that," Childress said. "That's . . . pretty awful. You think it's connected here?"

"I don't know. Like I said, I'm running down a thread. Where's Hanson's boat?"

"Here, in the garage. I got the key." He jangled a ring of keys, and led the way to the garage door.

The garage was no more than an old weathered shed, just big enough to keep snow off the boat and a collection of lawn care equipment, including a riding mower and a rototiller. There were axes and hoes and weed whips, a big block of wood, a chain saw sitting on a shelf; and it all smelled pleasantly of gasoline, oil, and grass.

The boat was an ordinary, ten- or fifteen-year-old aluminum fishing boat, a Lund with a red stripe down the side, scratched up like most fishing boats, from banging into docks. It was small for the lake, but perfectly usable, especially for walleye fishing, which is mostly done sitting down. As Virgil had said, the motor was nothing you'd want to pee over, and the boat-bottom was curved enough that peeing over the side would also be fairly unsteady, especially with the motor running.

As he was looking at the boat, Lucas gave Childress a brief explanation of Hanson's connection to the Jones case. He concluded with, "We know that the Jones killer is still active, and that he killed Marcy. We know that Hanson died the day after the Jones girls' bodies were found."

"That's a pretty heavy coincidence," Childress said.

"Yes, it is. But it could be nothing but that," Lucas said.

THE BOAT HAD NOTHING for Lucas, except the feeling that falling out of that particular boat, on a quiet lake, would be stupid.

"He got any fishing buddies around here?" Lucas asked.

"Two guys . . ." Childress took a little paper notebook out of his pocket, thumbed it, and said, "A guy name Tony Cole and another guy named Bill Kushner. They're golfing buddies of his, and they fish together. Couple of older guys, like him. They live out here . . . down the way."

"Ex-cops?"

"I don't think so. I don't know about Kushner, except that he's retired. Cole used to work at UPS out of Duluth. He's retired, too."

"They think he fell out of the boat?"

"They think it's possible, but they don't know," Childress said.

"You know if they're up here?"

"Yeah, they are. I can take you around after we get done here," the deputy said.

"I appreciate that," Lucas said.

As he spoke, they heard the crunch of a car's tires on gravel, and Childress said, "That's probably Miz Sedakis, that's Hanson's daughter."

"He got any other kids?"

"Got a son. He was up here, I guess, I didn't meet him."

They walked outside, and found a fortyish woman getting out of a gunmetal-gray Lexus RX350; she was tall, and fleshy, with blond-tinted hair and oversized sunglasses.

"Clark," she said. And to Lucas, "You're Agent Davenport?"

"Yes." They shook hands, and she asked, "Why are you up here?"

He told her, succinctly, about Hanson's work on the Jones case, and then his disappearance the day after they were found. "It's probably a coincidence, but it's an odd coincidence. When we were doing the investigation, we had guys running all over the place, on the smallest pieces of information. On rumors. Anything. I wondered if maybe he talked to somebody, who might have remembered."

Sedakis's hand went to her throat: "You mean . . . you think somebody might have killed him?"

"I've got no reason to think that, except for the coincidence," Lucas said. "I thought I'd come up here, talk to some of his friends, see if he said anything to anyone."

"I certainly remember the Jones thing, even though I was young. I must've been in tenth grade," Sedakis said. "I remember he was working day and night. We used to talk about it. He never was sure that the street person did it. He said there was some other detective down there who thought the street person might have been framed, and I think he half believed that."

Lucas said, "That was me," and then thought, *I never saw that in Hanson: never saw any skepticism about Scrape.* And he asked, "Did he say anything about it after the bodies were found?"

"I hadn't talked to him for a couple of weeks before this accident. We live down in Farmington, and he was up in Golden Valley. Most of the time in the summer, he was up here. So . . . no. I guess 'no' is the answer."

"When did he go back to the Cities?" Lucas asked.

"He didn't actually keep us up to date on his travels. He was up here most of the summer."

"He went back the night before he disappeared," Childress said. "We got that from his golf buddies."

"So . . . he went down the night the Jones girls were found."

Childress nodded. "And turned around the next day."

LUCAS ASKED to see the house. Childress took them in, asked them not to touch anything. Hanson had inherited the place from his father, who'd bought four acres on the lakeshore when the buying was good, back in the fifties. They'd had a trailer on the spot for twenty years, with the lakeshore prices rising all the time, and finally sold three of the acres for enough to put up the two-bedroom log cabin.

The cabin was well-kept, with two upstairs loft bedrooms, for kids or guests, reached by a nearly vertical stairway, with another small bedroom tucked in the back of the first floor. There were two small bathrooms, both with showers, neither with a tub. The kitchen was separated from the living area by a breakfast bar; the living room featured leather furniture facing an oversized television, fishing photos, a desk in a corner with a computer, hooked to a satellite antenna.

"Nice place; he kept it well," Lucas said. He pointed at three bright red Stearns life jackets hung on pegs by the door. "Life jackets," he said.

Childress said, "Yeah."

"We had some happy times up here," Sedakis said. And added, "I guess," as if she weren't quite sure. Then, hastily, "I'm more of a city girl."

A row of family photos sat on the fireplace mantel, including a woman who looked like an older, heavier version of Sedakis, and a dark-haired boy holding a thirty-five-inch northern pike on an old-fashioned through-the-gills rope stringer. "That's Mom," Sedakis said, "and my brother, Darrell."

Darrell, Lucas thought, with a thump of his heart, looked like Fell.

"I think I met Darrell once, maybe ten years back. I bumped into your father and him, coming out of Cecil's, over in St. Paul. . . . Big guy, black beard?"

"No, no . . . Darrell's never had a beard, as far as I know. We're not close; he's ten years older than I am, but I see him a couple of times a year. He's . . . I don't think he can grow a beard, actually. He's one of those guys who's never done so good with a mustache, even. It comes out kind of scrawny."

Lucas nodded. "Probably not him, then."

They went back outside, Sedakis talking about her father's career and retirement. Lucas learned that he was in reasonably good physical condition, though he was still too heavy. "A friend of mine wondered whether he might have had a heart attack."

Sedakis shook her head: "My family doesn't have heart problems. It's usually kidneys that get us, or cancer."

They talked a bit longer, and when Lucas ran out of questions, she left, waving as she pulled out into the lane.

"Interesting," Childress said. "I never worked a murder. . . . You think it could be a murder?"

"I'll find out, sooner or later. Or his body will come bobbing up, with his fly down."

"They mostly do that," Childress said. "But sometimes, they don't. They just stay down there. Too cold to rot, no bacteria, so they bob around like corks, still wearing their glasses . . . like a Stephen King story."

"Jesus," Lucas said. "You writing a screenplay?"

*

HANSON'S FISHING PALS, Cole and Kushner, lived three or four miles away, on another peninsula, and only a few hundred yards from each other. Both of them were in, and Cole volunteered to walk down to Kushner's place and meet them there.

The two older men looked like the kind of plaid-shirted guys who'd be waved back and forth across the Canadian border without so much as a glance: white, balding, too heavy, too much sun, soft canvas shirts from Orvis, fishing-boat hats, and jeans.

Cole was the taller of the two, and said, "I understand why you're looking into it—I already told the police that Brian was supposed to be down in the Cities. He coulda come back at the last minute, I suppose, but we play golf in the morning, and he'd usually want to make sure he had a spot."

"A spot?"

"We play a sixteen-man scramble with a regular crew," Cole said. "If you want to play, you have to let us know the night before. Otherwise, one of the extras will get put in your place."

"It's four hours from the Cities," Lucas said. "The neighbors saw him pull in around three o'clock, which means he left there late. Maybe he didn't want to take a chance of waking you up."

"Maybe not," Kushner said. "But there's another problem. He hardly ever went out fishing early in the morning. He'd get up late, have about six cups of coffee and some oatmeal, and then head out to the golf course. We tee off at eleven, five days a week. Then, we'd have a few beers, and head home, and then two or three days a week, down toward dark, we'd head out on the lake, do some walleye fishing. But he hardly ever fished in the morning."

Childress jumped in: "But if he got up here too late to play golf, he might've just decided to hop in the boat. He'd know he wasn't playing the next day."

The two men looked at each other, then back at Childress and simultaneously shrugged. "It's possible," Cole said.

"Ever see him pee off the back of the boat?" Lucas asked.

"Does a bear shit in the woods?" Kushner replied.

"Over the motor."

Cole frowned. "Really can't do that. Have to pee off a corner. You trying to figure out why he fell out . . . if he did fall out?"

"The boat doesn't look like one where you'd want to pee over the sides, because of the slanted bottom," Lucas said. "And the motor was running, and that doesn't seem likely—"

"My theory is, he hooked up with something big, a big muskie or something, while he was trolling. Maybe he hooked a walleye and the muskie took it, and he stood up and was trying to land him, and the fish came off and he sorta staggered backwards and went over," Kushner said. "If he fell over."

"Wouldn't he kill the motor when he got the hit?" Lucas asked.

"I guess he normally would," Kushner admitted.

"*He wasn't trolling*," Cole said suddenly. He looked at his friend. "The boat was going *forward*."

"Oh . . . shoot. That's right." Kushner scratched his forehead. "Brian was a back troller. He worked it slow. If the boat was going forward . . ." He shook his head.

"Interesting," Lucas said. "There are three red life jackets hanging by the front door. Did he usually wear one?"

Cole said, "If it wasn't too hot, he would. Law says you gotta have one in the boat, and there are crick dicks all over the place. No offense."

"Thing is, there wasn't one in the boat, and if he was wearing one, you think we might've found him," Lucas said.

Kushner said, "Maybe. It's a big lake. And the way that boat was driving around by itself, we don't really know where he went over."

Cole added: "He wasn't wearing one. He only had three life jackets—couldn't hardly get more than three people in the boat, so that was what he had. Enough for me'n Kush, if we came over in the evening, to go out."

There wasn't much more; on the way out to the cars, Childress asked, "You got what you wanted?"

"I don't know," Lucas said. "Is there a good motel in town?"

"The casino's just down the road, that might be best," he said. "Give me a call if you need anything."

Childress took off, and Lucas called Del: "You think of anything?"

"I went over to Hanson's house and asked around. One of his neighbors thinks he saw Hanson leave his house around eight o'clock," Del said. "He left his lights on, and they were still on when the news got out that he'd fallen out of the boat. One guy, named Arriss, said he was about to go over and look in the windows and make sure he hadn't had a heart attack or something."

"So his lights were on . . . and he wound up here."

"That seems to be the case. You get anything?"

"Maybe," Lucas said.

THERE WAS STILL enough light that he could go back to Hanson's cabin, so he did that. There were close-in cabins on both sides of Hanson's place, and he walked across the side yard and up the steps to the place on the south, and knocked on the porch door. A woman came to the door, saw him standing there. A worried look crossed her face, and he got the impression that she was alone.

"Yes?"

He held up his ID and said, "I'm with the state Bureau of Criminal Apprehension. I was just here a while ago with a Deputy Childress?"

"Oh, okay, I guess I saw you over there." She came to the screen door. "What's up?"

"Did you see or hear Mr. Hanson the night he disappeared?"

"I talked to my husband, and we both thought we heard a car come in, late in the night. We were both asleep. The next morning, we saw his car parked there, and then, a while later, the police came in. But that's about it. We never saw him or anything. We were really shocked when we heard."

The neighbors on the other side were named Jansen, she said, and she'd seen them come in a half-hour before. "They'll probably be going out fishing, so if you want to talk to them, you should get over there."

Mark and Debbie Jansen were eating dinner when he knocked, and Mark Jansen invited him in and offered him a cup of coffee and a chair at the kitchen table, both of which Lucas took. They hadn't heard Hanson come in, nor had they heard the boat go out. They found out he was missing when the police came around.

"Guess they traced him from the bow number on the boat," Mark Jansen said.

They chatted for another few minutes, Lucas finished his coffee, took their recommendation that he spend the night at the casino, and left. He was getting in the car when Mark hustled across the lawn and called to him, "Hey—Lucas."

Lucas waited until he came up, and Jansen said, "Did you go in his garage?"

"Yeah. Looked at the boat," Lucas said.

"Is his dirt bike in there?"

"No, I don't remember seeing one."

"This might be nothing, but later that night . . . it wasn't three o'clock, it was more like five o'clock . . . just getting light, probably . . . I heard a bike start up," Jansen said. "Like, up on the road. And it took off. I didn't think of it until just now, and there are a lot of trail bikes and four-wheelers around here, but I don' t know why you'd be *starting* one right there. . . . If that's something."

Lucas said, "Huh," and, "Thanks. Something to think about."

THE REASON TO THINK about it, he thought to himself as he drove away, was that if somebody drove Hanson's car up to the lake, whether or not it was Hanson faking his own death, or a killer faking an accident, he'd have to have a way to get out, once he got in. If he didn't have an accomplice, and he couldn't use the car . . .

"Then he'd have to know about the bike before he got here," Lucas said aloud.

He passed the casino turnoff a few minutes later and kept going. Called Weather and said, "I'll be home tonight, late. Don't wait up, but don't shoot me, either."

"I wouldn't shoot you anyway," she said. "But I'll warn Letty."

232

21

DEL WALKED UP the sidewalk to Lucas's house, saw Shrake's Cadillac pull to the curb. He waited, hands thrust in the pockets of his jean jacket, until Shrake and Jenkins had caught up with him.

"What's going on?" Shrake asked, as he came up.

"I don't know," Del said. "Weather called, but I just talked to Lucas, and he's still three hours out."

"Let's find out," Jenkins said, leading the way to the door.

Weather let them in and said, "We need to talk in a hurry, before Letty gets back. I don't want her to see you."

"What's up?" Del asked.

"You want a beer? We've got Leinie's and Negra Modelo."

They took two Leinie's and a Negra Modelo, and she went and got them, and brought them back to the living room, where the three cops were still standing, looking uneasy. Weather wasn't exactly a friend, except that she was married to Lucas: she was a little too smart, a little too commanding, a little too tight.

In other words, a surgeon. She said, "Sit down, everyone. You look like you're getting ready to stampede."

When they were sitting, she said, "The thing is, Lucas is going to kill whoever it was that killed Marcy. About five minutes later, people will start talking about how he and Marcy had a relationship back when they were both working for Minneapolis. Some people will say that Lucas murdered this man, whoever he is—"

"I already sorta mentioned it to him," Del said. "He didn't want to talk about it."

"And you might be a little early on getting concerned," Jenkins said. "Nobody has any idea of who the killer is."

"You have any doubt that Lucas will find him?" Weather asked.

Shrake, Jenkins, and Del exchanged quick glances, and then Del said, "I wouldn't bet against him. And when I talked to him, I got the feeling he's got a sniff of the guy. Something's going on, I could hear it in his voice."

"I could, too," Weather said.

They all looked around, and took nervous hits on their beers, and Shrake finally said, "So what?"

"He's going to find the guy, and then he's going to kill him. Even if what he does is legitimate, he'll be in a lot of trouble," Weather said. "Somebody will come up with the fact that they had this relationship, and it'll get in the papers and on television, and then the politicians will get involved, and the prosecutors will be talking . . . And Lucas is so angry, I don't think he'll be careful enough. I'm afraid he's so angry that he'll simply walk up and plug him. That's what I'm saying."

Jenkins shook his head. "He's too smart to do that out in public."

Weather interrupted: "But you see, it'd almost be better if he did it in public. But he can't. But if he does it where there are no witnesses but you cops, that's when all the speculation will begin. People will *imagine* what he did. . . ."

Shrake said, "Ah, shit . . . sorry."

Weather: "He feels terrible about the Jones girls, like he could have done more back then. And he thinks that letting this man go then probably got more girls killed. And now Marcy, and he sees it all going back to the beginning: he thinks it's his fault."

"That's nuts," Del said. "I worked with him on that case, and he was the only guy who *did* anything. Quentin Daniel was running the show, and Lucas freaked him out. He couldn't get Lucas into plainclothes fast enough. Lucas was the only guy who did *anything*."

"That's not the way Lucas thinks, though," Weather said. "And you know it. He blames himself when things go bad and he's involved—he thinks he should be able to control everything."

Del said, "Okay."

"What I wanted to talk about," Weather said, "is the possibility that you guys could kind of push him around. Make sure he's not there when this man is caught. Get him out of the way, somehow, so he never has a chance to kill the guy."

"So the guy can while away his old age playing checkers in Stillwater?" Jenkins asked.

"Oh, no. I don't particularly care if somebody kills him," Weather said. "I've got no problem with that at all. As long as it's not Lucas who does it. If somebody has to shoot the guy, I think one of you should do it. Or some other cop. If one of you shot him, especially Jenkins or Shrake, because you never worked with Marcy . . . I don't think anybody would question it, especially if the guy was carrying a gun."

"What if he isn't?" Jenkins asked.

"Let's not go there," Weather said. "But it would be convenient if he were."

Nobody said anything for a few seconds, taking it in, and then Shrake said, "We shouldn't talk about this anymore. The word 'conspiracy' comes to mind."

"Had to come out," Weather said. "We don't have to talk about what happens to this guy, because I'm just not worried about what happens to him. Thirty years in Stillwater would be okay with me. I'm concerned about Lucas."

"Ah, Jesus," Del said.

"You think I'm right, don't you?" Weather asked.

Del nodded, looked at Shrake and Jenkins, and they both nodded. Shrake said, "I figured that Lucas would waste the guy. The rest of it never occurred to me—the way it would look. You're right, there's gonna be a hell of a stink . . . if we don't do something."

JENKINS, SHRAKE, AND DEL were long gone by the time Lucas pulled into the driveway, their beer bottles trashed with the recycling. The house was quiet when he came in through the garage—he turned on the kitchen light, looked in the refrigerator, found a chicken salad sandwich left by the housekeeper, and a bottle of Leinie's. He sat down to eat in the breakfast nook, and heard bare feet coming down the stairs. A moment later, Letty stuck her head in the kitchen. "Hey."

"You're up late," he said.

"Yeah. Mom's cutting in the morning, so she went to bed at ten. Gotta be quiet when you go up."

"Okay. You know what she's doing?"

"Rhino, and then she's covering some burns," Letty said.

She watched him chew until he asked, "What?"

"Mom thinks you're onto something. You know who killed her?"

Lucas shook his head: "You might blab to Jennifer." Jennifer Carey worked for Channel Three, where Letty was an unofficial intern.

"Would not," Letty said. "Not unless you told me I could."

Lucas said, "All right. I've got a couple of ideas." He told her about Hanson's mysterious disappearance. "I'm thinking he knew the person who did it, and that person got worried and killed him."

"When are you going to find out?"

"Pretty soon," he said.

"So this is the time you gotta be really careful," Letty said. "If you're gonna take him out."

"You worry too much."

"You're right. And you're not worried enough."

HE SNUCK INTO BED, quiet and silent as a cat burglar, and then Weather said in the dark, "I hope your daughter gave you a good talking-to."

"Ah, yeah . . . she did."

"Good. I'm going to sleep now, so I don't cut off poor Mrs. Johnson's nose."

Rhino, Lucas thought, as he drifted away, for rhinoplasty. From the Greek *rhino* for nose, plus *plassein*, to shape. A nose job, in other words.

But he didn't dream of rhinos; he dreamed of the mysterious Fell.

I do not like thee, Dr. Fell . . .

WEATHER GOT UP at five-thirty, and Lucas at eight, early for him. He hadn't felt her go; he usually didn't. He stretched, yawned, did some push-ups and crunches, got cleaned up, got his gun, sat down in his den, and made a call.

Quentin Daniel picked up and in an old man's voice said, "What?"

"This is Davenport. I need to talk."

"That was a bad day," Daniel said. "That was about as bad a day as I've had since Carol died. On top of the Jones kids coming up—"

"That's what I need to talk about."

"When?"

"How about now?" Lucas suggested.

"You know where that Starbucks is, down the street from me?" Daniel asked.

"Sure."

"Meet you there in thirty minutes," Daniel said.

QUENTIN DANIEL HAD BEEN a ranking detective when Lucas first met him, and later, for eight years, the chief of police. He'd done some bad things in his time, and he knew it, as did Lucas, and they'd never been quite square since.

But Daniel was smart and had been a good investigator, and knew the Jones case and also knew his cops. That, in fact, had been his most serious strength: he knew his investigators so well that he'd match them to cases that he knew would catch their imaginations, and they'd work all the harder for it. He'd also had complete confidence in his own intelligence, and other smart cops didn't intimidate him. He saw the intelligence of others as simply another weapon in his arsenal.

Lucas had been his finest weapon.

Lucas crossed the street to the Starbucks just as Daniel opened the door to go inside. He'd always been a bigger man, but now had thinned down; his hair was longer, and silvery gray, and he was dressed for golf in a red shirt and white slacks, with athletic shoes. He must be in his middle seventies, Lucas thought.

He held the door for Lucas, said, "You're looking rich," and Lucas asked, "What's your handicap now?" Daniel said, "Same as always: my swing."

Inside, Daniel ordered a skinny half-caff no-foam latte and Lucas got a bottle of orange juice from the cooler. "Get a table while I'm waiting," Daniel said.

Lucas found a table in the corner, and when Daniel came over, asked, "How've you been?"

"I've lost twenty pounds and gotten my cholesterol lower than my IQ. Of course, I'm eating nothing but twigs."

They chatted for a minute, and Daniel asked about Lucas's kids, and Lucas filled him in, and then Lucas said, "You remember, way back when, on the Jones case, I was running after a guy named Fell?"

"I remember you were running after a guy," Daniel said. "There was something unusual about him."

Lucas filled him in and Daniel started nodding. "I got it now," he said. Then Lucas told him about the weird death of Brian Hanson, and the timing, and his thoughts about the possibility that somebody on the force had been talking to the killer.

"So what I want to ask you—you knew these people better than anyone—do you know anyone that Hanson might have been talking to? Did you ever have any feeling that he was worried about it, that there was anything going on there?"

Daniel took a sip of his coffee, then leaned back and closed his eyes, silent for so long that Lucas thought he might be into a serious senior moment; then he opened his eyes and said, "Hanson had some kind of a family problem. Something criminal, and it involved sex. Not here, though—not in Minneapolis. I remember hearing that he was maneuvering around, trying to get something done, and I had somebody tell him to take it easy. You know, unofficially. Be careful about asking for favors."

Lucas said, "Really."

"You're not surprised."

"There are some indications, if you have a suspicious mind, that suggest the killer was close to Hanson. I saw a picture of his kid, when the kid was still young, a teenager, and he sort of looks like the description of Fell, except that he wasn't fat. And the guy who shot Marcy had a black beard—and I've been told that Hanson's son can't grow a beard."

"Maybe if you were planning to gun somebody down in a quiet neighborhood, where it'd get noticed, you'd want to invest two dollars in a disguise," Daniel said.

"Could happen," Lucas said. "Do you remember anything else at all?"

Daniel leaned back, looked out the window for a minute—a young mom pushing a stroller, looking satisfied with herself—and took a hit on his coffee. Turning back to Lucas, he said, "You know, I don't. It was something serious, but not for us. Brian fixed it somehow—talked to some pals, got a lawyer. Never had any hint that his kid might have been involved in the Jones case. I think Brian would have told us, if he thought that. But if *you* think Hanson's death might be involved, I'd take a look at the kid."

"That's the biggest hint we've gotten so far," Lucas said.

"And that's all I got for you," Daniel said. "I wish I had more. Marcy being killed . . . goddamnit, I can't get it off my back. I didn't know her long, before I retired, but she was a comer. I keep thinking about her. I keep seeing her."

Lucas nodded: "So do I. I keep wanting to call her up, tell her some stuff."

LUCAS DROVE BACK to the BCA and found Sandy. She was wearing one of her long light hippie dresses, and a pair of round sunglasses that she thought made her look like Yoko Ono or somebody, but actually made her look like one of the three blind mice. He told her what he needed, and in one minute, she'd found Hanson's kid's driver's license information, including his current address, in a nice neighborhood in St. Paul. In two minutes, they'd downloaded his driver's license photo. They printed it; he told Sandy he needed everything they could get on him, and headed back to his car.

His cell phone rang as he was getting in: Sandy. "I dug through the records. He's got a Chevy van, white in color."

"Ah, jeez . . . *Sandy!*"

DORCAS RYAN, the onetime massage parlor hooker, worked the second shift, so she should be home, he thought. Twenty minutes later, he parked in front her house, and through the kitchen window, saw her looking out at him.

He walked up the sidewalk; she was opening the door as he came up. He didn't go inside: he simply handed her the digital copy of Hanson's driver's license photo, without saying a word. She took it, peered at it, said, "Just a minute," retreated back inside, returned with a pair of reading glasses, put them on her nose, and looked again at the picture.

She said, "Ah. It's been a long time."

"The kid . . . is that Fell?"

"It could be," Ryan said. "If I were in a court, and they asked me to swear to it, I don't think I could. I could say it could be. But it's been a long time."

"Don't tell anybody about this. If he's the killer, we want to snap him up."

"Who would I tell?" Ryan asked.

"Anybody," Lucas said. "You tell a friend, and she tells somebody else, and they call Channel Three . . . there you are."

"Won't tell a soul," Ryan said. "Not until I hear he's dead."

"He might not be dead—"

She snorted. "A cop killer, is what I hear on TV. A lady-cop killer. What are his chances?"

Lucas walked away, thinking, *Everybody thinks we're gonna kill Fell.* He remembered Letty's warning: gotta be cool.

AFTER LEAVING RYAN, he headed back toward the BCA, got on his cell phone as he drove, and called Del. Del had just gotten up, was eating breakfast. "I got a break," he said.

"I thought something was up," Del said. "I told Shrake and Jenkins to hang loose."

"See you at the office," Lucas said.

He started by pulling all of Hanson's DMV information. At the time of the Jones killings, he had been twenty-seven. Just right, Lucas thought. He ran the information through the NCIC and came up empty: Hanson had no criminal record.

Del showed up, and Lucas told him about Hanson. "If he's the one . . . you think he killed his old man? I mean, Jesus."

"If he's the one, he's a fruitcake. A psycho," Lucas said. "His old man was a cop, and Daniel says, knowing Hanson, if he smelled it on his kid, he'd have let us know. And the kid might have known that. This was a guy who set up that whole Dr. Fell routine . . . he's a planner."

Sandy came in. "Hanson went to the University of Minnesota, here in the Cities. Got a degree in horticultural science. Last job I can find was at a place called Clean Genes, whatever that means."

"Not quite right," Del said.

Lucas said to Del, "Did I tell you he drives a white van?"

"That's something," Del said to Lucas.

"Nothing to say horticultural scientists can't read nursery rhymes," Lucas said.

LUCAS ASKED SANDY, "How'd you do this? Some kind of weird computer shit?"

"I looked him up on Facebook," Sandy said. "His Facebook page says he graduated from the U, and I took a quick peek at his records—don't tell anybody about that. He did pretty well."

DEL ASKED, "What are we doing?"

"I want to look in Hanson's house," Lucas said. "Brian Hanson's. See what I can see. See if there's anything that would point us at the kid."

"St. Louis Park's been inside of it, when the deputies called from up north," Del said. "We could give them a call."

Lucas called St. Louis Park, talked to a Lieutenant Carl Wright. "I think we can get you in—I'd have to check with the chief," Wright said. "Part of the investigation into his disappearance?"

"That's exactly what it is," Lucas said. "When you went in the first time, did you move stuff around, or just walk through?"

"Walked through—for all we knew, he'd be coming back, so we didn't disturb anything."

"Excellent," Lucas said. "We'll start your way. If there's a problem, give me a call on my cell phone. Also, I don't want the relatives to know about this, if they get in touch with you."

"Why's that?"

"Tell you when we get there," Lucas said.

On the way out the door, Lucas said to Del, "Let's take your car. It's a little less conspicuous."

"Why can't we be conspicuous?"

"I might want to cruise Darrell Hanson's house on the way back. See if he's around."

★

ST. LOUIS PARK was a few minutes west of Minneapolis, and a half-hour after they left the BCA, they pulled into the redbrick police station, found Wright, who said they'd been cleared to walk through Hanson's house. "I'll be coming with you, to keep everything kosher."

"Fine," Lucas said.

"So what's this about the relatives?"

"There's at least the outside possibility that one of the relatives could be a guy we're interested in. . . ." He gave Wright a quick summary, without mentioning Marcy, and Wright said, "You know, if this is a criminal investigation, maybe we ought to get a warrant."

"We're not investigating Brian Hanson for anything, other than to find out how he died," Lucas said. "We're not searching for anything—we're just looking for signs that he expected to come back to his house."

"And it's better not to ask if it's okay," Del said. "We can always apologize later."

"That's true," Wright said. "All right. I can live with that. Let's go."

HANSON HAD LIVED in a fifties bungalow, on a tree-shaded side street not far from the station. The guy next door was trimming his hedge, and stopped when they got out of their cars—Wright was driving a patrol car—and asked, "No sign of him yet?"

"Not yet," Wright said.

"You see anybody checking around?" Del asked.

"It's been quiet," the neighbor said. "And we been kinda keeping an eye out."

Wright had a key. He explained that they used a locksmith to open the door the first time, and found the key on a hook in the kitchen. When Wright opened the door, they could smell the lack of activity: the house felt shut up, and still. And they could smell cigarette smoke.

"Guy's still smoking. Must be nuts, his age," Del said.

"Gonna kill him, for sure," Lucas said.

They walked through the house, moving quickly. Del stopped once to pop open the washer and drier. Both were empty.

"He'd been home for a few days," Lucas said.

In the bathroom, they found a dopp kit with a razor, shaving cream, toothbrush and toothpaste, and miscellaneous—antiseptic cream, SPF-30 face lotion, a tube of Preparation H, nose-hair scissors, Band-Aids. "There's a clue for you," Del said. "Did he have another kit up north?"

"No, he didn't," Lucas said. "The bathroom was empty. There was no suitcase, but that doesn't mean much, if he kept clothes in both places."

"Wonder why he didn't keep a kit in both places?" Wright asked.

"Because then you're never sure of what you've got," Lucas said. "I do the same thing with my cabin—I keep clothes there, but I take the dopp kit back and forth. And shoes . . ."

They found a pair of athletic shoes at the end of the bed. They were scuffed and dirty. "There's your fishing shoes," Lucas said.

Del said, "Speaking as a defense attorney, I can say that you're building a fairy tale."

In the kitchen, they found a carton of Marlboros sitting on the counter, one pack missing. "There you go," Lucas said. "He was coming back. At six bucks a pack, he wasn't going to leave those behind."

"I'll buy that," Del said.

"I gotta think about it," Wright said. "But I'm moving your way."

BACK IN THE CAR, Del said, "It looks almost too good."

"Let's take a look at Darrell's place," Lucas suggested.

Darrell Hanson lived in a well-preserved three-story Victorian across the street from Lake Como. A guy in a painter's white shirt and trousers was standing on a stepladder, painting the eaves a teal green.

They were parked on a narrow one-way lane, two doors down from Hanson's house, and Lucas looked around and said, "If you showed up at the right time of day . . . that side door."

Del said, "You're not thinking about bagging the place? Man, that's a *really* bad idea. This whole neighborhood is gonna be full of security—we could be on a camera right now."

"Come in from the back—"

"Aw, bullshit. That'd probably be *worse*."

Lucas took a long breath and let it out: "I'd like to bag it. See what

I could see. But I'm also thinking that Dwayne Paulson might give us a delayed report, if he thinks we got enough on Hanson."

"Maybe we got enough. Maybe. A half-ass photo ID, the white van . . ."

"When I make application, the photo ID could be 'probably.' I could get a 'probably' out of Kelly Barker."

"That's sorta . . . borderline, dude."

"Don't get all lawyer on me," Lucas said. "Look: we know Darrell's father disappeared from his house, leaving the lights on, his cigarettes out, and all the rest. We know that Hanson's death was faked, if it was faked, by somebody who knew about the cabin, how to get in and out, and about the motorbike. Had to know about the old man's habits. Had to know about the dirt bike so they could count on stealing it. So if he was killed, it was probably by somebody who knows him."

"And we thought we knew he was a schoolteacher, but it turns out he wasn't."

Lucas went on: "He was the right age—"

"I agree, he's probably the one," Del said. "I'm just saying, a lot of the stuff might not cut much ice with a judge. And why go to Paulson? We could just go to Carsonet."

Lucas said, "Because Paulson got divorced about five years ago, and he and Marcy went out for a while."

"Ah. That would help," Del said. "Still don't have any hard evidence."

"And once we go for a warrant, we're committed," Lucas said.

They thought about that for a minute, then Del said, "If you bag it, you gotta talk to me. I don't want you doing it alone."

"Then, if I get caught, two of us go down," Lucas said.

"So let's go talk to Paulson."

"I'm afraid he'll say no."

"So *then* we bag it," Del said. "Can't be in any more trouble, if we get caught."

Lucas put his head down and thought about it. If he black-bagged the house, he could only be inside for a few minutes. If he got caught, his career was done: and he might be looking at jail time. A lot of security around . . .

"All right," he said. "Let's go see Paulson. We can tell him what we've got, ask him if he'll give us a delayed report. We ask him before he makes application."

"Be right up front with him."

"He's no dummy," Lucas said. "If we try to bullshit him, we'll only piss him off."

THEY WENT BACK to the BCA to pick up some paperwork, and then Lucas talked to Paulson's clerk to make sure the judge would be around. Told that he had a relaxed schedule that morning, Lucas signed up for an appointment and he and Del headed for Minneapolis.

Paulson's chambers were on the eighteenth floor of the Hennepin County Courthouse. When his clerk ushered Lucas and Del into the office, they found Paulson with his feet up on his desk, picking on an electric guitar, listening to himself on earphones plugged into a tiny amp. He saw them, tipped his head toward two visitors' chairs, continued picking for another ten seconds, then shut down the guitar.

"I coulda been a Rolling Stone," he said. He was a tall man, with slicked-back hair, a long nose, and a thin white smile. He could have been a country singer, but probably not a Rolling Stone.

"And if you'd been a judge at the same time, you coulda sent yourself to prison for drug abuse," Del said.

"How are you, Del?" Paulson asked. To Lucas: "It's bad, ain't it?"

"It is. I've got to tell you, we're here to ask your advice about a search warrant, and it involves Marcy's murder."

"Uh-oh," Paulson said, dropping his feet to the floor. "Let's hear it."

Lucas explained what they had, and what they'd be looking for if they got a search warrant, and why they weren't yet applying: "We know it's a little thin, but we think the totality of the evidence should get us in. But if you don't think so, we don't want the application made official."

"And you came to me because you knew it was thin, and you also knew that Marcy and I dated for a while."

"That was a factor," Lucas said. "I won't bullshit you, Dwayne: we do think we've got enough, but we know we're on the edge."

"Give me one minute to think," Paulson said. He turned in his desk chair so that his back was to them, and tilted his head back. They looked at his small bald spot for a minute, then two, and finally he turned back and said, "This guy just walked into that house down in Bloomington and opened fire, with no warning."

"That's right."

"It sounds like he's an absolute danger to himself and others. He may be undergoing a psychotic break."

"Absolutely," Del said.

"I wouldn't give it to you without that. Make a note of that in your app, and I'll give it to you."

Lucas took the paperwork from his pocket: "I left space for additional notes," he said.

THEY LEFT with the warrant in their pockets, and Lucas said, "The more I've thought about it, the surer I am. No big thing pointing to him, but a lot of little ones. And he's a planner. He's not the kind of guy to leave big clues hanging around."

Back at the BCA, Lucas called John Simon, the director, and told him what was happening. Simon had almost no control over Lucas's unit, and resented it, but lived with it. "Just take it easy. I don't want a bunch of dead people," he said. "I don't want *any* dead people."

22

LUCAS, DEL, JENKINS, Shrake, and two crime-scene techs, Norman Johnson and Delores Schmidt, went into Hanson's house a little after three o'clock in the afternoon.

The place was empty, but lived-in: it smelled like good cooking, there were two dozen plants on the ground floor alone, and more on the stairway and through the second floor, where the bedrooms were. They were well watered and healthy, and the refrigerator was full of fresh food. A two-car garage faced the alley in back, but was empty.

"I was hoping we'd find a dirt bike," Lucas said.

They began pulling the place apart, starting in the bedrooms and the basement, where people tended to hide things. Schmidt, a computer specialist, went to work on a PC found in the den, and a laptop that was sitting in the kitchen. Using specialist software, she pulled up both passwords in a matter of minutes and began probing the files in the two machines.

"Look for porn," Lucas told her. "Image files."

The going was slow: two hours after they arrived, they hadn't turned up anything decisive, although Lucas found two file boxes full of photographs, and Schmidt found more on the computers—dozens of them included Darrell Hanson. Some of the photos looked exactly like Kelly Barker's Identi-Kit construction; others did not.

Then Hanson arrived home, driving the white van, a little after six o'clock. Shrake went out to meet him, and Lucas focused on him like a cat on a mouse, his breathing deepening, his eyes dilating. Wanted to smash him—

"He look like the guy?" Jenkins asked. Jenkins was standing shoulder-to-shoulder with Lucas as they looked out the back.

"Yeah," Lucas said. "He does."

Hanson had a screaming fit, and Lucas watched him have it, stalking around the room, staying one layer of cops away from him, watching him talk to Del and Shrake, Jenkins always at Lucas's elbow. Hanson was a short, dark-haired man, thick through the chest, with a sallow face and heavy black hair. Del slowed him down, but didn't calm him down: Hanson called an attorney, who lived a few minutes away, and twenty minutes after he arrived home, the attorney, a fleshy, sandy-haired man in a light blue suit, walked in.

Hanson showed the attorney the warrant that Lucas had served on him, and the attorney told him to sit down and shut up, and told Lucas to direct all questions to him, not to Hanson.

Lucas said, "That's fine. We may have some questions later."

Hanson said, "I want to know what's going on."

The attorney put a finger across his lips, but Lucas said, "I could give a speech, which doesn't include any questions."

The attorney scratched his neck, said to Hanson, "If you want to hear the speech, that's okay. Do not respond."

At that moment, Del came in, crooked his finger at Lucas. Lucas followed him through to the kitchen, out of earshot of the attorney and Hanson, and Del said, quietly, "We may have a problem."

"Yeah?"

"I just looked at the white van," Del said. "It's a white van, all right, but both sides and the back are covered with large red roses. He works with some kind of flower farm place, wholesaling flowers. The people who talked to Bloomington, who'd seen the van, didn't say anything about any roses. It'd be the first thing you noticed."

"Man . . . I think it's him," Lucas said. "He looks right."

"I don't know. I got a bad feeling," Del said. "I think we screwed the pooch."

"I'm gonna make a speech," Lucas said.

LUCAS MADE A SPEECH. They had reason to believe that Hanson's father had been murdered, had not fallen out of the boat and drowned. Evidence pointed to somebody who knew him well. The same person was believed to have killed a Minneapolis police officer and two other people, and the description fit Hanson. He said, "The whole issue can be solved with a DNA test. We have blood from the shooter, and the DNA processing is being finished this afternoon. Is probably done now. We do not have permission to take DNA from Mr. Hanson, at this point, but we will get it, unless he voluntarily wants to give it up."

"No," said the attorney, whose name was Jim.

"Wait, wait," Hanson said. "It'd clear me?"

"Yes," Lucas said.

"I'm telling you not to do it, Darrell," the attorney said.

"Jim, I know about DNA," Hanson said. "It'll clear me. It's not my blood. In fact, they don't even have to take any from me."

"Darrell, we need to spend a lot more time talking this through before we start volunteering anything," the attorney said. "We need to get a criminal attorney in here. I'm not really that hot on criminal law."

"You're doing fine," Hanson said. But he turned to Lucas and said, "Two years ago, I went to Iraq with a civilian contractor called Wetland Restorations from Caplan, Missouri. We were there to consult on some marshlands at the southern end of the country, that they were trying to restore. Anyway, before we went, they did DNA on all of us, you know, in case we got blown up. Wetland has a DNA file on me."

A TINTED-BLOND WOMAN in her forties came through the door carrying a Macy's shopping bag and wearing a look of shock: Carol Hanson, Darrell's wife, who, like Darrell, exploded at the cops, then began weeping.

Lucas went out back, while Del and Shrake tried to calm things down, and called the head of the BCA's DNA lab, told him about the file at Wetland. He agreed to go back downtown, make some calls, try to get the file. "We got the file on the blood from the Bloomington shooting. If we can get a legit file from this place, we could tell you pretty quickly if there's a match."

Lucas went back to the search: the woman, Mrs. Hanson, had gone into the family room and was lying on a couch, with Shrake sitting across from her, talking to her. Didn't want anyone to have a heart attack.

An hour after Lucas had talked to the man at the DNA lab, Hanson took a call, listened for a minute, then said, "Yes. You have my permission. Give it to them."

To Lucas, he said, "They're sending the DNA file to your lab. They'll have it in one minute."

"Aw, Darrell, that's . . . I can't be responsible for that decision," the attorney said. "We gotta get somebody else in here."

Lucas said, "Hey, if he didn't do it, we don't want to try to pin it on him. He's got me about sixty percent believing him now. We're gonna need another DNA sample, to be sure there isn't something tricky going on—"

"I'll do it," Hanson said.

His wife had moved into the front room with him, and cried, "They completely tore apart our bedroom. It's torn apart." She started weeping again.

Another hour passed. They'd almost finished with the house, and Lucas called the DNA lab, was told that the computer was still running the comparison: "Almost there," he was told. "The other file was good, and has Hanson's name and Social Security number right on the file. I don't think anyone's trying to pull a fast one, but we'll need to double-check."

"Call me," Lucas said.

"Twenty minutes."

Lucas sat on a living room chair, and Hanson started going through the "never been arrested routine" that Lucas had heard fifty times from people who'd just been arrested, some of them for murder. "Honest to God, I have never, ever . . ."

THE LAB DIRECTOR, whose name was Gerald Taski, called.

He said, "You're not gonna believe it. You're not going to believe it, that's all I can say. This is so weird, I only ever heard of one other case like it, out in LA. . . ."

"Well, tell me," Lucas said.

"It's definitely not him," Taski said. "You got the wrong guy."

"That's not good, but it's not weird," Lucas said. "What's weird?"

"Your guy knows the killer."

"*What?*" Lucas turned around and stared at Hanson, who flinched.

"He might not *know* he knows the killer, but the killer is very closely related to him," Taski said. "Not more than a few generations removed. They probably shared a grandfather. Maybe a great-grandfather, but I don't think it's that far back. We need more analysis."

Lucas listened for another minute, with Hanson, the attorney, and the other cops all watching him, then hung up and said, "Unless there's some kind of really unusual bullshit going on, you're clear."

"*I told you,*" Hanson said, and his wife started weeping again, and half shouted, "You ruined our house."

Lucas waved them down: "But—you're closely related to the killer."

Now it was Hanson's turn: "*What?*"

"You probably share a grandfather," Lucas said. "Who would it be?"

Hanson looked at his wife, then at the floor, and then his wife muttered something that Hanson didn't catch, and he looked around and said, "Oh, good Lord."

"Who is it?" Lucas asked.

"We're a big family," Hanson said. "I must have twenty cousins. That's what we're talking about, right? Cousins?"

"I guess so," Lucas said. "Cousins, but it could be uncles, or second cousins, I guess."

Hanson said, "I've got a cousin named Roger. Roger Hanson. If it's somebody, I'd say it was him."

"Did he know your father's cabin?" Del asked.

"Sure. But, most of the cousins did. It was like a family place."

"And he knew your father pretty well," Lucas said.

"Yes. But it's the same thing—everybody knows everybody. All the cousins. We all get together on the Fourth of July, and at Christmas."

"So why do you think it's Roger?" Lucas asked.

Hanson looked at his wife, and finally she said, "Because he's strange. In a bad way. He's angry and mean and he can be scary."

They talked for another twenty minutes: it became apparent that several cousins probably fit the description of John Fell, and were in the right age range. They said Roger Hanson had never taught school, as far as they knew. They didn't know anything about Brian Hanson cleaning up a legal mess made by one of the cousins.

"Does he have a white van?" Lucas asked.

Hanson ticked a finger at him: "I haven't seen him in a couple of years—but he's an antique dealer, a junk dealer, really, and he's always had a van."

Lucas told the other cops to pack up, and apologized to the Hansons for the mistake. "I'm sorry about it, but you have to understand, given what's happened, that it was worth it from my point of view. At this point, all we have to do is figure out which cousin is a cold-blooded murderer."

He added that they should not talk to anyone about the night's developments: "The last time somebody got under his skin, he went to

251

her house and shot three people, and killed one of them. So, stay quiet, and we'll clear this up. But stay quiet."

OUT IN THE CAR, Del said, "I been in a lot of clusterfucks, but nothing that ever ended like that."

"Not a clusterfuck," Lucas said. "One way or another, we broke the case." He got on his cell phone, caught the researcher, Sandy, as she was about to eat dinner. "Can you get back into the office pretty quick? It's kind of an emergency."

She could, she said: "I'm having pancakes. I can be down there in twenty minutes. What do you need?"

He gave her Roger Hanson's name, address, and phone number, which he'd gotten from Darrell Hanson, and told her to get everything she could find on him. "Are you coming in?"

"In a bit," he said.

"WHERE ARE WE GOING?" Del asked.

"I want to take a look at Roger's house. It's up on the northeast."

Roger Hanson lived in the prewar Logan Park neighborhood in northeast Minneapolis, on a street lined with shade trees and parked cars and pickups. His house was a modified bungalow with a narrow front porch, up three steps. Hedges ran down both sides of the house, separating it from the adjacent houses; a narrow, much-cracked driveway ran down one side of the house, to a one-car garage in back.

Nothing was moving around it: a car was parked out front, there was no other car in sight, no white vans on the street. There *was* that garage, and there could be a van inside.

"I could go knock, see if he comes to the door," Del said. "If he was hit, I might be able to tell."

"If he's hit, he won't come to the door," Lucas said. "Why would he? To get his Girl Scout cookies?"

"No lights," Del said.

They drove twice around the block, slowly, and then parked at the end of the block, in front of a house with a "Sold" sign on it. With any luck, Del said, the owners had moved out and wouldn't see them sitting there.

Nobody apparently did, or at least nobody was curious: they sat for an hour, talked in a rambling way about a few current investigations, none of great importance, a few personalities around the office, and about Marcy. In that hour, there was no visible activity around Hanson's house—no moving drapes, nobody at a window.

"It feels empty," Del said.

"Could be at work," Lucas said. "Could have flown the coop. Could be down at the grocery store . . . we don' t know shit."

"One thing we know," Del said, "is that the picture-window drapes are open, and so are the drapes on that room in the back, and that's probably a bedroom. If they're closed later on, or tonight, we'll know somebody is home."

"Let's go," Lucas said. "Take a few more turns around the neighborhood. Get the lay of the land."

"You're not gonna bag it?"

"I'm thinking about it," Lucas said. "Time's passing, and word is gonna get out. Maybe not exactly what we've got, but that we've got *something*."

They watched the house for an hour, and then Sandy called, and Lucas put it on the car speakerphone. She said, "All right. He's got a white van, number one. Two, he went to school in Moorhead, which has a big teachers' college, and he was there for four years. I couldn't get at any personal records, but I did find out that he didn't graduate. I could get at the graduation records."

Del said, "He didn't graduate because he diddled an eighth-grader in his last year."

"I could find no reports of diddling," Sandy said. "Maybe there'd be something, if I could crack the individual records, but they're *very* well-protected. I'd need a subpoena for that."

Nothing had moved in Hanson's house, and they gave it up after Sandy's phone call. On the way back to the BCA, Lucas said, "Another reason for bagging it: say we get a warrant, go in there, and find some trophies—the Jones girls' panties, or whatever. Or his old man is stuffed in the freezer. Then what? If we didn't put out a general alert, we'd take an ocean of shit. If we find anything, that'd be the end of our hunt."

"So what? Then we got him."

Lucas patted his chest, and his voice was grim. "*I* want to get him. Me. Me."

THEY CAME to no conclusion about bagging Hanson's house, agreed to talk it over the next day, and headed home. Lucas was too late for dinner, but had a sandwich, and called Bob Hillestad from Minneapolis homicide at home. Minneapolis, Hillestad said, had gotten nowhere, and everybody was waiting for the BCA to finish running the DNA file against the data bank.

Later in the evening, Lucas read a couple of online financial blogs, killing time, and as Weather was getting ready for bed, he went out to the garage, lifted a step in the back stairs going up to the housekeeper's apartment, and took out his burglary tools—an electric lock rake, a ring of bump keys, a small crowbar, a pair of white cotton garden gloves, an LED headlamp. He checked the batteries in the rake, thought they might be a little weak, and replaced them with two new C cells from the workbench.

He put them in a black nylon briefcase and dropped them behind the front seat of his Lexus SUV. That done, he went back in the house, got a beer, stepped in the bedroom to say good night to Weather, then leaned in Letty's doorway and watched her working through Facebook.

"I know women need to build social networks because it's wired into their brains to do that, but what a fuckin' waste of time," he said. "You oughta learn to play guitar or something."

"I'm working," she said, without looking up.

"Working?" The skepticism was right there in his voice.

Now she looked up. "Yeah. Some big newspaper, like maybe the *New York Times* or the *Wall Street Journal* or the Washington one—"

"The *Post*."

"Yeah, one of those, they did a big story about online bullies on Facebook and how some girl, like, hung herself, and they've got me going out to all my Facebook friends looking for people who got bullied, so we can do a story on it."

"They" were her mentors at Channel Three.

"Hanged," Lucas said. "Not hung. People get hanged, other things get hung."

"You mean like, 'He hanged up on me,' or 'She was really hanged up on that guy'? Or 'Jeez, he is really well hanged'?"

"I mean by the neck. People get hanged by the neck until dead. Everything else is 'hung.'"

"So what are you doing hassling me?" Letty asked. "While I'm working?"

"Not hassling. Just came by to see if you needed anything at the store. I'm gonna go buy some of that Greek yogurt."

"You could get me some Coke. Maybe some Hostess Sno Balls."

"I think Sno Balls are made out of pork liver," Lucas said.

"That's really funny. I'm laughing myself sick," she said. "Get me the Coke. And the Greek yogurt with peaches."

"Talk to you tomorrow."

LUCAS FINISHED THE BEER, ostentatiously banged around in the kitchen, then went out and climbed in the Lexus and headed over to Hanson's place. He could feel the stress building as he rolled along, and the excitement. The fact was, he liked it, always had.

He cruised Hanson's place once, saw no lights, was able to see that the position of the drapes was the same. Screwed up his guts, cruised it again. On his second pass, headlights flicked on from a car parked at the end of the block. He turned the corner, and the car followed. He turned the corner and the car followed again, and flicked its high beams a couple of times.

Lucas pulled over, the car followed, and in his rearview mirror, he saw Del get out and walk up to his driver-side window. He rolled it down and Del said, "Letty says you're way too obvious."

"Ah, shit."

"So you gonna do it?" Del asked.

"I am," Lucas said. "I think you ought to stay away."

"I'll tell you what I'll do. I'm too young to go to prison for burglary, but I've got you on speed dial. If I see him coming, I'll ring you, and you get the fuck out the back. If you go out the back, you'll see that you can jump a hurricane fence in the backyard, and I'll pick you up around the block."

"What about this car?"

"I'll take it. We'll drop my car somewhere, I'll let you out in front of the house, then go around the block and park where I can see his driveway."

Lucas nodded. "Thanks."

They did that, and when Del took the wheel of the Lexus, he said, "Not that I'm happy about it."

"You don't have to do it."

"Yes, I do," Del said. "I got this vague memory of talking you out of chasing John Fell, way back when. Saying it was pointless. I wonder how many girls are dead because of it?"

"I've been sick about it," Lucas said, staring stolidly through the windshield. "But even if we'd identified him, what were we going to do with it? We had no bodies, we had no witnesses, we had a dead guy whose fingerprints were on that fuckin' box. . . ."

"Still . . ."

"Yeah. Still."

THEY CIRCLED the block one more time, checking houses with lights: the house across the street from Hanson's had lights, as did the one on the left. "If we're gonna do it, best not to circle again," Del said.

"Drop me off," Lucas said, and pulled on the gloves.

Lucas climbed out in front of the lights-out house, walked quickly down the sidewalk and then up the walk to Hanson's place, and rang the doorbell. Rang it again, did a quick check around, pulled out the rake, rang the doorbell again, and slipped the rake into the lock. The rake sounded like somebody shaking a tray of dinner forks: not hard, just shaking it a little. Lucas kept the turning pressure on the lock, and felt it go.

He took the knob, turned it, called, "Hey, Roger. You home?"

No answer. He stepped inside, pushed the door shut, and turned on the light. Burglary notes: if you're burglarizing a house, don't go through the door and leave the house dark, and look around with the flashlight. The neighbors will call the cops. On the other hand, turning on the light is absolutely normal.

Lucas called out again: "Hey, Hanson? Hey . . ."

Silence.

He started moving, going swiftly through the living room, through the kitchen to the back door. He unlocked it, cracked it open. Then back through the house, checking the three bedrooms. One had been turned into an office, one was filled with what looked like junk, the other held a bed. The bed was covered with twisted blankets, as though the sleeper had been struggling with them.

He spent three minutes in the bedroom, quickly pulling out drawers, checking through them, finding nothing interesting but a switchblade and, in another drawer, two ball bearings in a sock, the ball bearings the diameter of a fifty-cent piece. He'd seen similar things used as saps, but the ball bearings were so heavy that if you hit someone on the head with them, you'd kill them. Must be some other use he was unaware of . . . or maybe Hanson collected ball bearings.

In the bedroom closet, he found a stash of what looked like old printed pornography, in a stack four feet high. The magazines were cheaply printed, apparently in Asia, and featured girls who were too young.

Lucas thought, *Yes*.

And he flashed back to the porn he'd found in Scrape's box. This was similar, but a decade or two newer. The same genre.

They had him, and it was time to go, he thought.

HE DIDN'T GO. His appetite whetted by the discovery in the bedroom, he checked out the office, and found a jumbled mass of income tax returns. He flipped through the recent ones, found declared incomes of $30,000 to $40,000, and business cards identifying Roger Hanson as an antique dealer, which explained the junk in the bedroom.

He found a file full of bank statements: the most recent one showed a balance of $789; and a file of Visa statements, showing a balance of $4,560. Hanson was broke. He found a drawer full of bills, thumbed them, pulled out a cell phone bill from Verizon and shoved it in his pocket.

He found a fat file stuffed with homemade brochures from Thailand, printed on color laser printers, advertising sex tours; and offering teenage girls. He put it back in place.

Listened. Nothing. No call from Del, yet. Risk was building. Looked at his watch: he'd been inside for eight minutes; the max he'd wanted to risk was five, and he was already three over.

But two more minutes . . .

He hurried through the kitchen to the back door. He pulled it closed, locked it as it had been. Checked a closet, saw nothing of interest. Opened another door, saw a steep stairs going into the basement. Flipped on a light, took the stairs, quickly as he could: two rooms: one a utility room with a washer, drier, washtub, furnace, water heater, a top-opening freezer.

The other side was filled with more junk—old, but not antiques. Weather bought antiques, and the antiquing trips had given Lucas the rudiments of an eye. His eye told him that this stuff was junk.

Glance at his watch: ten minutes. Time to run. His phone rang: Del.

"Yeah?"

"Get out of there, man," Del said. "You been in there ten minutes."

"Somebody coming?"

"Not yet," Del said.

"I'm coming."

He started up the stairs, caught the flash of the freezer. He stepped back, pulled it open, saw a pile of white meat packages, like the kind butchers use to package venison, and some boxes of sweet corn, and a shoe.

His brain said, *What?*

He brushed several boxes aside, and saw Brian Hanson's frosted face and hair.

He thought, *Holy shit*. After a few seconds, he pushed the boxes of sweet corn back across the dead man's face, closed the freezer top, and ran up the stairs. Remembered to turn off the basement light and shut the door. Walked to the front door, touched the speed-dial button on his cell phone, and Del said, "What?"

"I'm coming out."

"Fifteen seconds."

Lucas turned off the light, stepped out on the porch, pulled the door shut, walked as casually as he could down to the public sidewalk. Del pulled into the curb, and Lucas climbed into the Lexus.

"NO SIGN OF HIM," Del said, as they pulled away. "No sign of anything. We're clean. But Jesus, you were in there a long time."

Lucas said, "Yeah."

In his mind's eye, Lucas could see Brian Hanson's frozen face. He'd never particularly liked Hanson—too old-style for Lucas—but he hadn't been a bad investigator.

They turned the corner and Del was saying something, and Lucas backtracked: he'd asked, "What'd you get?" and now was looking at Lucas a little oddly. He said, "You in there?"

"I found Brian Hanson dead in the freezer."

Del laughed, and then stopped laughing. "You shit me. I mean, you were joking, you said something about finding him in the freezer."

"I shit you not. The guy is down in the freezer in the basement, frozen stiff. He's got frost all over his face. Freaked me out. And there's a pile of kiddie porn, and a computer that's gotta have more stuff—I didn't look at it—and there's a file full of stuff from Thailand advertising young girls for sale. Del, you can't believe the shit in there. He's some kind of antique dealer, the place is full of junk. . . ."

He went on for a while, and Del finally said, "That's . . . insane."

"It's insane. That's exactly right. It's insane."

They pulled up behind Del's car, and Lucas stripped off the garden gloves and shoved them in his pocket, and put the rake back in the bag behind the seat, and Del said, "If he's really insane, he's gonna wind up spending life at St. Peter."

St. Peter was the Minnesota hospital for the criminally insane.

Lucas shrugged.

Del said, "Man, if you kill him—"

"I've already had that lecture," Lucas said. "Let it go."

They sat for a couple of minutes, and then Del said, "If we can get a warrant from anyone, we can go in there tomorrow, clean the place out. We'll have him in a few hours."

"Gotta think about it," Lucas said. "But what we've got to do for sure is get Shrake or Jenkins over here, to sit on the place overnight. If Hanson comes in, we've got to know about it—we don't want him hauling his uncle out of there and getting away with it."

"What else?"

"I got a Verizon bill from him, with his cell phone number. We need to get in touch with Verizon, find out where he's calling from. Probably need a subpoena."

"All of this is tomorrow," Del said. "Let's get Jenkins over here to sit on the house. Then tomorrow, we drop on him."

"Don't want him to go to St. Peter," Lucas said. "I want to settle this now."

Del looked at him, then said, "Don't bullshit me: you're not doing any more tonight."

Lucas shook his head: "No. I'm satisfied. We got him—now I've got to figure out a way to *get* him. I'm gonna stop at the store, then I'm heading home."

"The store?"

"I'm gonna get some Greek yogurt and a six-pack of Coke, so I'll have it in my hand when Letty jumps me," Lucas said. He grinned in the dark. "She's a piece of work. And turn off your cell, so she can't call you. I want her up all night, worrying about what happened."

"That's mean," Del said.

"That's life," Lucas said. "You mess with someone, you can't bitch too much when they return the favor. Even when it's your daughter."

23

LUCAS CRAWLED INTO bed and lay awake for an hour, trying to work out how they would take Roger Hanson. He thought they might have two days, before word got around that his team was working on something solid. After that, the law enforcement bureaucrats would get into it, trying to slice off a piece of the credit for breaking the case—and capturing the killer of a well-liked cop. When they got involved, it'd turn into a snake hunt, with cops all over the state beating the bushes, trying to drive Hanson into the open.

Lucas had a couple of huge advantages: he *knew* who the killer was, and he knew how to find him, through the cell phone. But to avoid curiosity about *how* he knew—about the black bag job—he needed to lay down a logical trail of deduction. He had some help on that from Darrell Hanson and his wife, who'd pointed the finger at Roger. A pointing finger wasn't enough to get a warrant, then go on to an arrest, but it was a start.

What he needed to do was to ostensibly take Darrell Hanson's suggestion, as any cop would, and build a case against Roger. He could get some way down that trail simply by redoing everything he'd done to build the case against Darrell.

Was Roger's white van really white, and not covered with roses or something? Did he teach school? Darrell didn't think he ever had, but he could be wrong.

And Lucas wondered where Hanson had gone. What if he'd taken off for Mexico, or Thailand? What if he were sitting in the airport at Seattle or Los Angeles, waiting for a plane that would take him into some foreign obscurity?

But he hadn't done that, Lucas thought. The house was not torn up in the way it would be if somebody were fleeing the country. It looked like a house that somebody was coming back to: all the underwear still in place in the bedroom bureau, a pile of dirty clothes sat in front of the washing machine, a stack of computer equipment was blinking into the dark, still running, a jar of coins was sitting on the kitchen counter. And with as little money as Hanson had, he would have cashed the coins.

So he was out there, somewhere close by.

He thought about that, then snuck out of the bedroom in his underwear, went down to the den, and called Shrake, who was babysitting the house. Shrake came up and Lucas asked, "Anything at all?"

"Nothing. I've been sitting here thinking. Buster Hill hit him with at least one shot. If that's right, and Hanson knows he can't go to a hospital, I suspect he's holed up somewhere, taking care of the wound.

Maybe didn't want to come back home, where people could see him and know that he was hurt. I don't think he'll come wandering in—but if he does, I think he'll stay."

"I was hoping that he wasn't in an airport somewhere."

"I thought about that, too," Shrake said. "If I was a wounded guy, I'm not sure I'd want to take a chance with airport security, having a bullet hole in me. If they felt a bandage, and wanted to look at it . . . they find a bullet wound. It'd be taking a big chance."

"Hmm." Lucas thought about it, looked at the clock: a little after one A.M. "Tell you what: we're gonna need people around tomorrow, I think, and I'm buying what you're saying. Why don't you sit until two, then go on home. We'll see you at work tomorrow morning."

"Jenkins was coming on at eight."

"I'll call him in the morning," Lucas said. "I'll have him check, and if Hanson isn't there yet, I'll pull him in, too."

"You think we'll find him tomorrow?"

"I'm gonna get Sandy checking the big cell phone companies tomorrow," Lucas said. "If we can find a cell, we'll get him."

He rang off, went to bed, and slept soundly until nine o'clock, which he hadn't expected. He woke, realized that he felt too good to be up early, looked at the clock, said, "Aw, man," picked up his cell phone and turned it on, called Jenkins.

"Just sitting here. Nothing moving."

"Give it another hour," Lucas said. "We're gonna look at it from a different angle."

"Want me to knock on the door, try to sell him a magazine subscription?"

"No." Lucas didn't want to tell him that he *knew* the house was empty. Then he said, "But let me think about it. I may call you back."

He thought about it as he shaved and showered, then called Jenkins and said, "Go up to the door, and if he's there, tell him you're investigating the disappearance of his uncle, Brian Hanson. Ask him the usual: last time he saw him, if he seemed depressed. Tell him you're asking on behalf of the St. Louis County Sheriff's Office. I don't think he'll be there, but knock on the front door, and then go around and knock on the back door."

"The back door . . . ?"

"Just to make sure you're not missing him. But that'll get you right back by the garage. The garage has four windows in the overhead door, and I think there's a side door—it looks like there should be. If you should glance inside the garage, just as a matter of walking around the house . . . and if you should see a dirt bike inside . . . I'd be really interested if there's a dirt bike. And if you could see the license tag . . ."

"I can do that," Jenkins said. "Call you back in ten."

"I'll be on my way into work," Lucas said. "I'll just see you there."

He preferred to have the team around when Jenkins reported back. More trail, that way.

LUCAS ATE a fast nonfat vegetarian breakfast—Trader Joe's corn flakes with rice milk—and headed into the BCA; made a quick, impulsive stop at a diner, ordered scrambled eggs with link sausage, and a cup of coffee, and it all tasted and smelled so good he thought he might faint. He ate fast, didn't feel the slightest bit guilty, and knew he'd never tell a soul. And on to the BCA.

Sandy was waiting, and he gave her the name and the list: cell phone first, motor vehicles, photos, background.

She went away, and Shrake came in, followed by Del. "What're we doing?"

"Hanging out until I can give you stuff to do—errands, nailing it down," Lucas said. "When we get enough, we'll go for a warrant. But before we do anything official, I want to know where he is, and be headed in that direction. The word's gonna start leaking that we're up to something."

Sandy came back: "You were right. That's his phone number, and he is with Verizon. We need a warrant to find out where his phone is coming from."

"A warrant? Or just a subpoena? We don't want to listen to him, we just want to know where he is."

She said, "I didn't split that hair. I've got the name of the guy we need to talk to at Verizon."

Lucas said to Del, "Call the guy, try to whittle him down to a subpoena, then talk to the lawyers."

Del nodded. Lucas said to Sandy, "Photos, next. Everything you can get in the next five minutes. Start with his driver's license."

She and Del left together, and Jenkins came in with a piece of paper in his hand. "I happened to look in the garage, and there was a dirt bike parked in there. I wrote the tag number on this piece of scrap paper."

"That was lucky," Lucas said. "Be sure you put the scrap paper in the file. Did you run it?"

"I did. The bike is registered to Brian Hanson."

Shrake said, "We got him."

"I think so," Lucas said. "Listen, Sandy'll have those photos in a minute. I've talked to three different women about them, and I want you guys to run them down, have them look at Roger's face."

He gave them phone numbers and addresses for Dorcas Ryan, Lucy Landry, and Kelly Barker. They took the information, and as they left, Lucas said, "Make it as fast as you can. Get the IDs, and get back here."

WITH EVERYBODY OCCUPIED, Lucas walked up to the DNA lab and talked to the head of the unit, Gerald Taski, who was still excited about the hit on Darrell Hanson's DNA. "This is the first time it's happened with us," Taski said. "But it opens up lots of possibilities. Say you get some DNA, and you think you know who the bad guy is, but you're not sure, and you don't want him to know that you're looking at him. So you go to some other family member for DNA—you know, as a volunteer or you compel it with some other arrest—and use that DNA to nail down the first guy."

"That makes me a little uncomfortable," Lucas said. "Sounds like something the Nazis would think of."

"But think of the efficiency," Taski said.

"That's what the Nazis would have thought of," Lucas said.

"There's a thing on the Net known as a corollary to Godwin's Law, which says that the first guy to mention Nazis in a discussion, loses," Taski said.

"I don't want to know about Nazis," Lucas said. "What I want from you is a piece of paper I can put in a warrant application that says the

DNA from Bloomington is X number of degrees away from the killer. Like three or four degrees, whatever it is."

"You think it'll help identify him?" Taski asked.

"It already has. We got him, we just need a warrant," Lucas said. "So . . . the piece of paper?"

SANDY CAME IN and said, "Moorhead wants a subpoena. The universities are pretty tight."

"Isn't Virgil over there somewhere? I think he just told me he was over there." He stuck his head out of his office and called to his secretary, "Hey—where's Virgil?"

"Pope County," she said.

"Isn't that close to Moorhead?"

She said, "Let me look at the map," and she went off to a wall map, then called back, "It's a ways, but right up I-94. Probably a hundred miles or so."

Lucas went to his cell phone, and got Virgil: "You still in Pope County?"

"Until I finish eating breakfast," Virgil said. "Then I'm heading home."

"You're not far from Moorhead, right?"

"Ah, shit," Virgil said.

"You're gonna need a subpoena," Lucas said. "It'll be waiting for you when you get there."

LUCAS GOT EVERYBODY steppin' and fetchin', then retreated to his office and thought about it. He had enough for a warrant, but he really needed to find out where Roger Hanson was hiding out. He called Del: "What are we getting from Verizon?"

"I think we're okay, but their lawyers are talking to our lawyers, and I think we're gonna be prohibited from listening in . . . but we'll be able to get where his phone calls are coming from."

"That's all we need. How long?"

"Well, we gotta wade through all this legal bullshit, and then it should be quick. It's the legal bullshit that's holding us up."

"Stay on it. Push hard," Lucas said.

★

AN HOUR AFTER he and Jenkins left, Shrake came back from St. Paul Park, having spoken to Dorcas Ryan, and said, "She says he looks more like Fell than the first guy you showed her. Said she's still not a hundred percent, but she's ninety-five percent."

Jenkins called on his way in: he'd spoken to both Lucy Landry and Kelly Barker, and Landry agreed that the photo looked more like Fell than the first one—and Barker said she was a hundred percent that he was the attacker. "She says she's absolutely sure."

"All right. Get in here. We're going for the guy, as soon as we get his location."

"Something else," Jenkins said. "Todd Barker's having big problems. One of the shots sprayed bone particles all through his lungs, and they can't control the infection. They won't say it, but I think they're gonna lose him. We're gonna have a double murder."

Del walked in. "Hanson hasn't made a phone call this morning, but late yesterday afternoon he made a call from Waconia to a clinic in St. Paul. We don't know where it went at the clinic—it went into a main number—but if he's shot, he might be looking for pain pills or antibiotics."

Lucas said, "Have we got somebody who could make a credible call to him? See what we can see?"

"Let me talk to somebody," Del said, and he went away.

Jenkins came in, and Lucas told him and Shrake to get an early lunch: "I think we'll be rolling out of here in a couple of hours, as soon as we nail him down. We've got some running around to do, but it won't be long."

Del came back and said, "I've got a Chevy dealer making a robocall to him, offering complete service on his Chevrolet product. If he answers, we'll know where he is."

"How long?"

"Ten minutes."

"I'm going to start putting together a warrant application. I'll talk to Carsonet as soon as it's ready."

"You're not going back to Paulson?"

Lucas shook his head: "We've got enough that Carsonet will give it to us. And I'd just as soon not ask Paulson again. He might wonder what happened the first time. . . . I mean, I pretty much swore that Darrell Hanson was the one."

"Gotcha," Del said. He looked at his watch. "I'll go call my guy at Verizon."

LUCAS STARTED PUTTING TOGETHER a search warrant for Roger Hanson's house. He was halfway through when Virgil Flowers called from Moorhead. "There's not a lot, but it's suggestive. He majored in education with a minor in English, and dropped out halfway through the first semester of his senior year. He *was* practice teaching that semester, up in Red Lake Falls."

"Go home," Lucas said.

He looked up Red Lake Falls on the Net, called the superintendent, whose name was Lawrence Olafson, explained the situation, and was told that three or four teachers might possibly remember what happened when Hanson was teaching. He offered to have the teachers called out of their classrooms, and Lucas took him up on it, and asked him to keep the conversation confidential.

The first teacher, Steve Little, called fifteen minutes later: "I talked to George Anderson, he was also supposed to call you; he says he doesn't remember anything about that, so he won't be calling."

"Okay, but you're calling . . . do you remember the guy?" Lucas asked.

"Oh, yeah. Larry thought you might be wondering if there was sex involved, and there was. I'd forgotten his name, Hanson, I'd forgotten that, but he got tangled up with a young girl here. Pretty voluntary on her part, I remember, but she was like way too young for that to mean anything. They could have got him on rape, but her parents didn't want anything to do with that. As I remember. I could be wrong."

"So what happened?"

"They threw his ass out," Little said. "As they should have. And Moorhead threw his ass out, and that was the end of it. As I remember. Look, I'm not swearing to any of this, this was a long time ago."

"So they didn't do anything legal. No prosecution?"

"No, I don't think so. Except throw him out," Little said. "If you did the same thing now, of course, it wouldn't make any difference what the girl wanted or the parents wanted. They'd arrest him and put him in jail. Back then, things were different."

"Do you remember how old the girl was?" Lucas asked.

"Let me think . . . I mean, I still know her, that was almost thirty years ago, and I'd guess she must be in her early forties . . . So I guess she was thirteen. Maybe fourteen."

"Thin, blond?" Lucas asked.

"Yes. Is that important?"

"It could be," Lucas said. "Listen, Steve, we may be getting back to you. If you were lining up somebody else to call, that won't be necessary. This was just an informal check to confirm some information we had. If we need something more formal, we'll send some people up to take depositions from you all. And thank you. You've been a help."

"What's going to happen?"

"Read the *Star Tribune*. Or give me a call in a week or so, and I'll tell you," Lucas said.

DEL CAME IN and said, "He's still in Waconia. We made the call, he picked up there."

"So we're set," Lucas said. "We want to be out of here in half an hour. I'm going to talk to Carsonet—he knows I'm coming—so I'll be back pretty quick. I want you to get an entry team together. I'll give them the warrant, and I want them to hit Hanson's house at two o'clock. That'll just about get us into Waconia. Then Google Waconia, figure out what they have in the way of motels. And call Darrell Hanson, ask him if he's got any relatives in Waconia. See if you can figure out where Roger is, exactly."

"How many of us are going?"

"You, me, Jenkins, and Shrake. More than enough."

24

LUCAS GOT THE WARRANT. Del called Darrell Hanson, and was told that as far as he knew, he had no relatives in Waconia. Del did a search of Waconia on the Internet and found two motels, an AmericInn and what appeared to be a mom-and-pop called Wadell's Inn, on the far west side of town. He printed out satellite maps of the area.

When Lucas got back from the Ramsey County Courthouse, he gave the warrant to the entry team, made sure they understood that they weren't to serve it until two o'clock. "If he's home, be careful. He's shot one cop, and has nothing to lose by shooting another one. Call me when you're in, and call me if you find anything significant."

The team leader, whose name was Johnston, said he would inform St. Paul of what they were doing, and Lucas suggested that he not make the call until they were moving. "I got nothing against St. Paul, but I really want to keep this close. If it leaks, and a TV station gets ahold of it, and if they ran a teaser on it . . . we don't know for sure where Hanson is, and we don't want him running. If we lose him at Waconia, he could be anyplace from Missouri to the Canadian border before it gets dark."

They went in two cars, Lucas and Del together in Lucas's Lexus, with Del driving, and Shrake and Jenkins in Shrake's Cadillac; they pulled out of the BCA parking lot at fifteen minutes after one o'clock in the afternoon.

The day was hot and still, but there was nothing going on in the west: no sign of clouds. The air had the warm vibration that foretold of thunderstorms, but none were in the forecast for another couple of days.

"Great day to make a bust," Del said, as they headed south on I-35E.

"What was it, four days ago? I was bullshitting Marcy."

"Ah, well."

THEIR FIRST TARGET was the AmericInn. On the way out of town, Lucas looked at the satellite maps that Del had printed. Waconia was a good-sized town—several thousand people, anyway—set on the south side of a five-square-mile lake. The town was about an hour from St. Paul on the far western edge of the metropolitan area; State Highway 5 hooked it to the metro area.

Although it'd probably gotten started as a farm town, lying between Highway 5 to the south and the lake to the north, the satellite photos suggested Waconia had become another of the bedroom towns surrounding Minneapolis and St. Paul, with sprawling housing developments south of Highway 5. It wasn't far—twenty minutes—from the richest residential real estate in Minnesota, the towns lying around Lake Minnetonka.

They didn't talk much on the way out: Lucas was preoccupied with thoughts of Marcy Sherrill, flashing again and again to the image of her face as she lay dead on the floor at Barker's house. Del picked up his mood, and after making a couple of suggestions about how they might handle a room entry at the AmericInn—whether and when they should get in touch with the Carver County Sheriff's Office—he shut up and drove.

They got off the metro's interstate highway loop at the southwest corner of I-494, took Highway 212 west for a couple of miles, then split off again onto Highway 5, rolling through the heavily built exurban countryside south of Minnetonka. They came into Waconia on a four-lane highway, past a Kwik Trip convenience store and a strip mall on the north side of the highway, then past a bank and a hardware store and auto-parts places, past a Holiday station and a hospital; then the AmericInn, coming up on the right.

Lucas got on his phone, called the leader of the entry team at Hanson's house: "You in?"

"We're there, we're knocking, but we're not in. Be another two minutes."

"Call me."

JENKINS AND SHRAKE trailed them into the parking lot. Del said, "Got a white van."

"I see it," Lucas said. The van was halfway down the parking lot, among a scattering of other cars and trucks. They drove past it, and Lucas found a printout given him by Sandy, and as Del said, "Looks too new," Lucas read out Hanson's license plate number against the van in the parking lot: "Wrong number," he said.

"He may have taken off," Del said.

"We got another motel to look at."

"You want to check here, see if he's got a room?"

"Might as well."

They parked, with Shrake and Jenkins a couple of spaces closer to the entrance. They got out, and Shrake walked around the nose of his car, with Jenkins, and blocked the sidewalk between Lucas's truck and the motel entrance.

Shrake said, "We gotta talk before we go in."

Lucas, frowning: "What?"

Jenkins said, "Shrake and Del and I are afraid you're gonna pop this guy. You're gonna do it in a way that drags us all down. We gotta know that you're not going to drag three good friends through the shit, just so you can get even with somebody."

Lucas felt a surge of anger, turned to Del. "You're in this, too?"

"Yeah, and we're not the only ones. Everybody who knows you is worried. Your family."

"You've been talking behind my back," Lucas said, even angrier.

Shrake nodded: "Yeah. We have. We didn't want to insult you, if it wasn't a problem. But it looks to us like you've got a problem. The way you've been setting up this bust. You've got something fancy going on with the entry team, we could smell it."

"So what're you gonna do: try to take my gun?"

"Maybe," Shrake said. "If we've got to."

"You think you could do it?" Lucas asked, taking a step back. Both Jenkins and Shrake were big and hard, and specialized in physical confrontation.

Jenkins said, "The three of us could, yeah."

Lucas half turned to glance at Del, whose mouth was set in a solid line. Del said, "We don't want your fuckin' gun. What we want is a promise: you don't drag your three friends through the shit just to bring down Hanson. You're not an executioner. And we don't want to witness an execution."

Lucas looked at the three of them, shook his head, his voice cold: "You got no idea what this is doing."

"I think we do," Del said. "We've been worried about it for days. Talking about it. We couldn't think of anything else to do."

"All we want you to do is give us your word: no executions, no kind of fuckin' phony setups," Jenkins said. "We go in, we take him, the chips fall where they may. We do it straight up."

Lucas was breathing hard, as torn as he'd ever been in his life: the three men were among his half-dozen best friends. What they were doing felt like betrayal, but the little man at the back of his head told him that they were sincere enough.

He said, "Fuck you."

Shrake said, "You can't even do that, huh?"

"What're you going to do about it? I'll go alone if I have to."

"We'll fuck with you," Jenkins said. "We've got the Carver County Sheriff's Office on speed-dial. I'll call them, I'll get them over here. You go in and ask the desk clerk for the room number, and I'll embarrass you by telling him not to give it to you."

"You motherfuckers," Lucas said, suddenly uncertain; he felt cornered—and maybe wrong.

Del said, very quietly, "We'll believe whatever you say. You give us your word that we're not going to an execution, we'll take it."

They were all grouped up in a bunch, and Lucas felt as though he were about to start shaking with frustration, but the man in the back of his head was persistent: the three of them were serious, and sincere, and were his friends.

Finally, he nodded: "All right. Straight up."

"That's good enough for us," Shrake said, and he and Jenkins backed away, and let Lucas through, to lead them into the motel lobby.

THE MOTEL CLERK was a soft-spoken woman with carefully coiffed gold-tinted hair and a Fargo accent; her blue eyes got wide when Lucas showed her his ID. "We're looking for a man named Roger Hanson who would have checked in probably yesterday. Heavyset, black hair, maybe a thick black beard. He's driving a Chevrolet van."

She said, "That doesn't sound like anybody I've seen, but let me check."

As she went to her computer, Lucas's phone rang. He stepped away from the desk, and the entry team leader at Hanson's house said, "Man, you're not going to believe this. We've got a male body in the guy's freezer. We're gonna leave him until crime scene can go over the place, so we've got no ID."

Lucas said, "Older, maybe middle seventies, white hair, stocky—"

"That's him," the team leader said. "Who is it?"

"Probably his uncle, Brian Hanson. Former detective over in Minneapolis. There are a couple of older guys in Minneapolis Homicide who could ID him for you. Also, the former Minneapolis chief, Quentin Daniel, worked with him. Daniel's retired, and he could probably run over. I've got a phone number for him if you need it. Jesus: listen, anything else?"

"Lotsa porn, kiddie porn. This is the guy, Lucas. You got something going, right?"

"We're right behind him, we think. Maybe." He looked at Jenkins, who was standing by the motel counter. Jenkins shook his head. "Maybe not. I'll stay in touch as things develop. Call me if you get anything that might tell you where he is. Do not let TV close to the place. Nobody talks. We still got a chance to sneak up on this guy."

"Gotcha."

Lucas rang off and Jenkins said, nodding to the clerk behind the desk, "They've got no Hanson. She doesn't remember anybody who looks like him. There's no van—but there's that mom-and-pop place out at the end of town, and it's cheaper."

"Let's go," Lucas said. And to the clerk: "Please don't tell anybody about this. We're hunting the guy down, and if word gets out, he could be warned."

She said, "I won't tell anybody."

"You're welcome to talk all about it later," Shrake told her. "But not until we've got him. He's a dangerous man."

BACK OUT in the parking lot, Shrake asked, "Was that the entry team calling?"

Lucas nodded. "Yeah. They found a body in Hanson's freezer. From the description, it's almost certainly Brian Hanson. He's killed two cops now, and Todd Barker may go yet."

"And God knows how many kids," Del said.

"So let's find him," Jenkins said.

On the way to the other motel, Lucas said to Del, "We're gonna have to sit down and talk about this. It's like you don't trust me. We been through a lot of shit, man—"

"Ah, for Christ's sakes, I'd trust you with my life," Del said. "I *have* trusted you with my life. We're just not sure whether we can trust you with *your* life. That's what we're all worried about."

"I'm pretty fuckin' pissed."

"Ah, stick a sock in it," Del said.

WADELL'S INN WAS an older place at the far western edge of town, a single-story, L-shaped affair, gray with dirty white trim, fifteen or twenty small rooms stretching east from the entrance at the far end, all facing a gravel parking lot. Each room had a door facing the parking lot, and a window next to the door. The entrance lobby, the other arm of the L, was built as a ranch-style house, and might have doubled as the owner's residence. There was nothing behind the motel but farm fields; another mom-and-pop convenience store, called the Pit Stop, sat across the highway.

As they came up, Del said, "There's the van."

An older white van was parked halfway down the line of rooms. As they went past, Lucas looked at the numbers of the tag and said, "That's him."

Del rolled past the motel at full speed, followed by Shrake; they did a U-turn a quarter mile down the road and came back, sliding into the residence side of the L, where they couldn't be seen from the van.

They hopped out, and Lucas and Del went into the lobby, while Jenkins and Shrake stood at the corner of the L, where they could keep an eye on the van.

A THIN, OLD, sun-blasted woman sat in a closet-sized office behind the lobby desk, smoking a cigarette and looking at a computer screen. She stood up when Lucas came in, followed by the others, all of them blinking in the dim light.

Lucas showed his ID and said, "We're police officers with the Bureau of Criminal Apprehension. We are looking for a man named Roger Hanson, who owns that white van parked halfway down your lot. Black hair, heavyset guy. We need to know what room he's in, and we need a key."

"I don't know what his name is, but he's in Fifteen," the woman said. Her voice was a crow-like croak, rough from a lifetime of cigarettes. "I got a key here."

She went through a drawer and came up with a key on a plastic tag. Lucas took it and said, "Please stay inside. Lock the door when we leave. We'll let you know when it's safe to come out."

"He's dangerous?" she asked.

"He's a killer," Del said.

THEY WENT BACK OUT, heard the old woman lock the door. Lucas said, "All right. How're we gonna do this?"

Shrake said, "I went down and peeked at the first door. They're metal fire doors. We won't be able to kick it."

"I've got a key, but that'll be slower," Lucas said.

Jenkins said, "You turn it, get it open. I'll kick it, in case it's chained, and hop back. Shrake and Del can have their guns ready, and pop right through."

Lucas nodded. "That works. Let's do it."

They went down the walkway under the eaves of the motel, Del and Shrake pulling their guns. Halfway down to Fifteen, Jenkins whispered, "There's an eighteen-wheeler coming. If you get the key in then . . ."

Lucas spotted the truck and moved quickly to the door and knelt beside it, watched the truck. A few cars went by, and then the truck came up, and as the engine noise started to build, he slipped the key into the door lock, turned the key, pushed just a bit, felt the door come loose, and as the truck went by, said to Jenkins, "Now."

Jenkins kicked the door, nearly knocking it off its frame; no chain. Del and Shrake surged into the hotel room, straight through to the bath, and Shrake said, "It's clear. Goddamn it."

The television was playing, a suitcase sat on the floor next to the bed, and a ring of keys sat under a bedside lamp, along with a pair of sunglasses. Del kicked the suitcase and said, "Got a gun, here."

Lucas glanced at it: a Glock.

"He's close . . ."

"He's across the highway at that store, I bet," Shrake said.

They all looked out the door, at the store across the way. It was tiny. Lucas said, "If he's in there, there's a good chance that he's looking at us through the front window."

"Doesn't have a gun," Del said. "At least, not this gun."

Lucas said to Shrake, "I'm sticking by my word: there won't be any execution. But somebody's got to stay here, in case he's in one of the other rooms. Del and I were friends of Marcy's, and want to be there for the bust. Jenkins is faster than you, in case he runs."

Shrake said, "Go."

Lucas said, "Keep your gun out; he might be down in one of these other rooms. He might have met somebody, or something."

"I got it," Shrake said. "Go."

HANSON HAD HIS FACE in the soda cooler when the BCA agents went into his room. He was walking toward the cash register when they came back out, and he saw them at once, and knew who they were: some brand of cops.

He had no car, no keys, not much money, and no clothes but the ones he was standing in. His side, which seemed to be healing okay, nevertheless burned like fire. He saw them come out of the motel, and he turned and walked back through the store, past the restrooms, and out the back entrance, through a door marked "Not an Exit" and heard the counterman call, "Hey," as he went out.

He went through the back door only because he couldn't go through the front, but he had no idea where he was going. When he got out the back, he saw two things: the counterman's parked truck, and a small house, probably fifty yards away across the parking lot, with another car, an old Corolla, parked next to it. He ran that way. If he could get some keys . . .

Then what?

How far could he get?

He didn't think about it: he ran, and he thought, *Keys*.

He just ran.

LUCAS SAW A FLASH of what looked like daylight through the store window and it crossed his mind that somebody had just run out the back. He, Del, and Jenkins were lined up at the edge of the highway, waiting to run across, when he saw the flash, and Lucas took the chance and ran straight through the traffic, causing one car to swerve and another to hit the brakes so hard that they screamed, and Del shouted, "Hey," but Lucas was across the highway and running hard.

Del and Jenkins were slowed by more cars, but got across, now fifty yards behind Lucas, and instead of going into the front of the store Lucas went left, around the far end of it, saw the little shabby house out back and the fat black-haired man running toward it, and he half turned and windmilled an arm at Jenkins and Del, and shouted, "This way," and kept running.

Ahead of him, Hanson kicked through a half-closed gate on a hurricane fence, ran across a concrete-block porch and half turned and saw Lucas coming, only twenty-five or thirty yards back, yanked open the screen door and crashed through the inner door into the house's living room.

A woman was standing in the kitchen and she screamed at him and he saw a butcher knife on the kitchen counter and she backpedaled away from him, and then threw a towel at him, and he dodged the towel and grabbed the knife with one hand, and the woman by the hair with the other, and she twisted and screamed and then Lucas crashed through the door behind them.

Hanson tried to shout something—*"I'll kill her,"* or *"I've got a knife"*—but Lucas never gave him time, simply vaulting across a couch, reaching for Hanson's throat. His body smashed into Hanson's left side, the impact pushing the fat man back against the kitchen sink. He slashed at Lucas's face with the knife and the woman came free and fell on the floor, and Lucas tried to catch Hanson's knife hand but missed, snagged a shirtsleeve, but he felt the knife slash across his shoulder and the back of his neck, and he twisted away from the knife and the woman's body hit him behind the ankles and he went down, losing his grip on Hanson and then,

BOOM.

The gunshot, the sound not the slug, was like a bolt of lightning, and then another *BOOM* and Lucas, confused and half blinded by blood, scrambled across the supine woman, tried to pull her away from Hanson, and then realized Hanson was going down.

Jenkins said, "Stay down, stay down . . ." and he pushed Lucas down with his hand. The woman was squealing, and Del was saying, ". . . ambulance down at a place called Pit Stop right now. We've got a seriously injured police officer. . . ."

Jenkins looked down at him and Lucas said, "I'm not seriously injured."

Jenkins said, "Maybe not, but you're bleeding like you're seriously injured. So just stay down."

Del loomed over him: "Dumb shit."

"What about Hanson?" Lucas asked.

Jenkins looked behind himself, at the form on the floor, and Lucas realized he still had his gun in his hand, a big .357 revolver that he'd bought from a highway patrolman.

"You got what you wanted," Jenkins said. "He's stone-cold dead."

25

DEL PUSHED LUCAS flat and said, "Let me look at it."

Lucas let him look: Del used a paper towel to wipe the blood off Lucas's forehead, and then looked at his shoulder through a slash in Lucas's jacket, and said, finally, "It's not that bad. You've got a nasty cut right along your hairline, but I don't see any bone. It's bleeding like crazy, though. There's another cut on your shoulder, but your coat took most of the damage. You need to get sewn up."

They pressed more paper towels to his head, trying to stop the flow of blood, and he stayed on the floor, waiting for the ambulance. Carver County sheriff's deputies showed up two minutes after the shooting, and were handled by Jenkins. Then the ambulance came, and Lucas walked out to it on his own, stepping over Hanson's facedown body as he left the house. The woman who owned the house was unhurt, but in shock, and was taken out to the ambulance with Lucas.

At the hospital, they compressed the wounds to control the bleeding, and waited for a doc, and after Lucas had been waiting for fifteen minutes or so, a plastic surgeon showed up, took a long look at the cuts, and said, "Not too bad, but the recovery is going to be uncomfortable. Let's get them closed up."

They closed the wounds with a local anesthetic, plus some kind of intravenous relaxer. Before they started, Lucas made a quick call to Weather, caught her just as she was leaving the hospital, told her that he'd been dinged up in a fight and was getting some stitches. She wanted details, and he passed the phone to the surgeon, who, after a minute, said, "Oh, yeah, I know you," and told her that Lucas was worse than dinged up, but would nevertheless be home that afternoon.

When he got off, he said, "Weather Karkinnen, huh? I better do my best work."

THEN LUCAS WENT AWAY for a while, came back sewn up and bandaged, and found Del sitting next to the hospital bed.

"The doc said that when you're steady on your feet, we can drive you home. He's going to come by and talk to you, though."

"How's everybody?" Lucas mumbled. He was still feeling fuzzy.

"Jenkins shot Hanson twice, in the middle of the chest. He's over there, working through the shooting with the sheriff's department. The woman there, her name's Betty Ludwig, she's okay, she's maybe got some bruises; they brought her in with you and gave her some pills. . . . Shrake's with Jenkins, filling in the sheriff's guys on the investigation. They might be a little pissed that we didn't give them a call—and they want a statement from you, but it doesn't have to be today."

"Not a big problem," Lucas said. He was clearing up: Del's voice was giving him something to focus on. "Have you heard from Johnston?" Johnston was the entry team leader at Hanson's house.

"They got trophies. Locks of hair, underwear, a kid's necklace. And home movies," Del said. "They've got VHS movies of the Jones girls."

"Don't want to see that," Lucas said.

"I don't think anybody will—we know he took them, and now he's dead. No point."

THE DOC CAME IN a while later, looked at the bandages, asked Lucas a couple of questions, gave him a prescription for painkillers and antibiotics, and told him he could go. "Have your wife redo the dressing tomorrow, and every couple of days after that," he said. "You're welcome to come back to me, but you don't have to."

Lucas thanked him, and they walked out to the car.

"What I want to know," Del said, as they pulled out of the hospital parking lot, "is what the fuck you were doing?"

Lucas said, "I wanted to get my hands on him. I was right behind him when he went in the house, he didn't have a gun, so I went straight in and then he had the woman and a knife and I was moving so fast I just kept going. It seemed like the best way to keep her from getting cut. I wanted to get her away from him, to get between them. The guy was nuts. I was thinking he might kill her, just to do it. And I knew you guys were right behind me."

"You didn't get cut so Jenkins would have to shoot him?"

Lucas said, "I'm not that fuckin' crazy. From the time I went through the door to the time I got to him, was maybe half a second. All I was thinking of, was to knock him down and get him away from her."

THE SURGEON WAS RIGHT about the recovery being uncomfortable: the discomfort started when he got home, and Weather cornered Del and demanded details on how, exactly, Lucas had gotten hurt. When she found out, she chewed Lucas down to a stump, and then ordered him to bed. With cuts on both his face and back, he found that there was almost no comfortable way to lie in bed, and wound up half sitting, propped up by a pillow in the small of his back.

Jenkins and Shrake came by later in the day, to report on the crime-scene process. There'd be no problem with the shooting, they said, with the woman having been attacked, and Lucas having been slashed—and Hanson being a multiple child-killer.

Further, they said, Rose Marie Roux, the Public Safety commissioner and Lucas's real boss, had gone to Hanson's home, had viewed some trophies—underwear taken from victims, and VHS home movies from the eighties and nineties, including some that included the Jones sisters—and had then held a press conference. Hanson, she said, probably had murdered at least six or seven children, in addition to his uncle and Marcy Sherrill.

Weeks of investigation would be needed to figure out what he'd done, and who all the victims were.

ROSE MARIE SHOWED UP just as Jenkins and Shrake were leaving, ganged up with Weather to chew on Lucas some more. Weather said, "Shrake and Jenkins are worried that you're down on them, because they pushed you around a little. Lucas, they are your best friends in the world. You're not so dumb you can't see that."

Rose Marie nodded. "What she said."

"They're good with me," Lucas said. "I think they know that."

"Well, tell them," Weather said.

MARCY SHERRILL WAS CREMATED, and her ashes spread on her family's farm. Brian Hanson was buried in a veterans' cemetery. The two Jones girls were buried in a plot next to their grandparents, in St. Paul. Lucas went to all of the funerals. He had no idea what happened to Roger Hanson's body, and didn't care.

TODD BARKER ALMOST DIED from lung infections, but in the end, didn't. Kelly Barker made several more appearances on Channel Three, talking about the experience of being shot at, and then helping her husband with his recovery; she never made *Oprah*. Jennifer Carey, who did most of the interviews, told Lucas later that Todd Barker thought his main mistake was, he hadn't gone to the door with a gun in his hand. "He says he's never going to make that mistake again," Carey told Lucas. "He's even bought a couple of new ones. He's got a garage gun now, for when he takes the garbage out."

*

DARRELL HANSON and his wife went through some preliminary motions to sue the state for damage to their house caused by the search, but settled out of court for a minor payment. One of the state lawyers, whom Lucas knew, said that the prospect of being publicly tied to Roger Hanson had changed their minds, especially since the search had produced the DNA test of Darrell Hanson, and had pointed the finger at Roger.

THE BCA'S LAB BOSS did a number of interviews about the use of DNA to spot a killer through tests done on a relative. He suggested that it opened whole new doors to a time when, effectively, everybody in the country would be traceable through DNA. He had T-shirts printed that said "DNA," and, beneath that, "World Tour." Everybody thought they looked cheap and ugly, but Lucas's housekeeper found that they made excellent dust rags.

LUCAS WAS LARGELY HEALED in two weeks. Weather took the stitches out, humming as she did it. It hurt a little, but that didn't seem to bother her.

LUCAS FINALLY SAT ALONE in his den, when the house was momentarily empty, and thought about it all. He hadn't been responsible for the Jones girls' kidnapping—that'd been all Hanson. The VHS tapes suggested that Hanson hadn't had the girls very long before he killed them, so even if Lucas had pushed, and had been successful, he couldn't have saved them.

All those others, though . . . he might have saved them if he'd persisted in his hunt for John Fell. Weather kept telling him that it wasn't a perfect world, and anyway, he wasn't perfect. Things would happen. Good, hardworking, innocent people died of cancer all the time—and Hanson had simply been a cancer in the social system.

Lucas knew all that was true, but it was not something he could emotionally buy into. He didn't *believe* he could fix the world, but he *felt* like he could.

He just had to try harder.